DISCONTENT

JUDGEMENT
OF THE SIX

BOOK 5

MELISSA HAAG

(DIS)CONTENT

I hate. I thought I hated before the letter, before the werewolves, but now I understand that was nothing more than a chip on my shoulder. The urbat took what was mine. And they will pay.

Isabelle leads a very normal life...for an emotional siphon. If not for Ethan and his bar, she would have lost her sanity long ago. But everything changes with the crash of her fighting cage and a man who transforms into a wolf. There's something about Carlos—when he's not growling at her—that makes her do things she wouldn't normally do, like sigh and daydream.

Attraction aside, she is faced with the very real evidence that werewolves and urbat exist, and the urbat are after her. And the only way she can keep Ethan safe is to join with the werewolves and Carlos. It's a race against time to stop a war, fight for love, and find the last Judgement.

PROLOGUE

I THRUST THE KEY INTO THE LOCK AND SHOVED OPEN THE DOOR FOR the apartment building. My skin felt too tight from all the crap I'd dealt with at the office. I should have quit like Ethan had said. Who cared if I spent my life tending bar? It would be easier, especially with the setup Ethan had.

Stopping in the entry, I checked my mailbox.

"Hi, Isabelle."

The sound of my downstairs neighbor's voice just added to my bad mood. My skin grew tighter with the waves of annoyance that rolled off him and soaked into me.

As a rule, I didn't socialize with anyone in my building. It didn't seem right trying to be friends with any of them. After all, I robbed them of any negative emotion they might have, so they didn't have a choice but to like me.

Quickly grabbing my mail, I turned to give the man a tight smile and fled before he could pull me into a friendly conversation.

As a child, I'd always wanted friends. When Ethan came along and seemed to understand me better than anyone else ever had, I gave up on having friends and settled for having a friend. Singular. Ethan was enough.

I trudged up the stairs to the second floor, opened my apartment, and stepped inside with a sigh. My eyes fell on the bag hanging from the special support the landlord had installed for me. I wanted nothing more than to start hitting it but knew once I started, I wouldn't stop until I drained everything. First mail, then change, and then dinner. After that, I could have at it.

Kicking off my flats, I sorted through the mail while walking to the kitchen. I didn't need to pay attention to where I was going. My apartment wasn't that big. The living room and kitchen flowed together with a tiny island separating them. The living room had my bag dangling from the ceiling and that was it. My bedroom had a TV, bed, and dresser. I didn't need much.

I stopped mid-sort and stared at an envelope with a handwritten address. No return address. No postage. Weird.

I threw the bills to the side and set the envelope on the counter. The bills I'd write out later. The envelope had me curious, though. I would open it while I waited for food. The freezer had a nice selection of dinners waiting for me. I grabbed one at random and threw it into the microwave. As I listened to the hum of my dinner cooking, I tore open the envelope and pulled out a handwritten letter.

No MATTER *how I write this, you won't believe it. All I ask is that you don't throw this away. Just consider it.*

There are people looking for you. People who look human but aren't. They know what you can do. They must not find you. If they do, they will hurt us both, and so many more.

Don't trust anyone. Run. Stay hidden. Our time's almost up.

I TURNED it over and glanced at the blank back. There was no greeting and no closing. Just an unsigned note. My eyes fell on the one sentence that truly concerned me.

"They know what you can do," I murmured.

The microwave beeped, drawing my attention from the letter to the tension tingling under my skin.

I used a magnet to stick the letter to the refrigerator and drifted to my room to change. Dressed in spandex shorts and a tight exercise tank top, I padded out to the living room and ignored the cooling dinner that waited for me. I slipped on my gloves to protect my knuckles and started exorcising my demons.

The idea that someone might know about me didn't scare me. I found it amusing. No one really knew but Ethan. Even my parents didn't know, though they did have their own ideas about me; how could they not after raising me? But their suspicions weren't close. They thought I exuded positive energy. I'd like to blame their hippie thoughts on their habits in the '60s and '70s, but they weren't that old. The reality of what I did wasn't that I released positive anything. It was the exact opposite.

I mostly siphoned negative emotions. But if I wanted, I could pull the positive ones, too. I felt what the people around me felt. Like sampling ice cream, their emotions had different flavors, letting me know their moods. Unfortunately, the siphoning wasn't voluntary. No matter how hard I tried, I couldn't completely turn it off. But, boy, could I turn it on. If I wanted, I could drain a room in two heartbeats. Taking away all that negativity made the people around me happy, but it did the opposite for me. The more I siphoned, the less I felt like myself. I grew agitated, angry even. The more I absorbed, the more my skin tingled, until it felt painfully tight. The only thing that helped relieve it was physical activity.

I hit the bag, timing the backswing, and set a grueling rhythm. Who would even think someone could do what I could do? And, if they did, why would they come after me? Idiots. I'd leave them on the floor with a gap-toothed smile.

Good luck to whoever thought they could take me.

CHAPTER ONE

THE PHONE RANG BEFORE MY ALARM. HELL HATH NO FURY LIKE A woman woken before her alarm. I fumbled to find the phone in the dark.

"Hello?" My voice cracked.

"Hey, Z. This is your reminder to pack your bag. You promised to cover tonight."

"Ethan. You are sick to call me this early. I said I'll be there. Now, leave me alone." I ended the call without a goodbye.

The phone rang again before I could drop it back on the nightstand.

"What?" I answered.

"I've dusted your gloves, babe. You're overdue."

The call disconnected, and I smiled in the dark. Only Ethan, the huge pain in the butt I called friend, could annoy me and make me smile at the same time. He was right. I needed to go in and really purge.

Hitting the bag at home helped, but I suffered from a slow buildup. Ethan compared it to PMS. I grew moodier until I started an actual fight. Except the fights were never fair. In my anger, I pulled too much of my opponent's emotions, and they tended to just stand there with a stupid smile as I hit them. But I couldn't avoid the fights. I needed them. Hitting an actual person drained me way more than the bag, and it was the only thing that helped when I got like this. I hated fighting but didn't see any other choice.

With a sigh, I slid from the sheets and shuffled to the bathroom. My long, red hair was a tangled mess, and I scowled at myself in the mirror. The green of my eyes seemed vivid against the bloodshot background.

I should have slept longer. I already felt edgy and knew it would be a long day.

MANY HOURS LATER, I parked in front of Ethan's bar and spar—located in a less than desirable part of town—and leaned my head against the steering wheel. How could a day go so wrong? I cringed remembering how, in a fabulous fury, I'd stormed my boss' office, told her to shove her petty self-pity, which she'd been radiating all day, up her butt, and then left, slamming doors and pushing coworkers. Not one of my better resignations.

Ethan had been right; I was overdue.

Sitting back with a sigh, I started to change. I kicked off my flats and pulled my yoga pants on under my skirt. Someone walked by the car and stopped to stare in as I threw the skirt in the passenger seat. I pulled the curiosity right out of him, and he kept moving. The extra emotions bloated me and didn't help my mood. Gritting my teeth, I swapped tops, not caring who saw. In a hurry, I pulled on my socks and sneakers. It felt good. I knew what was coming.

I stepped out of the car, not worrying about the people I sensed in the nearby alleys. They were too busy getting high to notice me as I strode across the street. The emotions of those inside the bar drifted toward me, increasing the tension I carried. With a scowl, I yanked the door open. The warm air pushed past me, lifting my hair slightly. The heavy beat of music beckoned me, but I didn't pause. I shouldered my way through the bodies that crowded the room and made my way to the bar.

Ethan stood behind the cheap, laminate counter, filling orders. Tall and lean, he had the attention of most of the women in the room. The tight t-shirt he wore probably helped. He glanced at me as I moved around to the side and ducked under the bar to join him.

"E-Z!" a regular called out. I ignored him.

The bar came to life when Ethan and I tended together. We didn't do it too often, anymore. It called too much attention to me.

"Damn, girl!" Ethan shouted to be heard. "The more you sit on that thing, the better it gets."

I rolled my eyes at him, glad he'd chosen to comment on my butt rather than how early I was. The extra padding I'd acquired by taking up an office job only seemed to want to settle on my butt. It had to be those frozen dinners, I thought. It certainly wasn't lack of exercise. I'd hit the bag for forty minutes straight last night.

"Glad you decided to quit yet another job so you could come in early to help. Better start shaking that thing."

He just had to go there.

"Shut up, E."

A few of the patrons who sat listening to our exchange laughed.

"Which one of you idiots wants a drink?" My voice carried over all the noise. Happy faces turned my way. They knew me. They knew how this place would get soon. While they got high, I'd swell with every negative emotion they let loose. Oh, how I hated them.

"The spit's free," I said with a glare. One of the customers had

7

once told me my light green and amber-flecked eyes reminded him of snake eyes when I glared. He'd loved snakes. Of course he had.

Ethan bumped into me, drawing my attention and breaking my death glare.

"Don't be like that. They love you."

"Right."

He slid the drink he'd just poured across the bar and turned to face me. He arched a brow. Concern softened his light brown eyes. It had been almost two months since I last saw his beautiful face. Despite the rage boiling in me, I smiled at him; and he relaxed a little.

"You're going to love them more when you see who I have lined up for you, Miss Moody."

Ethan took care of me. He set up the fights, always seeming to know just when I needed them. He was careful, though, about whom he selected. It was a paid gig for the fighters, a flat fee no matter the outcome. It kept the extreme competitors away. They had too much emotion when fighting; and, often, I ended up worse off than when I started. I needed people who let out very little emotion. Not calm people. Cold people. Emotionless. They weren't always easy to find.

"Hope it's better than the last guy." I slopped some cheap booze into a glass and pushed it at a guy holding out a five. I took the money and slid it into the waistband of my pants.

Ethan laughed as he stole the money back out and put it in the register. He kept talking as we continued filling drink orders.

"He's a brick wall. He fried his brain on home-stewed goods years ago. If he's got any emotion to steal, it's nothing you'd want in you."

"Sounds interesting. If he doesn't do it, it's you and me again, babe."

We didn't fight; it was like we danced, but with fists and kicks.

With my help, Ethan had learned to block his emotions from

me—to a certain degree anyway—at an early age. After all, he was my sparring partner; I couldn't have him flopping to the ground after two minutes in my presence. When we were younger, he'd radiated so much anger the possibility of draining him had been slim, unless I would have purposely tried to. But as we grew closer, some of his anger had faded. At least, when we were together.

He grinned at me, winked, then turned to fill the next drink order.

We worked side by side for an hour. He filled most of the orders while I shouted insults at the patrons. They laughed, Ethan made money, and I struggled to hold myself together.

"E, if he's not here soon..." I shoved crumpled bills in the cash drawer.

Hands settled on my shoulders as I slammed the drawer shut. How many cash registers had I broken that way?

Ethan spun me away from the register, probably to save it, and planted a kiss on my forehead. Then, he pulled back with a grin and nodded to the stage. I turned to look.

The floor-to-ceiling chain-link fence had converted the stage into a fight cage. Mats lined the floors to protect anyone slow enough to get knocked down. A bag hung from the ceiling for warm-up; and, on occasion, it provided a place for my opponent to hide from me. A door led to a back hall restricted to employees and my guest fighters.

As I studied my sanctuary, the door to the cage opened, and a big brick of a man walked onto the mats.

Cheers erupted in the bar, and he raised his gloved hands over his head. Then, he did a few warm-up jabs.

Emotions soaked the room, and I could pinpoint where each one stemmed. But very little seeped from the man on the stage. It meant I wouldn't drain him as I fought. It meant Ethan had found me a real challenge. It meant I'd finally feel some peace.

I turned back to grin at Ethan.

"I love you."

He laughed.

"Now you feel love. Wait until after."

He swatted my butt as I turned away. The distraction broke the weak hold I had on my control. Emotions flooded me. The elation of the band when the crowd cheered, the lust from the dancers as they bumped and rubbed against each other, and the anticipation from those who turned to face the cage.

I pushed past people and made my way toward the employee door that opened to a crowded, dirty hall. Ethan's business wasn't legitimate enough for a cleaning crew. Which meant it was perfect for me and the fights. With a smile, I turned right and walked toward the door marked "Z's Play Room."

The big man turned when I opened the door, but he didn't approach. My gloves waited for me on the floor. They were clean and dust free as promised.

I looked through the cage, across the bar, and met Ethan's eyes. His smile was gone. He nodded at my opponent as if to say, "Get to it."

Tightening my gloves, I turned from Ethan and eyed the fighter with pity. I hated my need to fight. I hated that I would hurt him. I hated that I would never grow close to another person because of the drain I put on them. Most days I hated just about everything.

"What's your name?" I asked.

The man turned to look at me.

"He said you would ask. Call me Brick."

Ethan's idea of a name, no doubt. I studied the man a moment before stepping closer. Ethan was right. Very little spilled from Brick. I tasted a hint of contentment and nothing more, though the scent of stale cigarettes and old booze hung around him like a cloud. I gave Ethan one last look, then focused on Brick.

"Tell me when you want to stop."

The big man raised his fists and beckoned me.

All right, then. I swung first, relishing the feel of my shoulder muscles stretching and my stomach tightening. I connected, and a tiny bit of pent-up frustration burst from me like air set free from an overfilled balloon.

I ducked under his counterswing and swung again. Each time I connected, I released more of the pent-up emotion I'd siphoned. The crowd shouted encouragement to Brick, and their excitement refilled the depleting emotion before I could enjoy any relief. I picked up the pace.

Jab after jab, Brick stayed with me. He rarely landed a blow, but took plenty. Sweat trickled down my back and beaded on my upper lip. I danced around him, ducking and weaving. I kicked the back of his knee and brought him down but only for a heartbeat. He laughed and surged to his feet with an uppercut that almost connected. A quick twist saved me, and a glint of annoyance flickered in Brick's eyes. The emotions of the crowd still touched me, but Brick and I were moving fast enough now that I continued to drain myself faster than I could siphon.

Then, I felt a change in the room. A black hole, a vast, emotional nothingness approached. The unusual phenomenon momentarily distracted me.

Brick saw an opening and swung. The force behind his jab caused a breeze along my cheek as I dodged to the right. A reminder to stay focused.

Yet, I couldn't shake the feeling of that black hole and the sudden belief that something really bad was coming my way. Maybe it was the letter still on my fridge. Maybe it was because I was once again jobless. Maybe it was because I knew Ethan planned to talk to me again. Whatever it was, it filled me with dread, an emotion created by me alone.

I ducked under Brick's next swing and came back with a punch to his jaw. Something crunched, and I wanted to cringe for him.

Brick staggered back a step and shook his head. I didn't press him. Instead, I gave him a moment to clear the hit.

From the corner of my eye, I noticed the repetitious movement of a dark-haired man near the fence, but I didn't look away from Brick. His gaze looked a little unfocused, and I hoped I hadn't done any real damage. I still had a lot to drain. Sometimes, if a single fight wasn't enough to empty everything, I called out to the crowd for another contender. I might need to do that with Brick. He'd taken enough of a beating. The guy pacing beside the cage might be up for a round or two.

Brick brought his gloves back up and stepped toward me. A low growl, barely loud enough to hear over the noise, reached me. I turned to look and met the deep brown eyes of the tall, dark-haired man. My stomach dipped at the sight of him.

Just as I was registering the details of the stranger's strong, clean-shaven jaw, Brick swung and knocked my lights loose.

Time slowed as my head snapped back. Something crashed against the fence. I barely heard it over the ringing in my ears. I widened my stance to stay upright and saw one of the brackets pull from the ceiling before I straightened. Stunned, my gaze followed the dust down as I automatically brought my fists up.

I expected more from Brick, but he wasn't moving toward me. He wasn't looking at me, either. Something crashed against the cage again. Then, I saw it.

The metal of the cage bent inward as a huge dog crashed against the fence again and again. It didn't look at me. It only looked at Brick, who stared back at it blankly. I'd hit him too hard. I must have. Maybe Brick had hit me too hard, too.

Ethan shouted my name as a few more of the brackets tore from the ceiling. A memory surfaced of a video I'd seen earlier that year. A man had been attacked by a dog, just about the same size as the one that crashed against the cage. When the dog had fled, there'd been little left of the man. The memory shook me free.

"Brick, move!" I yelled, trying to jar him from his stupor.

I gave the man a shove toward the door, then ran past him when he showed no interest in saving himself. People in the main bar were screaming and running for the exit. Chaos reigned beyond the cage—every man for himself. Worried for Ethan, I pushed through the door to the hall so hard that it bounced back on me and banged my left shoulder.

The rhythmic slamming of the cage stopped as I stumbled out into the service hall and eyed my options. The employee entrance was too close to the dog. I'd need to go out to the alley, then circle around to the front to get Ethan.

Claws screeched on the employee door, and I almost tripped over myself in my rush toward the back exit. Behind me, the door shuddered as something hit it with enough force to make the metal groan. My heart stopped, and I twisted to look over my shoulder. I was still alone. But for how long? A burst of adrenaline helped me reach the end of the hall.

The cold metal exit bar of the back door gave way, and I flew outside, startling a few of the users who lingered amongst the trash. I pulled emotions from them as I ran past, fueling myself. The people sagged. I didn't stop running or pulling. I might need it to get to Ethan.

Ahead, the mouth of the alley beckoned. Already, people from the club ran past on the street. Screaming and shouting filled the air, along with my own rapid breathing and the pounding of my feet on the pavement.

Before I reached the mouth of the alley, the door burst open behind me. Taking a risk, I looked back. Just in time, too. The dog flew at me, knocking me backwards. I lifted my arms to block its snapping jaws as I fell to the ground under its weight. My head hit the blacktop with a burst of pain, and I lost my breath a second time.

My ears rang. I gave my head a tiny shake and blinked as I

looked up at my hands. They weren't braced on fur but a human arm. I blinked again, trying to focus. Beyond the snarling face and snapping teeth, I met the light grey gaze of an older man. He had wrapped his arm around the thing's neck in an attempted chokehold.

"Run," he said. The man pulled back, straining to win me some wiggle room.

The thing on top of me roared and tried shaking the man off, but it didn't budge from its position. Its front paws rested on the pavement, boxing me in, and its chest pressed me down. How did the man expect me to run?

I focused on the dog. I'd never tried pulling emotions from an animal before. But now, I stretched out my senses. I felt the worry of the man holding the beast but nothing from the beast itself.

"Get off me." I punctuated my words with a swing to its elongated nose. I connected and had the satisfaction of hearing its teeth click together.

It grunted, and the man above gave an extra heave. I had room to breathe. More than that, I had room to run. Twisting to my stomach, I pulled myself free.

When I won my way to my feet, I didn't look back. I ran to the mouth of the alley. If the thing had followed me, Ethan was safe. I wasn't.

Most of the people had already fled. I bolted across the street, almost knocking over two girls dressed in shoes not made for running, and slid into my car. The engine roared to life as I pressed the gas pedal to the floor and left behind a blue-grey cloud of exhaust, a path of burnt rubber, and my best friend.

Heart still thundering, I burst into my apartment. I locked the door and backed my way to the kitchen before I tried to start breathing normally. My keys fell to the floor, and I yanked the note from the fridge and read it again and again. Not human. My mind stuck on that phrase.

A man had been pacing beside the cage. When Brick had hit me, that man had changed. No, not man. It definitely was not human. Had it hurt anyone? Crap. Ethan. I patted my backside for my phone. I'd left it in my bag. The bag I'd dropped behind the bar. I shook inside and out. I needed a phone. I needed to check on Ethan. I needed to run and hide like the letter said.

There wasn't much in my stark apartment that I needed. I went to my closet, grabbed a bag, and started throwing clothes into it. Five minutes after storming my way in, I was ready to run out.

A knock startled me as I reached for the knob. My breath rushed out of me, and for a moment, I did nothing. Another sharp knock. I leaned forward and looked through the peephole. The familiar face had me yanking the door open.

"Ethan." A sob escaped me as I dropped my bag and threw my arms around him.

He caught me and held me close.

"I was so scared. Are you hurt?" he asked, pulling back. He looked me over and frowned at something he saw on my face. With a finger, he gently brushed my jaw. It felt tender.

"Brick caught you good," he said.

Screw Brick.

"What was that thing?"

He let go and moved to come in. I stopped him.

"No. I can't stay here. Let's go to your place."

He gave me a worried look.

"You sure?"

I nodded. He picked up my bag and held out a hand. Against my better judgement, I took it. I felt very little coming from him, though.

We walked around the back of the building to the parking lot.

In the dark, everything seemed scarier. My heart continued to pound, and I was glad Ethan was with me. He opened my car door; but before I could get in, he wrapped a hand around the back of my neck and pulled me close. I let out a shaky breath and laid my head against his chest. I felt the steady thump of his heart under his shirt.

"I thought I lost you tonight," he said.

He smoothed a hand over my hair, and I winced. He must have felt it because he dropped his arms, stepped back, and looked at me with concern. I reached up to gently probe the area on the back of my head. A large bump pulsed there.

"You almost did," I said, thinking of the beast that had brought me down. "But I'm fine now. I'll follow you. We'll talk when we get there."

He nodded and waited by the car until I closed the door.

WE PULLED UP TO A SMALL, boxcar house. Rusted pieces of metal that used to be parts of vehicles littered the dead lawn. Ethan's dad's house wasn't out of place in this neighborhood.

Ethan parked on the street and got out to wait for me as I parked. At this time of night, the neighborhood was quiet. Everyone was either high or already passed out. I grabbed my bag and joined him.

He offered his hand again.

"Better not," I said.

Ethan nodded, then followed me toward the house. I let myself in and smiled at Mr. Petnu. Regret poured from him when he saw me.

"Izza, whatcha doing here?" His words were slow, but he watched me closely.

"Hi, Mr. Petnu. I thought I'd stay for a while, if that's okay." I moved aside, so Ethan could step into the cramped room.

"You know it is. Want my bed?" Hope flavored the air.

"Um, no thanks." I waved a hand farewell and moved down the little hall to Ethan's cramped room.

A full-size bed just fit between the two walls, leaving no room on the sides and only two feet between the end of the bed and the closet. The bed was neatly made, and the closet doors were closed. I knew if I opened them, I would see all of Ethan's clothes tidily hung or folded.

"Explain to me again why you live here?" I said, setting my bag on the narrow dresser squeezed in between the end of the bed and the closet.

"I'm waiting for him to kick it so I can claim my inheritance."

Ethan never answered seriously. I flopped back on his bed, and he joined me. We lay together, looking up at the stained, foam-tiled ceiling.

"He asks about you all the time," he said, and I knew he meant his father. "He wants to know when I'll marry you and actually make something of myself."

"You still haven't told him about the bar?"

Ethan snorted. "He doesn't give a damn about what I do with my life, only who I settle down with."

It wasn't even that. Mr. Petnu wanted me to be with Ethan. Just me. Ethan's father wanted us to live there with him. I would be his permanent high. Cheaper and better than anything he could buy. And, that was the reason I wouldn't hold Ethan's hand coming in. If his father saw, he'd think it meant we were finally together.

"All the more reason to leave," I said before changing subjects. "Tell me what you saw."

"I was watching the fight and filling drinks. People kept coming in as usual. I didn't pay them any attention until that guy walked up to the cage."

He turned his head. I turned mine to meet his serious gaze.

"He changed. One minute a man, the next..."

I nodded.

"Yeah. That's what I thought. I just wanted to make sure it wasn't something new someone lit up in there."

Something flickered in Ethan's expression a moment before he closed the gap between us and pressed his lips to mine. All night, he'd kept himself closed off. I'd only caught hints of emotions from him, nothing long enough to taste. As his lips pressed against mine, though, some of them escaped. Desire. Fear. Love. He pulled back.

"I love you."

His words pierced my heart. Everything he felt for me drifted around us. It was a heady emotional mix that I wanted to drown in.

I pulled away and touched his face.

"I love you, too, just not that way."

He closed himself off once more.

"Because you've never tried."

"And I never will."

He shut his eyes with a pained and sorrowful expression.

"Did you feel anything tonight?"

It wouldn't do any good to pretend I didn't understand what he meant. This was a talk we'd had before. He thought, if he could keep his emotions locked around me, it meant we had a chance to be something more together.

"Don't lie and say you did. I know you didn't."

"Just now I did. When we're alone. When there are no distractions. When you're the only one I have to pull from. It will always be this way, Ethan. You know that. I have to be alone. I have to isolate myself." I turned to my side and held his face. He opened his eyes. Hurt filled them. "If I don't, I die."

"What if—"

"No, Ethan. I won't risk draining you. You're too important to me. You're the only friend I have. God, look at my parents."

My parents weren't much better than his. I'd broken them. Just by living with them as a kid. And, if I let myself love Ethan, like he wanted, if I spent every day of my life with him like he wanted, I'd eventually kill him. I would never be with anyone that way. Just holding hands on my first and only date had left that boy lying limp on the floor. Deep down, Ethan knew I would never do as he wanted. I loved him too much for that.

I sat up.

"I'm going to use your shower, then turn in."

He nodded but didn't move.

"I'll take the couch."

"Thanks."

CHAPTER TWO

AFTER JUST A FEW HOURS, I COULDN'T TAKE IT ANYMORE. THE FIGHT with Brick had been cut short, leaving me with emotions I didn't want. Now, Ethan's father snored loudly from his room, emanating too many emotions even in his sleep. I needed a break.

I tossed back the covers and scooted out of bed. My runners were side by side in Ethan's closet. He'd put them there while I'd showered. I laced them up and eased open his bedroom door. With soft steps, I crept past Ethan on the couch and gently opened the front door.

The encroaching sun had lightened the sky outside from black to not quite black. I shut the door behind me and breathed in the air. It wasn't fresh. In fact, it stank like rotten garbage and exhaust. But it was free of heavy emotion, and I breathed easy. The pavement called to me, and I jogged from the yard.

An hour later, I returned out of breath and bruised. I thought I might have even had a black eye. The idea just made my grin bigger. Jogging in Ethan's neighborhood was great.

The front door opened as I stretched and cooled down.

"Good run?" Ethan asked.

"The best. I may have convinced a few wannabe thugs to go to school today."

He laughed and offered me his coffee, which I took gratefully.

"So, what will the unemployed do today?"

"What are you going to do?" I asked, instead of answering. I hadn't given my lack of employment any thought. All night, my mind had kept replaying the scene from Ethan's place...the hit to my face, the cage bending inward, the teeth snapping at me.

"I have to go clean up," he said, and I knew he meant the bar.

"No." The word came out panicked, and I took a breath to calm myself. "You can't go back there. Not yet."

"What choice do I have? One of us needs a job."

He said it to tease me, but I didn't laugh. He didn't know; he didn't understand.

"I need to show you something."

I went into the house and grabbed the letter I'd shoved into my bag. When I turned, he was in the bedroom doorway, watching me. I handed the piece of paper to him, not saying anything. His eyes skimmed the page. He frowned and read it again.

"Shit."

Fear poured from him, his shock robbing him of control.

"Yeah." I sat on the bed.

"What are we going to do?"

I loved him for that. It wasn't my problem; it was ours. And I knew the fear he wasn't able to suppress wasn't for himself. It was for me. But, I couldn't pull him down with me. I wouldn't.

"I'm going to the bank, taking out everything I have, and doing what the note says. I need you to stay here."

He lowered himself to the mattress beside me. I'd expected an argument, but he sat there quietly for a moment, closing himself off emotionally as he stared at his hands.

"Want to know why I stay with him?" he asked quietly.

His question was unexpected. Though something about his tone had me worrying about what he would say, I nodded.

"You have your parents. They love you completely. You stay away from them to protect them, just like you do for me. But I saw..." He exhaled slowly. "Remember the day you came home with me?" He gave a pained laugh. "Your mom had put pigtails in your hair so it wouldn't fall in your face when we fought on the playground. I stood behind you, staring at your hair and cringing when you told my dad never to hit me again."

I remembered confronting Mr. Petnu. Ethan and I had both still been in grade school when I finally figured out why Ethan was angry all the time. I could still feel the rage that had consumed me as I'd stood before Mr. Petnu.

Ethan looked up at me before he continued.

"And when he fell to the floor, I wanted to cry I was so happy. But not you. Hurting him to protect me had hurt you. I remember how you'd whispered 'I broke him.' You didn't, though, Z. You fixed him. I've stayed because I never wanted you to regret what you did for me."

I couldn't speak around the tightness in my throat.

"All you've ever wanted was a friend. That's who I am. And that's why I'll follow you. Because there's nowhere else I'd rather be, and no one else I'd rather be with."

It hurt so much. For the second time in less than twenty-four hours, I threw my arms around him. He held me close while I fought not to cry. I was the reason he'd stayed with his dad. But, by staying his friend, I'd trapped him in more than just his home. He would stay with me to face the creatures the letter mentioned. I recalled the teeth of the thing that had brought me to the ground and knew Ethan would have no chance if they found me again. Yet, I couldn't bring myself to let him go.

"You are my best friend," I said with a tight voice. Finally, I pulled back. "I want one promise from you."

"Anything."

"If I tell you to run, you go...or I'll make you go. Run and find someone perfect and sweet who hates violence. Have lots of babies and name one after me. Okay?"

He closed his eyes and turned away before he nodded.

"Life should have been kinder and made you my brother," I said.

A sharp, rapid knock on the front door echoed through the small house and broke the moment. I quickly got off the bed.

"Might be one of the thugs," I explained when Ethan gave me a questioning look.

He smiled, and with a shake of his head, he stood. I followed him into the living room. Ethan had already folded his blanket and picked up while he'd waited for me. I wondered how often he did that for his dad.

Through the diamond of smoke-stained glass that decorated the window of the front door, I saw the top of a dark mop of hair. A step behind that head, I caught a glimpse of blonde. They were definitely not the thugs.

Ethan reached for the knob without looking through the window. His trust humbled me at times.

As soon as the door opened, anxiety, fear, and desperation flooded the room. It all came from the girl with the dark mop of hair. Her emotions were so loud, she drowned out what the girl behind her might be feeling.

"Hi," the dark mop of hair said, meeting Ethan's gaze. "Is Isabelle—?" Her gaze shifted to me. Some of her desperation faded as joy lit her face.

We stared at each other a moment while I waited for her to say what she wanted. But she kept quiet, staring at me as if I were her long lost relative or something.

Then, suspicion crept in. First the letter, then the weird dog attack, now strangers showing up at Ethan's and asking for me?

No one knew I was here. I didn't recognize her. How did she know my name?

"Who are you?" I asked.

Ethan shifted and started to close the door at my distrustful tone. The girl's expression quickly changed to one of frustration as she placed a hand against the door to stop it.

"Look, shutting the door in my face won't answer the questions you must have. How about letting us in so we can talk?"

Before I could tell the two girls to get lost, the blonde spoke up.

"My name's Gabby. This is Bethi. We've been driving for a week just to find you—"

Find me? Panic jetted my adrenaline.

Knocking Ethan to the side, I grabbed the door and slammed it in their faces. I heard one of them cry out as I grabbed Ethan's hand.

Run. Hide. The words echoed in my mind while my pulse jumped, and I felt a sliver of fear. I needed to get Ethan out of there. I pulled him with me to the kitchen, not ten feet away, and toward the back door.

"She's running," I heard a girl shout from the front.

Ethan kept up with me.

"Z, what is it?"

"It's them," I said, pulling the backdoor open only to stop abruptly.

A man stood outside and held up both hands in a pacifying manner. I wasn't in the mood to be calmed.

"We just want to talk."

"No."

I dropped Ethan's hand and breathed in, pulling the man's urgency and caution away. With the next breath, I took his concern and lifted my fists. I struck out, hitting him in the face. His brows rose, but he didn't move much. I didn't stop. I clipped him again and, like a breeze, I ruffled his russet hair.

The two women rounded the building just then, followed by another man. He had thicker shoulders than the first guy. Worried that I wasn't causing enough damage, I pulled from all of them. My skin started to itch.

"Stop!"

I didn't turn to see which girl yelled. I focused instead on the man before me. The next blow snapped the russet-haired man's head back. When he narrowed his eyes and came back around with a swing of his own, I stole his aggression and went for his ribs. He grunted in pain.

Humor burst from someone in the group. The unexpected emotion almost distracted me.

"Clay, don't laugh. Help him," one of the girls said.

Ethan moved to block whoever was coming to help. I knew he wouldn't stand a chance.

"Ethan, run," I said as I dodged a swing.

Anger and fear flared. I grabbed those emotions too, spun around, and hit the new guy in the face.

Someone cried out. The other man grabbed my arms, pinning me.

"Isabelle, enough," Bethi said. "You're only going to hurt yourself."

"I don't think so." I pulled hard from the emotional soup they'd made. First, the girls fell to their knees. Worry drifted from their men. I pulled again, and the arms around me loosened. Then, the men went down.

I turned and yanked Ethan to his feet. Despite his last minute effort to block me, he looked faint. When I pulled hard, I couldn't target.

"Sorry, Ethan."

"S'okay." He took a deep breath and managed a few stumbling steps.

The strangers were starting to move. I wanted to pull more and knock them out, but I couldn't risk Ethan. The men struggled to their feet. Ignoring us, they went to the girls and started to help them up.

"Come on." I pulled Ethan behind me, and I made for the front of the house where we'd parked. "Do you have your keys?"

Before we stepped around the rusted fender that separated the side yard from the front yard, I felt it again. The black hole. The void of emotion. With the group behind us and our car in front, we didn't have a choice but to face the thing that had chased me into the alley. I wanted to swear. Our chances of escape were slim. I tightened my grip on Ethan's hand and stepped forward.

The man I'd glimpsed at the bar, just before he'd turned into a dog, stood in the front yard. He had to be at least six and a half feet tall and close to three hundred pounds. Even with his hands loosely in the pockets of his dress pants, his biceps bulged beneath his shirt. I swallowed hard and eyed his neck. The width of it competed with the width of his jaw. He was built for fighting. My heart skipped a beat at the same time my stomach plunged to my toes. His precisely combed dark hair and pressed slacks were obviously meant to mislead his opponent. Was there any chance for us?

My gaze drifted to the older man who stood beside the fighter. He'd put the chokehold on the beast once before. However, he didn't look like he would offer any help this time. His light grey gaze studied me, and I felt a hint of hope and sorrow from him, an odd combination of emotions.

Focusing on the fighter once more, I tried to come up with a plan.

The man's dark brown eyes flicked to my hand, the one wrapped around Ethan's, before meeting mine. Something in that glance had me stepping protectively in front of Ethan.

"Isabelle," the man's low voice sent a shiver of dread through me, "let the boy go."

He was right. Ethan wasn't involved in this. They wanted me. "Ethan, this time listen."

I released his hand and gave him a nudge before sprinting at the man. Instead of trying to hit him—something he was sure to anticipate—I dropped. Balancing on my hands, I kicked out a leg and hooked him behind the knee with my calf. As he buckled, I used the hold on his leg to pull myself up behind him.

He landed in a three-point stance with his head bent as if in prayer. I twisted and grabbed a piece of rusted metal from a nearby pile. Ignoring the jagged edge that bit into my palm, I swung my ghetto weapon at his head. But he was too fast. He turned, caught my wrist, and tugged forward. He pulled me off balance, and I landed on his knee like a little girl on Santa's lap.

Our gazes locked. My breath heaved in and out as my stomach cramped with fear not my own. Crap. Ethan. I heard him struggling with someone. He hadn't run.

The man's eyes didn't waver from mine, and I realized he wasn't moving. Neither was I. I still had another hand free. I needed to pull more—

"You're bleeding."

The man's steady voice confused me. Why didn't he sound angry?

I could feel Ethan's fear, worry from three of the people, and annoyance from another, but nothing from the man holding me by the wrist. I hated not feeling anything from him. I couldn't steal what I couldn't feel. How could I fight him?

As he stood, pulling me up with him, his fingers trembled around my wrist. A weak hold? I swung with my left arm. Not a strong swing, but it was better than just standing there. He caught that wrist, too, leaving me no choice. If I couldn't pull emotion from him, I'd pull from everyone else.

I breathed in Ethan's fear, the group's worry and impatience, and the neighbors' desolation and hopelessness. Carefully, I pulled what I needed without reducing Ethan to an immobile puddle. Again and again, I stole from them. The man watched me breathe in and out. The emotions expanded within me, a ball of raw power. My insides hardened. My muscles twitched. The man before me frowned as he studied my face...my rage.

A quick twist freed my right hand. He didn't try to reclaim it, and I narrowed my eyes at him. What game did he play?

I breathed again, taking everything I could and stomped on his foot. He flinched, and I pulled my other hand free. My skin tingled painfully. Too many emotions swirled within me. I struck out and connected with his face. His head snapped to the side. My wrist crunched. It should have hurt, but I was too full of everything else and didn't feel anything. He frowned. I swung again, but this time he blocked it with an open palm. His warm fingers curled around my fist for just a moment. I pulled back and tried again.

He blocked each strike, moving fluidly with me. The pressure behind my skin eased. It was like I was back in the play yard with Ethan. A small smile broke free with that thought.

The big man's dark eyes drifted to my mouth, and his expression changed. He caught my next swing and pulled me forward. Off balance, I fell against his chest. His arms wrapped around me, and he buried his face in the curve of my neck. His chest expanded against mine as he breathed deeply.

Shocked, I wrenched on his ear and slipped out of his arms. Then, I did the most girly thing I'd done in a long time. I slapped him. With my cut hand. It left behind a bloody handprint.

He stared at me a moment, then reached up and touched his cheek. He looked at his hand, at my blood smeared on his skin, and his whole body began to tremble. Vaguely, I recalled seeing him do the same thing a moment before Brick had hit me in the face.

I backed up a step. He didn't try to follow. I backed up three more and risked a quick look behind me. The two guys loosely held Ethan. I understood why he didn't try to break free of their weak holds when he glanced at me, to the man, and back at me again. He had watched me take down some crazy huge men in the past. No doubt he'd figured out the mountain before me wasn't the same as those guys. The mountain wasn't normal.

The older man who'd stood aside and watched us fight heaved a sigh.

"Carlos..." he said.

My feet slid back a few more steps. Carlos' eyes drifted to the hand at my side. Though I knew better, I glanced down at it, too. The slap had caused it to start bleeding in earnest, and a drop fell from the tip of my middle finger to the ground.

"Isabelle, stop," one of the women said from behind me.

I rolled my shoulders. I couldn't take them all in a fight. If they were regular people, maybe. And I couldn't drain them, not with Ethan already weak and within range. What did that leave me?

"Isabelle, I promise, we're not here to hurt you," the same voice said.

"The world is full of promises waiting to be broken," I said.

I'd learned the truth of that at a young age. Even the promises made with the best intentions could crumble because of circumstance. I thought of the note and of Ethan as I took a deep breath, ready to pull everything in.

"The more you pull, the tighter you feel on the inside."

The words stopped me. I finally turned and eyed the speaker. She was the one who'd knocked on the door. She looked young and had vivid blue eyes that contrasted with her dark hair. She was also the one who leaked desperation and fear. Were they using her too? I thought not. The russet-haired man beside her hovered protectively close.

"Fighting helps." She stepped closer. "But if you pull too much in, your nose starts to bleed."

She was right. I'd learned that when I was still young, before

29

I'd met Ethan. I couldn't remember now what had made me angry with my parents, but I could remember what I had done to them and how my nose had bled afterward as I'd bent over their slumped bodies on the floor.

They know what you can do.

The phrase repeated in my head. I would not be used to hurt people like that. Adrenaline pumped through my veins.

"No." The word echoed off the houses.

I gave Ethan an apologetic look, and he immediately closed himself off. I hoped it would save him.

I pulled harder than I ever had before. First, the four by Ethan collapsed to the ground. Then, the older man went to his knees, his surprised gaze on me.

The man before me remained unaffected while Ethan slowly started walking toward the car. My friend's steps were measured and unsure. Yet, to save us both, I'd need to take more.

The man stepped toward me and lifted his hand. I pulled again as he reached forward.

"Stop...Isabelle...you'll hurt..." The dark-haired girl's head hit the dead grass, and her eyes rolled back.

My skin tingled as if all of me had fallen asleep and was just starting to come to. But he didn't stop. Curling my hands into fists, I wondered if I finally had enough to down him.

His fingers touched my cheek, then gently wiped my upper lip. I jerked back from his touch and saw the blood. My blood. I sniffled, realizing my nose was bleeding. That wasn't good.

His eyes bore into mine for a moment, then he stepped aside. Stunned, I watched him lift one of the girls from the ground then straighten with her in his arms. He walked toward the backyard, carrying her.

Ethan's car roared to life, pulling me from my shock. The big guy wasn't going to fight me.

I ran for the car and got in. Ethan didn't wait for me to close the door. We peeled away from the yard as the man stepped around the corner empty-handed. My last look was of him bending to pick up the other girl.

"HANDS UP, NOW," Ethan said. He paced the small space of our room, moving what he could out of the way.

My head hurt, and my eyes didn't want to focus.

"Now, Z!" He swung at me. I automatically blocked.

"Stop. Wait," I said. "I can't..."

He swung again and connected with my arm. My already tight skin throbbed.

"Stop being a girl and get those hands up."

I jabbed at him, but he dodged my pathetically slow move.

"Again," he said. His hits were more like nudges. He was trying to piss me off, and it was working.

I shifted my weight with my next swing and hit his arm. Long ago, I'd stopped aiming for his head or vital spots when we sparred. I didn't want to hurt him, not in a permanently damaging way, anyway.

"Come on, twinkle-toes. Dance. Move. Do something more than swing those little toothpicks you call arms."

Scratch that. He was going to lose some teeth. I swung harder, aiming for his mouth. He laughed. Jerk. He continued to block each pathetic blow. My swings were too loose.

Focus. I shook my head and stepped back to roll my shoulders.

"That's my girl." His soft voice and sad eyes told me just how worried he was. He'd kept his emotions tightly blocked the whole drive, but now they were starting to slip.

We fought quietly in the motel room for thirty minutes before my nose stopped bleeding and another thirty before my skin stopped throbbing. It still ached, but I called a stop regardless.

"We can't stay here," I said, moving to the bathroom. I grabbed a hand towel for each of us, tossed one to him, and used mine to wipe the sweat and blood from my face.

"I don't know what they are, but I think we need to listen to that letter." The towel muffled my words.

"All right." He snatched the keys up from the table. "I'll get what we need and be back in four hours."

I laid a hand on his arm as he passed, stopping him. His gaze met mine. I had no words for how much his simple agreement and willingness to help meant to me.

"Just come back."

He nodded and left.

Still in my running clothes from that morning, I went to the hotel's meager exercise room and hogged the treadmill for the next hour.

CHAPTER THREE

"THE CAR'S LOADED," ETHAN SAID WITH A NUDGE TO MY SHOULDER.

I lifted my head from my arm and wiped the drool from my face as I blinked at the clock.

"Good nap, princess?" He chuckled as he moved away.

"It was."

The hotel was pretty dead, given the time of day, which meant no neighbors, which meant no emotions to pull. Having drained most of the excess with sparring and running, I'd crashed as soon as I had returned to the room.

I sat up and caught the bag he threw my way. It wasn't the bag I'd packed for his house.

"Clean clothes," he said.

"You went back to my place?"

He nodded as he walked into the bathroom and turned on the water.

"Why? What if they'd been there waiting?" I stood and paced to the bathroom. He moved out and gestured for me to get in.

"Hurry up. I want to be on the road again in thirty minutes. It'll be the road trip we should have taken after you graduated," he said with a grin.

"Gah." I threw my hands up in the air and stomped off to close myself into the bathroom. There, I discovered he'd packed a lot of what I'd left behind. Half of my wardrobe consisted of exercise clothes. The other half, office clothes. Seeing it all crammed together in a bag looked weird.

I plucked out clean underthings, yoga pants, and a fitted tank before stripping. The shower felt great, and I lingered a bit too long. Threads of annoyance, twisted in with amusement, touched me as Ethan rapped sharply on the door. I turned off the water and towel dried before I quickly dressed. Steam billowed out the door as I stepped out.

What I saw stopped me. A man held Ethan by the throat. The sight of my friend dangling in the air wasn't as scary as the sight of the furred arm that held him there. The nails of the man's hand were long, black, sharp, and inhuman.

The bag fell from my fingers, a soft sound in the oddly quiet room. The man turned his head to look at me, and a smile curled his lips. Another man sat on the bed, watching the pair. He too turned to look at me.

"With a human?" the lounging man said. "That's worse than being with the werewolves."

Ethan's face had already turned an unhealthy red. His hands were still pulling at the hand at his throat. Yet, I felt no fear from him. He knew what was coming.

"Put him down." I bit out the words, anger surpassing my fear for Ethan. I didn't wait for them to comply. I pulled deep. Both men grunted.

"Stop or I snap his neck," the one holding Ethan said.

I laughed bitterly and pulled again.

"I'm not stupid. He's dead either way." I exhaled and was about to pull again when the sound of splintering wood interrupted me.

Before I could turn to look at the door, the man on the bed

reacted. His teeth erupted from his mouth while his nose stretched and thickened. The mountain flew past me. He reached the bed as the man's clothes split apart. In a blink, the mountain grabbed the man by his newly formed fur and tossed him at the window. The glass shattered, and the wolf cried out as he fell two stories.

The other man dropped Ethan and moved toward the mountain. I ducked around the pair and rushed to Ethan to grab his arm and start dragging him toward the door.

The mountain caught the man by the throat, causing an abrupt stop to the charge, and lifted the man up so his feet dangled like Ethan's had.

I gave Ethan's arm another urgent tug as I tried to get us out of the room. Then, I looked at the damaged door, and my heart plummeted. The other five people from Ethan's house stood in the doorway. I stopped tugging and glanced at the only other exit, the broken window.

The mountain caught my attention. He wasn't focused on the man clawing at his arms. He watched me. When I met his gaze, the man he held went flying through the window, too.

Silence reigned in the room for two heartbeats as we stared at each other.

"We need to leave," he said.

The sound of his voice made my stomach twist. Was it fear? Maybe. Or maybe it was preparing for what I would need to do next. Pulling would be easier if I knew what the giant was feeling.

Ethan, knowing what I was about to do, gave a feeble tug; and I realized I still held his arm. I dropped it and prepared to draw more. Ethan attempted to get to his feet, but I didn't move to help him. Touching him while I pulled would be so much worse.

"Come on, son," the older man said, moving to help lift Ethan. His tone and choice of words stopped me from trying to bring them to their knees a second time. I watched as he wrapped an arm around Ethan's back and gently lifted him to his feet. Ethan looked pale and shaky.

"Isabelle, I'm Bethi," the dark-haired girl hurriedly said, drawing my attention. "I dream our past lives. Mine, yours, hers." She nodded toward the other woman in the doorway.

"More of them are coming," the blonde said.

"Gabby can see their locations and the locations of the others like us. We need to leave. We can't let them find us."

Her words were so close to what the letter said. Did one of them write it? I glanced at Gabby then back at Bethi. There were obviously two groups here: the ones who went out the window, and the ones who got to stay in the room.

"Yes, let's leave," I said.

Maybe these people really were here to help, but I didn't care. I didn't want anything to do with either group. Ethan and I needed to get away from whatever madness was stalking me, and the faster we got out of the room, the faster Ethan and I could escape.

The older man helped Ethan walk toward the door. I stayed right behind them both and grabbed my bag from the floor on the way past the bathroom. The mountain took the extra bag from the bed and followed me. The skin on the back of my neck prickled as I imagined his eyes tracking me. I struggled to remember what the older man had called him.

One of the men held the hotel door open as we filed out—the one with the russet hair. He had a very faint bruise on his chin and watched me closely as I passed. In fact, they all kept looking at me. They were probably waiting for me to run again. It was tempting. But I wouldn't make a run for it and leave Ethan. And if others were coming, I couldn't afford to pull more emotion than I could handle without Ethan on his feet to help me run afterward. That meant I needed to have patience for just a little longer.

The group walked to Ethan's car, and I opened the front

passenger door. Ethan's eyes met mine as he slid in. He tried to say something but only managed a broken rasp.

"Keys?" I said.

He stuck a shaky hand into his pocket and fished them out. Before I could grab them, a hand reached around me and plucked them from Ethan's fingers.

"I'll drive."

I turned and met the brown eyes of the mountain. Sure, he'd saved Ethan. But did he think that meant I'd suddenly had a change of heart? I didn't know these people, and I sure as heck didn't like any of them.

"No thanks." I held out my hand for the keys.

His eyes flicked to the palm and the cut there.

"We don't have time for this," the blonde said. "They're grouping to the east. We need to go."

I didn't know what she was talking about, but the panicked look in her eyes influenced me; I'd let him drive for now. If I needed to, I'd siphon again.

"Fine." I moved to open the back door, but he beat me to it. He held the door as I got in and closed it gently as soon as I settled.

"Hang in there, E," I said quietly to Ethan as I watched the man walk around the car.

The big guy opened the driver's door and bent low to get in. He looked ridiculous behind the wheel, cramped and uncomfortable in the small space.

He pulled out of the parking lot, trailing the other vehicle heading west. He drove well for someone who wasn't looking forward.

I met his eyes in the mirror.

"What's your name, again?"

"Carlos."

Something about his voice made my insides twitchy. I didn't like the feeling.

"Eyes on the road, Carlos."

He held my gaze for a moment longer.

"You should buckle up," he said.

I ignored Carlos and reached forward to squeeze Ethan's shoulder gently.

"You okay, Ethan?" He'd kept himself closed off since the hotel.

He turned his head, winced as he did so, and gave me a what-do-you-think look. Faint blue marks punctuated the red skin of his neck. I rubbed his shoulder, and he reached up to pat my hand before facing forward once more. He would wear bruises for several days, a constant reminder of how I'd put him in danger.

The vehicle we followed took a sudden sharp turn onto a pitted side road, and I fell over in the seat when we mirrored the move.

"What was that?" I said, pulling myself up and buckling in.

"Gabby is trying to avoid—"

Brake lights came on and tires screeched a moment before something flew over the front vehicle and hit our windshield. A startled cry ripped from me. The glass splintered but held. The body rolled to the side and fell to the road, a smear of blood the only sign of its passing.

Everything slowed down as I gripped the seat and stared out the windows. Large dogs poured from the trees on the left. Like a wave, they washed over our car. The roof dented in as something heavy landed on it. Carlos floored the gas. I couldn't see a thing through the white web of the broken windshield. The back window shattered. A furred hand reached in, ripped the seatbelt from me, and yanked me backward through the opening.

A long jaw filled with teeth greeted me. I didn't think...I pulled. Hard.

Something hit the side of my head.

THE ACHE just behind my eyes almost consumed me. Only the rhythmic stroke of a hand gently running over my head provided any relief. My cheek rested on a leg, and my shoulder and side rested on a soft cushion. I couldn't lift my head. Words refused to form as the thump in my skull echoed my heartbeat. I groaned.

A feminine voice shushed me.

"We're in the back of a van. You have a huge lump on your head."

I recognized the voice but struggled to recall the face associated with it. Definitely one of the girls. Abby? No, Gabby. When I tried to ask what happened, it emerged as another groan.

"You've been out for a bit. One of them carried you, another me. They ran through the trees and tossed us in here. We started moving right away. Maybe ten, fifteen minutes ago. I don't know. It's hard to tell."

She kept running her hand over my hair. Anxiety poured from her, contributing to my headache. I took several slow breaths and closed myself off as best I could. After a few more slow breaths, I tried speaking again.

"The others?" I wanted to vomit at the effort it took to speak.

There was a moment of silence before she answered in a hushed voice.

"I'm watching. They've fought free and are following."

"Huh?" I finally tried opening my eyes, but there was nothing to see. My stomach lurched, and I knew I needed to sit up soon.

"I can see the locations of people in my mind. Little sparks. Humans, werewolves, and Urbat have differently colored sparks to designate their species. We're unique. I'm Hope, according to Bethi, and you're Peace."

Peace? That was laughable. I only felt peaceful when beating on someone. Everyone around me, though, loved me. I brought them peace. So, maybe she was right.

I struggled to sit up and barely made it upright before vomiting on the floor. It splattered on our shoes.

"Sorry." The throbbing in my head increased.

"It's okay." It sounded anything but okay. "I really wish there was a window to open." She gagged.

"Have you moved around? Is there a door?"

Her silence answered me. When I tried standing, I almost slipped. Had I fallen in my own vomit, I would not have been responsible for whatever happened next. Thankfully, I caught my balance on the cold metal side of the van. Crouched over, I felt my way along the seat, which was mounted to the wall, toward the back. Only a seam between two sheets of metal marked the doors. No latch or handle.

"No handles." My head would definitely explode soon. "I'm going to try something. If I pass out, please get me off the floor."

I pulled in her anxiety and fear and nearly threw up again. Breathing through my mouth, I channeled my energy and kicked the doors. The metal bowed, and I caught a paper-thin glimpse of daylight along the floor.

The van's speed increased.

"You okay?" I asked her. Thump, thump, thump; my stomach roiled with each dull beat in my skull.

"Yes." Her relaxed answer reassured me, and I pulled again.

My next kick saw more daylight, but I also fell on my hip. When I picked myself up, I was still dry.

"Can you stand it one more time?"

"Sure."

As long as she kept talking, she'd be fine.

I pulled and kicked, again and again and again. The fifth time something creaked, and the light didn't flash back out of sight.

"One more time Gabby. Okay?"

She didn't answer, but I couldn't stop to check. They were

trying to get us somewhere before I broke free or they would have stopped to check out the racket I was making by now.

I closed my eyes, pulled deep, and kicked again. There was a snap, and then the doors flew open. The driver must have heard it or seen the doors in his mirror because he swerved a little. I turned and fell onto the seat, almost landing on Gabby's head. She'd fallen over onto the cushion at some point.

The van braked hard, and the door slammed shut. The latch was broken, though, so I knew it wouldn't stay shut.

I braced us as gravel crunched under the tires, and the van moved to the shoulder of the road.

"Hold on, Gabby. Just a little more." I pet her head as she had mine. "It'll be over soon."

The van came to a stop seconds before the back doors flew open. Two angry men glared at me.

I gently set Gabby on the seat so I wasn't touching her. Please let her live through this, I thought.

"Hello, boys." I pulled hard, trying to focus just on them.

When they fell to their knees, I stopped pulling and stumbled out of the van. Then, I started getting me some peace.

I kicked one in the face and had the satisfaction of hearing a dry crunch. I kicked the other between the legs. There was no crunch there, just a raspy, broken exhale.

"You can't steal people!"

Yelling hurt my head just as much as kicking. I doubled over and heaved again but very little came up. Heaving just made me angrier. One of the men on the ground, the one with the crushed pecans, started moving. I kicked him again.

Satisfied they would stay down for a while, I tried to climb back into the van to get Gabby out. However, my arms and legs weren't working together. The world started to fuzz around the edges. Crapballs.

"Gabby." I wasn't sure if I was asking her for help again or checking to see if she was still alive.

She lay on the seat, her pale hand dangling over the edge, close to my puddle. Had I killed her? Shadow replaced fuzz, and it started to close in, choking out the light. I was losing this one. Too much damage to the head and too much bottled up emotion. I thought of Ethan as I started to slide to the ground. What would they do to him?

Hands grabbed my arms, stopping my downward slide. My head lolled back. Carlos' brown eyes met mine.

"I threw up," I whispered.

"You're alive."

For the first time ever, I felt something from him. Relief. It flooded me and made everything worse.

I gagged and closed my eyes.

"Stop. Please."

A cry of denial preceded a burst of anguish so profound, I almost wept.

"Gabby," a smooth voice said.

I opened my eyes again as Carlos helped me stand. The shadows at the edge of my vision hovered, waiting.

Inside the van, one of the men from the group scooped Gabby into his arms. He cradled her tenderly, trying to keep her head from moving as he stepped from the van.

"What happened to her?" He looked to me for answers, the pain in his eyes too clear. I hated myself just then.

"Is she breathing?"

He nodded.

"I happened to her. We couldn't go with them."

My eyes fell to the men on the ground. The nose of the one I'd kicked in the face had straightened. His open eyes met mine. I didn't even have time to gasp. Carlos set me against the van and turned to meet the attack. After the two in the hotel, the madness on the road, and the kidnapping, the man's swipe seemed a slow, pathetic attempt at a fight. Still, my head spun as I watched.

Carlos' large hands closed around the man's head, and he gave a quick twist. When he turned to the other one, I closed my eyes. I couldn't watch any more. My stomach's earlier rebellion wanted an encore performance. So, I listened to the scrape of dirt and a soft grunt, knowing what was happening. I swallowed with difficulty.

A moment later, something brushed against my cheek. I opened my eyes. Carlos stood before me, blocking out the world.

"Can we leave, yet?"

He nodded. I tried pushing away from the van but gagged at a wave of vertigo.

"May I help you?" He held out his arms.

I leaned around him enough to glance at Gabby up in the other man's arms. I didn't think he'd looked away from her yet. Her head rested against his chest, and she looked completely comfortable cradled there.

"Thanks, but I'll pass. I'd puke."

I tried again and managed to move several steps from the van. The sky rotated and the ground bucked. My knees shook. And suddenly I was up in Carlos' arms. The abrupt change in perspective did not help my struggle not to heave. He held me through it all and cradled my head to his chest when I finished. Then, he ran.

The breeze helped. I closed my eyes and either slept or passed out. I wasn't sure which.

"Is she okay?" Ethan's raspy, abused voice pulled me from my stupor.

I opened my eyes to blue sky, squinted, and looked around. Carlos still held me, but we were no longer running. Nearby, the man who'd helped Ethan stood with Bethi and the ginger. Their worry pooled around me, trying to drown me.

Ethan walked toward me, his gaze filled with concern.

"She's fine and wants to be put down," I said.

Carlos made a noise, something between a grunt and a growl, and bent enough to set my feet on the ground. With care, he helped me stand. The little drummer boy was still having fun in my head, and I winced. Ethan reached out with a steadying hand.

"You should rest," Carlos said, not taking his eyes from me.

A fleeting look of annoyance crossed over Ethan's face as he glanced at Carlos. Then, he focused on me.

"Is it the hit to the head or overload?" Ethan reached up and ran a gentle hand over the side of my head. The lump there continued to throb.

"Both, I think."

"When will they get here?" he asked, looking at Bethi.

He knew what I needed. I could see the calculation in his eyes. How much more could I handle? Not much. My skin was too tight, and my head wouldn't feel better any time soon if I didn't do something about it.

"Soon. They were just a few—"

A caravan of three vehicles pulled up. An older woman with white hair and an older man with grey hair rushed out of two of the vehicles. Both ran to Gabby, who still hung limply in her man's arms. In the third vehicle, I saw four people. A man and woman sat in front, and a younger couple in back. All of them were looking at Gabby.

"What happened?" the grey-haired man asked.

"I couldn't kick open the door without help. She's not hurt. Just the opposite. She's floating so high, it'll be awhile before she's back. As long as she's still breathing, she should be fine."

Ethan and I shared a look. It was close to the same thing as I'd done to my parents and his father. Guilt tore at me, and I moved away from Carlos and Ethan. The man holding Gabby watched me approach. His emotions continued to spill out, making it hard to get close.

"She'll be okay. I promise." I gave him a sad smile. "I accidently did this to my parents a ton of times while growing up." I didn't add that they used recreational drugs now because of it or that I almost killed them countless times.

He gave me a single nod, and some of his chaotic outpouring slowed. He didn't put Gabby down, though.

I sniffled and wiped at my nose. It was already bleeding.

"We need to go," Ethan said. The sound of his voice filled me with regret. He'd been strangled to the point he sounded like a chain smoker; I'd almost had my head bashed in and barely escaped being kidnapped. What had I gotten us into?

"Clay, put Gabby in the back with you," the older man said. The man who'd helped Ethan moved with them. "Bethi and Luke, there's room for you, too."

Clay moved to the vehicle as a man I hadn't noticed moved around to open a door for him.

"I need to go with Isabelle," Bethi said. "She needs to understand what's happening."

"No, she doesn't," I said. "She needs to be isolated."

She glanced at the blood dripping from my nose and nodded. She and Luke got in.

"You three are with me," the woman with the white hair said.

Ethan and I walked toward her small car, and Carlos followed closely behind. Ethan opened the door for me. He kept casting worried glances at my nose. My hand was a bloody mess from swiping at it, but the blood wasn't flowing too hard yet.

As I slid in, the woman got in behind the wheel and passed back some tissues. I pressed them to my nose and leaned my head back against the seat.

Ethan settled next to me, and the car dipped as Carlos sat in the front seat. As soon as his door shut, she started forward. The silence was nice, but her worry wasn't. My tight skin and aching head made my empty stomach twist. The shadows were back in my peripheral. White dots danced with them. I focused on them, and they started to lead me away.

An elbow jabbed in my side. I opened my eyes and turned my head to glare at Ethan. He arched a brow at me as if saying, "Whatcha gunna do 'bout it?" Right now? Nothing. But later...I closed my eyes. Two seconds after I started to follow the shadows and lights, he elbowed me again.

"Boy, you touch her again, and I'll rip your arm off," Carlos said softly.

My eyes popped open, and I lifted my head. Carlos was still facing forward. The woman had her hand on his leg. It wasn't a sexy touch. It was a keep-your-butt-in-your-seat touch. Who did he think he was? I'd like to see him try to lay a finger on Ethan. I narrowed my eyes on Carlos.

"How are you doing, dear?" the woman asked.

I met her eyes in the rearview mirror.

"Not good. How much longer?"

She was quiet for a few minutes. "There are too many in this town. We need to keep driving for a while to confuse our scent trail."

Ethan lifted my hand and gently squeezed it. "You've got an hour to get us somewhere reasonably safe. She needs at least thirty minutes when we stop."

I set my head back against the seat. He wanted me to hold this in for an hour and then was only giving me thirty minutes to exorcise it?

"I'll kill you."

His hand gave another squeeze. He knew what he was in for. A tear leaked from my eye.

"THIS IS GOOD ENOUGH," Ethan said, pulling me back from the edge yet again. "Stop the car."

The urgency in his voice didn't leak through his emotions at all. Or maybe it did, and I didn't notice. The human sponge was full. So full, she was ready to explode.

He removed his hand from my face—when had he taken over holding the tissue to my nose?—and gently pulled me from the car.

My legs didn't want to support me. If not for Ethan's arms locked around me, I would have fallen.

"Tell them to drive ahead. She needs everyone to stay back for a while. The bleeding has to stop."

While he spoke, he dragged me. My heels bumped along the ground for several yards, then he stopped.

"Z, stand up now, or I drop you," he barked in my ear.

That annoying, little—

He dropped me, but caught me again. The panic of thinking he'd actually let me go, gave me an adrenaline boost.

"Ass," I whispered.

"What are you going to do about it? Come on, stand up."

He jostled me, purposely annoying me. I yanked an arm free and swatted at him. He laughed and jostled me again.

I pushed back against him and found my own footing. Stance wide for balance, I stood there with my head hanging down. My skull pounded, and for a moment, the slight sounds of nature around us seemed as if they were under water.

"Poor little Izzie," Ethan said in a singsong voice.

He tapped my arm. I swung out at him, wide and loose, and he easily stepped out of the way.

"That's it? All you have is noodle arms?"

I didn't even have that. Tired and ready to let myself fall to the ground, I exhaled.

"No, Z."

A slap cracked against my right cheek, the one Brick had bruised. Rage ignited in me. Ethan. My eyes popped open at the same time a roar echoed in the air around us.

Ethan's eyes were wide. They should be. Then, I noticed his focus wasn't on me, but over my shoulder. I twisted and saw the mountain explode into a beast. It was just like the fight in the bar. One minute he was a man, the next a gigantic dog. Only, this time, we were in a field and there was no one else around.

The beast charged at us, his angry gaze on Ethan. I bent low.

"Ethan is mine," I yelled a moment before I ran at the thing.

It tried to jump over me, but I was too full of energy to let it pass by me. I jumped up and drove my fist into its soft underside. It grunted as it twisted and fell. I landed lightly on my feet and quickly turned, ready for the next charge. But it didn't come. Instead, the wolf stood there, growling its fury but otherwise motionless.

"Stop," someone yelled.

I turned and looked toward the road. A group of people stood clustered around the cars. The woman with the white hair and the man with the bright grey eyes ran toward us. They were so fast. I blinked and relaxed my stance, swaying on my feet.

"No," Ethan said, stepping close to me. His arms steadied me. "Let them go. Now."

"Boy," the man with the grey eyes said, "he means to kill you."

"Hear that, Z? He wants to kill me," Ethan said, nudging me.

"No," the woman said. "We don't have time for this. We need to move."

Ethan's slow exhale moved the hair at the back of my head.

"Fine. Ten minutes. Please."

He turned me to face him.

"Just me and you. Show me what you got."

My eyes watered. Ten minutes? I wished they wouldn't have stopped Carlos.

"It's okay, babe. I've got you."

A tear leaked over the edge as I rolled my shoulders and swung. I kept the first few strikes slow, so he would get the rhythm, and I stuck with traditional boxing moves. Jab, jab, uppercut. Always right then left. He blocked the first set with ease.

"I've got you," he said again. "Come on!"

Another tear fell, and I opened myself up. My hands flew. Ethan stayed with me as best he could. I kept my targets the same. Right shoulder only, until I noticed him favoring it. Then I pulled back a bit and aimed for the left. I always pulled back on the left side. It was too close to his big heart.

"Time's up," the woman said.

I immediately stopped punching. Ethan opened his arms, and I fell against him.

"I'm so sorry," I whispered as I sniffled.

His hand gently feathered over the lump on my head. It didn't hurt as much.

"I know you are, Z."

CHAPTER FOUR

When I lifted my head from Ethan's shoulder, I saw it was just us in the field. The others had moved toward the cars once again. The mountain was no longer a wolf. He was a shirtless, angry man dressed in loose black slacks.

I stepped away from Ethan and wiped at my face.

"There's no point to that," he said. "You're a complete mess."

I stopped wiping and gave him a look. He grinned at me. I almost grinned back.

"Did I hit you anywhere too hard?"

"Not too hard. Just enough to remind me to keep up with you."

"I'm—"

"Isabelle," he said, stopping another apology.

I narrowed my eyes at him, and he completely ignored it to jerk a thumb over his shoulder.

"Get your butt to the car before tall and half-naked goes caveman on you and drags you there by your hair."

I snorted at Ethan's description of Carlos.

THE CAR WAS QUIET. Now that my nose wasn't pouring blood and my head felt less like a drum, I looked around at what we passed —fields, open plains, and occasional wooded areas.

"I apologize," the woman said suddenly.

I glanced forward and caught her gaze in the mirror. "For what?"

"For preventing Carlos from helping you."

Carlos hadn't wanted to help. He'd wanted to hurt Ethan. But I didn't point that out.

"So, what exactly are you guys?"

She grinned slightly.

"I think you know. My name is Winifred Lewis, by the way."

"I'm Isabelle."

I felt Ethan's humor a moment before he closed himself off again. His control was impressing me. It had been too long since we'd last seen each other.

"Why did you come for me?" I asked.

"Bethi can probably explain better than I can. However, according to what she has told us, you are one of six women with special abilities. There is a group—Bethi called them Urbat—that is trying to find you all. Their leader held Michelle, one of the young women riding in the car behind us, for a time. And, according to Bethi, he has the last one of you with him."

"Yeah, that doesn't really answer my question. Why did you come for me?"

"Bethi said we needed to protect you."

I watched Winifred in the mirror and felt a wisp of some emotion from her. It was sour like regret and anger.

"What aren't you telling me?"

"We need your help."

My help? I was a bruised and beaten mess. Ethan, my best friend, was more so. How did they think I could help them?

Ethan's fingers threaded through mine.

"Where are we going?" he asked.

"A friend has a place about an hour from here. Gabby had been watching the area and thought we should be okay there for a few hours. Bethi will want to talk to you," she said, looking at me.

I nodded and glanced at Ethan. We shared a look, and I wondered if he was hearing the faint chords of dueling banjos like I was. They wanted to take us to a remote place to tell us why they needed me. The words of the letter continued to play in my mind. Were these the people the letter tried to warn me about?

I curled my right hand into a fist and winced. My sliced palm hurt. So did my wrist. Ethan, still watching me, looked down at my hand. He picked it up and started probing the wrist, somehow knowing the cut wasn't the issue.

"Did anyone happen to grab our bags from the other car?" he asked.

"I'm sorry, no," Winifred said.

The bags probably had my spare gloves and some wraps. Without the gloves, I'd continue to hurt my wrist. He and I both knew that taking a break from fighting wasn't an option. I'd just need to change my style. Ethan hated kicking.

I saw the barn as soon as we pulled up.

"Oh, yeah," I said under my breath. Ethan and I had a new hang out.

As soon as the car stopped, I had my door open.

"I'll be in the barn for an hour," I said over my shoulder.

"We need to talk first," Winifred said.

I stopped and turned back to her. Carlos was already standing beside the car, his gaze focused on me.

"No. There's no way I can sit in a room with a bunch of people right now."

The second vehicle pulled in and parked. The door immediately opened, and the dark-haired girl jumped out.

"It's okay, Winifred. Let her go."

I didn't wait for Winifred's permission but continued toward the barn. Ethan was right behind me. The structure was built into a hill, and we were at the top. I pushed one of the double doors open and stepped into an empty hayloft.

The floorboards held firm as I walked several feet in. Ethan's steps scuffed behind me.

"Shirt off, handsome," I said, turning on him.

His brows rose.

"I'm not lifting a fist until I see what I did to you the last time."

He hesitated a moment then pulled his shirt over his head, using just his left arm. That alone told me how badly I'd hurt him. The blue covering his right shoulder said the rest. I looked down at the floor for several minutes. Ethan moved close with a sigh and gently touched the bruise on my cheek.

"It's the price we pay. You know that."

"No, it's the price I should pay. Not you." I met his gaze, feeling pity for both of us.

"None of that." He took a step back and brought both hands up. "Let's go."

Shirtless, I could at least see if I did him any more damage.

"Fine."

We started out with a slow rhythm. It only lasted a minute.

"Ethan, this isn't working. You're blocking too slow."

Ethan dropped his arms and rolled his shoulders. A blast of frustration hit me. He quickly stifled it.

"Sorry."

"S'okay." But it wasn't. My head was starting to hurt again. If I only had a few hours here, I had to empty myself. Of everything. After that, I would need a nap and probably a bag of ice for my wrist and my face and Ethan's neck and his shoulder...

Ethan's gaze flicked to the double doors. Carlos stood there, arms crossed while he watched us. I hadn't even noticed that he'd followed. Not only was he quiet, but the country was quiet, which meant less emotional noise to notice a void. Plus, he was far enough away that I wouldn't have pulled in any emotion if he'd actually projected anything.

"Hey, big and broody," Ethan said. "Come here."

I smirked. Ethan always tried to rub people the wrong way. He was a product of his upbringing. He didn't make friends; he made frenemies.

Carlos walked toward us without any indication that Ethan had gotten under his skin. And maybe Ethan hadn't. I certainly didn't feel anything from Carlos.

"My shoulder's not going to cut it. I need you to step in. But there are a few rules." As he spoke, he walked around me. "You can't take it easy on her. Ever. Got it?"

Carlos looked from Ethan to me and nodded.

"This isn't a fight. This is a spar. A very fast, very intense spar. The goal isn't to hurt one another."

Carlos nodded again, and I turned to grin at Ethan. He was worried the big guy would hurt me.

"And no aiming for her face. She doesn't look good with bruises."

Carlos gave another stoic nod. I still didn't feel anything from him. If I didn't feel anything, it would be a lot easier to exorcise the emotions I held. This might actually be fun.

Ethan must have been thinking the same thing.

"Go get him," he said with a slap to my butt.

Before I could move, Carlos blurred. One second he was standing across from us; the next, he was standing before Ethan, his hand wrapped around Ethan's throat. Ethan's feet dangled in the air, and his hands flew to the fingers squeezing the oxygen from him.

Fear for Ethan made my temper snap.

"You son of a..." I let loose on Carlos.

His kidneys were my punching bags. I hit hard and managed five rapid blows to each before he dropped Ethan and turned on me. I punched him in the throat and brought him to his knees. He wheezed and looked up at me. I kicked him in the face. Once. Twice. The third time brought him to the ground. I straddled him and drew back, ready to remodel his face.

"Girl, that's enough," a voice said. "He's not fighting back. He won't."

I looked up and saw the man with the bright grey eyes standing in the doorway. Carlos moved ever so slightly underneath me, bringing my attention back to him.

His face was marked from the last kick. Why did I feel guilty for that? He'd had Ethan by the throat.

"No one touches Ethan. Ever. Got me?" I punctuated my words with a poke to his very hard chest.

Carlos nodded slowly, and I rose from him. I backed up a step and glanced at Ethan, who sat on the ground rubbing his throat. He gave me a thumbs-up. When I turned back to Carlos, he was standing, too.

"If he has more bruises from that, I'm coming after you."

"I will let everyone know Ethan's under your protection," the grey-eyed man said. "Though, we're all family here, so I don't think that's even necessary."

"Really?" I said. "Was that an example of how your family treats each other? Some family."

"Carlos misunderstood the situation when the boy patted your backside."

The man's worry carried a hint of humor with it. I didn't find anything funny. I glanced at Carlos. He was so damn hard to read, but I was pretty sure he didn't find anything funny, either.

"Ethan knows me. He knows my limits and what I need. There

are no situations to misunderstand because when it comes to Ethan, he's none of your business...unless he's giving you advice about what not to do around me. Then, you might want to listen. He's trying to save your lives."

"I think they get the idea," Ethan said.

I doubted it. Ethan had pushed me to the edge more times than I could count with his persistent interference. There'd been times I'd wanted to strangle him myself. But love always stopped me. And even when angry, I always knew, deep down, he was saving me from myself.

I turned to look Ethan over. There were new marks on his neck. I narrowed my eyes, and Ethan grinned at me. He knew what I wanted to do.

The mountain would go down for those marks.

"We sparring or not?" I said, focusing on Carlos again.

He lifted his hands. Good. I was ready to make good on my promise. Behind me, music started playing, and I flicked Ethan a dirty look. If he didn't cut it out, his body was going to hit the floor.

I turned, shifted my balance, and began. Putting my fists up, I edged forward. At the last minute, I kicked out and connected with Carlos' side and thigh in rapid succession. He tilted his head and studied me as I hopped back and guarded for his attack. Nothing came. Clever. He was learning my moves.

He wouldn't learn much, though. I wasn't going to keep this routine. I darted in and clipped his jaw with my damaged hand. He didn't even try to block the swing. I wanted to follow up with a swing from the other side but wasn't sure my wrist could take it. I would be a mess if I started to rely on my fists.

The music changed to violin pop. I grinned. Ethan was telling me to use my legs. He knew. Fine. I shifted my balance again and went for Carlos' head. He let one kick through but blocked the next. My momentum didn't stop. I twisted and kicked again.

When we were younger, Ethan recorded our fights so I could see how I moved. He compared it to a dancer. I compared it to a cat. Either way, I moved while in the air, looking for an opening and lashing out with feet, knees, or elbows.

Carlos started to block them all. His moves were different from Ethan's. Softer somehow. It didn't mean he was less of a fighter. He moved incredibly fast. There was something else to his touch each time we connected; it was like he was trying to maintain the contact, hold onto me.

Sweat trickled down my back, and I noticed a slight glisten on Carlos' forehead. Good. The music changed again.

I moved faster, spinning and bending, dodging and striking. Carlos and I moved together. It was as if he could read my mind. He met each move and pushed for more with his dark gaze. Several times, I unintentionally left myself open and felt the drag of his fingers on my cheek or sides. Was he just playing with me?

My breathing shortened from the exertion, but I didn't slow until Ethan called for a break. Someone had brought us water. Ethan handed me a glass. I knew better than to gulp it. But I took a healthy drink.

"Can I borrow that?" Carlos said from right behind me.

I turned and saw he was looking at Ethan's phone.

"Sure." Ethan handed it over, and Carlos walked away for a few moments. When he turned back, he tossed Ethan the phone.

"Play that."

Ethan looked at the screen, frowned for a minute, then caught my gaze and grinned.

"Back in there, kitty cat."

I gave him my glass and turned just in time to block a quick jab from Carlos. Why did that make me smile?

Music started behind me. It wasn't a song I knew, but I listened to the words as Carlos and I went through the motions. The beat was perfect and the lyrics inviting. He wanted me to come with him to lose myself tonight. And I did.

The coiled tension that I hadn't managed to fully exorcise with Brick began to ease as I fought Carlos. The relief made me smile as I kicked yet again. Then, Carlos changed the game. His hands closed over my ankle and held me there. His thumb rubbed a slow circle on the exposed skin. Something ignited in me. It wasn't anger. And it scared me.

I pulled myself from his hold; and without a word, I turned and left the barn. Though my steps were measured, I was all over the place in my head. What the hell had he been trying to do in there? He'd ruined a perfectly good spar, the best I'd had in a long time, by being touchy feely. Idiot. Hadn't he listened to a word Ethan had said? I breathed deeply, just a normal, human cleansing breath, and focused on my surroundings.

Outside, the light was starting to fade. Across the yard, the three vehicles were still parked in front of a small house. Ethan and I were stuck with these people. We had no car to get away from them. And, honestly, unless they proved to be a threat like those other things chasing us, I was starting to think we might be better off with them on our side. Except for Carlos. He'd gotten under my skin in there.

I headed in the direction of the house, glad I'd landed a few shots in the beginning that would leave a mark. The feel of his fingers lingered on my ankle, and I began to doubt why he hadn't landed any hits. Like Ethan, I had a feeling Carlos hadn't wanted to. Something about that thought had my stomach flipping weirdly.

"Wait up," Ethan said, jogging to catch up to me. "I thought it was a good fight. But you're acting like it wasn't. What's going on?"

I rolled my shoulders. I was tense again, but not because of an overload.

"I don't know. I'm drained." In that regard, the fight with Carlos was the best match I'd ever had. But something about him bothered me. Probably the way my stomach was acting. Then again, I hadn't eaten anything after emptying it.

"I think I just need some sleep and something to eat."

"I'll find the food. You see if you can find a shower. You need it."

I snorted and shook my head at him.

"You love my stink."

"I do." He grinned and pulled open the door for me.

Everyone was in the kitchen when we walked in. A few sat at the table but most leaned against counters or lingered in doorways. Their anxiety, fear, and impatience made me itch as much as their sudden silence and regard. Ethan moved close to me and threaded his fingers through mine.

"Are we interrupting something?" he asked.

"No," Bethi said. She sat at the table along with Luke. His gaze flicked down to Ethan's hand wrapped around mine.

"We're just waiting around for Isabelle to let off enough steam so we can talk."

I eased my hand from Ethan's and pulled out a chair.

"The steam's been vented. So talk." I sat. Ethan stood behind me.

Bethi glanced around the room.

"We should probably start with introductions and the basics."

"Sounds pretty smart," I said. I didn't quite manage to keep the sarcasm from my voice, and the man next to Bethi narrowed his eyes.

"How's the face, ginger?" I asked him.

Bethi reached over and laid a hand on his leg.

"This is Luke. My Mate," she said, watching me closely as if waiting for a reaction.

"I have a feeling you're not using an English term for friend."

"No. I'm not. Most of the people in this room are werewolves. A few of us are like you. Gifted humans."

"Gifted? I'd like to return mine. It sucks."

She actually smiled at me instead of being offended.

"Mine, too. I die just about every night. Fun stuff."

It sounded anything but fun.

"Anyway, to your right is Jim."

I looked at the man she indicated, and he nodded.

"Then, Thomas, Charlene, Michelle, Emmitt, Winifred," she turned to her left, "and Sam. Gabby and Clay are upstairs."

"She's still out?"

Bethi nodded but didn't say more about them.

"Behind you are Carlos and Grey."

I turned and eyed the older man. Everything about him matched his name from his hair to his eyes.

"Grey," I said. "Your name I'll remember. The rest of you might need nametags for a while. So, why am I here?"

"Because you're one of six Judgements. We're here to keep the balance between three races. Humans, werewolves, and Urbat. Urbat are the ones you met in the hotel room."

"Okay. Sure," I said. Ethan and I needed to ditch this crazy as soon as—

"I know you don't believe any of this. I didn't either. Not until I started having the dreams. I've dreamt of our past lives, some so long ago we still wore animal-skin clothes. Isabelle, I've already started dreaming details of our current lives. I saw the day you and Ethan met on the playground. I saw you walk him home the day he came to school with a black eye. I saw you cry when you brought his father to the floor."

My mouth hung open. No one knew about that. Even Ethan's dad didn't remember what happened that day. I'd drained him hard, broken him.

"I've been in your skin, felt how tight and angry you get. I've cringed with you over the bruises you gave Ethan when you sparred as children. And I've felt the shame you carried in the belief that you were as bad as his father was."

"That's enough," Ethan said. He sounded angry, but he was keeping it in so I didn't feel it. He gave my hair a gentle tug. "She's way prettier than my dad. A better fighter, too."

Great. Now I'd have to listen to him lecture me about how I wasn't anything like his father.

"Fine. You dream, I suck emotions. Which one levitates?"

Bethi smirked.

"Michelle is the lotto. She has premonitions that make other people rich."

"Why couldn't I get that one?" I said, looking back at Ethan.

"It's no picnic," Michelle said, drawing my attention. "If I don't share the information, it's very painful."

"Imagine putting your brain in a microwave," Bethi said. "It sucks, too. Gabby can see us in her head. Like an old sonar. And Charlene can control people with her mind."

I swiveled in my chair and stared at the blonde woman.

"If that's true, control me. Make me stop absorbing everything."

She looked troubled.

"I'm sorry. I can't. We're not like normal humans. Ethan I could control easily—"

"Hey," he said indignantly.

"—but we're different. Just like the werewolves are different."

Bethi heaved a sigh, and I felt her impatience.

"The five of us make up Strength, Hope, Prosperity, Wisdom, and Peace."

I stared at her. I could buy that she somehow saw our pasts, but the rest? No way.

"Do I look like I eat bullcrap with a spoon? What are you on? Seriously. I want some."

"She's as bad as you are," Luke said to Bethi.

Bethi grinned at him before focusing on me again.

"I wish I was on something. It might make some of my nights a little easier to bear. You asked why you're here. You're here because all six of us need to be together to pass Judgement on the races and end this cycle."

"Cycle?"

"We're reborn every one thousand years," she said as if it were an inconsequential point. "Isabelle, I think ending this cycle will turn off our abilities. Completely."

Now she had my attention. The idea of walking into a room full of people and feeling absolutely nothing...hell, yes. Maybe they were crazy. But she knew things no one could know. And I'd seen the way the werewolves and Urbat could change from man to dog. There was at least some truth to this craziness. And if there was some truth, why couldn't getting rid of our crappy gifts be true, too?

"All right. I'm in."

"Just like that?" she asked.

"Just like that." I stood. "I need a shower. Can anyone point me in the right direction?"

"To the left, down the hall," Carlos said from behind me.

I nodded and glanced at Ethan. Though I was willing to go along with them on the chance of getting rid of what I could do, I didn't trust them. Especially not with Ethan.

He gave me a slight shake of his head then turned to look at Carlos and Grey.

"Got any food around here?"

He always thought he was so tough. He was. But these people were tougher.

I looked at Bethi. She watched me closely.

"Go," she said. "Shower. Everything will be fine for five minutes, I think."

I went down the hall.

THE HOT WATER felt great as I washed and rinsed. I'd even brushed my teeth with a new toothbrush I'd found in the medicine cabinet before getting in the shower. It'd been long overdue. I felt fresh and, despite the emotions from those down the hall, tension free as I turned off the water. A towel hung on the bar toward the back of the tub. I grabbed it and dried off. Too bad I'd have to put my dirty clothes back on. I regretted that we hadn't had time to grab our bags.

When I stepped out of the tub, I found a full set of clean clothes on the toilet seat. I hadn't even heard the door open. I stared at the jeans. They weren't mine. I tended to avoid jeans because they never fit my butt right.

With a sigh, I tried to put them on. It wasn't going to happen. I tossed the jeans aside then put on the shirt and underthings. I didn't care if they were someone else's. They were clean.

Skipping any form of pants, I opened the bathroom door and squeaked at the sight of Carlos leaning against the opposite wall.

"Creep much?" I said, taking in his crossed, bulging arms.

He appeared completely relaxed as he gazed at my bare legs.

"Jeans didn't fit?"

His slow, deep words made my middle mushy. I didn't do mushy.

"Obviously not."

"I'll see if I can find something else," he said, straightening. "Stay here."

He walked down the hall toward the kitchen.

I couldn't believe he'd just told me to stay. Did I look like a dog?

I started following him, then stopped at the base of a narrow staircase. Grief and worry pulled at me. Sighing, I moved up the stairs into a loft with a slanted ceiling on both sides.

Clay sat on the bed, his back leaned against the headboard. In his lap, he cradled Gabby. He didn't look up as I approached or as I sat on the edge of the bed.

"When I came to, she had my head in her lap. She was stroking my hair like my mom used to do before I broke her. It was dark in the van. I could feel we were moving, driving further away from help. I felt Gabby's fear and her barely contained panic. Not far away, I felt the pitiless lust and eager aggression of the men who drove."

Clay finally looked up at me.

"I'm so sorry for what I did to her. But what they would have done..."

"I know," he said.

"If there would have been another way, I would have taken it."

He nodded and looked back down at her. I felt his love.

"Give her a few more hours. She's sleeping off the best high of her life." I stood. "And when she comes to, keep her away from me. I'm crack. Highly addictive."

He nodded but didn't take his eyes from her. I went back to the stairs. At the bottom, Carlos waited with a pair of black leggings.

"Perfect. Thanks," I said, reaching for them. He gave them up, and I went back into the bathroom. Walking around without pants didn't bother me. But the idea of being in the open and unstable while putting on pants did.

The hallway was empty when I opened the door again, so I veered for the kitchen. The same group of people still waited. Only this time there was a sandwich on the table right in front of an open chair. I sat and, without asking if the food was mine, dug in.

A sandwich had never tasted so good. After I swallowed several bites, I figured everyone staring at me wanted conversation. So I gave in.

"How long are we staying here?"

"It's not safe to move until Gabby's awake," Bethi said. "But, for all we know, the Urbat could be closing in around us now."

That wasn't very reassuring.

"We should be fine," Winifred said. Her words lacked conviction.

"If you need her awake, wake her up," I said. "A good slap will do the trick. However, she'll still be loopy."

There were two seconds of stunned silence. I used the time to take another bite.

"Clay can hear you and doesn't appreciate your advice," Sam said. "Neither do I."

I paused my chewing at the wave of irritation and glanced at Sam's surly expression. I definitely felt like the unwanted stepchild. I stood up and grabbed my sandwich, even though I didn't want it anymore.

"I'll be outside."

Ethan moved to follow me, and I didn't stop him. We walked to the barn.

"Keep eating, Z. They don't know you. They don't understand."

"Understand what?" I said, hating that he knew I'd lost my appetite.

"How much it's killing you that you knocked the girl out like that."

"Whatever." I took a bite and chewed.

"They don't all hate you, you know. Bethi seems to like you. And I think that big guy does, too."

I gave Ethan a dirty look.

"What? As soon as you disappeared down the hall, he started asking the girls if they had something clean you could wear. Although, maybe it wasn't consideration for you as much as consideration for us. You smelled like puke."

65

I shook my head and let out a laugh.

"You're ridiculous."

The barn door was still open, and someone had opened the door on the other side. We went to the opening and sat on the floor. My feet dangled over the edge as I looked out over the barren fields. Sunset was painting them gold and orange.

"I know I'm not like your dad," I said after a few minutes. "I just hate seeing you hurt."

"And that's why you're not like him. He could care less if I was hurt."

"So, you going to tell me when you learned to close yourself off like that?" I said, changing the subject to avoid a lecture.

He grinned at me. "Since the last time you came to the bar."

"Does it bother you?"

"It's not like I'm holding my breath. I'm just keeping tight control of what I'm letting myself feel."

"Hmm," I said with a frown. "I was going to say that I liked it, but it sounds a little cold."

He shook his head and looked out over the fields. "I guess it could sound that way. But how can anything be cold when it's done to protect someone you love?"

I studied his profile for a minute and then leaned over to rest my head on his good shoulder. Behind us, the yard light flickered on.

"When this is all done, maybe you won't need to turn yourself off. I hope Bethi's right and whatever's wrong with me will go away."

"There's nothing wrong with you." He wrapped an arm around my back and kissed the top of my head. His love for me leaked out just a bit, but I didn't comment on it.

CHAPTER FIVE

AFTER SEVERAL MOMENTS OF SILENCE, MY STOMACH RUMBLED. THE BIG releases made me so hungry afterward.

"I'll get us another sandwich," Ethan said.

I nodded and straightened away from him. He knew I'd stay in the barn and starve rather than go back in for more food. It wasn't just the emotions that kept me sitting but the group's attitude toward me. I hated myself enough for what I did to people. I didn't need them silently judging me too.

As his footsteps faded, I considered our situation. I hadn't thought everything through when I'd agreed to help. I'd only seen the end goal of getting rid of my siphoning. But, before I could get rid of it, I'd have to chum around with these emotionally uninhibited people. I had a feeling I'd be doing a lot more sparring with Ethan in the upcoming days. If it got too bad, he and I could take off for a while. I frowned as I realized just how dependent we were without a car or our bags. I didn't even have my wallet.

"Do you love the boy?"

The unexpected voice made me jump, but its familiarity kept me seated. I turned to glare at Carlos.

"I wish you'd stop calling him a boy. His name is Ethan. He's twenty-four—old enough to own the bar you trashed. And yes, I love him. He's my family."

Carlos studied me for a moment then looked out over the shadowed fields. His expression left no hint at what he was thinking or feeling. It was so strange not to feel anything from him. I wanted to ask him why he was so emotionally shut off but thought that might not go over so well. So, I joined him in his study of the horizon.

After a few seconds, he surprised me by sitting down in Ethan's spot. Heat radiated from him, and I found it unsettling.

"How often do you need to purge?"

At first, I thought he was talking about my throwing up in the van and was ready to deck him. Then, I realized he meant the fighting.

"It depends on who I'm around. The group inside is broadcasting emotions so loudly I can feel it from here. I'll need another round with Ethan before we leave, or if we stay the night."

"Not Ethan," he said. "His shoulder needs more time. I'll do it."

I glanced at him and found he was watching me. My stomach flipped wildly, and my insides warmed at the thought of us moving together like we had before. But something in his gaze bothered me.

"Why?"

He raised a brow in question, and I thought it might have been the first facial expression I saw him use.

"Why are you so willing to help me?"

"I like watching you move."

My mouth may have dropped open a little at his words. I wasn't sure. I was too stunned to notice anything but his intense gaze. It swept over my face then he stood and walked away. Before I turned, I heard Ethan.

"Hey, Carlos."

"Ethan."

I swallowed and closed my mouth. What the heck had the big guy meant by his comment? Without his emotions, I had no idea.

Ethan sat next to me while looking behind us, which I refused to do, and made a noise between a grunt and a laugh.

"He's a weird one. What do you get off of him?"

"Nothing," I said, accepting the sandwich Ethan handed over.

"Nothing?"

"Absolutely nothing. It's like he's a black hole. He's better at blocking than you are."

"Really? Interesting."

I didn't like the way he said that.

"What do you mean by interesting?"

"Absolutely nothing," he said before taking a bite of his sandwich.

After a few minutes of silent scrutiny, I changed the subject.

"Do you still have your wallet?"

"Yep."

"Good. At least we didn't lose everything back there. If we're going to be sitting here for a while, maybe one of them will let us use a car to grab a few things."

"Doubt it. You ran twice on them already. If we leave, I'm betting it's with an escort. Have you noticed that there's no friend here?"

I gave him a puzzled look.

"What do you mean?"

"The old woman said we were heading to a friend's place. Where's the friend? And why break the lock on the door if it's a friend?"

I hadn't noticed any of that.

"And do you know what else is weird?"

"What?"

"The women are all paired up."

That made me laugh.

"You're checking out women while on the run from things that look like people but can change into dogs? You overdue for a night out?"

"Nope. I'm waiting for you," he said with a wink before he got serious again. "All the women with abilities like yours...they're paired up. With a werewolf."

I cringed at the use of the word. It didn't seem real yet, despite the visual affirmations.

"So, what are you saying? They're going to try to hook me up with a werewolf?"

He shrugged and was quiet. I laid my head on his shoulder once more.

"I'm saying don't let your guard down," he said finally.

WHEN WE WALKED BACK into the house an hour later, the emotional soup almost pulled me under. I looked around at the people in the room, trying to pinpoint the source. There was too much of it, though. But, it wasn't Bethi. She and Luke were absent.

"Who the hell is worrying so much?"

The worry flooding the area immediately receded. Now, toward the back of the house, I felt fear and guilt. That was definitely Bethi and Luke.

"Gabby still hasn't woken up. We're trying to decide if we should move on without the guidance or continue to wait."

"I've seen people sleep twelve hours after that kind of hit," I said.

"My dad slept, what? Eighteen?" Ethan said from beside me.

I knew he was trying to help reassure the group, but it had the opposite effect. Worry clouded the air again. These people wouldn't relax until Gabby was awake. But everyone was too afraid to slap the girl.

"Okay, just hold tight for a minute." I marched for the stairs with Ethan right behind me.

"Bad ideas rattle around in that head of yours," he mumbled as we took the stairs two at a time.

Clay met my gaze as soon as my head cleared the stairs. His concern for Gabby battled with his anger at me. He obviously knew why I was there.

"What do you think's safer?" I said, getting right to the point. "Sitting here and waiting, or finding out if the bad guys are getting closer? I already told you what they mean to do to us."

"You're not touching Gabby," Clay said.

I grinned.

"You're right. I won't need to because you'll do it. You'll be gentler. Here's the thing. When she wakes up, she'll still be high and loopy. She won't act like herself. But don't let her go back to sleep. The effect will wear off faster once she's awake and moving around. You have ten seconds before I start pulling from you. I can't aim, so it'll just hurt her more."

He glared at me.

"Ten."

He looked down at her.

"Nine."

His hand reached up and stroked her cheek.

"Eight...seven."

He tapped her cheek.

"Pathetic. And six."

He growled.

"Five. Better hurry."

He closed his eyes and took a deep breath.

"Four."

He slapped her. It was harder than I thought he had in him.

Her eyes popped open, and her vacant gaze traveled around the room.

"Gabby," I said as if talking to the hearing impaired. "Check your sonar."

She blinked at me, and I could see her trying to focus.

"Check your sonar," I repeated.

"Is Clay safe?" she asked softly.

"You're sitting on him. He'll be safer if you can tell us if there are any bad guys around."

Gabby blinked again and looked at Clay. She reached up and ran her fingers through his beard.

"So handsome," she murmured.

"Focus, Gabby," I said loudly. "Check your sonar."

She sighed.

"They're netting again. None are close." Her eyelids fluttered.

"Keep her awake, Clay," I said, heading toward the stairs.

Ethan and I returned to the kitchen. The older man and woman were frowning at me. I struggled to recall their names. Winifred. I frowned back at the older guy as I tried to remember. Sam.

"Gabby says they're not close. I'm not sure you'll get specifics out of her for a while. Clay needs to try to keep her awake so she becomes more lucid."

A wave of desire and love hit me hard. It came from upstairs. Time for me to retreat.

"Since it sounds like we're in the clear, would anyone be willing to loan me a set of car keys and a map so I can grab some things to replace what I lost?"

All eyes turned to Grey, Sam, and Winifred. They, in turn, looked at each other.

"It's safer to stick together," Winifred said. "You're welcome to borrow what you need from us."

"Yeah, unless you have some stretchy clothes hidden somewhere, it's not going to work."

They looked at each other some more, and I got the creepy feeling they were somehow communicating with each other.

"I'm sorry, Isabelle. It's just not safe."

"Well, I'm asking to borrow a car, not for permission to leave. You're just deciding if I drive or go on foot."

Silence met my statement along with threads of anger. But I didn't back down and unease drifted through the room.

"Let's go check out the barn," Emmitt said to Michelle.

"We'll come too," Thomas said, placing a hand at the small of Charlene's back. Both men steered their women out of the house. The third man, Jim, followed.

Their departure left us alone with Grey, Carlos, Winifred, and Sam. They stared at me, and I stared back. Upstairs, Clay continued to flood the air with love potion number nine. I wasn't sure how much more I could take.

Grey broke the silence with a sigh.

"How do we know you'll come back?" he asked.

"Told you," Ethan whispered. I ignored him.

"I guess you don't. But, I'm telling you my plan is to get clothes and come back. It's a clearer plan than you've given us." I changed my voice to mimic Bethi's. "We need your help to make the next Judgement. It should make your powers disappear." It ended sounding more fairy godmother. "Look, I'm putting a lot of trust in complete strangers. Why is it weird for me to ask you to do the same?"

They glanced at each other again.

"You do know I could just knock you all on your butts and take the keys, right? I'm being nice and asking."

Ethan snorted. I gave him a quick glare. He'd be the first one lying on the floor.

"We're concerned for your safety as well as our own. Take Carlos with you and leave Ethan. If you run into trouble, Carlos can protect you. And, if you should need to use your ability, you won't need to worry about hurting Ethan," Winifred said.

Did they read minds?

I glanced at Ethan. He shrugged and handed over his wallet.

"Just remember what I said," he added.

Don't let your guard down. I nodded but was more worried about leaving Ethan alone than I was about any attempts at matchmaking.

"Be here when I get back," I said to Ethan.

His lips tilted up in a half-smile.

"I'm not the one leaving."

I looked at the old people. They had better keep Ethan safe.

"Let's go, big guy," I said to Carlos.

He took a set of keys out of his pocket as he opened the door for me. Feeling weird going somewhere alone with him, I stepped outside.

The temperature had dropped with the sun, and I shivered a little. Still, I was glad to be free of the emotions boiling inside the house and breathed deeply as I waited for Carlos to indicate which vehicle.

I kept pace with him as we walked toward the last car, then he stepped ahead to open the passenger door. Gallantry or security? Were they really afraid I'd bolt again? Without comment, I got in, and Carlos closed the door. I studied him as he walked around the hood, then I turned slightly to sit at an angle as he got in.

Carlos adjusted his seat, straightened the mirror, then turned to look at me. Every move he made was so constricted and concise.

"Are you a robot?" Ethan would have cracked up at the question. The big guy didn't react at all.

"Buckle up."

"Yep. Robot." I buckled in and continued to study him as we pulled from the driveway. He wasn't completely emotionless, though. I'd seen him shake and explode into a dog twice now. I'd felt his relief when he'd found me, and I watched him grab Ethan by the throat just because Ethan had patted my butt. I narrowed my eyes.

Was Ethan right? Were these people trying to set me up with one of their own? There were four single guys along and only one of them I could stand to be around for any length of time. Was that what Ethan meant by interesting? The human women were paired up with werewolves, and one of the remaining bachelors was a guy who didn't overload me emotionally?

"So, the old folks were pretty quick to send you with me. Why's that?"

"For your protection."

I made a noncommittal sound.

"Are they hoping we hook up?"

He twitched. It wasn't just his facial muscles; it was also his hands on the wheel. I tilted my head and considered his reaction.

"Why did that upset you?"

"It didn't."

I wished I could read something from him. If he wasn't upset, then what was the hand-clenching for?

"Are they hoping I'm going to hook up with some other werewolf?"

This time the steering wheel crackled under his tight grip.

"That upset you."

"Yes."

"Why?"

His driving continued to be precise. He even kept his speed exact. I couldn't imagine anyone wound any tighter.

After a minute of silence, I knew he wouldn't answer. It didn't matter. Whatever they had planned for me, I wasn't going along with it. But, as I continued to stare at him, I had to admit, he was good looking. He had nice skin, a warm light brown. Based on his name, I guessed Hispanic roots. Yeah, it was probably prejudiced of me to assume that, but his looks and name matched the part.

He kept his short hair neatly brushed, and it even looked like he'd used gel or something, which made me grin and wonder if his closet was as neat as Ethan's. My gaze drifted down as I continued my examination. Carlos' polo shirt hugged his shoulders perfectly. I leaned forward a little to eye the buttons. His collar was open, but I guessed he would have buttoned it if he could have. His neck was too thick. However, he did have the bottom of his shirt neatly tucked into the waist of his black dress pants.

This guy needed to loosen up big time.

"Do you own any gym shorts?" I asked. "T-shirts?"

The question seemed to surprise him because he glanced at me as he answered.

"No."

"I think we need to fix that if you're going to spar with me. I don't want to mess with what you've got going on there." I waved my hand at his clothes.

He studied my expression for a moment then focused on the road again.

Carlos definitely puzzled me. Ethan and I were flippant and often rude. We spoke what was on our minds and weren't afraid to express ourselves in other ways. It was as if this guy was the exact opposite.

"What do you do for fun, Carlos?" I said.

"I read."

That fit his meticulousness but not his bulk.

"What do you read?"

"Fiction mostly."

I felt like I was pulling the conversation from him. If there was some matchmaking scheme going on, someone needed to clue Carlos in because he wasn't putting in much effort.

"Why is it all the other girls are with one of you guys?"

"They're lucky, I guess."

Were they?

I turned away from him and looked out the dark passenger window for the rest of the trip. It didn't take long to reach a town with a clothes-for-everyone chain store.

Carlos followed me as I wandered around a bit. I grabbed four pairs of stretch pants, three black and one a calf-length hot pink, and several tops. Trying not to blush, I bought myself some new underwear and a few sports bras. Then, I went to the sporting goods department and found some gloves. They were cheap but better than nothing. I found my way to the medical supplies and grabbed three first-aid kits, bandages, wraps, and ice packs. Then, I went to the school supplies and grabbed two rugged backpacks.

"Let's hit the men's department," I said, trying not to smirk. Carlos was carrying half the stuff I'd grabbed. Ethan hated shopping with me. I never took a cart.

In the men's department, I picked out some clothes for Ethan and shorts and a t-shirt for Carlos. Arms full, we went to the register.

The woman rang everything up and told me the total. I used Ethan's card and signed his name. When suspicion drifted from her, I sucked it away. She smiled and wished us a good day.

Back in the car, I filled the backpacks as Carlos drove. I put two of the first-aid kits into Ethan's pack. He was the worrier. Everything else fit well. When I was done, I tossed the bags into the backseat and held up the shorts and shirt I'd gotten for Carlos. Black shorts with a true green top.

"What do you think?"

He glanced at the clothes.

"They should work," he said before focusing on the road.

There was definitely something different about this guy. Very little interpretable body language, succinct verbal responses, and tightly bottled emotions. I couldn't say I really minded any of it.

THE YARD and house were lit up when we pulled into the driveway. Ethan strode from the barn to the car as Carlos parked.

I opened the door and the breath whooshed out of me at the raw passion flooding the immediate area.

"What the hell," I said, looking at Ethan. The tips of his ears were pink. Even if he couldn't feel it, he knew what was going on.

"It's Clay and Gabby. Everyone else is in the barn."

I glanced at the house.

"They haven't stopped?" I'd known when I'd left that the emotion would spike. But after they'd gotten it out of their systems, it should have mellowed.

"Well, there appears to be a bit of a conflict. She's still high and saying yes; he's saying no."

"Ah." That explained the intensity of the desire. "Any baddies?"

"No. The group is planning on staying the night."

The group in question stood near the barn, talking quietly. If we stayed the night, there was no way I could sleep in the house with those two. The barn was mine. That meant I needed to get the group back into the house.

"Be right back," I said, moving toward the house.

Carlos quickly stepped in front of me.

"No."

I stopped and looked up at him.

"You have no idea what I intend to do, so what exactly are you saying no to?"

"Going inside. It's too dangerous."

"Puh-lease," I said as I rolled my eyes. "It's dangerous if I don't stop this emotional maelstrom. It will seep into my skin until my insides feel like they're bleeding."

He stared down at me for a moment, his jaw clenched. I found that interesting. He did have body language, then. Just very little of it.

Finally, he stepped to the side.

I walked into the house and found Clay and Gabby in the kitchen. She had Clay backed against the counter. His hands gripped the ledge of the sink, and his arms shook. Gabby's hands were in his hair, and they were tightly lip-locked. Based on what colored the air, I knew Clay was struggling not to touch her in return.

"Just give in to her already," I said.

He pulled back to look at me. Gabby made a small sound of protest and started to kiss his neck. His tremors got worse, but he shook his head.

"Fine. Then this is going one of two ways. I can rip that lust from her, which would keep her high, or you can man up and walk away."

His eyes narrowed.

"Believe it or not, I'm trying to be helpful. I just can't stick around with all this emotion. And according to grandma, I can't leave either. What Gabby's broadcasting needs to stop. Now."

Since opening the car door, I'd been slowly absorbing everything despite my effort to close myself off. My head was starting to ache with it. I needed to spar again, and I desperately needed sleep. This had been the longest day in history.

Clay leaned forward, kissed Gabby on the forehead, and tried to untangle himself. It wasn't easy. She kept clinging.

"Bethi," I called.

A minute later, the door opened behind me.

"Help Clay," I said. "I can't touch Gabby." If I did, I would pull in what I didn't want and set Gabby back further.

Bethi went to Gabby.

"Come on. Clay needs to go, and you need to make Sam some coffee."

As soon as Bethi grabbed Gabby's hands, Clay quickly fled. Gabby made a small, upset sound and tried to follow; but Bethi wrapped her arms around Gabby to keep her in place.

"I'll send the rest in," I said. Bethi would need the help.

I walked out the door and saw Clay pacing near the cars.

"Now you can help me," I said, waving him to follow me. He only hesitated a second.

As soon as we reached the barn, I looked at Winifred.

"Bethi won't be able to handle Gabby on her own, and I can't take anymore emotions. I need you all to go back inside, help Bethi and Gabby, and stay away from me."

I didn't really care that I sounded bossy. They all needed to go. Now. Except Ethan and Clay. Thankfully, no one protested. I moved into the barn as the group started back toward the house. It was then I noticed Carlos had followed me and was staying close. It didn't matter since he was still a lovely void.

Someone had rigged a flood light for the barn. It lit the area in the center. Perfect. I turned to the three men.

"Ethan, can you grab our new bags from the car? Carlos, can you ask around for some blankets? If we have to stay, I can't sleep inside the house tonight."

I looked at Clay and grinned at him.

"You look like you need to burn off some energy. How are you at fighting?"

I WOKE WITH A BONE-CRACKING, muscle-pulling stretch. When I opened my eyes, I wasn't tense thanks to Clay's sparring the night before and the lack of people around me. However, when I sat up, everything hurt. The blankets Carlos had provided had kept me warm throughout the night, but the hard floor lacked any cushion whatsoever. I felt like I'd been hit by a truck.

"Morning, sleepyhead," Ethan said. He was sitting at the door with his back against the wall, his blanket folded beside him.

"What'd I miss?" I rubbed my hands over my face, trying to ease the soreness from the spot where Brick had landed a hit.

"Gabby's sober. Breakfast is cooking. And we're ready to roll again. Guess there are some baddies headed our way."

"Figures. How's the shoulder?" I asked.

"Stiff. Sore."

"I have some muscle cream in your bag. I'll rub it in for you."

He held up the tube with a grin. I shook my head and stood.

"Should I be worried that you were waiting for me?" I asked as I went to him.

"Yep. All that making out last night got me worked up for your touch."

I snorted.

"Off with the shirt."

He met my eyes.

"You can help."

I bit my lip and reached for his hem. Despite how he was trying to play it, he was hurting bad. When I had the shirt off, the bruising made me cringe. It wasn't good. Not at all.

Squeezing some cream onto my fingertips, I kept my eyes down so he wouldn't see the threatening tears. Why did I have to hurt everyone around me? Even Clay last night had called Uncle before I was fully drained. He'd been nice enough to say thanks for the distraction, though I figured he was probably still mad about what I'd done to Gabby in the first place.

As gently as possible, I started to rub the cream in. Ethan sighed, closed his eyes, and tried to relax. He didn't let me wallow in silence long.

"Did I mention you bruised the top of my thigh, too? You should rub me there next."

"I think that older guy, Grey, might be able to help you with that. He looked like he had soft hands."

"I think I just threw up a little in my mouth." Ethan opened one eye to glare at me.

"Good. I call your share of breakfast." I rubbed the last of the cream in and helped him back into his shirt.

"No way. I'm starved," he said, standing.

I folded my blankets and carried them to the house. Inside, the kitchen smelled like sausage and eggs. Saliva pooled in my mouth, and my stomach rumbled. Charlene and Michelle stood at the sink, washing and drying dishes. Sam sat sipping coffee at the table. Clay and Gabby sat, too. Gabby had her head bent as she played with her orange juice. Her shame trailed through the air.

I snagged a plate from the counter near the stove and scooped up a healthy portion of eggs and sausage. Then, I joined the three at the table. Behind me, Ethan opened the refrigerator.

"I'm sorry about what happened," I said without preamble.

Gabby lifted her head and gave me a red-faced nod. Guilt joined the shame. I'd never be able to keep my food down if she didn't let her emotions go. With a sigh, I pushed my chair back and stood.

"Come on. Let's go for a walk."

She considered me for a moment then stood. Clay stood, too.

"No boys allowed," I said.

He didn't look at me. He kept his gaze on Gabby. Gabby, however, refused to look at him. When we moved to leave the kitchen, he didn't try to follow.

"Don't worry, Z. I'll protect your plate," Ethan called as the door closed behind us.

Outside, I took a deep breath and let it out.

"What I did might have killed you."

"It was the only option," she said.

I nodded, and we slowly walked toward the barn.

"When I was younger, I did the same thing to my parents. I'd thought I'd killed them; they were lying so still on the floor. I remember going to their bedroom and getting pillows to put under their heads. All day, I watched them, and that night, I went to sleep between them. Do you know how I woke up?"

She shook her head.

"With them making out right next to me. My mom wouldn't stop saying yes. Yes! Yes!" I mimicked my mom's passionate cries.

Gabby stopped walking, turned, and stared at me.

"I was so happy they were okay, I tried to hug them." I laughed, remembering. "They didn't even notice. It took a few more minutes to realize they weren't themselves." I sighed and looked at the ground.

"It took me a long time to figure out how to control my ability, how to block myself from people's emotions. But even when I try blocking, I still feel what people around me feel. So, tell me, why the guilt and shame? Nothing about what happened was your fault."

Her face darkened further, and her embarrassment soaked into my skin.

"I'm not asking to make it worse. I'm asking to help you through what you're feeling because if we have to travel together, I won't last long."

Gabby looked down at the ground.

"It's Clay. I remember..." She shook her head. "I was begging him."

"Trust me," I said with a grin. "He was loving every minute of it. If he could turn back the clock, he would do it all over again. Well, not the worrying, but he definitely liked what happened when you woke up. He respects you. I warned him that you wouldn't be yourself, and he didn't take advantage. That was really sweet."

She nodded and some of her shame disappeared as she looked toward the house.

"It was. He's always sweet. I just wish he wouldn't have said no. It would have made it a lot easier."

"What?"

"Finally saying yes to him." The guilt surged.

"Ah." So that was the problem. She was feeling guilty for holding out. "I hear the longer you wait, the more special it is. He seems like he's willing to give you whatever time you need. Don't sweat this. There are other things to worry about, right?"

"You're right."

"Are we good to go back in?"

"Yeah, I think we are."

"How's the sonar look?"

"We need to move soon. They are going to swing through this area in another hour or two."

An hour or two sounded a little too close for me.

We walked back to the house, and once we were inside, she went straight to Clay. He leaned against a wall, waiting for her. She gave him a tentative smile. He exhaled slowly, and I felt his relief. Some of my own guilt slipped away.

When I turned to the table, I saw Ethan scraping the last crumbs from my very empty plate. He'd actually eaten my food?

"You're dead," I said, stepping toward him.

He laughed and sprang up from the chair.

"It's on the stove. I swear!"

He grabbed a plate from the stovetop and held it out to me. The corners of his eyes wrinkled as he grinned at me. I shook my head at him, hiding my worry that he was only using his left hand.

"I'll let you live. For now."

I took my plate and gobbled the eggs.

ETHAN and I rode in the backseat again. Winifred drove. Emotionally, she was much quieter, and it made for a relaxing drive.

It was so relaxing that I leaned against Ethan and fell asleep for a few hours. When I lifted my head, his shoulder was wet.

"Sorry about the bath," I said, wiping my mouth. At least I'd crashed on his left shoulder and not his right.

"No problem. I was overdue."

I looked out the window. We were in a large city.

"Where are we?"

He shrugged, but Winifred answered.

"Evansville. We're going to stop for the day. Gabby said they recently swept through the area, so it should be safe."

"Good. I have to pee," Ethan said. "And dry off."

Within minutes, we were pulling into a hotel parking lot. The three vehicles parked close. I immediately felt the weariness and worry of the group as everyone got out and started grabbing bags. How long had Bethi said they'd been looking for me?

Ethan and I got out, already carrying our bags, and walked with the rest into the hotel. It felt good to stretch my legs.

Michelle and Emmitt broke off from the group to go to the front desk. They returned with four room keys.

"We'll stay with you," she said as she handed a key to Charlene and Thomas.

Then she handed a key to Sam, Winifred, and Grey.

"An Elder in each room allows for better communication."

Ethan and I shared a look. Better communication?

"We'll go with Sam," Gabby said, taking Clay's hand.

"Do these rooms have a couch or am I sleeping with Sam?" Jim asked with a grin.

"No pull out sofas. Sorry, Jim," Michelle said.

He didn't seem to mind.

"Bethi, you and Luke can stay with me," Winifred said.

Ethan and I looked at Grey and Carlos.

"I call dibs sleeping with you, Z," Ethan said under his breath. I nodded. There was no way I'd sleep next to either of those other two.

"Let's settle in," Charlene said. "I'll order room service, and everyone can meet in our room. We need to discuss what's next."

CHAPTER SIX

ETHAN AND I FOLLOWED GREY AND CARLOS DOWN THE HALL. THE pair didn't say much. Then again, neither did we. Grey unlocked the door, and Carlos stepped aside to let us in. As I passed, Grey handed me a spare keycard. Ethan set his bag on the far bed, and I took the side furthest from the other two. Ethan didn't comment.

I ducked into the bathroom for a much needed pee while the other two set their bags on the bed. When I came back out, Ethan was waiting with a clean change of clothes in his arms.

"'Bout time," I said, moving aside for him.

"Didn't know how bad you wanted me neck'd." He never said naked the right way. I couldn't even remember how it had started. Probably one of the first times I'd slept over at his house. Man, how old had I been? Eleven? My parents most definitely had been fried by then.

Ethan closed himself into the bathroom. The TV was on, Grey was gone, and Carlos sat on the end of his bed.

"Aren't we using the buddy system? You lost your buddy," I said, sitting on the end of my bed.

"He'll find his way back. He always does."

I couldn't be sure if that was a joke or not. A timid knock on the door distracted me before I could decide. Carlos stood and answered it.

"I'm here to talk to Isabelle," Michelle said.

Nervousness exuded from her. Carlos nodded and let her in. Then, he left the room, closing the door behind him.

"What's up?" I asked.

"Don't kill the messenger," she said with a cringe.

"Uh, that doesn't sound good."

The water turned off in the bathroom. World's fastest shower. He was worried about me.

"Did you even use soap?" I called. Michelle jumped at my sudden volume.

"Wanna come sniff me?"

His muffled reply made me grin. I shook my head and focused on Michelle again.

"What has you all nervous?"

"They asked me to come talk to you about—"

Ethan opened the door. He had a towel wrapped around his waist and the tube of muscle cream in one hand. When he saw Michelle, he froze.

"Good to know we have company," he said, giving me a hard look.

"Hey, Ethan," I called as if he were still in the shower. "Don't come out in a towel. We have company."

"You're useless," he said before turning around and closing himself in the bathroom once more.

I loved all this Ethan time. Between the exercise and his constant snarky humor, I was feeling great. It was hard to remember I'd been bashed in the head and was on the run from people who could change into dogs. Why did I just think that? Way to ruin a mood.

"Maybe I should come back later?" Michelle said.

"Nah, you've scared him for now. We should have at least five minutes before he's ready to show his face again."

She moved to sit on the bed that Carlos had occupied.

"Bethi told you the basics about us, but no one's told you anything about them, the werewolves. The Elders thought you might have a few questions."

Her term for the old people in the group made me want to smirk.

"If the Elders thought I had questions, why didn't they come here?"

"You don't seem to like any of them."

"Yeah, well, they're a bit bossy. Since I am too, you can see where there might be some personality conflict."

She remained silent for a heartbeat.

"Do you have any questions?" she asked hesitantly.

"Nope. Honestly, I haven't stopped to think about it, and I'm not sure I'm going to. I'm along for the ride. I just want to get rid of this emotion siphoning thing and move on with my life."

She looked down at her hands, fidgeting. There was a message they'd sent her to share. I was sure of it.

"What questions should I be asking?" I asked.

"When I first saw Emmitt, he felt familiar, almost as if I'd recognized him, even though we'd never met. My stomach went crazy, and I just couldn't stop staring. It turns out, the werewolves have this built-in sensor that goes off when they see their Mate. A pull. That's what Winifred calls it. And, apparently, we feel it too." She stood and moved to the door. "Let me know if you think of any questions."

I stared at the closed door for several minutes, too stunned by the bomb she'd just lobbed at me to react in any way. Ethan poked his head out the door, looked around, and stepped out fully dressed.

"I hope food's been ordered. I'm starving," he said, crossing the room. He shoved his dirty clothes in his bag. "And you can rub me in tonight."

Shaking myself from my shock, I stood before Ethan could notice anything wrong.

"Sure."

As we left the room to meet with the others, I refused to read into what Michelle had just said. It was information. That was it. Nothing more.

THE DOOR TO Charlene's room opened before Ethan could even knock on it. Grey stepped aside to let us in. Everyone else was already there, and there wasn't much room to move. Ethan and I stayed near the door and leaned against the wall.

I glanced around the room. When I saw Carlos, my stomach did a happy dance. Had it done that before? If it had, I'd never noticed it. Usually I was too focused on everyone else's emotions and responses to pay much attention to my own. Why did Michelle have to go and point it out? Now, my reaction to Carlos was probably just like that time in elementary school. Someone had gotten lice and when the school nurse had shown up and explained why she needed to check our hair, I'd started scratching at my head like crazy.

A sudden wave of anger and frustration brought my focus back to the present situation, and I realized Ethan and I had arrived in the middle of a tense conversation.

"We need to decide," Bethi said impatiently with a look at Winifred. "There are too many of them to keep running like this. We almost lost Gabby and Isabelle. The drive to find us is only going to increase as the end of the cycle approaches."

Everyone else in the room seemed to be watching Winifred, who was giving Bethi a troubled look.

"The risks of trying to remain hidden are still better than if we expose our existence. Once we do that, we'll have both the humans and the Urbat hunting for us," Winifred said.

I glanced at Ethan while Bethi nodded. Was he as lost as I was?

"You're right, we will," Bethi said. "But that's what will make it safer. The pressure won't just be on us. It will be on them as well. Thanks to Gabby's sonar, when we reveal ourselves, we can also reveal the Urbat and their location. They'll have to scramble. During that chaos, we might just have a chance to find Olivia. With her, we can end this."

The importance of what they were discussing hit me. They wanted to reveal themselves to the world.

"It could work," Michelle said. "If we use Blake's name."

"What's to stop him from revealing ours?" Winifred asked.

"Blake needs all six Judgements," Bethi replied. "And he'll know he won't stand a chance at getting us back from humans if we are taken. He can't risk revealing anything about us because of that."

It surprised me that they were even considering revealing themselves. The panic it would cause...I shuddered. I didn't want to be anywhere near that wreck when it went down.

"If we do this, we'll need to go through a reputable source so it's not brushed off as a hoax," Michelle said. "A news station would be best. Preferably one with broad coverage."

"I agree," Bethi said. "We need to decide where and when, soon. We can't just keep running around aimlessly. Gabby's got to sleep sometime, and that's all it'd take for them to get lucky again."

"The where will help determine the when," Michelle said.

"If we're looking for broad news coverage," Gabby said, speaking up for the first time, "New York would be the place to go. But, it puts us much closer to the danger because the Urbat are primarily in northern New York."

"That's actually perfect," Bethi said. "Blake knows we need Olivia; I think once he sees we're headed that way, he'll call his troops back in. You know, fortify home base. He won't expect us to stop at a news station."

I liked how Bethi's mind worked, but there were still some large holes in her logic.

"How are you going to get anyone to even listen to you, let alone put you on air?" I asked.

"Charlene will convince them," Bethi said.

I glanced at Charlene. She looked uncomfortable, and I felt a wave of worry roll off her.

"Will you?" I asked her.

"I'm capable of manipulating wills. I'm not sure I should, though. Yet, I agree that Bethi's plan has merit. It's better than a life on the run."

"Why aren't you sure?" Winifred asked.

The worry grew stronger.

"Once we expose our existence, there's no going back."

I studied her for a moment longer. It wasn't just worry but a hint of guilt. I spoke up.

"It's not just the existence of the Urbat and werewolves we're exposing. We're risking exposing ourselves too, right?"

She held my gaze as a subtle thread of fear flavored her emotions. Then, she nodded. Something more was scaring her. What? Silence reigned for several minutes as the rest of the room thought over the situation.

Ethan shifted slightly beside me. He was probably bored. He had no real stake in this, and I just wanted to eat and then see if one of these guys would spar with me. Each second standing here meant that much longer I'd need to exercise.

"Seriously. If anyone has a better option, say it. Otherwise, we're just postponing the inevitable," Bethi said.

I applauded her impatience.

"You're asking a lot of us," Winifred said. "We need time to consider all the possibilities."

"You've had over a week," Bethi said, tossing her hands up in the air. Luke immediately reached for one of her runaway hands, and she calmed slightly.

Winifred looked at Grey, then Sam. Then, she sighed with a slight shake of her head.

"For better or worse, we agree with you. We can't remain as we are."

Thankfully, we were saved from more discussion by a knock on the door. Grey turned to answer it. A man with a cart waited outside and started passing in covered plates. Since I was third closest to the door, I had to pass twelve plates. Twelve delicious smelling platters warmed my palms. I wanted to raise the lid of each dish and lick whatever I found under it before passing it on, just because.

As soon as Ethan had his plate, he lifted the lid.

"Two burgers? Z, hit me. I'm in heaven."

I had my own plate in my hand and lifted the lid. A single third pound patty rested between the two halves of the toasted bun. I glanced at everyone else's plates. Michelle, Charlene, Bethi, and Gabby also only had one cheeseburger. I scowled at Ethan as I took a bite of my puny patty. Stacked with lettuce, tomato, fried onions, and two slices of cheddar, it made my mouth happy and lifted my mood a little. In all likelihood, I wouldn't have finished a second burger. Ethan would probably be hard pressed to finish his. But I still would have liked to try.

Charlene turned on the TV. I appreciated the noise. It covered the sound of fifteen people chewing.

I watched TV with everyone else and gradually cleared my plate. Ethan drastically slowed down halfway through his second burger. I was half-tempted to steal it but knew what it would be like sparring on a packed stomach.

"Hey, Ethan," Jim said. "If you're not going to finish that, I will." Jim had been checking out everyone else's plates as soon as he finished his. Charlene shook her head but said nothing.

"All yours," Ethan said, handing over the plate.

Everyone started passing their empty plates and lids back toward the door. Grey stacked them in the hall.

"If that's all, I want to go check out the fitness room." I stood, waiting for someone to object.

At Winifred's nod, I left the room before everyone was done passing their plates.

Ethan left with me, as usual. Once the door closed behind us, I sighed in relief.

"Want company?"

"Nah. I'm going to run on the treadmill for a while." Despite his amazing blocking, I needed some distance, even from him.

We walked back to our room. I changed into my three-quarter length exercise pants, then left him watching TV.

The fitness room was empty when I found it. I closed the door behind me, found the stereo, and turned on a local pop station. There was a certain smell to the exercise room—plastic, sweat, and metal—that relaxed me. I went to the treadmill and studied the panel. It had a bunch of preprogrammed options. I chose to control my own speed.

After ten minutes of warm up, I opened up to a run.

WHEN I OPENED the door to our room, I found Ethan passed out on the bed. The room was otherwise empty. I quietly shut the door behind me and grabbed my bag so I could go shower.

Ethan hadn't moved by the time I reemerged. He lay on his back, one hand on his shirt over his stomach and the other almost behind his head. It was a familiar position.

Wisps of emotion drifted from him. Worry, mostly. After I set my bag on the floor, I eased myself onto the mattress beside him. I let myself take his worry until only happiness remained. He needed more of those kinds of dreams.

"Z, they're going to leave without us."

Ethan's voice penetrated my dreamless sleep.

"Good. Let 'em."

I rolled over, away from him. He swatted my butt, hard. My eyes popped open.

"They're going to dinner. Still want them to leave without us? It's an Italian place around the corner. All-you-can-eat pizza."

That had me sitting up and rubbing a hand over my face. All-you-could-eat pizza sounded good. I was happy until I noticed we weren't alone in the room. Carlos and Grey waited by the door. Grey had a hand on Carlos' shoulder, and Carlos was completely focused on Ethan. My stomach flipped before I tore my gaze from Carlos. Nothing flavored the air but Ethan's twisted humor and Grey's concern.

What was up with Carlos? He acted so detached most of the time. Not when someone touched me, though. Then he went all weird. Michelle's words came back to me, and I shook my head. Nope. That wasn't it. It definitely wasn't attraction. I didn't do attraction.

"I'm up. Let me brush out my hair." I hadn't done anything to my hair before falling asleep.

They all waited as I yanked a brush through the tangles until it pulled through smoothly.

"Let's go," I said, tossing the brush back into my bag.

Carlos led the way. Ethan and I followed. Before we reached the lobby, Ethan reached over and took my hand in his.

"Thanks, by the way."

I knew he meant the dreams and shrugged away the thanks then gave his hand a squeeze. His love poured out for a moment before he let me go.

The rest of the group waited in the lobby. As soon as we appeared, they started out the doors. The walk to the pizzeria was short, and the aroma inside the place made my mouth water. Several long buffet tables were set up with different pizzas, and another table had salad and bread sticks. The best part was that we were the only people there. Heaven.

One of the waitresses saw our large group and started pushing tables together. I ended up sandwiched between Carlos and Ethan. Once everyone ordered drinks, it was a mass exodus to the buffet. I stayed sitting, unwilling to let Ethan trample me on his way to his favorite food.

Carlos remained sitting, too.

"Good call," I said. "We might want to wait a few minutes. They can clear out the old pizza, and we'll get the fresh stuff."

His eyes drifted to my lips as I spoke, and my pulse jumped. Heat flooded my cheeks, and I looked away. Darn Michelle and her little talk. She'd planted thoughts in my head, and now I was reacting to a stupid glance. Werewolf pull, my butt.

Unwilling to sit there uncomfortably for the next five minutes, I stood and went to the salad bar to reluctantly fill a plate. I had nothing against salad. I just liked pizza better. When I returned to the table, half the group was back with their own food.

I noticed Michelle and Charlene both had salads on their plates, too.

Conversation floated around me as I ate. Charlene's words caught my attention.

"I raised you better," she said to Jim. He had an obscene stack of pizza slices on his plate.

I turned to Carlos.

"Are they related?"

"Charlene and Thomas are Emmitt and Jim's parents. Grey is Thomas' brother," he said.

As I studied the group, Ethan's words rang in my head like a gong. Two men from the same family paired up with one of us. How weird was that? I glanced at Ethan. He either hadn't heard or didn't care. He continued to scoff his pizza with abandon.

Finished with half my salad, I set my plate to the side and went for pizza. I'd been right. They'd brought out fresh stuff. The gooey cheese gave me some trouble, but it was trouble I willingly dealt with.

Gabby wandered over to the salad bar. Her slow steps caught my eye, and I noticed her semi-vacant stare. She was checking her sonar again. No one ever asked her to do it; she just did it all the time. Her brow furrowed ever so slightly then cleared again, and I wondered what she saw. Since she continued to fix herself a salad, I figured it wasn't too big of a deal.

Happy with the cheesy goodness that loaded my plate, I headed back to the table. When I sat down again, I picked up my fork and licked the salad dressing from it.

A storm of desire hit me so hard I dropped my fork. Metal clattered against china, and just that fast the desire disappeared. It didn't fade; it vanished completely.

I looked up from my plate and found everyone watching me.

Where had that come from? I glanced at Clay. He didn't look the least bit guilty, and I felt his curiosity when he found himself under scrutiny.

Beside me, Carlos slightly shifted in his chair.

"You okay, Z?" Ethan said softly.

"Yeah. Fine."

I refused to look at Carlos. It couldn't have been him. I picked up my fork and carved out a bite of my pizza as if nothing was wrong. But I had a feeling there was a lot wrong.

And most of the wrongness sat to my left, quietly eating his food.

Gradually, everyone started to eat again and conversation resumed. I remained physically focused on my pizza while my thoughts drifted.

Why was Carlos so detached? It took Ethan years to hold back his emotions, and he only just recently discovered how to close himself off. However, even closing himself off didn't completely save him from me when I pulled. Yet, when I'd pulled, Carlos hadn't seemed affected at all. If things went south and this group turned on Ethan and me, Carlos' ability to block me could very well screw any chance of escape.

Yet, with all the leaking emotions around me, I didn't feel one bit of dishonesty or disloyalty. Instead, there was a ton of happiness and gratification. I lifted my eyes from my food and traced the source to Jim as he sat with another plate piled with pizza. A glance at the buffet table showed the decimated remains of three pizzas. Geez, had he been eating while putting more on his plate? He lifted a piece and consumed the triangle in four bites. The piece wasn't small.

Jim caught me watching him, grinned, and lifted the next piece in a salute before eating that one, too.

"How long do you give the manager before he comes out and asks us to leave?" Ethan said, following my gaze.

"I think Jim intends to find out."

Jim winked at me.

The rest of the men ate just as heartily but were more discreet about it. Since the women, except for Winifred, didn't seem to have the same aggressive appetites, I guessed it was a werewolf thing. I went back to my pizza.

By the time I finished what I had on my plate, I was full of pizza and emotions. Though Jim broadcasted his satisfaction of his gluttony the loudest, Gabby's emotions drew my attention.

Something was bothering her, but never to the degree that she stopped eating or spoke up about it.

A waiter came with the bill, even though the guys were still eating, and asked if we would care to order any dessert.

"Is it all-you-can-eat?" Jim asked.

Charlene shot him a warning look.

"No, sir," the waiter answered.

Jim shook his head and went back to his pizza.

"I think we've eaten our fill," Thomas said, as soon as the waiter walked away. However, I caught his gaze straying to the buffet table as he ate his last piece.

Emmitt went to pay, and the group began to stand. I felt a burst of amusement and looked up in time to see Emmitt swipe two slices of pizza on his way back past the buffet. He discreetly passed a slice to his brother, Jim, as we walked to the door. The amusement had come from Grey.

If I hadn't felt so tight with overload, I would have been amused too.

THE FIRST MILE on the treadmill took the edge off; the fifth mile saw the immediate tension drained. I was used to running after eating. When I'd had a job, I had often gone to the gym over my lunch break, just to make it through the day. That midday relief hadn't always been enough to keep me from wanting to punch someone in the face, though. But hopefully, this run would be enough to get me through the night.

I slowed the treadmill to a walk and reached for the towel I'd draped on the handle.

"Want to spar?"

Carlos' voice made me yip and miss a step. I stumbled backward and shot off the end of the treadmill. Thick, bare arms wrapped around me, catching me before I hit the ground. A tingle of awareness zipped through me.

I quickly straightened away, and he let me go.

"Thanks, but I'm good for now," I said as I hid my blushing face by wiping it with the towel. Other girls reacted to boys. I didn't. What the heck was wrong with me?

"Z, you need twenty minutes. Running's not enough."

I pulled my face from the towel and caught Ethan leaning in the doorway of the exercise room. He arched a brow at me when I scowled at him.

"I'm drained."

He grinned at me.

"If that were true, you wouldn't be scowling at me."

Damn him, he was right.

"Fine. Whatever."

I tossed the towel aside and faced Carlos. He wore the clothes I'd bought for him. The sleeveless t-shirt stretched across his broad, muscled chest. The material clung to his chiseled abs, too. His shorts encased his massive thighs. I swallowed and met his eyes.

"You make it look like I shopped in the junior's section."

He didn't react one way or another, but Ethan chuckled.

"I'll be in the room watching Bonanza. There's a marathon."

He turned and left, and I shook my head at the empty doorway. Ethan's taste in TV was weird. A person would never guess his love of Westerns by the way he spoke or dressed.

A brush along my spine had me spinning; but Carlos was a distance away, watching me.

"Kicking," I said. It seemed a good idea to keep him at a distance.

He nodded.

We settled into a rhythm, and once he had my pattern, I picked up speed. I loved sparring against these werewolf guys. I could go as fast as I wanted, and they met each move. And I didn't seem to hurt them like I could Ethan.

Fingers stroked my ankle as Carlos deflected a kick. The lingering tingle returned my focus to the sparring. I bounced back a step and eyed him. Was he playing with me again?

He waved me forward. I balanced and kicked twice, turned, and jabbed at his right shoulder. The unexpected combination caught him off guard, and I connected with him. He flashed me a quick smile. It was like lightening, there and gone again.

After that, I kept things random. He never attacked me, only blocked. But whenever I left an opening, he would let me know with a soft, trailing touch. When I focused on kicks, I usually felt his hands on my legs. When it was my fists, he left the skin on my face and neck prickling.

Fifteen minutes later, I stopped. My chest heaved and sweat soaked my back. I could feel a trickle trailing down my lower spine. I'd depleted everything and dodging his roaming touch was now impossible.

"I'm done," I said, bracing my hands on my knees.

"Five more minutes."

Something in his tone stopped my panting breaths. My lungs screamed for oxygen as I looked up and met his focused gaze. He stood before me, balanced on the balls of his feet as if ready to spring. His hands shook. No, his whole body shook. Did that shaking mean he wanted to go full wolf? Right now? I'd seen him like that twice before and didn't want to see it again.

I forced myself to inhale slowly and keep still.

"For you or for me?"

He closed his eyes as if struggling for control. He'd never seemed to struggle before. That he did now worried me. I knew how fast he could move. Could I make it to the door? I shifted my weight to my right foot, ready to turn and find out, but his eyes popped back open. I stopped moving again.

"Five more minutes."

Dude was like a broken record. I would have laughed if not for the shaking. Where was that old guy when I needed him?

"Is Grey going to need to put a choke hold on you again?" As I spoke, I eased back a step.

The shaking grew worse.

"Come here." The softly spoken command made my stomach flip weirdly.

I took another step and gasped when Carlos blurred before me. One second he was five feet away; the next, he was coming at me with open hands. He brushed my forearm, and I batted him away. He caressed my bare shoulder, and I jabbed him in the gut. He leaned in, and I freaked out and slapped his face.

Why did I always go girly on him? Next time, aim for the nuts, I scolded myself.

The slap did the trick, though. He straightened away, and the shaking eased.

"I apologize," he said.

Then he left the room.

"What the hell was that?"

Unfortunately, the exercise equipment had less of an answer than I did.

I took my time walking back to the room and opened the door warily. Ethan lay back on the bed, his head propped up with several pillows. The room was otherwise empty.

When he heard the door click, Ethan turned and looked me over.

"Looks like Carlos worked you good. I like it when you're all sweaty," he said, grinning at me.

I stepped into the room and closed the door behind me.

"Yeah. I'm empty for real, this time." But I shouldn't have been. As soon as Carlos had started acting weird, I should have started pulling. Even though I couldn't pull from Carlos, there had probably been other people nearby. Enough to feed me the energy I would have needed to protect myself. Why hadn't I tried?

I crossed the room and grabbed some clean clothes out of the bag.

"I'm hitting the shower."

"Want some help?"

"Keep dreaming," I said; and, with a laugh, I closed myself into the bathroom.

When I came out several minutes later, clean and refreshed, Ethan hadn't moved.

"So, are we going to talk about the big guy?" Ethan said without taking his eyes from the TV.

"What do you mean?"

"He keeps watching you. You move; his eyes follow."

"Yeah, right." I stretched out next to Ethan on the bed. It felt good to lie down despite the recent nap. Some days that felt like my routine. Sleep, eat, exercise, repeat.

The show Ethan watched didn't interest me, so I closed my eyes.

"I'm serious," he said. "What do you feel from him?"

"Nothing."

"Ever?"

"Ever."

"Don't you find it weird that he doesn't have any emotions to pull? You always said you couldn't be with anyone because you'd drain the guy. Z, you can't drain him."

I opened my eyes and turned to look at Ethan. He was still facing the TV. He looked relaxed, and I couldn't feel anything from him, but his words told me he was feeling something. What, though? Worry? I gave a little pull, testing his hold.

"Don't, Z."

"Then tell me what's going on in that head of yours."

He turned and met my gaze.

"I never had you, and I'm losing you."

My heart went "aw!" and my brain went "oh, crap." I took a moment to sort through the two emotions.

"You've always had me, and you always will."

"You know what I mean."

"I've never loved anyone more than I love you, Ethan. What we have has to be enough. If it's not, if you push for more, I'll leave because I love you. I won't hurt you." Guilt hit me. "More than I already do."

He closed his eyes and heaved a sigh.

"I can handle a bruise from a girl." The derogatory way he said that made me smile. He lifted his right arm and pulled me to his side. I gently laid my head on his chest, avoiding his bruised shoulder.

SOFT SOUNDS BRUSHED my consciousness enough to pull me from sleep. I lifted my head from Ethan's chest. The room was dark, and Ethan breathed evenly beside me. The clock showed it was the middle of the night.

The hushed rustling stopped. No doubt one of the other two had shifted in their sleep.

I eased myself from Ethan's side and stood, needing to go to the bathroom. I kept my hand on the mattress to guide my way around the bed. Where was the light from the hall? I didn't think hotel rooms got so dark. I moved slowly, so I wouldn't trip on anything.

A thread of worry soured the air, and I paused by the end of the bed. Someone wasn't sleeping.

"Who's awake?"

I strained to hear something and was rewarded by a whisper of noise right in front of me. Something brushed my cheek. I jumped a little, and a hand gently cupped my bruised jaw. I knew the hand...that gentle touch. My pulse leapt when both of his large hands cradled my face, and his fingers burrowed into my hair.

His hold should have made me feel trapped or threatened. However, I felt anything but. For a moment, neither of us moved. Then, his thumb brushed over my lower lip.

My breathing hitched, and my lips parted in surprise. I felt him move closer as his thumb continued its soft caress.

"Z?"

Ethan's tired voice stopped the gentle touch on my mouth, and the fingers at the back of my head twitched.

"Going to the bathroom," I said quietly, as if Ethan and I were the only two awake.

I listened to him roll over and grunt when he jarred his right shoulder. Guilt poked a hole through the moment and whatever might have happened next. I turned my head slightly, freeing myself from Carlos' hold and walked the rest of the way to the bathroom.

I closed the door before I turned on the light and almost screamed to see Carlos standing right behind me in the mirror. He spun me around and backed me against the wall before I could blink. My eyes grew wide when he leaned in, and my heart started to feel like it was trying to beat free from my chest. But he didn't kiss me. He rested his cheek against mine, breathed deeply, and spoke close to my ear.

"You're sleeping in the other bed."

His words were a rumbled growl, and my insides went crazy. He wanted me to sleep in his bed? I didn't think so. I remembered my knee and lifted it with every intention of bringing him down.

One of his hands dropped to deflect the move with ease. At the same time, he brushed his lips against the shell of my ear. I struggled to breathe.

Then, he moved away and plunged us into darkness. The door

clicked softly. I reached out, found the wall, and then the light switch. I checked the mirror. My reflection looked pale and shaky. Pale was my norm, given the red hair. The shakiness wasn't.

Ethan had been right about everything so far. It was weird that the other girls were all matched with a werewolf. And, though I desperately wanted to deny it, the black hole was interested in me. Worse, my pulse jumped and my stomach reacted like I'd swallowed a bowlful of butterflies around him.

I took a calming breath, used the bathroom like I'd intended, and then opened the door with the light still on. If Carlos thought I was going to sleep with—

Grey lay on the far side of his bed, closest to Ethan. Carlos lay near the window. In the same bed as Ethan. The light reflected off Carlos' eyes as he watched me. He wanted me to sleep with Grey? I studied Grey. His eyes were closed, and he was on top of the covers. A thread of worry drifted from him.

What was Grey worried about? Maybe he was afraid I'd spoon him. I shook my head, turned off the light, and shuffled to my new assigned spot. As long as it wasn't with Carlos, I was too tired to care.

I pulled back the covers, and as I slid under, another wave of worry washed over me.

"Relax, Grey," I said softly. "Your virtue is safe with me. No spooning unless requested."

Rolling on my side, I grinned as amusement replaced the worry. It tapered off, and I let myself relax.

I hadn't lied when I'd told Michelle I didn't care about what made werewolves tick. I was just along for the ride. The almost kiss in the bathroom, Carlos' apparent jealousy, and my sudden girly hormones didn't change a thing. Once I was done with these people, it would be just me and Ethan again. An E-Z future.

Why was I having such a hard time believing that?

CHAPTER SEVEN

"I KNOW YOU'RE HOT, BUT I'M NOT INTO GUYS."

Ethan's wry words cut through my light sleep. My eyes popped open as I recalled Carlos in bed with Ethan, and I sat up. Light from the parted curtains illuminated the room enough so that I could see.

Ethan was on his back with his head turned so he eyed Carlos, who lay on his side facing Ethan. It looked a bit too cozy, and I could understand Ethan's concern.

Grey remained still with his eyes closed, though by the smile tugging at his lips and the waves of humor rolling off him, I could tell he was awake.

Carlos opened his eyes and glanced at me before eyeing Ethan. "You're safe with me."

I wasn't sure that was the reassurance Ethan was looking for.

Ethan turned his head as he searched for me. He eyed Grey for a moment before meeting my gaze.

"Did he spoon me? I feel recently spooned."

"Minor spooning," I said, keeping a straight face. "Pants off, but boxers on."

Ethan sat up and swung his legs off the bed.

"You're warped. How can such a twisted mind hide behind that pretty face?"

"You like warped." I couldn't stop the grin.

"Lucky for you. If no one is calling dibs on the bathroom, I'm grabbing it for the next ten minutes."

"All yours," I said, lying back down.

As soon as the bathroom door closed, Grey got out of bed and left the room.

Don't look. Don't look. I turned my head and looked. Yep, Carlos was staring at me.

"Want to tell me what that was about last night?" I asked.

"No."

"You keep too much in. You're going to give yourself an aneurism."

He didn't say anything, but I didn't expect him to.

For the next ten minutes, we stared at each other. It drove me crazy that I didn't know what he was thinking or feeling.

When the bathroom door opened, I bolted out of bed to grab my bag and claim some alone time. It wouldn't pay to take a shower yet; I needed some time on the treadmill before we headed out. So, I splashed some water on my face before brushing my teeth and combing out my hair. After pulling the mass back into a ponytail, I braided it.

Ethan was the only one in the room when I reemerged. He sat on the bed with the tube of cream in his left hand.

"I think you're milking this," I said, setting the bag down.

"Guilty. So, you wanna tell me how I ended up in bed with Carlos?"

Ethan handed me the tube. Then, he managed to pull off his own shirt while I squeezed some of the athletic cream onto my fingers.

"You were right," I said as I started to rub it in.

"Hold up. Say that again. Only this time, say it like you're selling it."

"Shut up." I poked his side, then went back to spreading the salve. "Carlos caught me on my way to the bathroom last night. He said we were switching and took my spot. At first, I thought he meant I should sleep with him."

Ethan snorted.

"Like to see him try," he said.

I grinned, remembering how I'd tried to knee Carlos.

"I think he's jealous of you," I said as I stepped back to signal I was done.

"Good. Guess what he did before he left?"

"What?"

"Changed into workout clothes."

That sneaky giant...

"Want to go for a run outside?" I asked.

Ethan bent down and lifted his running shoes. He knew me too well.

IT WAS EARLY ENOUGH that the sidewalks were still clear. Ethan and I ran in unison. We didn't run together often, but when we did, he stuck to me. I liked the sound of our feet hitting the pavement together.

The gestapo caught up to us seven blocks from the hotel. Grey's worry gave them away. I didn't slow down or give any indication that I'd noticed them tailing us. Ahead, I spotted a fast food chain restaurant. I veered that direction.

Sweaty, but not yet breathing too hard, Ethan and I stepped inside. I ordered double of everything we would normally eat. To go.

"You always play nice," Ethan said under his breath.

He was right. I did. When I could. I tried to make up for the times my mood swings wouldn't let me be nice.

Ethan carried the bags, and I carried the large orange juices. Grey and Carlos were waiting just outside the doors. The sight of Carlos in his tight exercise clothes made my palms sweaty. I ignored the weird phenomenon and pushed my way through the doors. Carlos' gaze swept over me then locked on my face. I pretended not to notice and focused on Grey instead.

"Grey, you're going to need something other than jeans if you plan on taking up running." I handed him an orange juice.

"If the point of the exercise is to burn off the emotion you absorb, doesn't stopping for breakfast defeat the purpose?" he asked.

"Sleeping in a hotel defeated the purpose before the breakfast run did. If you would have felt what was coming from the room above us..."

He winked at me and took a bite of his breakfast sandwich.

"I'm going to have to tell Gabby to stop ratting me out," I said, handing a juice to Carlos.

"She didn't."

"How did you find us?"

Grey answered by tapping the side of his nose before taking another bite.

"You should have showered," Ethan said to me under his breath.

"Shut up. I don't stink." Did I?

He laughed at my frown and dug into his sandwich.

"Might as well walk back," I said as I unwrapped my own food. I wasn't about to run with the two of them following us. The whole point of leaving the hotel was to give myself some distance from Carlos.

Grey turned and started walking. Carlos hung back, waiting for me to follow. What did he think I would do? Run away? Where would I go? They had the cars. I rolled my eyes and sped up to walk beside Grey.

"Hey, Grey...do you fight?"

He grinned at me, a twinkle in his eye.

"Nah. I'm a lover, not a fighter."

Darn. I needed a partner before we left. And it wouldn't be Carlos or Ethan.

My partner happened to find me as we rounded the corner near the hotel. Luke stood waiting by the doors.

"Isabelle, may I speak with you for a moment, please?"

His proper speech made me grin.

"Sure thing. What's up?" I stopped to talk to him while everyone else went inside. Carlos lingered just on the other side of the doors. I wished Michelle had never said anything because my stomach wouldn't settle down around him.

"Bethi wants to speak with you. Alone."

"Alone seems to be pretty hard to do around you people."

"You're safe with me. He knows it." Luke tilted his head toward Carlos.

What did I care if Carlos thought I'd be safe? And why was Luke concerned about what Carlos thought?

"Because I'm Mated," Luke said as if I should have asked why. "Werewolves don't stray. Ever."

Luke smiled. I didn't like his smile. And I didn't like how he glanced at Carlos. I hated conversations with hidden meanings. It was like those stupid picture books where you had to find the guy with the red and white striped hat. I didn't have time for games.

"Yeah...I don't really care. I'll talk to her. But after, you owe me twenty minutes in the exercise room. Deal?"

He appeared to like the idea.

"Deal."

No doubt, he was remembering the beating I'd dished him at

Ethan's back door. Good. It would make the sparring more interesting.

Luke reached for the door and held it open for me. After we passed him, Carlos silently fell in behind us. I should have bought him a bigger shirt. There hadn't been any bigger shirts.

Luke went straight to the exercise room, and I was surprised to see Bethi already there.

"You look like crap," I said, taking in the shadows under her eyes and her pale complexion. Worry, fear, and desperation clouded the air.

"The dreams...you need to help me," she said.

I knew what she meant. And I wanted to help her; I couldn't imagine dreaming about dying over and over again. But I also knew what would happen when I did what she wanted.

"You're going to turn into a crackhead."

"I hear it's a sexy look," she said with a shrug.

I glanced at Luke. He watched Bethi with concern. When he felt my regard, he met my gaze and nodded. He'd seen Gabby. He knew what could happen. I sighed.

"Fine. You can sit on the sidelines. I'll pull a little while I can drain it. But you have my back at the next stop."

She eyed me for a minute then nodded. I liked her more for not asking what I wanted from her before agreeing to my terms.

"Ready to dance, Luke?" I asked with a grin. He moved to the center of the room.

I felt a wisp of vengeance and smirked at him. Yep, he was remembering the punch to the face. I rolled my shoulders and shook out my arms. I'd be using my fists this time.

"Luke."

The way Carlos said his name had me turning. Carlos remained focused on Luke.

"Relax. She knows what she's doing," Luke said.

I wondered what Carlos would do if Luke managed to make contact.

Facing Luke once more, I waved him forward. He went right for my face as I'd expected. Pay back. I blocked it easily and let him stay on the offense. He grinned wickedly and started moving too quick for me to deflect. I winced at the openhanded whack to my side.

Carlos growled behind me. He actually growled? It almost distracted me. Annoyed, I pulled. Bethi's desperation flooded me, as did Luke's smugness. I grinned at him as he lost his momentum. Then, I jabbed at his face. He jerked his head back at the last second, so my knuckles only whispered along his jaw. Bethi giggled.

"Luv, who are you rooting for?"

"My sister," she said with a grin. "She needs to win."

Her giggle wasn't real. I felt no humor coming from her. Just more worry and fear. I breathed again. Her fear filled me, and Luke's annoyance burrowed under my skin. I scowled when he slowed further.

"Focus, Luke. You know what I do. I steal emotions. It weakens you. So stop feeling. If you're not feeling, I'm not stealing." I jabbed at his face again. This time I connected. It wasn't hard, though. I didn't want to hurt him.

I felt his burst of frustration.

"No frustration," I said, dancing away from his slow counter-jab. "Get rid of it, or I'm taking it."

I pulled again. He'd managed to get rid of his frustration because I didn't get a thing from him. However, Bethi's worry seeped into me. She heaved a relaxed sigh.

"Carlos, she needs to go," I said without taking my eyes from Luke.

Luke grinned at me and swung again. I leaned to the side,

ducking under his arm, and came back up with a fist to his jaw. I caught him in the same spot as before. He grunted.

"I'll be right back," Carlos said.

Out of the corner of my eye, I watched him walk Bethi from the room. I stopped pulling and laid into Luke.

I STARED OUT THE WINDOW, resisting the urge to ask if we were there yet.

"Are we there, yet?" Ethan asked in a whiny, high voice.

I grinned. God, we thought alike.

"No. And if you ask again, I'll pull this car over," Winifred said.

Winifred had learned to keep her emotions in check, so it made it hard to tell if she was teasing. I looked at the mirror and caught her smile. At least someone else in the car had a sense of humor besides Ethan and me.

Carlos sat in the front with Winifred. His precise posture and silence annoyed me after his stunt last night. He obviously felt something. Why keep it so hidden? I shook my head slightly. No. I didn't care. I didn't want to know. However, I did appreciate that his emotional nothingness helped make the ride somewhat bearable.

Ethan, on the other hand, had grown a little lax in his boredom, and I felt something from him every now and again. I couldn't blame him, though. It had been a long car ride so far, and we hadn't made much progress as we zigzagged across the state.

Despite the emotional ease within the cab of the car, every time we passed another vehicle on the road, I inadvertently absorbed emotions. It tended to happen too quickly for me to block; Winifred drove like a demon.

As the sun crested the sky, so did my impatience to get wherever we were going. My skin tingled with it, and I struggled to resist the urge to smack Carlos in the back of the head just because he was so annoyingly calm...and because I was itching for a fight.

"Seriously, are we almost there? I need a break."

Ethan glanced at me, studying my face.

"Gabby is guiding us through their nets. As soon as she finds a safe place for us to stop, Michelle or Charlene will make arrangements for somewhere to stay the night," Winifred said.

"So, in other words, you don't know when we'll stop." The thumping behind my eyes intensified, and it had nothing to do with anyone else's emotions. It was plain ol' annoyance from me.

"Try taking a nap," Ethan said.

"It's past that."

He frowned, and I could see him flex his right hand. He was testing his shoulder, most likely trying to gauge if we could pull off onto a back road for a little sparring.

"Not happening," I said, taking his left hand.

He didn't ask what I meant, so I knew my guess was right. I'd just have to sit in the car and wait out the ride like everyone else. Carlos shifted in his seat and glanced back at our hands. I narrowed my eyes at him.

I managed to contain my irritation for another two hours; although, I did have to give up my hold on Ethan's hand. Ethan remained quiet beside me, his worried glances telling me I wasn't successful at hiding my problem. My grip on the door handle tightened with each passing mile. A tiny part of me was thinking about opening it and jumping out. Not to die but to escape. What, I wasn't sure. The car remained soothingly mellow.

"Gabby's found a safe spot. She apologizes that it has taken so long. She said the Urbat changed their pattern slightly, and she wanted to watch it for a while to be sure they wouldn't come back."

"How could you possibly know that?" I asked.

Winifred met my gaze in the mirror.

"As an Elder, I can communicate with our kind in my mind. I asked Sam, Sam asked Gabby and relayed what she said to me."

What she was saying twisted in my head. Werewolves could do everything, it seemed. Everything except leave me alone. I almost twitched with the need to glare at Carlos. This was all his fault. I so didn't want to know anything more about what his kind could do.

"Whatever. How long till we get there?" I bit out.

"It's another hour away. But she said the way is completely clear now. Would you like me to find somewhere to stop?"

"Yes."

Winifred took the next exit. She didn't go far. Two turns brought us to a semi-rural road with fields between the houses. She pulled over beside one field.

My breath clouded as I stepped out. It was cold enough to shiver, but I barely noticed. The rest of the cars pulled up behind us. I didn't bother searching out one of the other guys in the group. I walked into the dead field, knowing Carlos already followed.

When I turned, his gaze swept over my face. His expression gave nothing away. I grew even more annoyed and realized my need to vent wasn't so much the emotions I'd absorbed but rather my own emotions I had tried to ignore.

Once he was close enough, I attempted to punch him in the head. I was irritated that he could so successfully block his emotions from me. I kicked out at his knee. And, pissed as hell over the stunt he'd pulled in the bathroom, I spun close and drove an elbow into his ribs—a new move for him. His grunt made me grin; and I spun around, trying to hit the side of his head. He caught my arm and pulled me close.

"Behave."

What? Me, behave? I saw red. Sparring went out the window, and I attacked. Who the hell did he think he was to tell me what to do? My body obeyed every thought, and my moves blurred as I hit, kicked, elbowed, and kneed him. I used everything. Some moves connected, and I had the satisfaction of hearing a grunt. Most moves he deflected. Within just a few minutes, I was panting and less angry.

I stepped back, signaling an end to the fight, and looked up at Carlos. His eyes burned with an unnamed emotion.

Eh, maybe I should have behaved.

Before I could apologize, he seized me and tossed me over his shoulder. The cold wind bit into my overheated legs, and below me, the ground zipped past. Just as quickly as the movement had started, it stopped; and he set me on my feet.

"What the hell was that?" I asked, pushing my hair out of my face so I could see.

He stood too close, leaning over me in a menacing way.

"I was about to ask you the same thing," he said softly.

I swallowed hard.

"I'm sorry. I was angry."

"Yes. I know. Why?"

"I don't want to talk about it." I glanced over his shoulder and saw the cars in the distance. They were no bigger than an inch. I could barely discern the people milling around them.

He reached out and held my face between his large hands.

"Isabelle, I'm struggling to control my patience with you. Why were you angry?"

My gaze flew to his, and I snorted.

"Struggling? You? I don't think you even have emotions to struggle with."

A flood of complete, hopeless wanting hit me so hard my knees buckled. Carlos didn't let me fall, though. He shifted one arm to my waist and held me tight against him. The contact along with the deluge of want hazed the world around me. I swam in his need and grew just as desperate with it.

He tipped his head forward, his lips brushing the curve of my ear.

"All of what I feel would frighten you."

The tickle of his breath against my skin made me shiver. I pressed closer, needing his touch, wanting his attention. The compulsion to wrap myself in him, in who he was, robbed me of any other thought.

I brought one hand up to place on his shoulder and turned my head to breathe him in, deeply. He shuddered and groaned.

Humming with need, I touched my nose to his neck, nuzzling him, drowning in my want. Gently, I trailed my nose along the column of his neck, exhaling as I went.

He whispered my name. Then, suddenly, it all disappeared. The desperation. The need. The heat inducing desire. It all vanished. Only a lingering ache churned in my stomach.

I froze in Carlos' embrace and shook with my anger, realizing what he'd done.

He exhaled slowly and with a gentle kiss against the shell of my ear, stepped away.

For a moment, despair pulled at his expression, then that too carefully closed off. Though I was mad at him, I was angrier with myself. Ethan had warned me to watch my back. I hadn't been watching.

With an irate toss of my hair, I turned away from him and started the walk back.

Enough emotion had been vented that my skin didn't feel tingly and tight. I frowned, considering the emotion he'd just shared. Though I'd felt every ounce of it, I'd absorbed very little. And it had only been one emotion. I hadn't felt whatever else he'd been feeling. No one felt just one thing. Ever. What kind of control did Carlos have?

THE REST of the drive finished in silence. Ethan wouldn't look at me, and I wondered what he thought of the scene he'd witnessed in the field.

When we pulled up in front of the hotel, I moved to stand near Bethi. She gave me a curious look but didn't say anything. Michelle and Emmitt went to check in. When they came back with four room keys again, I spoke up.

"I need a separate room."

Michelle glanced at the Elders.

"Why?" Winifred asked.

"I'm going to pass out if I have to keep sparring at this rate. I need more isolation."

"She's right," Bethi said. "She can't help herself. Isolation protects her."

Winifred glanced at Grey. Grey looked at the ground. I refused to look at Carlos.

"Emmitt, will you check to see if they have another room?" Winifred asked.

It felt like I was committing a crime with the way everyone silently watched me. Emmitt came back with another room card and handed it over.

"Thank you." I looked down at the number. "If it's all right, I'll just keep to my room." I didn't wait for them to approve but grabbed Ethan's hand.

No one stopped us, and when we were halfway down the hallway, I exhaled in relief. Ethan didn't say a word as I unlocked the door and motioned him inside.

Once the door closed behind us though, he turned to study me.

"Talk to me, Z. What happened?"

I sat down on the bed and looked up at him.

"Turns out he's not a robot."

"What made you think he was?"

119

"He didn't leak anything, Ethan. Ever. He was a complete void. Even when you're blocking, I have a sense of what you're feeling."

Ethan sat next to me.

"That's because you know me better than anyone else."

"That's just it." I set my head gently against his damaged shoulder. "I know you. I don't know him. I don't want to be near him anymore."

"Z, what happened out there?" he asked softly.

I sighed.

"He opened himself and let me feel just one emotion. It was too much. It burrowed under my skin, and I felt what he felt. It was like it was my own emotion. I couldn't tell the difference."

"What did he feel, Z?"

I closed my eyes and turned my head to hide my face against Ethan's shoulder.

"God, he wants me." My stomach tightened at the remembered emotion.

"Lots of guys have wanted you, but you typically don't kick their butts for it. You really laid into him, Z. You were nicer to Brick."

I cringed, knowing he was right.

"I was so mad. At the car ride. At the people chasing us. At this dumb trip. At him for being so damn nothing all the time. I thought coming with them to see if I could get rid of this thing I do was a good idea, but maybe it's not. I just want to go."

He finally wrapped his right arm around my shoulders and gave me a squeeze.

"This is the right decision for now. You're just afraid."

I lifted my head.

"What?"

"Carlos made you feel something you didn't want to feel, right? It freaked you out."

Yeah, it definitely freaked me out. I set my head back on Ethan's shoulder and exhaled heavily.

"Do you need to spar again or are you feeling all right?" he asked.

"I'm good. Bored after the long drive, but good."

"What do you want to do?"

"Let's just watch some TV." I didn't want to leave the room and risk running into Carlos again.

"Sounds good to me." He stiffly dropped his arm, stood, and moved to the head of the other bed. He got comfortable then waved me over with his left arm. I gave a weak smile and joined him. I needed Ethan to get better.

I just needed Ethan.

THE NEXT MORNING we packed up and joined everyone in the lobby. I wasn't looking forward to another day in the car or facing Carlos. The negative emotions drifting from the group told me no one else wanted to spend another day driving either.

"We thought we might go out for breakfast," Winifred said as we approached.

"Good," Ethan said. "I'm starving."

There'd been no room service the night before since the hotel didn't offer any. And raiding the snack machine in the hall had been unsatisfactory. It had either been understocked, or the rest of the group had hit it first. Fruit snacks and chewing gum had done little to curb Ethan's appetite.

We threw our bags into the car then walked the three blocks to the restaurant. I enjoyed the stroll and lingered at the back of the group with Ethan. Despite my intention to ignore Carlos, I found myself studying him. He walked beside Grey near the front of our procession. Everyone else chatted, but they were quiet. I couldn't help wondering what Carlos was thinking. Had he been upset by the separate room? Was he worried I'd shared a bed with Ethan? Why did I even care? He had to know we'd want a separate room after he'd made me switch beds. I mean, I wasn't about to make Ethan sleep next to Carlos again, though I didn't think Ethan had actually minded. Yet, if Ethan wouldn't share with Carlos and Carlos didn't want me bunking with Ethan, that meant I'd find myself snuggling with Carlos.

The remembered sensation of Carlos' mouth against my ear made me shiver.

"We need to get you a better jacket," Ethan said.

His hunched shoulders were near his ears as he struggled to stay warm, too.

"We'll be warm enough once we're eating or back in the car," I said quietly. The cold didn't bother me as much as the idea of sitting in the car with Carlos.

The quaint restaurant had the typical breakfast offerings. Jim made me smile when he hopefully asked if they had a buffet. The small dining room obviously didn't have one. I didn't know why he bothered asking.

I ordered an omelet then played tic-tac-toe with Ethan on the back of my placemat. He won most of the games.

"You cheat," I said, setting down my blue crayon.

He grinned and shook his head at me.

"It's tic-tac-toe. Cheating's impossible. Don't be a sore loser."

Playing the game and the banter never fully distracted me from Carlos' steady gaze from across the table. What would he do if I kicked him in the shin? I was so tempted to find out. Only the possibility that he might turn into the mad dog I'd seen in the alley stopped me. I didn't want Ethan to get hurt because I was annoyed.

When the food arrived, Emmitt immediately asked for the bill. I glanced at Gabby. She was in her sonar world again, and I wondered if she'd seen something to cause the need for speed. I ate quickly as did everyone else.

"Ethan," Winifred said as we walked out the door. "Could I speak with you for a moment?"

I slowed down with him, but she waved me ahead.

"It's all right, Isabelle. You go walk with Gabby."

I was obviously not wanted. Ethan nodded that he was okay, so I turned and caught up with Gabby and Clay.

"I'll be your third wheel for this walk," I said.

Gabby didn't answer, just stared straight ahead. I leaned around her to look at Clay.

"She been doing this a lot?"

He nodded and cast her a worried glance.

I nudged Gabby with my elbow, and she blinked and turned to look at me.

"What are you seeing?"

"I'm not sure yet."

"Meaning..."

Her brow wrinkled.

"They've been sweeping for us since we ran into them at your hotel. It's like they're doing a grid search. I've been slipping us through the holes in the lines. Sometimes, it seemed as if they caught a scent trail and repositioned to net us. When that happened, I would confuse our trail with a highway or high population area.

"They're still sweeping for us, but there are larger gaps in some of their lines. Not many. A few. I've been trying to see where the men might have gone, but I don't see any large groupings other than the one in northern New York. The holes are random so far. It's making it easier for us to slip by them."

She paused for too long.

"But..." I prompted her.

"It feels too easy," she said, fully looking at me.

I knew what she meant. When the river of life gave you a floatie, there were definitely rapids ahead.

"Ignore the big gaps then and go for the smaller ones."

"That's what I was thinking, too," she said with a nod.

"Did you talk to grandma and grandpa about it yet?" Grey felt more like an Uncle than Winifred and Sam.

"I haven't mentioned it yet because I was trying to figure it out. But I'll talk to Sam when we're on the road again."

I nodded as if I cared whether or not she shared the information, then looked over my shoulder. Ethan kept pace beside Winifred. His gaze swept the sidewalk before him as he listened to her. He looked sad. What was she saying to him?

At the hotel, the groups separated into their designated cars. Except Winifred and Ethan.

"Z, I'm going to ride in the party bus and give you a break for a bit. Have the big guy pull over if you need something."

My mouth dropped open as he pivoted and climbed into the SUV with Winifred. There were three vehicles. Winifred's car, the SUV that Sam drove, and the car that Thomas drove. Thomas, Charlene, Jim, Emmitt, and Michelle had climbed into one car. Sam, Gabby, Clay, Bethi, Luke, and Grey had already disappeared into the eight-passenger SUV.

Slowly, I turned my head and found Carlos watching me. My eyes narrowed. I rolled my shoulders and went to the car. It didn't pay to sit in back in protest. I went to the front passenger seat and made myself comfortable.

Carlos immediately joined me. He didn't even seem to notice I was there as he adjusted his seat, mirror, and steering wheel. He buckled then glanced at my seatbelt. I buckled in, glaring at him the entire time.

I waited until we cleared the city limits before I spoke to him.

"So, this is how we're playing it? I ask for a room that doesn't include you, and you finagle a car ride alone with me? What are you hoping to prove? How fast you can piss me off?"

His fingers twitched on the steering wheel.

"I thought we could talk," he said evenly.

"About what?" If he mentioned the field, I'd punch him in the head.

"Michelle said she spoke to you."

Oh, hell no. That subject was just as bad. I debated telling him to shut up then decided to play dumb. Maybe he'd give up.

"About what exactly?"

When he spoke, his voice was soft like the lull in the eye of a hurricane.

"I know you feel the pull. I see it every time you look at me. Why are you fighting it?"

Because fighting is what I do, I thought.

"I don't know what you're talking about. What pull?" I kept my voice curious and confused. Stupid man. Did he think I was about to talk about *him* with him?

His hands tightened on the wheel again.

"Do you know why we're alone in this car?"

Well, that was an abrupt change in topic.

"No clue. Fill me in."

"I'm barely in control, Isabelle. Grey thought you'd be safer if I was busy driving." He completely looked away from the road to stare at me. "But you're not."

The car stayed perfectly in the lane. Not even a tiny bit of veering. That was scarier than his words.

"Okay. Okay. Just look at the road already." He was freaking me out.

He didn't listen.

"Tonight, when we stop, we'll go back to four rooms. Not five. Do you understand?"

Did he just try to tell me what I was going to do? Yes. He did.

"If you value Ethan's safety—"

I reached out, grabbed the steering wheel, and yanked it to the right. The car swerved with a screech as he immediately counter-steered. He braked hard and pulled over to the shoulder. We were still on back roads. As soon as the car stopped, he turned to look at me, thunder in his eyes.

"Don't ever try to threaten me," I said in a low voice.

"Don't ever risk your safety again."

I shivered at the menace in his words. His intense gaze made my stomach dip and my middle heat. He inhaled slowly, deeply. Both his hands still gripped the steering wheel. Yet, they shook.

Emotion flooded the air. This time there was no question regarding its origin. Helplessly, I breathed in his absolute, desperate need. His steady gaze never left my face as he lifted one hand from the steering wheel and reached out toward me. His need to touch me became my need to be touched. I could barely breathe because of it. I closed my eyes, trying to deny the feelings that I knew weren't my own. But I was helpless against his need. It was too all consuming.

I leaned forward.

When a fingertip brushed my cheek, I exhaled shakily and my eyes flew open. I wanted more, but he was still in the same spot, only allowing himself a small touch. The pads on his fingers feathered over my skin from cheek to jaw, a light, gentle stroke that left a burning trail. The need for more consumed me.

No, this wasn't me. It was him.

I was drowning in what he felt and couldn't save myself.

CHAPTER EIGHT

IF I GAVE INTO CARLOS, I WOULD LOSE ETHAN. I WOULDN'T ALLOW that. I let the fear of losing Ethan fill me, robbing Carlos' need of its potency. Willfully, I turned my head, trying to dislodge his touch.

The heat in Carlos' gaze turned to frustration, and his fingers twitched against my cheek.

Suddenly the back door opened, and the car dipped as someone got in. The door closed again.

"I think you two need a chaperone," Grey said.

The emotion immediately vanished, and Carlos slowly dropped his hand. I sagged against the seat and a shaky exhale escaped me. Grey's gaze bounced between Carlos and me.

"Did Carlos manage to discuss anything with you?" Grey asked. "I'm guessing it's the reason behind the swerve and the sudden stop."

Neither of us answered. I wasn't sure I could talk yet without quavering.

Carlos straightened in his seat, checked his mirrors, then signaled that he was ready to pull out. A distance ahead of us, I saw the other cars had pulled over as well.

MELISSA HAAG

"You two are a chatty pair," Grey said with humor.

"We're not a pair," I said and looked out the window. I refused to play their little matchmaking game.

Silence reigned for several long minutes. It was enough time for me to relax and notice Grey's sadness.

"You've been with us a handful of days. You know we're different from you, but you haven't asked any questions. Aren't you curious about us?"

"No."

"I'm curious about you. Will you tell me about yourself?"

I kept my gaze focused on the horizon. Damn Ethan for abandoning me with these people.

"What do you want to know?" I asked in a flat voice.

"What's your favorite color?"

His question surprised me. I'd expected questions about my power or my relationship with Ethan.

"I don't know. Blue?"

Grey laughed.

"You sound like Carlos. I'm guessing you've never given something like that any thought because there were always too many other things that needed your attention. My favorite color is green. Blue would be a runner-up. What about a favorite food?"

That question was easier.

"I don't have a favorite food. I have a food trinity. Pizza, burgers, and cereal. I could survive forever on all three."

"Burgers are good," Grey agreed. "Have you ever had a fajita? Those are good, too. I think my trinity would be Carlos' fajitas, burgers, and Winifred's cookies."

I immediately saw what Grey was doing. I didn't want to know anything about Carlos. I knew enough. He thought we had some magical connection. We didn't. End of story.

"I appreciate the conversation, but I think I'm going to try to take a nap. I'm not a fan of long, boring car rides."

I curled my legs up on the seat and leaned on the window.

A SUDDEN BURST of worry nudged me from the light doze I'd managed out of sheer boredom.

"Carlos, get ready to turn left."

Hands settled on my shoulders as the car lurched at Carlos' sudden turn. Tires squealed. My eyes flew open, and my pulse leapt. I gripped the door as the car's speed increased significantly before Carlos even straightened the wheel. The other cars raced just a bit ahead of us.

"What's going on?"

The hands gave my shoulders a quick squeeze then released me. I turned to look at Grey as he settled back into his seat. He gave me a shadow of a reassuring smile. I wasn't fooled. His concern perfumed the air.

"Gabby didn't like the way they were netting to the north. She thinks we can pass by to the west. But it's a small window, and we need to get there as quickly as possible."

I stared ahead at the SUV, at Ethan.

"How close are they?"

"Close enough that Carlos is willing to speed."

I glanced over at the speedometer. We still drove on back roads. There weren't any other cars in sight. The three vehicles moved in tandem, a little too close given the high speeds. My grip on the door tightened.

Carlos glanced at me but said nothing.

In the backseat, I felt Grey's frustration. "We might not make it."

"How many are we talking?" I asked. My gaze swept over the tree-studded landscape as I wondered how close they really were.

"Five."

All my tension melted. "There are fifteen of us, right? Why are we freaking out over five Urbat?"

"Right now, none of them know where we are. If we're spotted, they'll all know."

The next few minutes passed in silence. We turned twice before hopping onto a highway. As soon as we hit the ramp, Grey's worry vanished.

"Now, we were talking about favorite foods, weren't we?"

I sighed and curled up for another nap. It didn't work.

"What kind of music do you like?"

"It depends on my mood."

"Do you like rainy days or sunny ones?"

"Rainy."

"Are you a morning person or a late night person?"

"Neither. I'd rather sleep all day." He didn't take the hint.

"What—"

"Is the point of all these questions?" I turned to look at Grey.

"You're only encouraging him," Carlos said. I glanced at him. He watched the road.

Grey's amusement floated around me. Too bad for him I was out of patience.

"One more question, and I knock you out."

Grey winked at me but kept silent.

"How much longer until we get where we're going?" I asked Carlos.

"A few more hours."

The car ride from hell...

My bladder was ready to burst when we finally turned into the hotel parking lot. My door was open, and I was out before the car stopped moving. I beat Emmitt to the door.

"Bathroom?" I said loudly.

The man behind the reception counter looked up and pointed to his left. I veered in the direction he indicated and closed myself in the small bathroom.

After the day I'd had, I officially disliked werewolves. And when I found Ethan, I was going to hit him. Gently. I'd only leave a tiny bruise.

I finished using the bathroom, washed my hands, and stalked out. Not only had they deprived me of a bathroom, I was starving.

In the lobby, Carlos stood holding my bag.

"Where's everyone else?"

"Dropping off their things. Everyone's hungry."

Instead of handing over my bag, he handed me the keycard. Good. I'd have two hands free to deal with Ethan. I glanced at the number on the card then took off in the correct direction. Our room wasn't far. I unlocked the door and pushed it open. Grey looked up from the bag he had on the foot of his bed. The room was otherwise empty. My gaze drifted to the bathroom door. It was closed.

I marched up to the panel.

"Ethan, get out here."

His muffled refusal confirmed my suspicion that he was hiding from me.

"I invoke my tenth grade birthday present."

That sneaky jerk. I pounded on the door in frustration.

"You can't. You used it already. Like, three times."

"That card had no expiration or number of use limits."

I slapped the door. That gift had been my worst mistake. I'd made a card with a coupon on it. *The holder of this card can piss Isabelle off and not get hit for it.* I'd written it out of guilt because the day before his birthday, he'd tried kissing me for the first time. And I'd punched him in the face. Not for the kiss, but the overwhelming flood of teenage-boy horny emotions that had come with it.

"Fine. Come out." I backed away from the door and looked pointedly at Grey and Carlos.

"We'll wait for you in the lobby," Carlos said.

Ethan didn't emerge until the door closed behind the pair. He eyed me warily. Looking at him hurt.

"How could you?" I said. "You're supposed to have my back, and you just left me with him."

His tension eased, and he took a step toward me. In a heartbeat, I was wrapped in his strong arms. His hold felt like home.

"I'm sorry, Z. Winifred was persuasive. Plus, I had questions I knew you wouldn't want to listen to."

I didn't ask what. He knew me well; and if he thought I didn't want to listen to him, he was probably right. I wrapped my arms around his waist and talked into his bruised shoulder.

"I don't want to do this anymore."

"You know we're stuck with them, right? On our own, the group that's hunting you girls would find you. And on your own, you wouldn't stand a chance."

He was wrong. On my own, I *would* stand a chance. But I wasn't on my own. I had Ethan. He was my weak spot.

He smoothed a hand over my hair.

"What's making you want to run? Same thing?" he asked.

I pictured Carlos, cringed, and buried deeper into Ethan's shoulder. He sighed and kissed the top of my head.

"How do you feel? Need to spar?"

I shook my head. Despite the long ride, the back roads meant fewer accidental pulls; and Grey had kept most of what he'd felt to himself.

"Then, let's go eat."

We left the room together and walked the hall side by side. The rest of the group already waited in the lobby. When they saw us, Jim was the first one out the door, all the while mumbling about starvation.

Instead of walking, we drove; and Ethan stuck with me. The Chinese buffet we pulled into didn't surprise me. After skipping a meal, I was willing to bet the men would be ready to wolf down anything, as long as it was in quantity.

A long table in the center of the place fit us perfectly, and I found myself between Ethan and Carlos. Jim led the charge to the six buffet stations. The variety of food amazed me. They had standard Americanized Chinese fare such as beef and cashews with broccoli; they had straight up American food such as mac and cheese and chicken nuggets; then they had the atypical foods such as crawfish, eel, and shark bites. When Charlene walked past the crawfish, she shuddered. Thomas, who wasn't far behind her, chuckled.

I didn't blame Charlene for her shudder. Anything with eyes still in place was off the menu for me.

Plate loaded with Crab Rangoon, General Tso's Chicken, and fried rice, I made my way back to the table. Carlos was already sitting. He barely had anything on his plate. He had a bit of rice, a bit of something that didn't look familiar, and that was it.

I studied him as I sat. As usual, he gave nothing away.

"You sick?" I said.

He exhaled slowly and turned to look at me. His dark eyes hinted at sadness, though he continued to be an emotional void.

"No."

"Don't you like Chinese food?"

He glanced at his plate.

"I'm not sure I've had it before."

Not had it? It wasn't in my trinity but it was darn close.

"Then you need to start with one of these," I said, holding up a

Crab Rangoon. He didn't even look at what I offered him, just leaned forward and took a bite while maintaining eye contact. My hand started to shake. He reached out to steady it, eating the second half in one bite. His lips brushed my fingertips.

"Thank you," he said.

I cleared my throat before I attempted to speak.

"No problem."

For the rest of the meal, I kept my food to myself. Slowly, the emotions of everyone else in the room started to bleed into me.

If Ethan thought I was unusually quiet, he didn't mention it.

GREY BEAT me to the room, and I saw my bag on the bed with him.

"Werewolves are ridiculous," I said before closing myself in the bathroom to change into my exercise clothes and pull my hair back. When I stepped out again, Ethan was on the opposite bed, reclined and watching TV.

"You game for a little exercise?" I asked him.

He glanced at me and gave me a reassuring smile.

"Nah, I'm going to milk it another day."

I shook my head at him and left the room. He probably wasn't milking it. He hadn't asked me to rub any more ointment into his shoulder, and I was willing to bet it was because he didn't want me to see the ugly colors his bruise was turning.

The exercise room in this hotel was almost nonexistent. The tiny room had a treadmill, an elliptical, a TV, and a Carlos. He leaned just inside the door and straightened when I walked in.

I debated turning around but knew I would regret it if I did. My skin already itched. He was here and sparring was always better than running. So I stayed.

Ethan had made a valid point before we'd eaten. Running

wasn't an option. That left tolerating these people. Most days, I didn't tolerate well. I needed to set things straight with Carlos.

"We'll need to be careful in here," I said, looking around at the foot room.

He nodded and got into his ready stance. I started out slow with easy jabs. He blocked each one with an open palm. His stoic silence, both emotionally and verbally, bugged me.

"What did you think talking would accomplish?" I asked, just before I picked up the pace.

He shrugged.

"Not good enough."

I dodged around his block and caught him in the ribs. He exhaled slightly, so I knew he felt it, but otherwise gave no other indication I'd even touched him.

"It was obviously planned," I said as I continued with a few jabs. "I mean, you had Winifred say something to Ethan, so he wouldn't ride in the car with us. And you said Grey wanted you to drive, so you would stay calm. Meaning, you talked to him about it beforehand. If you planned something, you had to have an expected outcome.

"So, what did you hope to accomplish?"

"Alone time."

"We've had alone time. This is alone time."

"Alone time where you weren't angry."

"Then you picked the wrong topic."

He stopped blocking and straightened. I automatically stopped hitting.

"Why did it make you angry?"

"Are you kidding me? I've known about you people for what? Three days? You flipped out when I first met you. The girls in this group—my 'sisters'—are all paired up with a werewolf; then, the first night Ethan and I join the merry men, Michelle comes to my room and mentions how she was attracted to Emmitt. Next, you try to start talking about 'the pull.' Three days. How would you react?"

"So, it has nothing to do with him?"

I knew he meant Ethan.

"It has everything to do with me. Just me. I will never be with anyone. Ever. I kill people, Carlos. Slowly. I leave behind burnt-out shells of who they used to be. Ethan understands that. He jokes, and I know he would be there waiting for me if things ever changed; but he knows that, to keep him safe, I have to keep my distance."

"I'm not like Ethan."

"No. You're not. You're scarier. The control you have over your emotions is incredible. But, you're a volcano. When your emotions finally erupt, you will leave devastation behind. If I'm around you when that happens, I can't imagine how it would feel under my skin."

I sighed and rolled my shoulders.

"Now, are you going to help me purge or not?"

He nodded and got back into a ready stance.

"ISABELLE, GET UP AND GET DRESSED." Grey's loud, firm voice startled me awake. I sat up as a light turned on.

Grey was out of bed, grabbing my bag. Carlos was reaching out to shake Ethan. Grey tossed the bag to me. His urgency seeped into me.

I quickly got out of bed.

"E, get your lazy ass out of bed. Now."

Ethan sat up and looked around at us.

"What is it?"

"Gabby said we need to leave immediately," Grey said. "A

group of ten are netting this way. We have five minutes to be a mile from here."

Crap. I shouldered my bag and slipped on my shoes. I had a tank top on and leggings. Good enough.

Ethan bounded out of bed, grabbed his shoes and bag, and went to the door. As soon as he opened it, I heard movement in the hallway.

"Hurry," Winifred said.

I hustled to the door with Grey close behind me. The others were already speed walking the hall, heading toward the lobby. I kept pace with Ethan. The glass door showed the lit parking lot. The sun wasn't even close to rising.

Ahead, I saw Clay walking near Gabby. She was speaking softly.

Ethan went straight for the car and slid into the backseat. I got in and closed my door a second before Grey and Carlos closed theirs. Ours was the second engine to roar to life. We were in the middle of the procession out of there.

"Talk, Grey. I want to know what's happening."

"There are more now. They're closing in fast. Gabby says they aren't veering at all, almost as if they know right where we are."

We sped through the streets. The city wasn't overly large, and it didn't take long to reach its outskirts.

"They've made city limits and have split up. Five in each group. They'll find our trail."

The vehicle in front of us accelerated suddenly. Carlos pressed the gas to keep up.

"Buckle up, Isabelle," he said, glancing in the mirror.

I hadn't realized I'd skipped that part. I clicked the belt and reached out for Ethan's hand. His strong fingers wrapped around mine.

"We'll put as much distance between them as we can. It should be fine," Grey said. He faced forward, watching the road, so I wasn't sure who he was reassuring.

For the next two minutes, only the sound of the wheels devouring the blacktop kept us company. I wasn't sure if it was because Grey had no update or because he focused on something we couldn't hear.

His uneasiness worried me, though.

"Grey?"

"They have our trail. The net's closing." The quiet way he spoke sent a spike of fear through my chest. Ethan's reassuring fingers squeezed mine lightly.

"How many?"

"At least sixty, more closing in behind them."

My pulse spiked. Sixty? I looked around. Fields and trees and a few houses.

"Stop the car by the next field," Grey said.

"There's no way to avoid them?"

"None."

I turned to look at Ethan. He met my gaze steadily. He'd already closed himself off.

"Keep that wall up," I said, squeezing his hand. He nodded.

"Grey, warn the rest. They need to close themselves off from me as best they can or stay away from me." My insides quivered with what I knew I would need to do, what I didn't want to do. But I needed to protect everyone. I needed to protect Ethan.

"Done."

The vehicles pulled over and doors opened. I wanted to tell Ethan to stay in the car, but given our last experience with Urbat, a car wasn't any safer than out in the open. We moved into the field. Emmitt, Clay, and Thomas pushed their women into the middle of our loose circle. Winifred stayed near them. Bethi came to stand beside me after handing something to Ethan. She oozed fear.

"Take a hit," she said.

I pulled her fear away from her like the thick, unwanted skin it was. It filled me with energy. She pulled out a wicked knife from her jacket and held it with ease.

"Have you used that before?"

"Yeah. You taught me how in another life."

"Good."

After that, no one spoke. We waited in silence under the stars.

CHAPTER NINE

THE THUNDER OF FEET HITTING THE GROUND REACHED US FIRST, THEN the Urbat came out of the darkness like a swarm of locusts. My pulse leapt at the sight of so many creatures devouring the distance between us. They sprinted on all fours, and their teeth glinted in the moonlight as their challenging snarls filled the air. I shivered, rolled my shoulders, and stepped a few feet ahead of the group. I needed room.

I glanced over my shoulder, a look that took less than a moment, but the details seared into my memory.

Luke and Bethi stood together, just slightly back to back. Clay crouched in front of Gabby. She had a hand on his back as if restraining him. Emmitt and Jim had Michelle pinned between them, her pale, frightened face seeming to glow in the moonlight.

Thomas was pushing Charlene closer to Michelle, so he could box the women in with his sons. Sam, Grey, and Winifred encircled them with Sam near Gabby and Clay. Ethan stood directly behind me, the knife he clutched in his hand very similar to Bethi's. His gaze focused on the oncoming horde. My breath hitched in concern for him, and I shifted my gaze to Carlos, who stood a step away from Ethan and me.

Where Ethan looked nervous, Carlos appeared calm. A mountain, unyielding against the approaching storm. His gaze met mine. Maybe it was his stoic presence or maybe I caught something more in that brief connection, but whatever I saw firmed my resolve.

I turned back to face the approaching mass. One hundred yards away, two branches split off the main group to surround us.

"Give me your fear," I shouted. It didn't matter if it came from my companions or the beasts.

As soon as the dogs were within range, I pulled hard. A few staggered. My skin tightened and energy heated my blood. I bent my knees slightly and brought up my fists.

Then the beasts crashed upon our group like a wave upon a shore.

The men shouted. My sisters screamed in fear.

Kicking out, I caught one of the creatures in the face. Teeth and blood flew. I inhaled his fury, grabbed his head, and twisted. I didn't break his neck, but I did turn him. Bethi dove forward and used her knife to finish him. Luke moved with her, shielding her from another attack. She immediately withdrew her knife and spun to help him. I dropped the wolf and swung out at the next beast.

The brutes pushed against us, a wall of furred bodies bent on our destruction. I kicked and hit and pulled in emotion until I felt bloated with it. When one beast fell, another took its place.

Someone screamed again. Gabby. I risked a look.

The wolves were trying to get to us, the Judgements. One beast had caught Gabby's arm, but quickly lost his hand with a swipe from Grey. Grey, the liar, fought beautifully, his moves a testament to his strength and precision. The wolves around him fell rapidly, a few seemingly helped by an invisible hand. Sam fought much the same as Grey, taking on three or four wolves at a time. Winifred was gone. A white wolf now guarded Charlene,

Michelle, and Gabby. The Elders weren't letting any Urbat near the three.

Ethan and Carlos fought together behind me.

Seeing everyone protected, I turned again, hitting a wolf hard enough that he staggered toward Bethi. He noticed her and started to change, growing human arms to try to grab her. Before I could move forward to intercede, another animal lunged for me. It met my fists. From the corner of my eye, I saw Luke turn and attack the wolf going for Bethi. The distraction cost Luke, though, and another wolf's claws raked bloody gashes into Luke's chest.

Bethi started yelling obscenities, and her anger flooded the area. It gave me the power I needed to push back the beast I fought and gain enough room to bring both hands up and shove a thumb in its eye. The creature yowled and screeched as it fell away from me.

Something crashed into my back. The weight nearly brought me down but immediately disappeared. I almost turned but caught myself in time. There were too many circling us for even a moment's distraction.

"Back to back," I yelled. I shifted positions and felt Ethan move closer. We'd sparred together so many times, we now moved in a fluid harmony that seemed surreal in the violent chaos around us. I knocked an Urbat to the side, and Ethan lashed out with his knife, silencing the snarl.

"More coming!" Gabby yelled.

More? We couldn't handle more.

Behind me, I heard Carlos growl. The sound gave me shivers.

A wolf in the wake of the one I currently fought, crouched low, its hind legs bunching. It sprang in the air, sailing over its fellow monsters, right toward me. Carlos jumped and intercepted it with a thud. Midair, as they fell, Carlos wrapped his massive hands around the wolf's head and twisted, successfully executing the move I'd tried earlier. The body fell to the ground.

My arms were growing tired. Even while sparring with the werewolves, I'd never moved so quickly, hitting and blocking seemingly within the same second. I needed more juice.

"Walls!" I yelled, only giving them a moment before I pulled hard.

I used the new power to push away yet another attack. But my narrowed focus enabled another wolf to lurch closer.

Carlos reached out and grabbed the creature by the throat, stopping its forward advance. In the second before he yanked the beast away, it lashed out with its claws, raking my side. I grunted at the pain but didn't stop moving.

Behind me, Ethan's anger slipped. He'd been holding his guard well, trying to shield me from his emotions as much as to shield himself from my pull. Now, he fought furiously, irate that someone had actually hurt me. I also felt his exhaustion and pain. He favored his right shoulder. I'd done that to him.

Turning, I caught one of the attackers by the throat and threw him away before he could touch Ethan. Ethan swiped out with his knife and caught another man's forearm.

The rumble of more feet vibrated the ground, and I felt a flicker of fear. My own. There were too many. Sweat coated Ethan's face and wet the back of his shirt. Even the infallible Carlos strained against five partially shifted men.

I fought harder. We needed to reduce their numbers before more came. I stepped forward, slamming my fist down on a muzzle. The crack I heard should have worried me—my bones or his?—but I was already turning to face the next creature.

Then, the world stilled.

Pain ripped through me, sudden and sharp. I struggled to breathe and clutched at my middle. My gaze fell to my hands. But there was nothing there. No blood. My eyes widened as I realized the pain wasn't my own.

Lifting my head, I saw the unthinkable. A half-formed wolf

stood toe to toe with Ethan. Ethan's mouth was open in a silent cry of pain, his knife paused in the air, mid-swing. I saw why. The thing's furry arm had vanished into Ethan's stomach, piercing him. As I watched, the creature pulled his bloody hand out. A drop of red fell to the ground in slow motion.

No, this wasn't right. It wasn't real. I blinked and made a sound of denial when the image remained. The thing before Ethan cackled and turned toward me.

Like a marionette cut from its strings, Ethan crumpled to his knees. The knife fell from his loose fingers. His arm pressed against his bloody stomach, and he fell to his side.

I barely noticed Carlos jump between the creature that had hurt Ethan and me.

The thing cried out in pain while I dropped to the ground beside Ethan. Someone shouted something at me but I couldn't hear.

Ethan's gaze found mine, and his lips twisted in a sad smile as the chaos around us seemed a world away. His ragged breathing filled my ears, and I felt everything.

His hopelessness and pain.

His love.

His acceptance of his death.

The acceptance cut me deep. I clutched at his hand and petted his cheek.

"No, Ethan," I said. "Stay with me. Come on."

Memories flashed through my mind. Us walking to school together. Me defending him when kids would pick on him for his crappy clothes. Him convincing me to go to my first high school dance.

His hand rose and touched the loose ends of my hair.

"I love you."

The pain in my gut intensified, and tears tracked down my cheeks at his words. He wasn't just saying he loved me. He was saying goodbye. I wanted to scream. He wasn't supposed to die. It was E-Z all the way. We'd made that promise so long ago. Together, always. I held his hand tighter.

"I love you, too." I bent forward and kissed him. My lips trembled against his. His fingers touched my cheek. I tasted blood, and my tears fell faster. I couldn't let him go like this.

Slowly, I inhaled, pulling in emotions from everyone around me. Bethi's anger and fear. Luke's devotion to Bethi. Clay's determination to keep Gabby safe. Gabby's despair and resignation. Sam's outrage when someone clawed Gabby. Grey's deep sorrow.

I couldn't feel Ethan's pain.

I breathed again, pulling harder, tasting Emmitt's steely resolve that no one touch Michelle. Jim's boiling anger that one of the monsters had tried for his mother. Charlene's absolute love for her boys and Thomas.

Something dripped from my nose. A bit of blood. I wiped it away along with the tears still flowing freely.

"Stop, Z. Don't take my pain." He pulled in a shallow breath. "It'll keep me here just a little longer."

My breath hitched on a sob. I hadn't taken any of his pain. It was already gone. I knew what that meant.

"I can't do this without you," I choked out. "Please. You just have to wait." For what, I didn't know. There were no sirens rushing toward us, no doctors running to stanch the blood flowing from the hole in his stomach.

Ethan's gaze shifted away from me, finally drawing my attention to Carlos. The man moved around us in a blur of speed as he kept away those who Bethi and Luke couldn't.

"When I'm gone," Ethan said, his raspy voice barely above a whisper, "fight her. Don't let her keep the pain in; it'll kill her. Keep her safe for me. Promise."

Carlos and I spoke at the same time.

"I swear."

"No. You fight me. Stay, Ethan."

Ethan kept his attention on Carlos.

"She'll need you and hate you for it."

His fingers lightly tugged my hair, and he met my gaze again.

"I'll love you even after I'm gone. Remember, without you, I would have died years ago. Thank you for saving me."

He coughed, and I waited for him to breathe again but he didn't.

"No." My denial echoed over the growls and Bethi's cursing.

I reached forward.

"Ethan?" Nothing.

Devastation emptied me. Then rage filled me.

"No!" I screamed. And as I screamed, I pulled. I tried to find a wisp of Ethan. I wanted to inhale him and keep at least that part of him inside me forever. But there was nothing. He was gone.

Fury took me.

I yelled my anguish and pulled.

My nose started to bleed harder. Still, I pulled more.

I stood as those around me started to stumble.

"Run!" someone yelled.

Distantly, I was aware of Carlos moving away from me. He left me surrounded by an enemy that had lost its crazed determination. I reveled in the fear and pulled harder. The brutes fell to their knees.

I saw Carlos pick up Gabby and Bethi. He tossed one over each shoulder and ran with them. Their men staggered behind them, struggling to follow. Grey had Charlene in his arms and naked Winifred had Michelle. They all fought to move away from me.

One of the beasts before me weakly swiped at my legs. I looked down at him.

"He was mine." My voice broke on the last word.

I clenched my fists at my sides and pulled hard, harder than ever before.

I would kill them all for taking from me the only thing I'd ever wanted in life. My friend. The only one to stand by me. I screamed Ethan's name and pulled again.

Vaguely, I felt my skin split and blood trickle down my arms, but didn't stop. The anguish of Ethan's death consumed me and the lingering feel of the wolf's hand inside my stomach blinded me to the world around me.

Something hit the back of my head. It wasn't a blow; it was an annoying slap.

I spun out with a kick and almost caught Carlos in the head. He blocked just in time. I flew through moves. My blood sprayed him. Faster and faster, I tried to kill the man before me. Pain filled me, inside and out.

"He was mine," I yelled at Carlos. "I was supposed to keep him alive."

I hit harder and kept pulling. But there was nothing to pull. Angry, I kept attacking Carlos. A few times something on the ground almost tripped me.

Then, suddenly, I was empty. I fell to my knees. The pain of all my cuts and bruises were nothing compared to the hollow ache that existed inside of me. I was nothing without Ethan. I turned and saw him lying where I'd left him. I crawled to him and laid my head on his chest.

"Since I first saw you in the play yard, you were my friend. I loved you too much...but not enough. I should have let you go."

I let the pain take me away.

EVERYTHING HURT. Especially the drag of a wet cloth over my arms.

"Ow," I said without opening my eyes. The word was thick and slurred. "I think Brick hit me too hard."

"Not Brick."

The voice wasn't familiar at first. Then, everything came crashing back. I moaned and pulled my arm from Carlos' grasp. A sob escaped me.

"Ethan...oh, God, why?"

An anguished cry filled the room, and I realized it was me. Ethan. Ethan was gone. I started to fall apart all over again. A hand settled on my head.

"I'm sorry, Isabelle."

Wrapping my arms around myself, I curled into a ball.

"Go."

"I can't."

He gently pried one arm away from my middle and started washing it again. It didn't seem to hurt anymore. But, the pain from the hole in my chest consumed me.

While I cried, Carlos cleaned every gash, scrape, and tear. Then, he left me to my tears.

THE NEXT TIME I WOKE, my head pounded. Before I could start crying again, the bed moved.

"Here."

I kept my eyes closed, uncaring what Carlos might be offering me. I didn't want anything except to be left alone.

"You should drink something."

He smoothed a hand over my hair. It almost comforted me. But I wouldn't let it. I didn't deserve comfort. Ethan was dead.

The ache in my chest grew.

"You should go away," I said.

The door closed, and I cried until I couldn't anymore. I laid there in numb silence, not thinking of anything; the past was too painful and my future nonexistent. Eventually, I slept.

LOUD VOICES WOKE ME.

"We need to talk to her."

"No." I recognized Bethi's voice. "You go in there now, pushing like you want to, you'll either destroy her, or she'll destroy you."

"We can't stay here." Impatience and frustration laced Winifred's words.

"And you can't push her to leave."

Leave? And go where? New tears wet my cheeks.

"What are we supposed to do then?"

Bethi sighed.

"None of you understand. I'll talk to her."

The door opened, then softly closed again. A moment later, the bed dipped. I didn't want to talk, so I didn't open my eyes. It didn't matter. She didn't leave.

Sorrow flooded the air as Bethi lay down beside me. Her breath brushed my cheek, but she didn't say anything. Caving, I opened my eyes to look at her.

She was lying on her side, facing me. Her face was pale, and the dark smudges under her eyes competed with the red puffiness. Her exhaustion was a living thing. Yet, I knew the concern she radiated wasn't for herself, and it made my tears fall faster.

"Does anything hurt on the inside? Organ-wise?"

She was smart to clarify; everything hurt on the inside.

"No." My voice was raspy and faint. I didn't sound like me. I wasn't me.

"Good. I was worried about that."

I didn't ask why. I didn't want to know. I didn't care. Nothing mattered anymore.

She reached over and gently touched my tear-streaked face.

"They haven't suffered real loss yet. None of them understand." She gave me a sad smile, then rolled her eyes. "And now Luke's scolding me. They can hear what I'm saying."

She sighed and shook her head as she tucked both her hands under her cheek.

"He and I have been through a lot together in just a short time. I love him, and I know he loves me. But he still doesn't understand me, not like Ethan understood you. It takes a lifetime for that, a lifetime you and Ethan had already shared."

She searched my gaze, and I felt a surge of grief and fear from her before she pulled it back.

"I remember our past lives, Isabelle. Each tragic one of them. I've felt what you're feeling, a pain so deep it's hollowed me out and has left nothing good behind. A pain that steals your breath and eats at your mind." Tears gathered in her eyes. "I've felt it countless times, and I'm destined to feel it again when I remember your life. I will love Ethan as you love him, and I will die on the inside when he dies. I will never forget him. But please, please, don't make me suffer more than I need to when I relive your life."

The tears ran across her cheek to wet her hands and pillow.

She truly understood my hell, and I pitied her for what she would have to remember because of this life. I wrapped my arms around her, and she started crying in earnest.

"I think Ethan would hate what you're doing now, and it's killing me, too."

I held her while she cried, too damaged to take her sorrow from her.

"Why, Bethi? Why did they come after us?" But the real question drilling through my mind was why Ethan had to die.

"Urbat are power hungry. Blake knows that if he controls us, he might be able to influence the Judgement we make. He wants his people to rule."

Blake.

The hollowing pain shifted a little at her words, leaving room for me to feel something.

I'd seen his people, now, and knew what they were capable of. Under Blake's rule, how many more Ethans would die?

That empty space inside me expanded, and a hot ball of hate formed.

"No," I said. "Never."

"Then we need to stop Blake." Her earnest gaze held mine.

A shaky exhale escaped me. I didn't want to keep fighting. Look what my need to fight had caused. I'd lost my only friend. I should go home and tell Ethan's dad he'd lost his son. As soon as I had that thought, I realized the man probably wouldn't care; and his indifference would cause me to do something I'd regret. More tears slid down my cheeks. Ethan and I...we'd really only had each other.

And now Ethan was gone. If I wanted to keep Ethan's death from being pointless, if I wanted to avenge him, I needed to stop Blake.

The hate inside me grew.

I would kill Blake, just as he'd killed Ethan.

AFTER BETHI LEFT, the others gave me solitude. Though she hadn't directly touched on the subject of the group's need to keep moving, our conversation must have appeased them in some way. That or they'd realized the truth in her words; if they pushed me, I'd push back.

With a broken sigh, I closed my eyes and slept some more.

When I woke with tears already wetting my cheeks, it was light outside. How much time had passed? A day? Two? How long had Ethan been gone, taken from me? I hurt inside, but more than that,

I hated. I hated deeply. And it was all mine. In fact, I didn't feel a single emotion around me.

Someone knocked on the door, startling me enough that the tears stopped. I knew who it was. Carlos.

"Come in." I didn't sit up. I didn't look at the door. I didn't want to see him. He'd pulled me back from the edge, and I wasn't yet sure if I was thankful or angry about it.

"Today's the funeral," he said softly. "We should leave in twenty."

His words made my heart stop. I nodded but curled tighter under the covers as the door closed again.

Bury Ethan? I hadn't thought beyond losing him once I'd woken up again. Now, I could see him one last time. It wasn't how I wanted to see him, but it was all I would get.

With effort, I pulled myself from bed and padded to the bathroom. I'd gotten up several times before but always in the dark with the lights off. On this trip, I finally caught sight of myself in the mirror and stared in shock. I looked scary as hell.

Bruises, interspersed with hairline abrasions, colored my face. Capillaries had burst, giving my skin a mottled, red hue. My eyes were freakishly bloodshot. I leaned closer to the mirror and realized they weren't just bloodshot; capillaries had burst there, too.

The marks on my side hurt and were covered with gauze. But there were many more bloody lines crisscrossing my skin that weren't bandaged. Most of those fissures had already scabbed.

As if seeing the damage made it more real, I started to ache all over. Only then did I realize the pain I'd felt inside had blocked the reality of the damage to my outside.

I stared at myself, seeing what happened when I pulled too much. It wasn't good. Bethi's question about hurting on the inside took on new meaning. I'd been so close. Ethan would have been pissed if he'd seen me. Bethi was so right. How close had I been to joining Ethan? Fresh tears started as part of me wished I had joined him.

Reaching into the shower, I turned on the water for the first time in days. I didn't wait for it to warm but stepped into the cold stream and shivered. As the water cascaded over me, I carefully washed, trying to keep the bandaged parts dry. The water warmed as I rinsed, but it didn't penetrate the cold in my soul. I turned off the shower and stepped out.

The motions were right—I dressed and combed my hair—but the life behind them was wrong. Tainted. The hate I carried inside was so alien. Sure, I'd thought I'd despised people before. But the new hate that dwelled within me...I wanted to burn the entire planet.

It wasn't just the hate, though. The consuming guilt that was trying to drown me weighted each movement. Still, I forced myself to keep going.

It felt odd walking out of the bedroom. I wandered down a hall and found Carlos waiting by the door. I didn't look up at him. I couldn't. I stared at his shoes.

"Ready?" he said, moving to open the door.

Was I ready to face Ethan?

"No," I said, my voice barely a whisper. Guilt ate at me. How was it that I couldn't save him?

Carlos stopped and turned back to me.

"I just left him. How could I do that? How long did he lay there, alone?"

"He wasn't alone. You stayed with him. I didn't move you until..."

I liked that he seemed to know I didn't want to hear more. Swallowing hard, I thought about how I'd pulled after Ethan had fallen.

"How many did I hurt, Carlos?"

"All of them."

"How bad?"

"Dead."

I took a slow, deep breath and exhaled. That meant there were fifty less of Blake's men. It also meant that I'd killed the man who'd taken Ethan from me. A little of the hate stopped boiling.

"Good."

But I knew the fight wasn't done yet. I still needed the man who'd sent the Urbat. Blake. I wrapped my arms around myself.

"Are there more of them coming?"

"No. Since the attack, they've stayed clear. Gabby says they seem to know where we are but aren't making any moves toward us. The way north is open for us when we're ready."

The group's willingness to leave me alone for a few days made more sense now. It would give me some time to heal. Luke, too, I thought, recalling his injuries. I couldn't remember any of them fighting after Ethan fell, though.

"Was anyone else hurt?"

Carlos was quiet for so long, I finally gave in and looked up. Faded bruises and scars from healed claw marks riddled his face.

"No one else," he said softly.

I looked away. Shame filled me. I'd done that to him. I couldn't remember most of the fight. Just the rage.

"I'm sorry," I said softly.

"Would he let you apologize?"

I knew he meant Ethan.

"No. He wouldn't."

"Then, I won't either. I'm here when you need me. However you need me."

I nodded, and Carlos opened the door. Outside, the rest of the group waited by the cars. Their pity swamped me. I took it away, just so I wouldn't have to feel it anymore.

"Isabelle, don't," Bethi said. "You need to keep it under control. You can't handle another break like that again. Trust me."

I didn't look at her. Instead, I turned to Carlos. "Which car?"

"We'll ride alone," he said and motioned me to the last car.

I went to it, got into the passenger seat, and waited while he shut my door and walked around the car.

Today, I would bury Ethan, our past, and our future. The thought robbed me of breath, and my eyes began to water.

The door opened, distracting me, and Carlos slid in behind the wheel. While he went through his pre driving checklist, the first two vehicles pulled out of the driveway. We followed at a distance. It was a quiet ride. My thoughts whirled around what-ifs and should-haves. Regret burned my stomach, and grief ate a hole through my chest. It hurt to breathe.

The ride didn't take long. We pulled into the empty parking lot of a funeral home. As soon as I stepped from the car, I felt disconnected from reality. The wind brushed my hair aside as I walked toward the building, but I couldn't feel the temperature of it.

Carlos held the door for me. The smell of potpourri greeted me as I stepped inside.

I kept walking down the hall then turned into the open parlor on the right. A coffin waited at the front of the large room. There were only a few chairs before it, the sum of Ethan's life. Like a sleepwalker, I moved forward.

He lay as if sleeping, his serene face powdered with life-like color. I stepped up onto the platform with him and laid my hand over his stomach. How could someone do this to him? Silence him? Ethan brought laughter. Ethan was life.

I was angry, hurt, confused, and alone. I needed someone to talk to, someone to help me through the chaotic thoughts in my head. But whenever I'd had a problem, I'd always talked it out with Ethan. And Ethan wasn't there anymore.

"How do I live with this much anger?" I said softly.

"You learn to lock it away," Carlos said beside me.

I hadn't even realized he'd stayed with me.

"It doesn't ever leave, but the wall you build around it grows thicker with time, making it harder for you to reach the anger."

"Why would I want to reach it?"

"Because it helps you remember."

I turned to study Carlos. His steady brown gaze held me. He knew the pain that currently devoured me from the inside. How could I have ever teased that he was a robot? No one who felt this much ever could be.

"Will I ever feel happy again?"

"I hope so."

I looked away and stared at Ethan. Who was Isabelle without Ethan? I had no idea. I'd barely known myself when I'd still had Ethan. A bleak, questionable future lay before me, and I didn't want to face it without him.

I didn't stay long. I just needed to say goodbye and try to memorize his face one last time. Then, I turned away.

They all faced me, a loose group of people I'd met only days ago.

"They will do a short service in an hour," Charlene said.

I didn't want to stay for that. Ethan wouldn't want me to, either.

"Did you arrange all of this?" I asked.

She nodded.

"Thank you. Where will he be buried?"

"The local cemetery."

"A headstone?" When this was over, I wanted to be able to find him again.

"Of course."

I nodded, then walked to the exit.

CHAPTER TEN

WE PULLED INTO THE DRIVEWAY. WHILE THE REST GOT OUT OF THEIR cars and went toward the house, I got out and started walking toward the fields. A void silently followed me.

I walked until I reached the center of the area then stopped.

All I wanted to do was cry. I was the lonely kid back on the playground. I needed to do what Carlos said, and I tried to lock away what I felt. However, indifference was like trying to wear a toddler's coat. It didn't fit me, and I doubted it ever would. Yet, I continued to try to push away thoughts of Ethan. Then, I realized I had very little else to think about. I had no job, no friend, and a family barely coherent enough to remember my name.

How did a person pick up the pieces of who they were after being so thoroughly shattered? I decided they didn't. They sweep the old pieces of who they were away, and they rebuild themselves into who they need to be.

Those creatures killed the nice girl in me when they killed Ethan. These people, Bethi, Charlene, Michelle, Gabby, they needed me to be their fighter because, with the exception of Bethi, they couldn't fight for themselves. They would end up just like Ethan.

After several moments, Carlos came to stand beside me.

"Do you need to spar?" he asked softly.

"No."

Whether I needed to or not didn't matter. I couldn't spar. Carlos still wore the bruises from facing me. What if more of those other werewolves came right now? Had I damaged Carlos like I had Ethan? I pushed the scary thoughts away and looked out over the field.

"Just avoiding the pity party in the house."

It was something I would have said before I'd lost everything. But now, the words felt wrong. No, I felt wrong.

Carlos seemed to notice, too, because he moved closer.

"Tell me what you need," he said.

I closed my eyes against the pain. What I needed was Ethan, but that wasn't going to happen. I needed to face reality. But telling Carlos about either of those needs wouldn't help them come true.

"I'm tired." I wasn't. I just wanted to go back to the house and shut myself into my room again.

"We can go back. The rest will leave."

"Where are they staying?" I asked to try to be polite. I didn't really care.

"A neighbor's place not far from here. Grey has been sleeping in the car."

When I started walking, Carlos fell into step beside me. Ahead, the house seemed a welcome sanctuary. I wondered how much time Bethi had won me.

"How long are we staying here?"

"As long as you need."

Forever. But they wouldn't allow that. Pain and guilt came back with crushing force.

"I want to go back to bed."

"Isabelle—"

"Don't." I wasn't sure what he'd been about to say, but I knew from his tone I wouldn't have liked it.

He studied me while we walked. Before we were halfway to the house, all but one vehicle pulled from the driveway.

"Why doesn't he just go with them?" I asked as I watched Grey get into the back of the car. I wanted to be isolated again.

"He's here just in case."

In case of another attack. The heaviness in my chest wanted to consume me, and I focused on placing one foot before the other until everything else faded away. At last, I reached the door to the house. Mindlessly, I found the room I'd used and shut myself in.

Everything remained quiet and emotionless as I lay on the bed. In time, I closed my eyes and dreamt of Ethan.

A hand on my arm woke me. I opened my eyes and looked at Carlos. He held a plate of food.

"I'm not hungry."

He glanced at the plate.

"If you're not hungry for this, I can take you—"

"No. I don't want to go anywhere. I just want to be alone."

"You need to eat."

"Go away." I rolled away from him.

Several moments of silence had me thinking he'd listened.

"I can't," he said softly.

He lightly touched my hair then moved away from the bed. After a moment, the door closed again. I went back to sleep.

At some point during the night, a noise woke me. I immediately breathed in, testing the emotions around me. Nothing. I lifted my head and spotted Carlos' outline in the shadowed room. He sat in a chair near the bed.

"What are you doing?" I sounded angry and ready to fight, and it surprised me.

"Listening."

"To what?" It came out less harsh this time.

"To you crying in your sleep. For him. I can't take your pain away. I can't make this better. But I can share it."

I laid my head back down and stared at his outline, not knowing what to think or how to feel about what he'd said. It took a while to fall back to sleep.

When I woke, it was light out. My head hurt from sleeping too much. With a groan, I shuffled to the bathroom. My eyes looked a little better. Less red, more yellow. I turned on the shower, and this time, I let it warm. While I waited, I slowly peeled away the bandages from my side and the few that were on my thighs and arms. The claw marks on my side were no worse than the rest. Long, yet shallow and scabbed over. Physically, my wounds would heal. Eventually. Unlike the rest of me.

I tossed the bandages in the garbage and stepped into the shower. The hot spray felt good on the numerous bruises. Standing there, feeling any form of relief from my physical pain added to my guilt. The same thoughts kept repeating themselves. Had I not sparred so intensely with Ethan, his shoulder wouldn't have been bruised. Without the injury, maybe he would have been fast enough to avoid dying.

The water washed away my tears as I scrubbed and rinsed. It didn't ease the pain I carried inside. I was fairly certain I'd died with Ethan and my body just didn't know it yet.

Once I dressed, I left my room; the bed no longer looked like the haven it had been.

Carlos was near the stove in the kitchen. When I entered, he turned off the burner. I moved to the table and stood just behind one of the chairs. I didn't know what to do. I was so lost.

"Sit."

"No, thanks."

He glanced at me. His face looked better today. Barely bruised at all.

"Bethi's coming. She knows you're not eating."

I felt her before I saw her. Anxiety clouded my senses, and I automatically blocked myself as best I could. She stepped through the door and studied me.

"Good morning," she said.

"Morning."

"Carlos says you're not eating."

"Carlos has a big mouth." I said it without rancor as I sat.

He turned away from us and made two plates, which he set before us. Then, he started to clean up the kitchen. Bethi dug right in. I slowly did the same, not really tasting what I ate.

"Why are you here?" I asked as soon as she'd eaten everything. I pushed my plate aside and Carlos gave me a look before he took it away to wash it.

"We need to leave today. Two Urbat came last night. Grey took care of them. But we think it was just a test to see if you were still out of action. More are gathering to the east."

Images flashed in my mind. Shapes pouring over a dark horizon. Teeth and blood. Ethan on the ground.

If they came again, it would end the same way, with one or more of us dead. I glanced at Bethi, and my imagination painted her eyes with Ethan's vacant stare. What little I'd eaten twisted in my stomach.

"I agree. We can't face them like that a second time."

We'd been unorganized and ripe for the death they'd handed us. I pushed my chair away from the table and stood, knowing what needed to happen. Yes, we needed to leave. But more than that, we needed to organize ourselves. To fight, we needed to be fighters.

Before I could move to the bedroom to get my things, Carlos spoke up.

"I'll clean up everything in here. Go outside and get some fresh air."

Bethi and I walked out the door. Grey stood by the car, casually leaning against it.

"The rest of the group will be here in a few minutes," Bethi said.

"Good. We need to talk about what happened."

She gave me a surprised look.

"Really?"

I didn't answer. Instead, I watched the road for the caravan of vehicles. As Bethi had said, it only took a few minutes. By the time they were pulling in, Carlos was walking out the door with our bags.

I didn't miss how Winifred and Charlene glanced my way as soon as I stepped away from the car. They were worried about me. Why though? They barely knew me. I hated the pity I felt.

"We can run some more, but it won't stop the bad guys from trying again," I said. "Not if what Bethi says is true. They need us. But we can't fight like that again." I looked at Charlene, Michelle, and Gabby. "You three need to be more than helpless."

Clay and Emmitt growled at me.

"Shut it," I snapped. "You want them to die?"

I refocused on the three women.

"What do you have in mind?" Charlene asked.

"When we were fighting, we couldn't see overall movement." I walked up to the three of them. "Stand back to back." Michelle glanced at Charlene but all three moved to do as I asked.

"Back to back, you can have a 360 range of vision if you work together. Gabby has the ability to see long range, but when we're fighting, it's the short range that will keep us alive. The three of you have to be our center and our eyes. You watch and shout out what you see."

"Like what?" Charlene asked. "There was so much motion, nothing made sense."

"We'll work on that," I said.

I glanced at Winifred.

"And we can't have two layers of protection. Not against the numbers we faced. The rest of us need to form a single ring around them."

No one looked convinced.

"Trust me. Fan out around them. Grey, Jim, Carlos, Thomas, Winifred, Clay, Sam, and Emmitt."

Everyone moved around the women so that I stood between Jim and Carlos. I turned to face outward. The rest did the same.

"This is how we'll practice," I said. "This is how we'll learn to fight together. And this is how we'll keep anyone else from dying." I swallowed hard. "Gabby, your job is to find us two quiet places each day where we can stop for thirty minutes to practice."

I stepped away from the circle.

"Let's go."

NUMBLY, I stared at the passing landscape.

"Are we there yet?" Ethan's words echoed in my mind, as did Winifred's response. My stomach churned sickeningly.

The car started to slow, and I lifted my head from the seat.

"Why are we slowing?"

"Gabby found the first quiet place."

So soon? Trying to pull myself out of the dazed state I was in, I looked at the clock and saw we'd actually been on the road for two hours. It hadn't felt that long.

I unfolded my legs and opened the door as soon as Carlos parked on the shoulder. Gabby's quiet place was on another rural road with long stretches of fields and trees. I waited impatiently as the rest of the group climbed from their vehicles.

"In the same position," I said as I walked a few yards into the field.

Everyone remembered their spots and faced outward.

"Grey and Sam, you'll attack us. Your goal is to try to pull any of us from the circle."

Grey and Sam stepped out and moved around us. Bethi squatted down into her ready stance but didn't pull her knife out.

"Call out where they are, girls," I said when Grey moved out of my line of sight.

"Grey and Sam are both by Emmitt," Michelle said a moment before snarls broke out.

I spun around to see both Emmitt and Jim had broken the circle in their effort to fight off Grey, leaving an opening for Sam, who was batting Clay aside to grab for Gabby.

"Stop," I called. Everyone immediately stopped.

"Two opponents," I said, looking at the three in the middle. "That's all it took to get to you. You need to call out what's happening." I pointed to Emmitt and Jim. "Michelle, they were in your direct line of sight. This is what you should have said, 'Two coming at Emmitt.' Then, when Grey drew Emmitt out, you should have yelled that the circle had been broken. We should have then tightened up and closed the gap. Together. Jim, rushing to help your brother will get us all killed. If he's dumb enough to break the circle, don't be dumb enough to follow."

Anger swamped me. I turned on Emmitt.

"I hope that's self-directed. Don't break the circle. Ever. I don't want to watch anyone else fall."

A hand settled onto my shoulder, and I shrugged it off.

"This isn't a game, so I won't be nice. You want to live? We need to work together. Now, back in place and do it again."

We practiced for another fifteen minutes. Sam and Grey always managed to break the circle, and I tended to piss off the defending men with my criticism. None of the women harbored any hint of anger toward me. They listened. However, Bethi radiated frustration. I wondered if it was because of the group's lack of skills or because Sam and Grey were mostly attacking the side away from her. I didn't care. I did care that with each attempt, the two always managed to get to one of us.

"Time's up," Gabby said.

"Good." Jim scratched his stomach. "I'm getting hungry."

I marched back to the car. Idiots. They weren't taking this seriously. If Blake's men found us again...I slammed the door shut and curled up in a ball on the front seat. Carlos didn't say anything when he got in and started the car. As soon as we were moving, I closed my eyes. I didn't sleep, though. I couldn't. Images of the fight and of Ethan's bloody stomach haunted me.

When we next stopped, it was for fast food and a bathroom break.

Without much of a choice, I went inside the diner with the rest. Before I could step away to use the restroom, Carlos caught my hand.

"What can I order for you?"

"I'm not hungry," I said, tugging my hand from his. Even when I turned my back on him, I could feel the weight of his disappointed gaze.

The bathroom didn't provide any escape from censure because Bethi was waiting for me.

"You have to eat."

"No kidding. Good thing you're here to tell me that."

I stepped into a stall and closed the door on her.

"I get that you're broken. I know broken."

"I'm peeing. Stop talking. It's weird."

She sighed then left me alone. I took my time to leave the bathroom. When I stepped out, only Carlos waited inside. He had a bag of food in one hand and a drink carrier in the other.

"Thirsty?" I said, eyeing the four drinks.

He shrugged and moved to the exit, standing in the doorway to hold the door open for me. It was a tight squeeze past him.

He beat me to the car and set the drinks on the roof to open the door for me, again. The guy had a thing for doors. Once I was inside, he passed me the drinks and the food. I glanced at the chocolate shake as he walked around to the driver's seat.

"I got it for you," he said as he slid behind the wheel.

"Thanks." I set the food on the floor and put the chocolate shake in my cup holder.

"Which one do you want first? Soda, water, or vanilla shake?"

"The shake." He started the car and pulled out to follow Winifred.

I put his drink in his cup holder then leaned over to put the drink carrier on the floor behind the driver's seat.

"Want your food?" I asked as I straightened.

"Not yet. Help yourself."

I hadn't been lying. I wasn't hungry. Even a few sips of the chocolate milkshake turned my stomach. Setting the cup aside, I curled up and watched out the window. My mind remained blank as the towns slipped by.

Hours later, Carlos once again pulled off to the side of the road. I opened my eyes, not remembering closing them. By my feet, the bag of food remained untouched.

Behind us, I heard a door slam and turned to see everyone exiting their vehicles. I knew we needed to practice, but I didn't want to do it. Still, I opened my door and joined them. I didn't need to tell them to form up or to give direction to Sam and Grey.

Like earlier in the day, they broke through each time, teaming up to find or make a weak link.

"Stop," I called after the third attempt. "If the ring collapses, Clay, Emmitt, and Thomas should fall back to protect the center three. Jim should pair with Grey, Winifred with Sam, and Carlos with me, and Bethi with Luke. Pair off and spend some time fighting back to back."

When everyone grouped into fours, attackers versus defenders, I rolled my shoulders and turned to go back to the car.

"Shouldn't we practice?" Carlos asked, following me.

"Not now. Not today. I'm tired of fighting."

He kept quiet as I shut myself into the car again.

I CURLED INTO THE SEAT, turning slightly to stare out the window.

The sun started to set and cast shadows over the landscape. My stomach dipped at the haunting familiarity, and my gaze searched the darkness for the nonexistent, approaching horde.

I shivered and turned away from the window. My gaze settled on Carlos' profile.

As usual, I felt nothing from him. How could he stand closing himself off like that? My emotions were all over the place. Sorrow. Anger. Regret. But most of all, loneliness.

"Can I lean against you?" I asked softly.

"Yes."

There'd been no hesitation in his answer. Would he have answered differently if he knew why I wanted to lean on him?

I shifted in my seat, inching closer to him. His wide shoulders took up more than his share of space, so it didn't take too much leaning to reach him. Warmth seeped through his shirtsleeve the moment my cheek rested on it.

Closing my eyes with a sigh, I pretended I leaned on Ethan. He was alive, and we were driving. His right shoulder wasn't hurt anymore.

The ache in my middle eased. Eventually, my breathing slowed, and I drifted to sleep.

THE SUDDEN STILLNESS and absence of noise tickled my awareness. A door opened, and Carlos left me leaning against the seat. A moment later, an arm wrapped around my back and another slid under my legs. I floated for a second before he cradled me against his chest.

Struggling against sleep, I opened my eyes and looked up at him. Light chased the shadows on his face. Stubble coated the curve of his jaw. I couldn't remember him ever having whiskers.

He glanced down at me, shadow covering his face, so I couldn't read his expression.

"Go back to sleep. I have you."

I sighed and closed my eyes again.

AS I ROLLED from my back to my side, something told me to burrow in deeper and let sleep pull me under once more. My eyes refused to be team players.

Dim light shone from behind drawn curtains, giving the space around me definition. A bed across from mine. A table with a lamp attached to the wall above it. I gazed at the unfamiliar sights as my groggy mind tried to place where I might be.

The car. Carlos carrying me.

I blinked at the bed across from me. As if sensing my regard, Carlos rolled from his back to his side so he faced me. He wasn't under the covers but on top of them, fully clothed. I could just see his face. His eyes were open.

I could feel the fear of a young child and the annoyance from another person further away but nothing nearby.

"Where'd Grey sleep?"

"With Jim, I think."

Carlos made no move to get out of bed, so I didn't either.

"How long have we been here?"

"Since two. About six hours."

"Anyone else awake?"

"No." He was quiet for a moment. "How do you feel?"

"Fine."

"I know you're not fine. It's been days since you sparred with anyone. You should—"

"No."

He inhaled deeply then exhaled slowly.

"All right. Are you hungry?"

I shrugged.

"Get dressed," he said, sitting up. "I'll be back in a few minutes." He stood and left the room.

With a sigh, I left my warm nest and shuffled into the bathroom. The light nearly blinded me. I ignored my scabbed face in the mirror and paused at the sight of my brush, toothbrush, and paste neatly laid out on the counter. The bottom of each item was precisely in line with the rest.

Carlos had serious OCD going on.

It took me less than two minutes to use the toilet and brush my teeth and hair. I didn't bother with clean clothes. What I'd slept in was good enough. I felt like crap on the inside and could care less how I looked on the outside.

In the main room, I found my runners at the end of the bed. I slipped on socks then laced up my shoes.

When I opened the hotel room door, Carlos waited in the hallway.

"Good morning, Isabelle," he said softly.

I'd thought we'd already covered that in the room.

"Good morning."

It seemed the correct response because he turned and started walking down the hall. I followed him, watching my feet. Carpet changed to tile, and I looked up. We were in a room just off the lobby. Actually, other than the change of flooring, it was essentially still the lobby. A counter ran along one wall. Three steamer trays, a clear display of muffins and mini-bagels, and a waffle maker summed up the hotel's complimentary breakfast.

Carlos went to the steamers and lifted the first lid. I peeked around him and saw eggs. They smelled good, and my stomach actually rumbled. I picked up a plate and held it out like a kid in a cafeteria. He scooped a helping onto it then lifted the next lid. Bacon. He put three pieces on my plate. He lifted the final lid. French toast. I shook my head.

"I'd rather have a waffle."

"I'll start it for you. Sit down and eat."

I did as he said. He brought me a cup of milk before he returned with a plate of his own and joined me.

Carlos watched me as I speared a clump of eggs and put it in my mouth.

The flavor took me off guard. It tasted good. My stomach rumbled until I finished the eggs. I set down my fork, using my fingers to bite into a piece of bacon. The saltiness was delicious. I chewed slowly, wondering why this food tasted so different. I wasn't starving. I'd been eating. A little.

I realized the food hadn't changed. I had. I was still angry, still devastated, but something was different.

A beep distracted me. I started chewing again and watched Carlos get up and go to the waffle maker. The thing he brought back was the size of my head. Probably the right portion size for werewolves.

Carlos set the plate before me then sat. I drowned the waffle in syrup and took a bite. It was good, just like the eggs had been. We ate in silence, and I tried not to think too much. When I did, my thoughts always found a way back to Ethan.

Just before I took my last bite, Clay, Gabby, Emmitt, Michelle, and Jim came in.

"I smell pancakes," Jim said. He looked at Carlos and me for confirmation.

"Waffles," I said when Carlos remained quiet.

"Just as good." Jim playfully pushed his brother out of the way to get to the waffle maker first.

I turned away from their playful antics and waited for Carlos to finish. When he stood, he took both our plates.

"We're supposed to meet in room 237 at ten," Emmitt said to Carlos when he noticed us getting ready to leave.

Carlos nodded and threw our plates in the garbage. I followed him from the room with no intention of going to another one of their little packed-room meetings. Just the thought of it made me twitchy. Hiding out in my room sounded like a better plan.

When Carlos turned down a side hall, I didn't question it; I'd been watching my feet on the way to the lobby. He turned again, and I absently followed until he stopped. I looked up, realizing I'd been watching my feet again, and saw where we were. An exercise room. The food in my stomach soured.

"No."

He was too quick, though. He moved around me to close the door and stand in front of it.

"Yes."

I narrowed my eyes at him and almost got mad. But I didn't. It was too much effort. Besides, my anger was reserved now. For Blake and his kind.

"I don't feel like it."

"Just five minutes."

"No."

He studied me for a moment then stepped away from the door. His gaze didn't waver as he advanced. There was something predatory in his moves that had me taking a step back.

"No," I said again.

He seemed not to hear as he slowly stalked me. He would step forward. I would step back. Until there wasn't anywhere else for me to go.

"I don't want to spar."

He didn't stop until we stood toe to toe. Then he tilted his head to the side.

"I know."

If he understood, why had he just broken my personal bubble? I stared at him, trying to guess what he meant to do. Did he really think he could make me fight?

After taking a moment to study my face, he slowly lifted his hands. My pulse leapt when they settled on my shoulders. His gaze didn't waver from mine as his thumbs moved on my skin. Just tiny circles. It wasn't aggressive, but it gave me an idea of what he was thinking. And that made me angry.

"Back off, Carlos."

"No."

His hands started to move, tracing down until his thumbs rested on my collarbones.

My arms were up between his, breaking the contact before he could move further.

"Got a problem?" he said calmly.

His words gave away his intention, but it didn't change my answer.

"Yeah. You."

"I'm not your problem, Isabelle."

His calm tone worked its way under my skin, and before I knew I'd fisted my hand, I jabbed him in the right shoulder. The image of Ethan's bruised shoulder flashed in my mind. My stomach pitched and tears threatened until Carlos spoke.

"You don't need to baby me, Isabelle."

Like I'd babied Ethan?

"Shut up and finish what you started."

I gave him twenty minutes instead of five.

He didn't comment when I finally stepped back. Nor did he say anything as he followed me down the hall. Ethan would have been making little comments, trying to tease me into a better mood. Guilt hit me with that thought.

I used my keycard to open the door to our room, then quickly grabbed my bag and shut myself in the bathroom. Staring at my reflection, I let the tears fall. I'd hit Carlos repeatedly in the right shoulder, just like I had Ethan. What was wrong with me? Why did I have to be that way?

Turning away from my reflection, I started the shower. I let the warm water wash away my tears. After a good cry, I felt a little better.

When I reemerged, my skin was pink from the long, hot shower; and a billow of steam followed me out despite my use of the bathroom fan. My clean leggings had been a bugger to tug on.

Carlos sat at the end of my bed. The TV was off. He wasn't reading anything, just sitting there. Apparently waiting for me. My stomach gave a little jump. It hadn't done that in days.

"Sorry. Was I hogging the bathroom?" I said as I pulled the towel from my head.

"No."

His gaze traced over my face and wet, tangled hair, then drifted down to my tank top and further still to my legs. Once he reached my toes, he let his gaze travel the same path back up.

"Get a good look?"

"For now."

My gut clenched. He stood and moved close. A thread of panic wormed its way into my heart.

"Two thirty seven. Don't be late," he said, then turned and walked out the door.

I stayed where I was for a moment. So many thoughts wanted to surface, but I wasn't ready for any of them. I needed to keep things simple. Simple tasks, simple thoughts. I went to the bathroom and picked up my hairbrush. On autopilot, I ran it through the wet strands.

Before the clock showed five to the hour, I was out the door. Though I didn't want to go, I wasn't ready for the implied "or else" of Carlos' words if I didn't show up.

The room wasn't hard to find; it was at the other end of our hallway and had the door propped open. The heat coming from the room explained why. Too many bodies in too small of a space. Someone had even opened the room's window. It didn't help much. My cheeks flushed as soon as I stepped in.

Carlos leaned against the wall near the door. He turned and studied me for a moment.

Bethi stood from her place on the bed and walked toward me. When she reached me, she grabbed my hand and tugged me into the hall.

"How are you doing?" she said quietly.

"Fine." It was such an automatic answer. Why did I bother saying it? She studied me for a minute, and I could see she knew it was a lie.

"You're still bouncing between numb and angry. Numb might seem like it's better, but it's not. Not for you. You need to be angry, Isabelle. Very angry."

"Why?" I wanted to slap myself for asking.

"Because they aren't done yet."

Her vivid blue eyes seemed violet in the light of the hall as she earnestly watched for my reaction to her words. I noticed the dark circles under her eyes and the redness.

"You can sleep by me tonight if you want." I didn't know where these words kept coming from.

She smiled at me. It started small and grew into something that made me want to grin back.

"Not sure how Luke would feel about room sharing. Can you picture Luke spooning with Carlos?"

"Bethi!"

Luke's voice made my lips twitch.

"Luke's smaller than Carlos. He knows he'd be the spooned, not the spooner," I said.

"If you don't go out there, I will," I heard Luke say.

A second later, Carlos emerged from the room.

"Hey, Carlos," Bethi said with good cheer.

"Hello, Bethi. I think Luke would like you to join us again."

"I'm sure he would. So, can we share a room tonight?"

"Yes."

Poor Luke. I realized my lips were curving into a smile. What was wrong with me? Nothing. It was Bethi. She was over the top. I found it hard not to like her. She reminded me of Ethan. That thought sent a spear of sorrow through my chest.

"Let's get inside and get this over with before my skin starts to crawl," I said, brushing past both of them to step into the room once more.

Bethi was only a step or two behind me.

"All right. We all know what needs to happen. We need to outline a plan and execute it," Bethi said, moving to sit beside Luke, who looked slightly annoyed.

"Hold up," I said. "Can you recap for me?" My brain was fried, and I had no idea what needed to happen.

"Sure. We need to stop Blake from coming after us or, at least, make it really hard for him. When I started having the dreams of our past lives, I ran. I was terrified the Urbat would find me. They had destroyed me in so many ways in so many lives, I was sure there was nowhere safe from them.

"Then, I realized something. In this life, they couldn't just come for me directly. They had to be careful. Why? Because humans outnumber them. For all the strength the Urbat and werewolves have, it is nothing compared to the collective strength of humanity. We need to use the Urbat's fear of exposure to our advantage.

"By exposing the two races publicly, the Urbat won't be able to move as freely."

"Correct. They will be hunted," Winifred said, "and so will we."

Bethi turned to face Winifred. "What other option do we have?"

"I'm not refuting your plan, only stating the truth. Our lives will be in greater danger afterward."

The room fell silent.

I thought they'd already discussed that part and made peace with it.

"You guys have remained hidden for how long? Why do you think public awareness will make it more difficult to hide?" I asked. "You look human. You blend."

"The plan is that Winifred will be exposing herself on TV. Her face will be all over the place. So will anyone who goes with her," Bethi said.

"No," Charlene said. "We all go. I don't want to split the group for this. I think that would be bad. I can make people forget the rest of our faces. Just not Winifred's once it's broadcast."

"I'll be fine," Winifred said. "I'm more worried about the rest of our people."

"They should be fine as long as they keep blending in," Bethi said. "The point of this meeting is to decide which station and then how to get on the air because I doubt anyone will take us seriously if we just walk up and tell them the truth. Plus, we need to figure out our route. According to Gabby, the way north is perfectly clear."

"They've pulled back but are still following us at a distance," Gabby said. "Occasionally, one will get close, almost as if verifying our location, and then retreat. All netting movement has stopped. There's a wall of Urbat to the west two states long. The same to the east. It's as if we're in an almost empty alley."

"Almost?"

"There are still clusters of them. It took me a bit to figure it out, but I'm pretty sure they're guarding the airports, train stations, and bus stations between here and New York."

That didn't sound good. Why New York? Because they already knew we were headed that way or because they wanted us to head that way?

"We need to decide this," Bethi said again. "What station?"

Charlene picked up the remote. "We don't watch TV often. I wouldn't even be able to tell you what our local stations are back home."

She started to surf through channels, pausing at anything that looked like a talk show or morning news.

"Any suggestions on how we can get someone to talk to us once we pick a station?" Bethi asked, looking at everyone.

"When I called the local news station, they agreed to send out a reporter after I said I had money and wanted to donate it," Michelle said.

"That could work," Bethi said, looking excited.

"No," Charlene said. "I've got something better." Conflicting waves of fear and excitement rolled off her.

I followed her gaze and stared at the TV. A woman was speaking. I looked at the newsreel at the bottom of the screen. Penny Alton was reporting a short, feel good piece about a man who'd saved a kid from a train.

"We're pushing someone in front of a train?" I asked.

"I vote Emmitt," Jim said quickly.

"Cut it out," Charlene said, giving Jim a censuring look. "I know her. Penny. She wasn't Alton back then, though. But I recognize her. And I think, no matter what I have to say, she'll talk to me."

Thomas wrapped his arms around Charlene.

The surprised understanding on Bethi's face as she stared at the reporter had me curious.

"Why?" I asked.

"She knows what I can do. And she hates me for it," Charlene said, her fear winning over the excitement.

"Is it smart to use her, then?" Winifred asked.

"Yes. Because she will do anything to try to expose me to as many people as she can."

"Good," Bethi said. "We have the where and the how. I don't think we should call her, though, until we reach the city. No sense in giving anyone an advantage."

"I agree," Charlene said. She looked so pale.

Winifred clapped her hands together, commanding attention and breaking the mood.

"Let's pack up and start moving, then. We have a long way to go. Michelle, perhaps your lawyer can help us find somewhere more secure to stay while we're in New York. Gabby, even though they seem to be hanging back, I want to steer clear of the Urbat."

Gabby nodded.

I didn't envy her job. Navigator. Did the girl ever sleep?

CHAPTER ELEVEN

MOST OF THE MORNING DRIVE I SPENT LOST IN MEMORY. IT DIDN'T hurt to remember my life with Ethan. What ate at me was the realization we wouldn't be creating new memories.

When the caravan stopped for lunch at a restaurant just outside of yet another town, I was ready for a break from my thoughts.

Inside the place, seeing the long table and watching everyone crowd around it, brought a pang. It didn't last long. Jim sauntered over and gave me a grin. Sitting in Ethan's spot, Jim picked up the menu and began making enthusiastic noises as he read. Then, he nudged me as if unaware he'd had my attention the whole time.

"They have a one pound burger." He tilted his menu to point at the option, then started to read. "This one pound behemoth is grilled to your preference, topped with a slab of deep-fried cheddar, three jumbo onion rings, and enough bacon to grease your arteries."

He closed the menu. "I'm getting two."

"Jim," Charlene said. "Just one."

He nodded then leaned toward me. "Order the same. I'll help you finish it."

He looked at me so earnestly that I nodded.

"Want a beer, too?" he asked hopefully.

"I don't drink."

"Yeah, I've heard that before," he said with a grin.

The waitress came around and started taking orders. All the men were asking for the Behemoths.

When she looked at Jim, he put his arm around my shoulders.

"We'll have two of the Behemoths, medium, and two beers."

The waitress made a note on her pad then looked at Carlos. He reached over and knocked Jim's arm from me before ordering.

"A Behemoth. Medium, please," he said as Jim laughed.

Amusement drifted from most of the group. But not from Grey, who sat across from us. A thread of worry tickled my awareness. I glanced at him and the thread disappeared, even though he wasn't looking at me to notice my attention.

The rest of the group finished ordering. Within a few minutes, the waitress started to bring out the drinks. When she set mine in front of me, I asked if she could bring me water, too.

As soon as she left, I pushed the beer toward Jim.

"Can't," he said. "I'm driving."

"I don't drink," I said again.

"Maybe you should."

"You're not a good influence."

He winked and nudged the beer back my way. I shook my head.

"If I drink, my guard slips. People get hurt when my guard slips."

Jim leaned back in his chair.

"You've never let loose?"

His aghast tone definitely felt staged.

"Once. I put the bar to sleep."

"I'll drink yours," Bethi said, reaching across the table. She'd just sat down again with the drink in hand when Luke snagged the bottle and drained it.

"Not today," he said, setting the empty bottle next to her plate.

"Killjoy."

Jim sighed and absently scratched his chest.

"We should have ordered appetizers."

At the far end of the table, Charlene and Winifred started discussing hotel options for the night. They pulled Gabby and Michelle into the conversation. Bethi and Luke were having a stare down. No doubt over the beer.

That left our end of the table pretty quiet.

"Have you ever been to New York?" Grey asked when I met his gaze.

"No. This is the furthest I've ever traveled from home."

"Are there any sights you want to see?" Carlos asked.

"I doubt there will be time for that. Sounds like it will be a lot more hotel fun."

My response seemed to kill the conversation attempt. It was fine with me. I stared at my placemat and remembered playing tic-tac-toe with Ethan. My chest started to hurt. I embraced it; I never wanted to forget.

By the time the burgers arrived twenty minutes later, I wasn't very hungry. I nibbled on some fries and managed a few bites of my burger. Before Jim could snag the Behemoth from my plate, Carlos took it and set it on his. Jim grumbled, and took the remaining fries.

When the waitress came back around asking about refills, Carlos asked for a to-go box. I glanced at him.

"You'll be hungry later," he said.

We left the restaurant and only managed to drive a few miles when the vehicles ahead of us pulled into a tavern. We were the only cars in the gravel parking lot.

Carlos frowned but pulled in behind the rest.

"What's going on?" I asked.

"Jim. He needs the bathroom."

Sure enough, the driver's side door opened, and Jim jogged toward the building. I watched him disappear inside, then turned to keep staring out the window.

After a few minutes, Carlos growled and turned off the car.

I glanced at him. He didn't look at me. His tight hold on the steering wheel conveyed something. But what?

"Are you impatient, annoyed, angry?"

"All of the above."

"Why?"

"Jim's been in there for five minutes. Grey said he's not answering the Elders."

"So?"

"We don't have time for his fooling around."

"You sound like you know Jim."

"I grew up with him."

"Why doesn't someone go in to check on him?"

"Because that's most likely what he wants."

I shook my head and opened the door.

"Isabelle, wait."

I ignored Carlos and started toward the building. When I was almost to the entrance, I heard Carlos open his door to follow. I pushed my way into the tavern and spotted Jim at the bar. He had a row of shots lined up. When he saw me, he spread his arms wide.

"Time to let loose. There's no one in here."

Except the bartender, but I didn't point that out. I reached Jim and glanced at the shots.

"Carlos is annoyed with you." No doubt, Luke would be too. There were twenty little cups waiting. I doubted Luke would keep Bethi from them all.

"Really? That's new."

I couldn't tell if Jim was being sarcastic or not.

"The rest are going to be annoyed with you, too."

"Not if you stick up for me."

"And why would I do that?" I asked, looking up at him.

"Because deep down, you want to let go for a little while." He grabbed a shot and held it out to me.

His sudden seriousness brought back the ache in my chest. He was right. I desperately wanted to let go of the pain and loneliness. I took the shot and tossed it back just as the door opened.

"Jim," Winifred said. "Outside, now."

The liquid burned a pleasant path to my stomach. I set the glass aside, arched a brow at Jim, and turned around.

"Before you take him outside and beat him like he probably deserves—"

"Not helping," he mumbled.

"I was wondering if we could take a break. From our lives. Just for an hour. Before it all gets crazy again."

Winifred's gaze had shifted from Jim to me as I spoke. Her expression softened, and a wisp of pity drifted to me. She was still plenty angry, though.

I shrugged and gave my best innocent face.

"Nothing will be the same once...well, things will change even more than they already have."

More of her anger faded. She sighed and eyed Jim.

"You are not always right."

"I understand," he said, sounding contrite.

"I'll tell everyone we're staying." She walked back out.

"Quick. Drink two before Carlos gets in here and rains on the festivities."

Accepting the two shots, I lifted one to my mouth as the door opened again.

"We don't have time for this," Bethi said, stomping in. I turned without drinking and held the extra shot up to her.

"Can you beat Luke this time?"

183

Gabby and Clay were just coming through the door. I couldn't see anyone behind them.

Bethi squealed and raced forward. She snatched the shot from my hand and slammed it back.

"Like drinking much?" I said.

"Nah, I like annoying Luke." She grinned at me and stole the other shot from my hand.

"Bethi."

Luke's word of warning made her eyes pop. She quickly tried to drink, but his hand closed over her mouth. The shot spilled all over. Luke shook his hand and gave me a dirty look.

"She's seventeen."

I glanced at Bethi.

"Wow, your dad looks really young."

She snorted behind his hand then bit him. I knew it was a bite because of his grunt and the immediate removal of his hand.

"We need music," she said. She took my hand, and we went over to the digital jukebox on the wall. "Gabby! Michelle! Come help," she called.

Our tastes in music led to an eclectic selection of pop, rock, and ballad. When I wandered to the bar, Carlos stood near the shots. Jim was talking to Thomas and Emmitt. Charlene and Winifred were sipping glasses of wine. The quiet conversation and relaxed atmosphere felt nice. It wasn't the usual bar vibe of lust, mistrust, and disgust.

I reached around Carlos, grabbed a shot, and held it out to him.

"Want one?"

"No. If I drink, my guard slips. People get hurt when my guard slips."

I eyed him. Was he mocking me? Scolding me? He met my gaze steadily, giving no hint why he'd just thrown my words back at me. It annoyed me.

"Fine." I tossed another shot back and grimaced at the cloying sweetness.

"Ew. What was that?"

Carlos took the shot from my hand, sniffed it, and shook his head.

"Jim said they're all different."

"Really?" I eyed the shots again. "That makes this kind of fun."

I picked up another shot. Before I could get it to my mouth, Bethi ran up to me, grabbed my hand, and poured the liquid into her mouth.

"Daddy's going to put you in a time out," I said, looking back at Luke.

"Just remember your promise," Luke said. "She's sleeping with you tonight."

Crap. He was right. But the sun was still up, and we had plenty of time before we needed to worry about that.

"No puking," I said.

She laughed. "Come dance."

The shot I'd managed to drink had warmed me enough that I nodded.

I loved music. I loved moving to music. Granted, usually my moves involved kicks or jabs, but I knew how to dance. What girl could work in Ethan's bar and not pick up a move or two?

So for a while, I lost myself on the dance floor. There was no pain or sorrow, just the moves and the moment.

Bethi and I had moves. Gabby and Michelle...well, they tried. Eventually, Emmitt joined Michelle, and Thomas and Charlene gave the floor a try. It was fun. A lot of fun. Their laughter clogged the air as much as their happiness. I soaked it up without meaning too. They didn't seem to notice. They kept being happy.

I slipped from the group and went to the bar. Carlos still guarded the shots. I took two and downed one after the other.

The last one made my nose burn.

MELISSA HAAG

"Ugh! Keep me away from exposed flames."

He didn't comment. I turned to face the room and stood beside Carlos. He had a view of everyone having fun. Even Grey was to the side, joking with Jim.

"Why aren't you out there?"

He turned his head and met my gaze.

"Are you inviting me?"

"Is that what it takes? An invitation for you to have fun?"

He shrugged and went back to watching everyone. I shook my head at him, reached back, and picked up a couple more shots. I took a sip from each.

"These aren't bad. This one's minty. This one's..." I took another sip. "I think my taste buds are checking out for the day because it doesn't taste like anything."

I held the two shots up. He glanced at them, looked up at me, then took both. After he swallowed, he set the glasses to the side.

"Second one was water."

"Hope Jim didn't pay for that."

"Come on, Isabelle!" Bethi said. She was shaking it to some party rock. I went to join her.

I danced. I drank. I danced some more. Time slipped away as I let loose.

And I started to smile more than not. A warm glow filled my belly. I wasn't sure if it was the alcohol or the emotions of those around me. All I knew was that I felt happy. There wasn't a smidge of negativity around me, not even from Bethi.

I grinned and made my way toward Carlos and the drinks. Carlos studied my progress across the floor. He was probably trying to judge just how far gone I was. Not too far. I felt like I was still walking fine, until I almost tripped.

I leaned against the bar beside Carlos.

"Done drinking?" he asked, looking down at me.

"Nah. Just wanted to relax and check out the view."

Charlene laughed and danced with Thomas and Jim. Jim kept the shots lined up on the bar and his mom's wineglass full. None of the werewolves seemed even the least bit tipsy. Bethi definitely was. She was surprisingly good at tricking Luke. Michelle's cheeks were rosy as she swayed in Emmitt's arms. Gabby definitely wasn't drunk. However, I did see her sip from Clay's beer a few times.

So much joy. I felt bloated with it. And I didn't want to stop to spar with Carlos. So I exhaled and tried to push some of it away from me.

Almost everyone staggered. The bartender bumped against the bottles behind the bar and laughed.

In fact, everyone seemed happier. A weird, crazy, might-need-to-be-locked-up kind of happy.

I started to worry when I saw Winifred laughing and leaning against Sam. He supported her and laughed just as hard.

"Carlos?" I said, tearing my gaze from the pair.

Carlos looked at everyone with a frown.

"Did you do something?" he asked.

"I don't know. Maybe." If I had, it wasn't something I'd ever done before.

"I'll take Thomas, Charlene, and Grey outside and see if that helps clear their heads."

I nodded and watched him as he moved across the room and convinced the three to leave with him. When he opened the door, I noticed how late it had gotten and turned to the bartender.

"We're ready to close the tab," I said.

"He's been paying along the way. No tab to close," the man said, his random amusement still clinging to him. I tried to ignore it.

"Good. Make sure no one else buys any. We need to get going soon."

He nodded. I looked at the seven shots still waiting.

"Can I get a glass of water?" He moved to get me one, and I downed two more shots.

When he brought the glass, I filled the shots with water.

"Bethi, come help me," I waved her over.

Luke didn't scowl at me this time. I handed her the waters, and Luke got two of the real thing. I grabbed another shot to join them. Bethi kept giggling and spilling her water as she tried to drink it. Luke helped her aim for her mouth, chuckling the entire time.

I needed to get away from everyone. The mad laughter was starting to grate on my nerves. I went over to Jim.

"Can I have your wallet?" He reached into his back pocket and willingly handed it over. He still had sixty dollars left. I took it all, since he seemed to be the instigator, then walked out the front door. The cool air felt good.

Grey, Charlene, Thomas, and Carlos stood near the road. They spoke quietly and no one seemed to be laughing anymore. I did, however, feel their lingering amusement. Whatever it was seemed to have faded for them. It gave me hope for everyone inside.

I leaned against the building and waited for the discussion to finish. They couldn't blame me for what happened. I mean, I'd warned Jim. And I didn't think spreading some happiness was a bad thing. Not with this group. Besides, I'd really enjoyed myself for the first time in a very long time.

The tension I'd held slowly evaporated, and I sighed happily as the world seemed to turn soft and wavy. Drinking was a great idea. I owed Jim big time. And I needed to tell him that. I stood and reached for the door. It moved away from me, and I had to reach for it a second time.

Inside, Jim was laughing at something Emmitt had said. He had a nice laugh. It made me smile.

Forgetting why I'd come back in, I let the song on the jukebox draw me to Bethi's side where I started dancing again. I closed my eyes and just moved. Not too much though. I didn't want Luke and his wild dance moves to take me out.

It took two fast beat songs for me to notice the laughing had stopped. And it took a slow song for me to open my eyes. The bar was empty. Except for Carlos. He leaned against the wall near the jukebox, and he watched me.

My pulse leapt and my belly warmed. He straightened away from the wall and held out his hand.

I gave him a small smile and moved toward him. Once I slipped my hand in his, he closed his eyes for a moment.

"Home," he whispered.

I didn't understand what he meant.

When he opened his eyes again, he pulled me toward him. We moved together to the music, a gentle sway that beckoned me to lean in further. I rested my cheek against his chest and sighed, floating in peace.

The music ended too soon. I lifted my head, but he didn't stop dancing with me. Our gazes locked. Something there made my pulse flutter. In excitement or in warning, I couldn't tell. My head was too fuzzy to think straight.

"I need some air."

I pulled away from him, but he kept hold of my hand and led me toward the smoker's exit near the back. Trees surrounded the overgrown patio, and he tugged me toward them.

We walked a ways into the woods then he stopped and turned toward me, only inches separating us. The distance reminded me of the night in the bathroom, and I tilted my face up toward him, wondering if he'd try something like he had that night. Part of me hoped he would. I didn't want to be alone. I wanted him to hold me, but I didn't want it to mean anything.

He turned away from me, confusing me. It took me a moment to notice that the hand holding mine shook.

"Carlos?"

"Will you do something for me, Isabelle?" he asked softly.

A shiver coursed through me at the rough edge in his voice. I tried to focus, to feel what he might be feeling, but my head was swimming too much.

"Do something?"

"Yes. For me."

I hesitated. He wanted me to do something for him but wouldn't turn around and look at me. Even with my head swimming, I knew that, along with the shaking, couldn't be a good thing. Yet, he was still talking. Asking nicely. That couldn't be too bad, could it?

"What do you want me to do?"

"Run," he said.

I wasn't expecting that.

"Why?"

He turned and using my hand, tugged me closer to him. My breath caught when his other hand rose to my face. His fingertips trembled against my skin as he touched me lightly along my jaw.

"Because I want to chase you."

At first, I thought he was joking. But his serious expression told me otherwise.

"Just run?"

He nodded.

"Like tag?"

Slowly, he shook his head. I searched his face for a hint of what he might be thinking. The shaking got worse as I backed up a step, then another. He growled low, and like the insane person I'd always guessed I was, I tore free from his touch and ran.

A rumbling growl sounded behind me a moment before something came crashing through the trees after me. I let out a squeal and pushed myself to go faster. I dodged around trees and squeezed through bramble. A few times, I thought I might have gained some distance, but then I'd hear another splintering crash or growl.

Either the running or the adrenaline seemed to burn off enough of the alcohol that I realized what I was doing was crazy. I stopped suddenly and spun around to face Carlos. Only it wasn't Carlos that burst through the trees.

A dark beast prowled closer on all fours. Its lips were pulled back in a snarl, and a spike of fear dissolved the rest of the alcohol's effects. It looked just like the things that had attacked us.

"Carlos?" Fear pitched my voice higher than usual.

It jumped forward and knocked me down, not giving any indication that name meant anything. The beast stood over me and lowered its muzzle to my face. I could barely breathe past the terror filling me.

"If you're Carlos, you better show me now, or I'll make you bleed."

The beast gave a shudder and fur started to disappear, exposing familiar tan skin. His ears receded and his teeth retracted. Within seconds, the beast leaning over me became Carlos.

His gaze locked with mine. There was no anger. Instead, everything in his expression hinted at the want he'd once let me feel, a desire so potent, a need so consuming, I'd let him hold me. My breath caught in my throat at the sight of it.

"Isabelle..." He slowly lowered his head, his breath fanning my face as he glanced at my lips.

Panic surged through my veins.

"I'm not ready," I whispered.

He sighed, closed his eyes, and dropped his forehead to mine.

"I know."

He didn't move, and I became very aware of just how close we were. His inside thighs touched the outside of mine. The heat of his chest warmed me but didn't press against me. His arms, braced on either side of me, prevented any further contact. But for how long?

"Can we get up?" I asked nervously.

He nodded, but didn't move further.

"Carlos. Are you all right?"

"Thank you, Isabelle."

"For what?"

"For running."

Then he got up and offered me his hand. My eyes bugged.

"Where are your clothes?"

He looked down at himself then at me.

"I'll need to get some new ones from the car."

As he grabbed my hand and pulled me to my feet, I forced my gaze to remain locked on his face.

"Do you think everyone is ready to leave?" I asked, pretending my face wasn't fire engine red.

"Yes."

He turned and started walking away. I had no choice but to follow the full moon out of the woods. It was a nice walk back.

When we reached the building, Carlos pointed at the back door as he veered left to walk around to the parking lot. I went inside and found everyone sipping water at the bar.

The seat next to Bethi was open, so I carefully made my way to it. It seemed the clarity from the run in the woods and those intense moments on the ground had started to fade, and my eyes refused to focus as they should. It made walking a little tricky. That my head felt light and fuzzy didn't help either. No one else looked like they felt any better than I did. I couldn't be sure if it was the alcohol or the mysterious and slightly creepy mood change they'd all gone through just before I'd left.

"Are you all right?" I asked Bethi as I sat next to her.

"Yeah. I'm fine."

"What happened to all of you?"

"You did."

"What do you mean?"

She glanced at the bartender. Winifred, at the far end of the bar, called the man over to her and started a conversation.

"You can take people's emotions, pulling so many that people lose their will to live. Like those Urbat you..." She cleared her throat. "Anyway, when you're full of emotion, you can also push it back out, forcing foreign emotions into the people around you. When there's enough of it, the emotions seem to overload their brains and make for a very violent death."

"How do you know this?"

"Been there, dreamed it."

"Why didn't you say something before now?" I asked, getting angry. I might have done something different the night that Ethan—

"You didn't survive in the dream."

That cut off my growing anger.

"Oh."

So when I'd felt so full of happiness before, I hadn't pushed it out into the air but into everyone around me. It hadn't hurt me, and it hadn't hurt them. But I hadn't been that full of emotion, either. I realized what that meant for me. The next time I faced the Urbat, I could pull/push emotions like a pulse. They wouldn't be able to get close to me. And, I bet the more I held in before pushing it out, the more it would affect the people around me.

Carlos came in just then, drawing my attention. Dressed once again in slacks and a polo, he looked just like his old self. However, the image of his naked backside was burned into my retinal memory.

"Are there any other hidden talents I should know about?" I asked Bethi, trying to distract myself.

"If there are, I haven't dreamt them," she said. "I really hope you'll be able to fix the hangover I'm going to have tomorrow."

"Sorry, babe. Hangovers aren't emotions."

Carlos strode across the room, his focus entirely too intense. I looked away and caught sight of my flushed face in the mirror behind the bar.

A second later, Carlos stood behind me. Our gazes met in the mirror. My chest felt tight, and my heart didn't want to beat right. The dumb organ couldn't make up its mind if it wanted to be fast, slow, or just stop.

"You should try to eat," he said, placing the leftover container in front of me. "Please."

I nodded, flustered by my reaction to him, and opened the box. The burger was cold from being in the car so long. I took a bite anyway. It was good and made my stomach feel better. Bethi stole a piece of my bacon.

By the time I managed half the burger, I felt normal. Still drunk but not flustered. I set the rest of the burger back into the container.

"Finished?" Carlos asked.

"All yours," I said, nudging the container to the side. He reached around me, and his arm brushed mine. The skin under my sleeve tingled at the contact. So much for normal. I kept my gaze locked on my glass of water. Twice, I almost used the mirror behind the bar to see if he was looking at me.

A stool scraped along the hardwood floor.

"Looks like it's time to go," Bethi said.

I glanced up and saw the Elders standing. Winifred was handing the bartender a decent tip for a thankfully slow weekday afternoon.

Carlos set the empty container next to my elbow and offered me his hand. I knew he only meant to help me from the stool, but I couldn't touch him.

"I've got it," I said. My ungraceful slither from the stool didn't support my words.

He followed closely as I moved toward the door.

When Jim passed Winifred, she held out her hand. He sighed and handed over the keys. I doubted it was due to his alcohol consumption. Rather, it was most likely due to our detour. Everyone piled into the same vehicles, leaving Carlos and me alone.

He didn't comment when I hesitated before veering toward our car. He waited patiently for me to get in then closed the door for me. Once he was behind the wheel, I leaned my head back and closed my eyes. The disorienting movement of the car as Carlos pulled out of the driveway had me opening my eyes again. I swallowed hard.

"You can lean on me again," Carlos said.

CHAPTER TWELVE

His offer didn't help settle my stomach.

"I don't think that's a good idea. How far do we have to go?"

He was quiet a moment.

"We'll be there soon."

The whole in-the-head communication thing was still weird. So, instead of wondering how it worked or who he'd asked, I replayed our run through the woods. What had possessed me to say yes to that? I glanced at Carlos' profile and felt a tug in my stomach. Stupid pull.

My head still felt fuzzy when Carlos pulled into the hotel parking lot, and Bethi's comment about a hangover had me regretting the last few shots I'd consumed.

I couldn't wait for a shower and bed. Thanks to the weird happiness burst, I didn't feel twitchy or edgy, so there was no need to spar before I crashed. However, thanks to our afternoon binger, we hadn't practiced either.

Everyone moved a bit slower than normal to get inside. Someone must have called ahead and reserved the rooms because it didn't take long for Michelle and Emmitt to hand out room keys. When Michelle handed a card with the same room number on it to both Carlos and Luke, I didn't complain. I had promised.

Bethi and I walked together up the stairs then down the hall. She was very quiet and not radiating too much of anything. In fact, everyone in the group seemed emotionally subdued.

Luke reached around us to open the door.

"Does anyone need the bathroom before I shower?" I asked.

"Yes," Bethi said, making a beeline for it.

It didn't take her long to step out and give both Luke and Carlos a chance at the bathroom. Once everyone finished, I closed myself in and started the shower. Who knew what was in my hair after being chased through the woods and knocked to the ground. I wasn't a fan of anything with more legs than I had. The thought made me grin as I recalled werewolves had four legs. Then, I frowned as I remembered how Carlos had shifted from four legs to a very naked two. I shook the thought away, stripped, and stepped into the shower.

The hot water felt good, but I didn't linger. I wanted sleep.

After I dried myself, I found a clean pair of shorts in my bag. I was pretty sure they weren't mine. At least, I didn't remember buying them. They looked the right size though, so I pulled them on followed by a clean tank top.

When I opened the door, the room was already dark. After the bright light in the bathroom, I couldn't see much but was able to discern that one bed had two lumps and the other just one. I carefully shuffled to the bed with one lump, lifted the covers, and slid in.

Exhaling slowly, I let myself relax.

AN ARM over my waist prevented me from rolling over like I wanted to. So I threw it off and repositioned myself on my other side. The weight settled back on my waist and pulled me toward a heat source that warmed my face. I scooted closer until my nose touched skin then sighed and went under once more.

THE ALMOST SILENT click of a door closing nudged me to consciousness. I wasn't ready to wake up yet. My head hurt a little, and I still felt so tired. I snuggled in closer to Bethi, then froze as I registered every little detail about my snuggle buddy.

My hand was on the chiseled ribcage of my bedmate. Chiseled didn't quite describe Bethi. My nose pressed against a sparsely haired chest. I couldn't picture Bethi sleeping with me topless, let alone having chest hair. And the fingers of a strong, large hand stroked my back.

Anger rode in on top of my panic-pony.

"Is anyone else in the room with us?" I asked, without moving.

The hand on my back stilled.

"Why are you asking?"

"Because I don't want to hurt anyone else when I go after you."

"Bethi thought you might feel that way. She and Luke just left."

He didn't move or try to defend his position. I lifted my head and met his gaze. His darkly lashed chocolate eyes held me for a moment before I noted the rest of his face. His strong jawline...the slight curve of his lower lip...the dimple in his chin...his corded throat...his chiseled, bare chest. I swallowed hard and didn't check any lower. Instead, I met his gaze again.

"Good morning, Isabelle," he said softly, like it was an endearment or a declaration.

It made my heart flutter, and I had to look away. Focusing on his bare chest didn't help. It was perfect. Tanned skin dusted with dark hair. Who was I kidding? I liked where I was.

I sighed and closed my eyes.

"Good morning, Carlos."

His arm tightened fractionally around my waist.

"Why, exactly, aren't you on your half of the bed?"

"I am."

I lifted my head again. He lay on his side, on the very edge of the bed.

"This doesn't mean anything," I said, trying to move away.

"Not a thing. Go back to sleep."

His fingers started tracing paths on my back. I wanted to sigh again and settle in for some more sleep, but I couldn't. I'd only ever been this close to Ethan. And Ethan had known and respected the boundaries I'd set to keep him safe. My boundaries kept everyone safe. Look at what had happened the night before. A few drinks and I was pushing happy like the newest drug on the street. The affirmation of my need to isolate myself hurt as much as the memory of Ethan.

"Carlos, I can't do this. I can't deal with what you want. It hurts. Don't you understand? It was supposed to be Ethan."

His fingers twitched against my skin, then curled into a fist.

"Because you loved him or because you thought you owed him?"

For the first time, Carlos sounded angry.

I tried to pull back and look at him, but his arms tightened around me.

"It doesn't matter. I'm telling you, I can't deal with any of this right now. Let go."

All he did was pull me closer. His body shook.

"Bite me."

"Excuse me?"

"If you want me to let you go, bite me."

Last night, he'd asked me to run. I had and ended up on the ground with a big, naked Carlos hovering over me. Biting was definitely not a good idea. I could imagine where it would lead.

And my very vivid imagination killed what little anger I had still clinging to my backbone.

"I'll scream if you don't let go," I said. I inwardly cringed. Way to sound like a scared little girl.

He made a noise. It was a cross between an angry growl and a groan of frustration. His shaking continued.

He was freaking me out, and I didn't know what to do about it. He had no emotions to pull and was obviously stronger. I was out of my depth with him.

"Please." It was a desperate last attempt before I really did start yelling my head off.

He exhaled slowly then lifted one of his arms. I scrambled out of bed and rushed to lock myself into the bathroom. The cold of the tile barely registered as, with a quiet thump, I leaned my forehead against the door and released a shaky breath.

After taking a few seconds to calm down, I turned to the sink and started to brush my teeth. I took my time, singing the alphabet in my head three times before spitting. How long would it take for him to leave? The problem with not sensing his emotions was that I didn't know if he was out there waiting for me.

I used the toilet, washed my hands, and brushed and braided my hair. Hoping sufficient time had passed, I gingerly opened the door just enough to peek out. The room was empty.

Bethi wasn't going to get another chance for a sleepover after abandoning me like that.

I stalked out of the bathroom and bolted the door to the room before changing for the day.

FOLLOWING MY NOSE, I found the breakfast area on the main floor near the lobby. All the tables, save one, were empty. Carlos sat alone, slowly eating his breakfast of eggs, bacon, and yogurt.

He didn't look up when I entered, and I hated the swift guilt that hit me. I had nothing to feel guilty about. He'd taken advantage. He knew I was off limits. I'd made it clear. Yet, he continued to be annoyingly intense.

I stomped over to the counter, scooped some eggs onto a plate, grabbed a milk, then purposely ignored him and went to the table near the window.

Since finishing high school, I often found myself alone, watching the world when I wasn't so angry at it. At times like those, I would pick up the phone and call Ethan.

We'd tried working together after I'd graduated, but the emotions from him and everyone else in the bar had been too much for me. He'd come up with the cage idea after the first time I'd quit. I'd tried again, working for a few hours then fighting. It'd been great. But I'd started drawing too much attention, and Ethan had worried. Thus, I'd found myself in the white-collar employment pool, only working at the bar when I needed a fight. Still, I'd known Ethan was only a phone call away whenever I needed to talk.

It felt like we were on one of our long stretches where we were both busy, and all I needed to do was pick up the phone. If only it were that easy. I missed him.

"Isabelle."

Carlos' voice, so close to me, made me jump. I turned and found him next to the table. He was looking down at me, his dark eyes focused on my face.

"We leave in thirty. I'll get your bag, unless you need to go back to the room for something."

"Thanks."

He looked at me for a second longer then left. I breathed a sigh of relief and went back to not eating my cold eggs.

"You gunna drop kick me into fairyland?"

Bethi's voice penetrated my misery, and I pulled my blank stare from the window just in time to see her flop into the chair across from me.

"I should. When you asked to sleep with me, I thought that meant me and you in a bed."

"I know. I'm sorry. Luke wasn't willing to bend." She smirked at her choice of words.

"No more sleepovers for you," I said, balling up my napkin and tossing it on the plate.

"Come on. You looked like you were pretty comfy."

"Don't go there."

"It's funny that you're doing everything you can to stay away from Carlos. I was the complete opposite with Luke."

"Why?"

"Once I realized he was one of the good guys, I thought he might be my ticket to a few dreamless nights. After all the memories of dying..." She shook her head. "I was desperate. Still am. Anyway, I tried to bite him countless times. He dodged every attempt. I can't even count how many times I ended up with his hand in my face."

"Wait, bite? Why bite?"

"Yeah. It's the werewolf version of being engaged, I guess. I was hoping that Claiming him would stop the dreams. It didn't. Then, I'd hoped Mating would do the trick. It didn't either. But at least I'm safer. Mating is essentially tying the unbreakable knot. No, seriously. It's unbreakable." She leaned forward and grew serious. "If they catch us, they can't force us to bite one of their own if we're Mated. It won't work as long as our Mate's alive."

I heard the words and even registered their meaning on some level, but I was still stuck on biting meaning engaged. My eyes narrowed. I knew biting would have been a bad idea.

"Excuse me," I said, picking up my plate and standing. "I need to talk to Carlos."

I tossed my food in the garbage then took the stairs two at a time. He was just leaving the room as I turned the corner. I marched up to him and put my hands on his chest, pushing him back against the door.

"Still want that bite?"

In a blink, I was the one against the door. One of his hands was in my hair and the other gently held the back of my neck. His entire body seemed to curl around me, shielding me from everything. My anger slipped a notch as a burst of desire exploded inside me.

"Yes," he breathed.

It took me a second to recall I'd asked a question. I pulled my anger around me like a protective blanket and kicked the desire in its teeth.

"Did you maybe forget to mention that biting you would have meant we were engaged?"

He gave an angry growl.

"Yeah, that's how I feel. What was that run last night? Another trick?" I pushed at him. When he didn't move, I pinched the inside of his bicep. He winced and pulled away from me. "I don't like liars, Carlos. Watch yourself."

I picked up my bag and left him standing in the hall.

By the time I reached the lobby, I saw everyone was already outside, milling around in the parking lot. As soon as I pushed through the doors, they started piling in their assigned vehicles, and I slowed as I realized I'd be stuck in a car alone with Carlos again.

The door opened behind me, and Carlos moved past me, his bag over his shoulder.

"I'm not getting in the car with you," I said, crossing my arms.

He stopped walking but didn't turn.

"Why not?"

"Because you're not following the rule."

He turned to study me.

"What rule?"

"The   don't-touch-Isabelle-or-she'll-break-your-damn-hand rule." I glared at him.

He considered me for a moment and slowly closed the distance between us.

"You're afraid," he said, sounding too much like Ethan.

I wanted to hit him. Instead, I marched over to the car to yank the door open and get in. Hopefully the echo of the slammed door let Carlos know just how angry I was.

IT WAS A LONG, tense ride. I spent the time staring out my window.

Three hours into the drive, Carlos suddenly spoke, taking me by surprise.

"What is it you don't like about me?"

His hesitant tone launched a pity party in my heart. I quickly closed the door on that noise.

"Your persistence."

I felt him glance at me but refused to look.

"I don't understand why you keep trying. Nothing's going to happen. I'm not biting you. I'm not dating you. I'm not doing anything with you."

"Okay."

That was it, just a calm, measured okay. I finally turned to look at him. He met my gaze.

"I just want you happy."

The words made my insides churn with emotion. I could easily gage the mood of those around me, except for Carlos; but when it came to how I felt, I couldn't look deep. I didn't want to.

"Then just be my friend," I said. "I need one."

He returned his attention to the road, and I went back to watching out the window.

It wasn't long after our little talk that the first vehicle pulled off the shoulder for another practice session. This time, we started paired off, fighting back to back. Carlos and I moved together pretty well. He was fast and kept up with me easily. When we stood back to watch the rest, I saw Luke and Bethi were in sync too. Jim paired well with Grey, Emmitt, and Thomas. Winifred seemed to work him a bit harder than the rest. No doubt punishment for yesterday. The normal people radiated frustration, with Bethi adding a special blend of melancholy. Probably her hangover. The not so normal people didn't emanate as much, for which I was grateful. My tender head and stomach were getting worse by the minute. Thankfully, after our allotted thirty minutes, we were on the road again in search of somewhere to eat.

We pulled into the first restaurant we saw. It looked like a little ma-and-pa place from the outside, and the inside confirmed it. There were maybe ten tables, and three of them were taken. The cook's eyes rounded when he saw our big group come in. This time, we didn't try to push tables together.

Carlos stopped at a table furthest from the other customers and pulled out a chair for me. Why did that make me hesitate and my heart skip a beat? He watched me closely. I'd asked for friendship, I reminded myself as I sat.

He didn't sit next to me, but across from me.

"Can we sit with you?" Michelle asked. Emmitt stood just behind her.

"Sure," I said.

Michelle sat to my right and gave me a shy smile. Emmitt pushed her chair in for her before moving to the other side of me.

"I'm sorry if it seems like I'm being hard on you," I said.

"You are being hard on us, but I understand why."

I felt Michelle's burst of pity and knew what she would say before she said it.

"I'm really sorry about Ethan."

My eyes stung and my lungs burned for a few seconds until I locked the new wave of grief away behind the wall that held the rest. Then, I nodded.

"Bethi said you two grew up together. How did you meet?"

A smile tugged my lips as I remembered.

"At school. On the playground. He was the new kid, two grades older. He wasn't like the other kids who'd fall asleep if I tried to play with them. He was angry. All the time. He took a ball from a girl I knew." I could still picture his face, so stubborn and set. "When I asked him to give it back, he tried hitting me. I was already in self-defense classes so I blocked it. It was our first spar."

"How did you learn self-defense without putting the instructor to sleep?" Michelle asked. I was glad she didn't ask more about Ethan.

"Back then, my pull wasn't as strong unless I really tried. Plus, grownups hide what they feel more than kids do. Where I put a kid to sleep, a grownup usually barely felt it. It wasn't until I hit my teens that what I could do grew."

I remembered when I'd first figured out something was changing. A boy in my eighth grade class had asked me to go to a movie with him. I'd been flattered. Ethan had insisted on going with us as a chaperone. He hadn't trusted the boy.

Once we were in the movies, the boy had reached over to hold my hand. My excitement at the contact had quickly turned to horror when the boy had slumped next to me. Ethan, sitting two rows behind us, had jumped the seats before I'd made a sound and pulled the boy away from me. That was when I'd known relationships beyond friendship were out.

The waitress came over with waters for everyone and asked if we wanted anything else to drink as she handed us menus.

"We're fine. Thank you," Emmitt said politely.

From a table over, I heard Jim say, "We're going to starve."

He was sharing a table with Charlene, Thomas, and Winifred. Charlene shushed Jim and continued to eye her menu. Jim caught my eye and looked at me hopefully.

"He misses Liam and Aden," Emmitt said.

"Who are Liam and Aden?" I asked.

"My brothers," Michelle said. She reached into her purse and pulled out a photo of two little boys standing in the spray of a sprinkler. "This is from this summer."

Pride and love clouded around her.

"They mean a lot to you," I said, studying their faces.

"The world. That's why I'm here. Blake, the man controlling the Urbat, kept me prisoner for my premonitions. He used my brothers to keep me in line."

I really did not like Blake.

"Where are your brothers now?" I asked.

"Somewhere safe, I hope."

Her melancholy rained down on me. I gently pulled it from her. She smiled at the photo once again, and I handed it back to her.

We talked about her brothers a bit more as the waitress slowly took everyone's orders. When it came to me, I asked for a simple BLT, no fries. Carlos gave me a calculating look, but I ignored him. My stomach wasn't ready for anything heavier than what I'd ordered.

I ONLY MADE it halfway through my BLT before I set it aside. The emotions in the little diner were making my already upset stomach worse. The cook was worried, probably that he'd undercooked the burgers, which he had. The waitress emanated impatience and irritation. She probably wanted a smoke break. And the restaurant's other customers were just as dreary.

I felt over-sensitized to every little mood swing. My gaze shifted to Jim, and I scowled at him. Stupid drinking. I put my elbows on the table and rubbed my face. My stomach gave a lurch as a burst of concern came from the right.

"Are you all right?" Michelle asked.

"I want to kill Jim," I mumbled through my hands.

She set a sympathetic arm on my shoulder.

"I've been there. Hungover because of Jim, I mean."

"And because of yourself," Jim said from the other side of the room.

"Quiet," someone said in a low voice. I thought it was his mom.

"Do you want something for your head?" Michelle asked.

I dropped my hands. Everyone was watching me.

"No. I think I'll just step outside for a while."

Even the simple motion of standing made me feel worse. My skin crawled, my head throbbed, and my stomach squeezed and rolled in a sickening way. I made my way outside and gulped in the fresh air. The emotions of everyone inside still drifted to me. I moved away from the building, walking toward the sparse trees near the back of the property. Passing the dumpsters made me gag.

I leaned against the first tree I came to.

"It's more than a hangover, isn't it?"

Carlos' voice made me jump. I should have known he would follow.

"The hangover isn't helping. I think I'm more sensitive to everyone's moods because of it."

He moved around me so we faced each other.

"Then we need to do something about it."

I cringed.

"I'll throw up if I have to spar. I just need a few minutes."

He studied me and shook his head.

"No, I think waiting will make it worse."

"I'm not fighting, Carlos."

"What if you tried pushing again?"

I frowned.

"We're too close to people."

"Then let's go for a walk." He held out his hand.

I ignored his hand and shoved away from the tree.

"It would be better if I did this alone. I don't know what I'm doing, and I don't want to hurt anyone."

"I was fine yesterday."

I walked as I thought it over. I doubted he'd leave, even if I asked him to.

"Fine. Stay."

I stopped walking. I could hear the occasional car pass in the distance, but felt nothing around me. A squirrel chittered at us from its branch above. Glancing up, I considered it.

"You know, I'm going to be really upset if dead rodents start falling on my head because of this."

I closed my eyes, rolled my shoulders, then tried to relax. I took several slow breaths, and on an exhale, I tried to push out. After my third attempt, I opened my eyes and looked at Carlos.

"Why isn't it working?"

"What's different from last night and today?

I shrugged.

"Last night you were more relaxed."

"I'm trying to relax."

"But you're still worrying. You need to let it all go."

"You think I'm worrying? About what?"

"Hurting me. Hurting the squirrel."

He was crazy. I wasn't worried about that. I looked up at the squirrel staring down at us and realized it had stopped chittering.

Why? And the sudden worry I felt affirmed Carlos was right. I sighed. How did someone let go of all worry?

No matter how hard I tried, I cared about whether or not I would hurt someone around me. If I couldn't push the overflow out, that meant I needed to spar. My stomach shook its head at the idea.

"It's not working." Facing Carlos, I gave him an unhappy look and put my hands up. He shadowed my move. "I might puke on you. If I do, I'm really sorry."

"I can handle it."

"I can't." I gave a half-hearted jab.

He swatted it away and returned the swing. It was so unexpected that I almost didn't block in time.

"What the hell?"

"Fight," he growled.

"I hope I do puke on you." I started to swing like I meant it.

I gagged twice within two minutes, and he was quick to dance away. But after that, some of the nausea started to ease. He seemed to sense I was feeling better because he drove me harder. Sweat started to glue my shirt to my back. I hated that feeling. And it was unlikely that I'd get a shower until after dinner. The thought of yet another restaurant dinner made my stomach twist. I didn't understand why it would be so picky now after months of feeding it TV dinners.

"Do you know what?" I said, trying to find a way under his guard.

"What?"

He blocked my jab to his head.

"I want a sandwich. Just a plain 'ol PB and J." He was a second too slow on raising his arm, and I caught his jaw. I almost apologized, but he was too quick to return the blow. Blocking became more of a priority than saying sorry.

"What kind of jelly?" he asked.

"Doesn't matter. I'm just tired of the heavy restaurant food. And I want cereal for breakfast." When I stopped talking, I stepped back. "I'm done. For now. If I get any more sweaty it will just annoy me more than we're helping me."

He nodded and relaxed.

"Thanks, Carlos."

"Anytime, Isabelle."

My stomach dipped in a pleasant way as he said my name like it was an endearment and a secret promise. I awkwardly nodded then started walking back to the restaurant as Carlos' request to run and later to bite him bounced around in my head along with Bethi's words.

"Would it be all right with you if Winifred and Bethi took your place in the car? Just for a little while?"

"Why?"

He didn't sound objectionable to the request, only curious.

"I have some questions." Questions that might result in me wanting to beat him again. Or me blushing. Either way, I didn't want him around.

"All right. When it gets to be too much, tell Winifred to let me know. We can stop for a break."

"Thanks," I said, glancing at him. The slightly pink mark on his cheek caused a pang of regret. I was tired of hitting people. Well, I wouldn't mind hitting a few more of those Urbat. Better yet, Blake. But it wasn't like Blake or his men would just hold still for me while I—

I grinned.

"You're happy," Carlos said, opening the door for me.

"I am. I think I just had a brilliant idea."

I didn't tell him, though. Instead, I stepped inside and smiled at Bethi who was watching for me. I doubted Carlos would be onboard with what I had in mind. But I had no doubt Bethi would be. She didn't seem the type to back down from anything. And she knew I needed to realize my full potential in order to help them deal with the Urbat.

"I was wondering if you and Winifred would drive with me for a bit," I said, moving toward Bethi.

"That's fine with me." She patted Luke's arm when he frowned at her.

I glanced at Winifred, and she nodded. When I turned to look for Carlos, he was talking to the waitress.

"We've paid the bill and can leave if you're ready," Winifred said, reclaiming my attention.

"I'm ready."

CHAPTER THIRTEEN

BETHI TURNED IN HER SEAT TO LOOK BACK AT ME. WE WERE IN THE car, waiting for Winifred and Carlos to come out of the restaurant.

"What's up with the switch?"

"I have some questions about what you said this morning. And I have an idea that I'll need your help with."

"Intriguing."

The driver's door opened, and Winifred got in. I turned to see Carlos climb into the front of the SUV with Jim. Our gazes met as he closed the door. My stomach did its weird twist thing.

"This is for you," Winifred said, breaking my focus. She passed a to-go box back to me. I took it but didn't open it. The portion of BLT still in my stomach was enough for now. Winifred watched me in the mirror as she started the car.

"Carlos said you didn't eat this morning and barely ate anything before you went outside."

"Yeah." I set the box aside. "Still, I think I'll save this for later."

A wave of annoyance rolled over me as Winifred mumbled something about Jim. Then she shook her head and cut off the emotion.

"Sorry about that. So, what questions do you have?"

Now that it was time to start asking, I was nervous. Did I really want answers? I settled back into my seat as I decided it didn't matter what I wanted. Ignorance would get me into trouble, not just with Carlos and the whole pull thing but with werewolves in general.

"Let's start with what werewolves can do. I've noticed some differences. Obviously, you change forms, but when in your non-fuzzy form, you guys are hard to dent. Do you have thicker bones or something?"

"I don't believe so, but it might explain why we're harder to injure. We tend not to go to doctors for obvious reasons. Besides additional strength, we have better hearing, better vision, and quicker reflexes than humans. We generally heal faster, too."

"Same with the Urbat?" I asked.

Winifred glanced at Bethi.

"Yeah," Bethi said. "From what I've seen, werewolves and Urbat are about the same body-wise. Their differences seem to lie in their beliefs and values."

I thought on that for a bit. It would have been nice if the werewolves had an upper hand, physically. Yet, it was better to be equals than the Urbat having the advantage.

Now to the harder questions. I glanced at Winifred and caught her watching me in the mirror. I heaved a sigh, hoping everything I said would stay with the two women in this car.

"When I said I'd help, I didn't care who you all were or what was going on. I just wanted to get rid of this thing I do, so I could be with Ethan."

I glanced down at my hands and tried to swallow past the lump in my throat. It took a few tries before I could speak again.

"But things changed. Before Ethan..." I cleared my throat, skirting around his death. "He noticed that all of us girls seemed to be paired up with one of you. Not long after he pointed that out,

Michelle said something about a pull, and Bethi said something about biting."

I lifted my eyes and met Winifred's gaze.

"Am I supposed to be Carlos' Mate?"

"Do you want to be?"

I shook my head in frustration.

"Don't answer questions with questions. It's annoying. According to your beliefs, does Carlos think he and I are supposed to be together?"

"Yes," Bethi said when Winifred wouldn't.

Winifred gave her a look.

"What? He nearly tore down Ethan's bar when that guy hit her. What else could it be?"

"That's why he came at the cage?" I asked.

Bethi, still turned in her seat, grinned at me.

"Werewolves are protective."

"Okay. Fine. So I get that he wants me to bite him—not going to happen by the way—but why did he want me to run?"

Shock hit me.

"I beg your pardon?" Winifred said.

"Last night, after I blasted all you guys. Carlos took me into the woods and told me to run. I blame my agreement on the alcohol."

"What happened?" Bethi's rabid curiosity coated my skin like lotion.

"I ended up on the ground with a growling fur-beast straddling me," I said.

"Did he hurt you?" Winifred asked.

"He thanked me and helped me to my feet. So, can you tell me why he wanted me to run?"

Winifred's sudden need to watch the road had me curious. That she took a moment to answer had me planning all the ways I'd make Carlos pay if he'd talked me into doing something bad. Gradually, Winifred's shock died down.

"It hasn't been long since we shed our fur as daily wear and started to wear clothes. At heart, we're still animals," she said. "And a chase still gives us a thrill." She glanced at me in the mirror.

"Wait. You're saying he wanted me to run because it turned him on?"

"I'm totally going to get Luke to chase me," Bethi said with a grin.

I ignored her.

"And the shaking?" I asked.

"Struggling for control over the change," Winifred said. "When we're emotionally—"

"I get it. Do I have a choice? Am I going to be forced to pair up with Carlos?"

"No one will force you," she said. "You will always have a choice."

"Good," I said with a long exhale. "I didn't sign on to be a new candidate in this werewolf dating service you all seem to have going on. Now, for some serious business," I said, ready to change the subject.

"I thought that was serious," Bethi said.

"When I tried to push out the sludge inside me just a little while ago, it didn't work. Carlos thinks it's because I'm too worried about hurting the people around me. He might be right. But, I need to figure out how this thing works."

Bethi was already nodding.

"Yep. I agree."

"Okay. So, pushing with everyone around is out. But I thought of something else. Gabby said the Urbat are spread out. I want to see if we can isolate one or two, so I can use them as practice."

I could already see the rejection in Winifred's gaze. Bethi, on the other hand, thought it was a great idea by her excitement.

"Yes," she said. "That would be perfect. We can hang back, and you can easily take on one or two. As long as Gabby's watching, they can't really go anywhere with you if it doesn't work.

"We don't think this is a sound plan," Winifred said. She opened her mouth to say more, but Bethi turned on her.

"Did you see what happened to her when Ethan died? Her skin split. From the inside. Her eyes were seconds from hemorrhaging, based on how they looked just after. She's lucky she didn't liquefy her liver. If she doesn't learn how to push out the excess emotion the next time something bad happens, she won't have an out. Denying her isn't an option."

Bethi's angry waves of frustration made me twitch. I needed to call my attack Chihuahua off.

"Down girl. You're back on my sleepover list," I said, nudging her with a finger. "Just cut back on the overload, okay?"

She took a breath and muted some of what she felt.

"Can we pull over to talk about it? After that, I think I need to drive with Carlos again.

"Sorry," Bethi mumbled.

"Don't worry about it." As I spoke, the lead vehicle put on its blinker and braked.

When Winifred came to a stop on the shoulder, I breathed a sigh of relief and climbed out. Carlos was already out of his seat and walking toward us. His gaze swept over me. He'd been worried. I couldn't feel it or see it in his gaze, yet I knew and felt a flutter in my middle because of it.

"I'm fine," I said when he walked up to me.

"Why did we stop?"

Winifred indirectly answered his question as she spoke to Sam and Grey while everyone else joined us.

"Isabelle wants to find a lone Urbat. She needs to figure out how she released her emotions yesterday and can't do it with us around."

"Alone?" Sam said.

Carlos studied me.

"Isolated. Not alone," I said.

"It's not up for debate," Bethi said. "If she doesn't learn how to do this, the next time she overloads, she could kill herself."

Carlos' hands, which had hung loosely at his side, curled into fists.

"How does the route look?" Sam asked Gabby.

"Clear. It's been clear since we left. Although, one of them came near the hotel last night then left again. Since then, none of them have moved."

"It's bugging me that they've backed off like that," Bethi said. "They don't back off. They fight."

"Maybe what Isabelle did scared them," Winifred said.

Bethi seemed to consider it, then slowly shook her head.

"I think there's something more to their actions."

"We need to find out what," I said, agreeing with her. "Maybe we can kill two birds with one stone."

"What do you mean?" she asked, looking at me.

"They are obviously trying to steer us north, right? So let's go west and see what happens. As soon as we find an Urbat, we'll stop and I'll say hi. Maybe the lucky guy will be able to shed some light on why they want us to go north. If not, I'll still get my chance at figuring out my newest trick."

"What exactly do you mean by isolated?" Grey asked.

"You just need to be far enough away that when I pull or push emotions, you won't be in the blast zone."

He nodded and looked at Winifred and Sam.

"If the rest of you stay back by the vehicles, Carlos and I can walk Isabelle as close as possible. Then, she can go the rest of the way on her own. Gabby and Sam can keep Carlos and me informed of any movement. We'll be close enough to protect her if need be, and the rest of you will be far enough away to stay safe."

They debated it for a while, then finally agreed. Gabby would take us to a thin spot. Not too close. Within a mile. Then Carlos, Grey, and I would walk the rest of the way.

Before we got back into the cars, we practiced again. Emmitt was getting better at trusting the circle to protect Michelle and his mom. The three in the middle were working together seamlessly to announce the fight. Our weakness would be in the numbers. There was no way we would survive without casualties if we were attacked again like we had been. We needed to get to New York.

I SAT in the front again, enjoying the emotional silence as Carlos drove. My stomach rumbled, and I unbuckled to reach back for the sandwich I'd forgotten.

"Isabelle, that's not safe."

"Not feeding me isn't safe. I'd hate for you to lose an arm because I'm hungry."

I settled back into my seat and set the box in my lap before I buckled again.

"See, nothing to it."

He didn't comment.

With a grin, I opened the box and saw a whole sandwich inside. It wasn't the toasted BLT I'd half eaten. I lifted the top and saw peanut butter and grape jelly. I'd mentioned I'd wanted one, and he'd gotten it for me. It wasn't the first thing he'd quietly done for me. He'd been taking care of me since Ethan had died. And how had I treated him? Like a pariah.

"Thank you," I said quietly.

"You're welcome, Isabelle."

My stomach dipped and danced at his use of my name. I had a feeling he knew exactly what he did to me when he said it, too. Thoughtfully, I lifted the sandwich and took a bite. Ethan had been right; the big guy did want me. But watching my back wasn't going to be enough because Carlos wasn't attacking. He was worming his way in.

"This pull won't go away, will it?"

"No."

I nodded slowly.

"I don't do relationships," I said softly. "It's not just to protect the guy, you know. It's to protect me, too. I don't want to spend my life hitting the people who mean something to me."

"Maybe you'll feel differently when you learn how to release what you pull in."

I finished my sandwich in silence then turned in my seat to study him. He really wouldn't give up. For some reason, the idea didn't annoy me as much as it probably should have.

"And maybe I'll be so overcome by my awesome new skill that I'll bite you."

His hand tightened fractionally on the steering wheel. The bite thing was really messing with him.

I smirked when he cleared his throat lightly before speaking.

"Michelle found a place in New York already," he said. "Three apartments in a secured building. Bethi is arguing that you need better isolation."

"It's New York. How isolated does she think she can get me? Tell her to stop worrying."

"Will it be too much?" He glanced at me.

"It will be what it will be. We need to expose the Urbat, and everyone agreed New York is the place to do it. So, we have to go there. But, this side trip will be helpful. If I can master pushing out the emotions, pulling won't be an issue anymore."

We drove west for almost an hour before we pulled over again.

I got out and stretched. I was tired of all these car rides and just wanted to get where we needed to be already.

"He's about a mile up the road," Gabby said as she walked toward me.

"He?"

"Just a guess," Gabby said. "They've all been men so far. I figured the Urbat are just as hard up for females as these guys are. I'll keep an eye on things from here and report any movement to Sam. Sam will keep Grey and Carlos informed."

I nodded.

"Ready for a country stroll?" I said, looking at Grey and Carlos.

"Lead the way," Grey said.

My palms started to sweat as I walked away from the group.

"I want you to stay as far back as possible, Grey."

"You have my word," he said. Yet, Grey's worry drifted on the wind.

I didn't bother trying to reason with Carlos, who strode beside me. I doubted he'd listen.

The sound of the idling engines faded as we walked. Ahead, in the road, I spotted a little figure.

"Gabby says there's movement north and south. Reinforcements," Grey said. "We'll only have a few minutes."

We picked up our pace, and I watched the distant figure rapidly grow. Whoever it was approached us, too.

When I could make out the worn pants and stained shirt of the man, he stopped advancing. So did Grey. Carlos and I kept going.

"I won't let you pass," the man called.

I could see the superior smirk. Oh, how I wanted to wipe that look from his face. His people had killed Ethan.

"I'm not here to try to get past you," I said. I kept walking until I felt his disdain. Then I stopped. I couldn't feel Grey or Carlos so I began pulling a little.

"Here for some more fun, human-lover?"

My nervousness fled at the rise of my fury. He knew about Ethan? How could he know when I'd killed them all? Could they do that mind thing, too?

"No. I'm here to see how many more of you I can kill before I die."

His humor faded, and I waited for his reaction.

"The others are turning back," Carlos said. Grey was obviously feeding him information.

"Your friends don't want to come and play?" It didn't surprise me. "Why not? What are you and your kind afraid of?"

His anger washed over me. I pulled some of that into me as well. My skin tingled but didn't feel tight.

"Nothing. Certainly not a little bitch like you."

I laughed, pulled hard on an inhale, and pushed it all back at him on the exhale. The man fell to his knees, holding his head. His nose bled.

"Tell Blake I'm coming for him."

"He's counting on it." The man spat red.

"I doubt he's counting on what I'm going to do to him."

His twisted, feral smile made me itch to do worse to him.

"Blake's got far worse planned for you," his gaze flicked to Carlos, "and a few others in your group."

I tried to step forward, but Carlos' hand on my shoulder stopped me.

"You know what you need?" I said to the man, ignoring Carlos. "Obedience training. When I'm finished with you, you'll be fetching my paper."

I pulled hard again. The man grunted and wavered.

"Do you like how that feels? Mmm, your fear is delicious. I like the taste of coward."

His anger spiked, and I pulled it all. The man slumped to the ground. Though his face rested against the asphalt, his eyes tracked my progress when Carlos finally released me. I squatted beside the man and poked his forehead.

"Don't threaten what's mine."

"When we're done with you," the man slurred, "you'll have nothing." He started to laugh.

I wanted to push out the anger I still held, but I didn't. I couldn't kill him. Even though it seemed like a really awesome idea now, I'd regret it later.

"Night," I said standing. Then I kicked him in the head.

His eyes rolled back and closed.

I stood and stayed there, staring down at him for a moment.

"Isabelle?"

Turning, I glanced at Carlos. I felt twitchy with the unspent energy still crawling through me. It wasn't anything I couldn't handle. But it made me frown at him irritably.

"Get rid of it," Carlos said.

I started walking. Grey was a good distance away, and I waved him to move further. When I was an equal distance between the fallen man and Grey, I glanced at Carlos.

"Do it," he said.

His dark gaze held mine. What if I hurt him? I swallowed my fear and pushed. This time, it worked. Carlos didn't stagger or fall, but I did see his fingers twitch.

"Did you feel that?"

"No. There are others coming this way. We need to run."

I didn't need to be told twice. He and I ran back to the vehicles. It was obvious he was holding back so he kept pace with me. All the engines were running. Winifred was at the wheel of our vehicle.

"Kicked the hornet's nest, did I?" I said as I slid into the backseat. To my surprise, Carlos joined me.

"Not too badly. There are only a few headed this way," she said as she turned the car around. We followed the other cars back the way we'd come.

"How are you feeling?"

"Fine. Let Bethi know it worked."

Winifred nodded.

WE DROVE FOREVER. My butt went numb, and my patience wore thin. The clock on the dash flashed two a.m. Sure we'd stopped for bathroom breaks, practice, and slowed down for a fast food dinner, but we still continued to push further north as if trying to make up for the westward detour.

The Urbat alley remained a beehive of activity with many leaving their posts to follow us north. Though Bethi felt more assured by the response to our test, no one else did.

"Seriously, are we there yet?" I asked, letting my head fall back against the seat.

"Almost," Winifred said.

Thankfully, she wasn't sugarcoating it. We pulled into a motel parking lot a few minutes later. The neon light flickered like a horror movie, and the burned-out bulb of the yard light cast shadows on the long, narrow building. The weathered exterior doors to each room needed new paint—at least, on the bottom half.

"I changed my mind," I said, looking out the window. "Let's drive all night."

"Gabby needs a break. She said this area's been clear for a while."

"Gee, I wonder why," I mumbled as I opened my door. I waited for Carlos as he grabbed our bags from the trunk. The rest of the group shuffled toward the shady "office."

"Not that I expect five star hotels or anything, but a single star would be better than this."

"We'll be safe," Carlos said, coming to stand beside me.

I tipped my face up to look at him. "From the Urbat, yes. But I bet there's a lot nastier stuff crawling around in those rooms.

"Come on." He led me toward the office. The rest were just coming out with keys.

"The rooms only have one bed each," Emmitt said as he held up a fistful of old-fashioned keys.

I glanced at the numbers on the doors. One through lucky number seven.

Carlos took a key and watched me. My guilty conscience had me wondering if he was expecting me to throw a fit.

"Well, come on, snuggle buddy," I said. "You can protect me from everything that skitters away when the lights go on."

I heard Michelle make a concerned noise. She looked less pleased than I did. Bethi, on the other hand, seemed to have no problem with the situation.

I followed Carlos to the door and peered around him as he turned the light on. The inside was far better than the outside. The room smelled fresh, was bright, and looked clean.

"Thank God!" I flopped onto the bed and didn't move.

CHAPTER FOURTEEN

SOMETHING TICKLED MY HAIR, AND FOR A CONFUSED MOMENT, I WAS certain I had a cockroach crawling on me. My eyes flew open, and I almost yipped in surprise when I saw Carlos not far from me.

As my mind tried to sort through the lingering dream and the recalled impression of our current motel, I noted other things. The sunlight that poured through the window. Carlos shirtless and on top of the covers. My bare feet comfortably tucked under the same covers.

I blinked at Carlos' sleep-relaxed face as I tried to shake the dream that still clung to me. Ethan had visited me and a bittersweet pang remained.

In my dream, Ethan hadn't said anything to me, just smiled gently and held my hand. We'd been sitting somewhere, but I couldn't recall that detail, only the feel of his hand holding mine.

Something moved in my hair again, and I twisted to see what. Carlos lay with his arms behind his head, and his fingers tangled in the ends of my hair. I made to move away but saw his fingers delve deeper. Despite his closed eyes, he was awake.

I rolled toward him, trying not to stare at his chest.

"I dreamt of Ethan last night," I said softly.

Carlos turned his head and looked at me, his dark eyes fathomless.

"I'm sorry he's gone."

"Why? You didn't like him."

"No, I didn't. But you did. And I see how much it hurts you. I would do anything, even put up with another man in your life, to erase the pain I see."

I hated when Carlos said stuff like that. I wasn't emotionally ready to deal with it.

"Maybe that's why he came to you last night," he continued. "Maybe he was telling you he's okay."

"No," I said, shaking my head. "He was letting me know he's still waiting for me. He'll be there on the other side, ready to hold my hand."

Carlos remained quiet for a moment.

"I won't leave you like he did."

I scowled at Carlos and got out of bed.

"Given a choice," I said as I rifled through my bag, "Ethan would have stayed with me."

A hand settled on my shoulder.

"Let him go."

"How?" I said, whirling to face him.

My budding anger fled at the sight of Carlos standing before me without a shirt. His gaze traced my face for a moment, then he stepped close. My breath caught as his hands curled around my arms. I could feel each finger pressing firmly into my skin. With slow deliberateness, he drew me closer until I was flush against his chest. A tremble passed through him at the contact. I wasn't unaffected, either. I raised my hands to try to brace myself and win some space.

His thumbs skimmed over the skin of my arms, and his gaze fell to my mouth. Then I knew how he meant for me to let Ethan go.

My pulse leapt, and I struggled to come up with something to distract him.

"Aren't you supposed to say some stupidly sappy thing to win me over first?"

"I could tell you I'd die for you," he said in a low, measured voice. "But that would be cruel. I would never leave you alone like that. I'd rather die with you. So, even at the end, we're still together. Do you understand? I don't just want to be with you. I want to be with you forever."

His hand rose, and his shaking fingers touched my cheek.

"He may be waiting for you on the other side, but I'm here...right now...waiting for you."

He slowly bent toward me. My face flushed, and I felt a rush of yearning as his mouth hovered over mine. Conflicted feelings tore through me as he waited, watching me so closely. My attraction to Carlos was undeniable, but how could I feel anything like this right now?

I tipped my head down, away from the temptation and stared at my fingers on his bare chest.

"I know you're waiting. And my answer hasn't changed. I can't." I was still too raw on the inside to consider it. How many days had it been since I'd buried my friend? Now Carlos was asking me to let him go. Some part of me understood what he'd said. He wasn't trying to pull Ethan's memory from me, just my hold on our past. The hold that kept my chest aching hollowly and kept me from moving forward.

"I'll still be here, waiting, when you can," he said softly.

Why did he have to say that? The gentle press of his lips against my forehead along with the tremble in his hand nearly had me clenching my fists to keep from reaching for him. Then, he stepped away and left the room.

I groaned and hit the bathroom door in frustration. Why did

everything have to be so damn complicated? No, not everything. Feelings. Emotions. I hated them.

Grabbing my clothes didn't erase the feel of Carlos' skin from my hands. And shutting myself in the bathroom didn't stop my wayward thoughts. I was frustrated with how I felt, the direction of my life, everything. I didn't want to be alone anymore. But more than that, I liked Carlos. He was an amazing spar partner and easy to be around. Sure, his detachment might annoy me at times, but mostly because I envied it. Plus, I knew he wasn't really detached. He'd let me feel how he felt toward me. I braced my hands against the sink and hung my head for a moment.

He wanted me, and I wanted him. I really did. And that was the problem. Wanting Carlos felt like I was cheating on Ethan. I stepped away from the sink and turned on the shower before stripping down. The water didn't wash away the guilt for Ethan or the guilt for turning away Carlos.

By not accepting Carlos' kiss, I was sure I'd hurt him. Yeah, he'd said he understood my hesitancy and that he would be patient, but I wondered if he truly understood. I wanted him to understand. It wasn't him. It wasn't even Ethan. It was me.

I sighed and turned off the water and started drying off. Pulling on clothes over my damp skin was a pain, but I knew I needed to woman up and talk to Carlos and try to explain. If I didn't hurry, I'd change my mind.

Just as I yanked open the bathroom door, someone knocked on the outside door. Panic, not my own, washed over me. Something was wrong. I ran to the door.

Gabby stood there, her eyes wide, with Clay right behind her, looking concerned.

"Carlos..." she said.

My heart seemed to seize in my chest.

"Carlos what?" I grabbed her arms and pulled in her panic. Clay grunted as she sighed.

"He's a few miles from here. He went for a run. There are seven Urbat closing in on him. Grey is heading toward Carlos now."

I glanced behind them and saw the rest of the group in the parking lot, staring off to the south.

"Carlos knows the Urbat are coming and that Grey is, too. And he knows Grey won't make it in time."

"Wait. What do you mean in time?" I asked, focusing on Gabby once more.

"The Urbat will catch Carlos."

I saw red. This wasn't going to happen. Not again.

"Phone," I said, holding out my hand.

Gabby quickly pulled out her phone and gave it to me. I turned and searched for Jim as I started walking. Our eyes met.

"Keys." I held my hand in the air, and he threw them to me.

"Isabelle, stop," Winifred said.

"Make one move to stop me, and you all fall down," I said without pausing my progress.

I opened the door to the SUV and looked at Gabby.

"Call me and direct me."

I closed the door as I started the engine; then I wheeled the big boat of a vehicle around to the direction they'd been looking. Gravel flew, and the tires squealed when I hit the blacktop. A car honked at me because of my wide swing, but I ignored it and accelerated. Seconds later, the phone rang. I put it on speaker.

"Where?" I said, talking loudly so she would hear me over the roar of the engine.

"Keep going. I don't have a map, so I don't know how close they are to the road you're on."

I went from zero to one hundred in no time and kept it floored.

"You're almost to Grey," she said after a few moments of silence. "And they've reached Carlos."

"Where, Gabby?" Carlos is strong and fast, I thought to myself. He'll be fine. He isn't Ethan.

"You're halfway there."

My foot was already pressing the pedal to the floor. Ahead, I saw a bend in the road.

"The road's curving left," I said.

"No...that will take you further..."

I eased off the gas.

"Jim's got a map up on his phone. Keep following the road. After the curve, there's a road to the right. I think you'll want to take that. I won't know until you're closer."

I took the curve going sixty.

"Keep talking, Gabby."

"The right should be coming up."

I flew past the faded marker on a gravel road and slammed on the brakes. The tires made a god-awful noise. Thankfully, there was no one behind me. I'd barely come to a jolting stop when I slammed the SUV into reverse and added to the blue smoke hovering in the air.

"Got it," I said as I cranked the wheel.

"Go, Isabelle," Gabby said. "Grey's almost there, too."

I gunned it down the road. Something ahead and to the left caught my attention. Not far into the trees, men and wolves fought, a sphere of piled, thrashing bodies. I could guess who was at the center.

"Slow down," Gabby said. "To your left."

"Got it."

I skidded to a stop, threw the SUV into park, and shoved open the door. All movement stopped as both wolves and men turned to watch my approach. Carlos roared from somewhere under the pile of bodies. A wolf flew. Then another.

The rest backed away before Carlos could touch them. One wolf remained, his teeth sunk deeply into the spot where Carlos' neck met his shoulder. Carlos, on his hands and knees, tried to lift his head.

One of the men moved toward me as if to intercept me.

I held up a hand.

"Stop."

Whether because of my impatient tone or my angry glare at Carlos, the man halted.

One of the wolves transformed from wolf to man. He stood with his legs braced apart and crossed his arms as he smirked at me.

"Go ahead and pull a stunt like you did on the road. He'll die."

After giving the man the briefest of glances, I returned to glaring at Carlos.

"You read fiction and go for a run the morning after I pissed off Doofenshmirtz here? How did you not see this coming?" I asked, waving a hand at the seven men around him.

Carlos said nothing. I felt only a small twinge of pity for him at the moment. I was too full of the group's anger and aggression that I'd been slowly siphoning since I'd stopped the car.

"Fine," I said between clenched teeth. I stalked toward Carlos.

"Isabelle, go," he said with his head still hanging low.

"I don't think so. I have something to say."

I reached him and bent, gently touching his cheek.

"You promised."

Growls sounded behind me as the men realized I wasn't angry with Carlos. I grinned, then twisted to come up swinging.

Something flew through the trees and crashed into three of the wolves coming at me. The new wolf tore into those Urbat while I tore into the four who were trying to rip into Carlos.

My knuckles cracked and bled with each furious swing. I kicked out and solidly found my mark. The half-formed man bent as if in slow motion then collapsed to the ground, wheezing. Behind me, I heard Carlos move.

"Stay..." I ducked under a man's swing.

"out of..." I came back up with a jab to his throat.

"my..." Swinging wide, I caught another in his ribs as he tried to feint around me.

"way, Carlos."

The half-formed man fell. Suddenly, everything was quiet.

"Wouldn't dream of interfering," Carlos said softly behind me.

I looked around and found all the men on the ground. Grey was still in his fur, standing over one. Blood covered his muzzle.

"Thanks, Grey."

"He wants to know if you're all right," Carlos said. He reached around me and touched my fisted hand. I hadn't realized I was still clenching them. His fingers skimmed over the skin just below my bloody knuckles.

"I'm fine."

"Grey's going to the SUV and getting some clothes. Gabby says things are clear now. Before we go, you need to get rid of what's left."

How did he know my skin still tingled with anger and aggression? It wasn't much. I waited until Grey walked away, then moved further into the trees for extra protection before pushing it out. When I turned, I saw Carlos—really saw him—for the first time.

His face was swollen, and he had bruises around his neck. Bloody bite marks covered the base of his neck and his shoulders, his shirt was torn, and he was missing a shoe.

"You big, dumb fool," I said in a burst of frustration.

He shuffled forward until he stood just before me. I could barely look at his face. Fear was pummeling my frustration. Images of what could have happened tormented me.

He reached up and gently wiped his thumb on my cheek. Once I realized I was crying, it just got worse.

"It could have been you, too," I said.

He wrapped me in his arms.

"Never. I'll keep my promise. I'll stay with you."

I cried, and he held me.

One of the men moved on the ground behind us. The sound brought my head up from Carlos' chest. The man weakly shifted his hand from his side, bringing it up level with his shoulder. His pathetic attempt to lift himself landed him right back in the dirt.

My tears evaporated with my anger.

I pulled away from Carlos and went to the man. He attempted to right himself again and ended up on his back. It was the same guy from the road. Tilting my head, I considered him. There was no fear, only anger and resentment.

I squatted beside him, ignoring Carlos' soft warning to stay away.

"Don't like being my bitch twice, do ya?"

The man said something rude.

"Now, why would Blake send you after us when I told you I was coming for him?"

He didn't say anything, just stared at me with his jaw clenched.

"Maybe you didn't tell him. Or maybe he sent you because he doesn't want me coming to him, but I doubt that. He sent fifty men to try to catch us. So why only seven this time? Unless...someone's not being a good boy.

"Here's what I think. I think you lost your temper the last time we met and convinced these idiots it was a good idea to chase one of us down. Not smart. You're going to be in trouble when Blake finds out."

A sickening crunch cut off the man's laugh as his chest moved oddly, almost as if inflating. I knew humpty dumpty would be ready to move again soon.

"You're Blake's," he said. "But I told you, we're going to leave you with nothing."

Nothing. They'd meant to kill Carlos. And would probably come after Thomas, Emmitt, Luke...all of the men.

I stood, placed my foot on his chest, and pushed down hard.

Whatever little boney bits that were trying to knit back together, collapsed again under my weight. The man rasped in pain.

"Don't push me. You won't like it if I lose *my* temper." I lifted my foot. "Tell Blake he's wasting his men. He'll need every one of you when I get there."

Carlos' hand settled on my shoulder. I took it as a sign to go. Turning away from the idiot on the ground, I moved closer to Carlos and walked with him back to the SUV where Grey leaned, casually watching us. He was dressed, thankfully.

"You get to drive," I said.

The SUV was still running, and Grey had Gabby's phone in his hand.

"Everything okay with the rest?"

"Just fine," he said, moving to the driver's seat.

I opened the back door and stepped aside to motion Carlos in. I hadn't looked at him since he'd let me cry. A gentle touch under my chin had me lifting my gaze to his.

"Sit with me."

I nodded and waited for Carlos to ease himself in. Blood smeared across the back of the seat as he slid over. The sight of it worried me. I quickly got in and closed the door. Carlos sighed and leaned his head against the seat as he closed his eyes.

The touch of his fingers on my hand almost made me jump. Instead, I turned my hand so he could wrap his fingers around mine. He gave a gentle squeeze of reassurance a second before a faint rhythmic sound caught my attention. I looked down and saw blood dripping onto the seat from a bite on his arm. I wasn't reassured.

The drive back took longer because Grey actually obeyed the speed limit. When we pulled into the parking lot, everyone still waited outside. I hopped out and worriedly turned to Carlos. He slid toward me and seemed to exit with more ease than when he'd entered.

Charlene gasped when she saw Carlos, and Thomas wrapped a comforting arm around her.

"He'll be fine," he said softly.

Fine? Carlos didn't look fine. He had stopped bleeding, though.

"You two, go inside," Thomas said, meeting my gaze. "Help him clean up. We'll clean and load the car."

I nodded and walked beside Carlos as he made his way to our room. The back of his shirt hung open in two flaps. Claw marks created jagged, bloody valleys in his skin, and my temper flared at the sight.

When he reached the door, he opened it and stood aside to let me in first. Courtesy over injuries. I would have said something snarky about that, but my voice wasn't ready for snarky. It was still set on throat-closing worry.

Moving ahead of him, I went into the bathroom and turned on the shower. My thoughts raced to what I would need for Carlos' wounds. I still had the first aid kits, but I didn't think there was enough salve or bandages to take care of everything.

When I turned, Carlos stood right behind me. His shirt was gone along with his shoe and socks.

"Isabelle," he said softly. "Stop."

I looked up and met his gaze.

"Stop what?"

"Worrying." He kissed my forehead, then stood to the side, obviously wanting me to leave.

I hesitated, looking at the open wounds, drying blood, and coloring skin.

"Call me if you need anything," I said, lingering at the door.

"I will."

I closed the door then went to sit on the bed. Someone knocked on our door, but I ignored it. I couldn't deal with anything else. Not right now. My chest hurt just as much as my hands. And though my gaze was trained on my hands, I didn't see the dirty, bloody knuckles. Instead, my mind brought back the images of the blood smeared on the seat, the bite marks on Carlos' arms, and, finally, the hole in Ethan's middle. Life's fragility hit me hard.

Never had I felt so vulnerable than right then. My gift, the way people always seemed to like me, the way I always managed to come out on top, had given me a sense of invincibility that I'd never recognized. My hands shook harder.

I could die. Everyone around me could die. And why? Because we were trying to stop some guy from a power trip. Who cared? Let Blake have his power. This Judgement business was probably a line of bull anyway. Yet, deep down, I knew that was a lie. It wasn't bull, and we couldn't let Blake have any power. He was a killer.

The water turned off in the bathroom, and I stood to get the first aid kits. One had an icepack, which I cracked and shook. It cooled in my hand as I set the case on the bed. The door opened, and I turned to watch steam roll out along with Carlos, a towel wrapped around his hips. His gaze immediately found mine. His left eye was almost swollen shut. I lifted the icepack, holding it out to him.

"Thank you, Isabelle."

I nodded and looked away to grab the salve. The cap didn't want to unscrew, and the tremble in my hands didn't help. When I turned back to him, he was in the same spot, both hands at his side, the icepack seemingly forgotten as he watched me.

"I'll start with your back," I said, circling him.

Without his gaze on me, I allowed myself to wince at the gashes. As gently as possible, I soothed the salve over the cuts, big and small, then grabbed the bandages and tape to cover everything I'd treated.

After I finished with his back, I moved to the front. He tracked my every move. When he watched me like that, it made me think he didn't care about the cuts, bruises, and swelling as much as he cared about me standing just inches from him.

I squeezed some more salve onto my finger and gently spread it over a cut above his right nipple. The skin under my fingers quivered.

"Sorry," I mumbled.

"You have nothing to apologize for."

"Don't I? You went for that run because I wouldn't...I should have—"

"Don't, Isabelle," he said, lifting the hand that wasn't holding the icepack. He gently ran a finger along my cheek. "You spar to release energy. I go for a run. That's all that was."

I nodded and eyed the next cut. He let his hand fall to his side and continued to study me.

"You're still worrying."

"I think you need stitches," I said, adding more salve to a particularly deep gash.

"We heal quickly. By tomorrow, the shallow ones will be scars and the deep ones scabbed over."

When I had all the cuts coated, I grabbed the bandages and tape and started covering everything. He held still through it all. I finished with the bite on his neck.

"I don't see why anyone would ever want to be bitten."

"It would have been different if it were you," he said softly.

He was right. I wouldn't have tried to remove a chunk of meat with my teeth.

"I'll see how the others are doing," I said, moving toward the door so he could dress.

SINCE CARLOS' eye was mostly swollen shut, Winifred drove the car. Carlos again sat in the back with me. I didn't mind.

He kept the icepack on his eye and leaned against the door for the next four hours. I couldn't be sure if he slept or not. Winifred must have thought the same because she didn't try to make conversation.

So, I endured the boredom until my stomach rumbled loudly in the silence.

"We should stop and eat," Carlos said, making me jump.

"How are you feeling?"

When he lifted his head, I noted he was careful to sit forward before he tried to straighten. I hadn't considered how it would feel having those cuts pressed against the seat. He set the icepack aside as I studied his face.

"Better," he said, meeting my gaze.

He didn't look better. He looked worse. Purple-black skin painted his swollen eye.

His hand crept across the seat, and he tugged my pinky. My heart turned over at the playful gesture.

"Gabby says that there's been absolutely no movement since your altercation. We'll stop at the next place we find."

The next place turned out to be an ice cream and burger joint with outdoor seating.

"Forget lunch," I said when I saw the sign. "I'm going for dessert."

Everyone piled out as soon as we parked. I hung back to hover near Carlos as he eased himself from the seat. Once he was out, he stood there for a moment. There was nothing in his expression or in the air to give away the hesitation, but I was sure he had to be in pain.

"Why don't you sit, and I'll get us food," I said, waving him toward the tables.

He nodded and veered off that direction. I went to stand behind the rest of the group and stared at the board. A gust of wind blew past, and I shivered, recalling Ethan's comment about getting me a jacket. So much had happened since then, and the need for a jacket as we traveled further north had completely slipped my mind. I wrapped my arms around myself and studied the options on the board. They had ten different kinds of burgers, including a half-pound burger. I heard Emmitt tell the boy at the register he'd cover the order. Since everyone else was still deciding, I stepped up.

"Can I get two of the half-pound deluxe burgers? And can you add another patty to one of them?"

"Sure," the boy said.

Behind me, I heard a happy noise from Jim.

"Anything to drink?" the boy asked.

I frowned trying to remember all the times Carlos had sat next to me during a meal. I couldn't recall what beverage he'd ordered.

"Two colas, whatever you have."

The boy nodded, and I moved away. Did Carlos like soda? Turning, I walked back to the tables where he sat waiting.

"What kind of soda do you drink?"

"A cola is fine," he said.

I moved to sit across from him, but he stopped me.

"Come sit next to me. Please."

It took a moment to untangle my half-completed bench mount on the picnic table. Then, I walked around and joined him on his side. Heat radiated from him, warming my right side.

"So, what's your favorite, though?" I asked, continuing my train of thought.

"I prefer tea over soda and water over tea."

He liked water. And I'd ordered him a soda.

"Sorry."

He reached over and wrapped his hand around mine.

"Thank you for ordering for me, Isabelle. The burger sounds delicious."

My insides went hot then cold, flustering me. I carefully extracted my hand. Well, at least I'd gotten part of the order right.

"What about ice cream? What flavors do you like?" I asked.

"My favorite is butter pecan. What about yours?"

"Anything vanilla with chocolate and caramel mixed in."

The rest of the group started to come back from the window. Gabby and Clay were first and sat down across from us.

"You look tired," I said to Gabby.

She just gave me a weak smile. I glanced at Clay. His attention was on Gabby. So I wasn't the only one thinking she looked like she needed a nap?

"How much is she sleeping, big guy?"

"Not enough," he said without looking at me.

"Gabby, you need to start sleeping. You won't do us any good if you pass out when we need you most. They aren't moving, right?" She nodded. "I don't think they're going to. Blake's waiting for us."

She sighed. "I just don't want anything to happen again."

"Again?"

"Ethan..."

My heart ached. "That wasn't your fault. It was Blake's and his men. I've put the blame where it belongs. You should too."

Her gaze flicked to Carlos.

"And Carlos is a big idiot. He knows we need to use the buddy system now...don't you, Carlos?" I said, turning to give him a look.

"Yes, ma'am."

I turned back to Gabby. "Are you more tired or hungry?"

"Tired."

"Then, check one last time and go take a nap in the car."

"That's what I've been telling her," Charlene said, joining us.

"We'll be fine," Sam said.

Gabby looked at Clay, and a small smile tugged at his beard. I looked at Carlos' clean jaw in comparison. It had a hint of shadow to it. I liked it that way.

I caught that he was watching me study him and quickly distracted myself by watching Emmitt and Michelle pay the bill. The boy said he'd bring out the food as soon as he had it ready.

Another gust of wind brushed over us, and I shivered despite my warm right side.

"I'll be right back," Carlos said.

It was hard for me to watch him rise to his feet. He didn't have his normal graceful moves.

"Here are the sodas," Michelle said, distracting me from my observation.

She and Emmitt each held a tray. I half-stood and took one of the trays from her. We sorted through the different flavors until everyone had what they'd ordered. When I sat back down, I twisted to look for Carlos. He was just shutting the trunk of the car. He had something in his hands. I stood again and went to see if he needed help. As I got closer, I saw he had a sweater.

He held it out to me.

"It'll keep you warm."

He was beat up and probably hurting all over and he'd thought of me? Swallowing hard, I reached for what he offered.

The soft knit of a neatly folded brown sweater warmed my hands. I shook it out and grinned. It was huge. I looked up at him and eyed his shoulders and chest. I was so used to facing bigger opponents I never really realized just how big Carlos was. I put the sweater over my head, and the bottom of it fell to just below my butt.

I held out my arms and laughed at the drooping sleeves that covered my fingertips.

"This is great," I said. "How does it look?"

"Perfect."

I glanced up at him and caught a fleeting look in his eyes. Yearning. My heart skipped a beat in response.

"Come on," I said.

He followed me to the tables. Gabby and Clay were missing, and I was glad she'd decided to nap. Jim somehow had an order of fries and was devouring it, a handful at a time. The Elders sat together talking about the route we'd take since Gabby was napping instead of navigating. There was nothing to do but sit and wait for the food. And with Carlos' sweater covering me, I didn't mind the wait or the cooler weather.

Not only did the sweater keep me warm, it wrapped me in Carlos' unique smell. It wasn't something I'd committed to memory, but I recognized it nonetheless. It tickled my stomach and made it hard to breathe without blushing.

"Better?" he asked as we sat.

"Yes. Thank you."

It only took a few more minutes for the boy to carry out the first tray of food. We ate quickly, then got back into the cars.

CHAPTER FIFTEEN

NEW YORK WASN'T WHAT I'D EXPECTED; IT WAS ANNOYING. Irritation, impatience, and indifference surrounded me. And that was just on one of the main arteries leading into the city. I rolled my shoulders and shifted in my seat.

"Are you all right?" Carlos asked.

"I'm getting the itch to hit someone. So yeah, I'm good."

"We'll be to the apartments soon," Winifred said from the front seat.

I looked out the window at the traffic crawling around us and doubted it. So, I leaned my head back against the seat and closed my eyes.

It took almost an hour before the car turned off. By then, my skin tingled with what I'd absorbed. The indifference would have been cool if that was all I had. But the irritation and impatience infected me, too. It wasn't just the energy but also the moods seeping into me. It was like the slow PMS build up again. What took three months to accumulate back home, only took an hour in New York.

Pushing the door open, I thrust myself from the car and looked around at the parking garage.

Bethi was just opening her door and eyed me up and down.

"Not good, huh?"

"No."

"I thought you'd have this problem. You and Carlos should go take a walk in an alley or something. I'm sure you'll be able to find someone willing to help you."

I cracked my scabbed knuckles and glanced at Carlos, who was watching me over the roof of the car. After almost twenty-four hours, his eye was no longer swollen shut, but the discoloration remained.

"If you come with me, no fighting."

He nodded.

"We'll be back in a few," I said to everyone and no one as I strode toward the parking garage exit. The man by the door nodded to Carlos as we left.

Outside, the cold air should have chilled me. It was a testament to what I contained that it didn't. I breathed deeply of the metallic tang of exhaust and lengthened my stride until I jogged. Very few people paid us any attention. As the blocks melted away, the buildings took on a less polished appearance. I ducked into the first alley I found and slowed to a walk.

My breath puffed out, and I strained to listen as I walked from one end of the alley to the other. No one disturbed us. Stepping out onto the street, I looked for the next alley. It took twenty minutes to find what I wanted. Or, rather, for what I wanted to find me.

Two men stepped out of the shadows. Both had their hands in their pockets. Aggression oozed from their pores.

"Cash," the one said.

"Sure, I'll take some," I said with a grin.

I shifted my weight as I struck out with a kick to the man's knee. He surprised me by blocking with a downward thrust. We both pulled back and eyed each other. Meanwhile, his sidekick had moved nervously to the mouth of the alley. That was when I realized I was alone.

Crap. How had I lost Carlos? I needed to move this along so I could find the big guy.

"Why do you need the cash?" I asked.

Ethan would have shaken his head, but he would have understood. I needed to know I wasn't kicking some down-on-his-luck dad who had starving quadruplets at home or something.

"Why do you need to know?"

His aggression hadn't slipped to concern or desperation, so I knew there were no extenuating circumstances to prevent me from kicking his butt.

I let him have it.

FIFTEEN MINUTES LATER, I found Carlos leaning against one of the buildings across the street. My knuckles were bruised and my foot sore, but it was nothing compared to what I'd done to the two men.

"Better?" he asked, eyeing me.

"Much." But for how long?

"Want to run back?"

I nodded. I had a feeling I'd need to do a lot of running and hiding here.

We made it to the parking garage in less time than it took to find my marks. Bethi and Luke were a few feet back from the guard at the door. When they saw us, they spoke to him; and he buzzed us through.

"Come on. We'll show you to your apartment."

We followed Bethi up three flights of stairs and opened a heavy metal, yet nicely painted, door to a plush hallway.

"Here's your key," she said, handing it to me. "It's for the third door on the left. If you keep walking, we're around the corner a ways. Carlos has Luke's number if you need anything."

They left us just outside our door.

I shoved the key in the lock and turned the handle, opening the door to a spacious apartment. I did a quick walkthrough. Comfortable couch positioned in front of a huge TV. Treadmill behind the couch. Nice. Breakfast bar in the kitchen. Cupboards stocked with dishes and fridge loaded with food. Then, I walked down the short hall. Bathroom on the right. Bedroom on the left. That was it.

"One bedroom?" I said, staring at our bags, which were already on the bed.

"The rest are sharing two bedroom apartments. Jim is taking a couch in one and Sam a couch in another. They thought it would be easier if you were kept separate. Michelle said bigger apartments are harder to come by, especially short term."

"I wasn't complaining," I said quickly. "Just observing."

"Would you help me with the bandages? I think I'll take a shower then go to sleep."

"Sure."

And right there in the hall, he tugged his polo shirt over his head. I'd seen his bare chest several times already. Yet seeing him take off his shirt was completely different. I loved the roll of his muscles as he moved. He turned his back to me.

Carefully, I peeled the tape back and removed the bandages. Scabs clung to the deep wounds; however, the lighter abrasions showed recently healed pink skin.

I ran my fingers gently over the marks, unable to believe how incredibly fast they were healing. It took a few seconds to realize he was holding still for me.

"Sorry. You're all set."

He nodded, grabbed his bag, and went into the bathroom. The water turned on, and I walked to the kitchen to open the fridge. Inside, I found fancy sandwich fixings, including croissants instead of bread. There was some type of green stuff in a jar and carved, seasoned turkey. In the crisper were avocado and sprouts. Shrugging, I slapped it all together then took a huge bite.

Carlos stepped out of the bathroom in time to catch my groan. He stopped to watch me.

"You have to try this," I said after I swallowed.

I hurried to him and offered up my sandwich. His lips twitched then he took a bite.

"Whoa! Was that a facial expression?"

He chewed then swallowed.

"Almost. That was good. Is there more?"

"Sure. I'll make you one."

I walked away wondering why he'd almost smiled. Maybe he wasn't used to people sharing food with him. After watching werewolves eat, I could understand why.

He disappeared into the bedroom with his bag and came back a minute later to sit at the island and watch me put together his sandwich.

"How is it in here?" he asked.

I knew he meant the emotions.

"Not bad. I don't really feel too much of anything. A wisp of this or that every now and again. That's it." I slid the plate with the sandwich over to him and took another bite of mine. "So, what's the plan for tonight?"

"Charlene and Michelle are trying to find a way to contact that reporter, Penny, to set up a meeting. It won't be tonight. Tonight we rest."

Focusing on the sandwich, I considered the night ahead. Staying in for the evening wasn't new to me. But usually I did it alone, and my idea of relaxing involved hitting the bag. I glanced at Carlos, eyed his multicolored face, and didn't think he'd be up for that much fun. What exactly would two people do on an evening in? The first thought that came to mind had me blushing and turning away from him.

"Want to watch a movie?" I asked, walking over to the couch. I picked up the remote and surfed through the selection guide. "Oh, look. *Werewolf in London* is on." Giving him a quick grin, I turned to that movie.

"I like your sense of humor," he said, moving to sit beside me.

"Really? I can't tell. You never let anything show."

"Because you're not ready."

Sitting sideways, I gave him my full attention.

"Why did you say that?"

"I didn't say it. You did."

I recalled when I'd said those words—just before he'd been about to kiss me.

"Of course I'm not ready for that." My face was never going to cool. "We barely know each other."

"I disagree."

"You think you know me?"

"I know that when you need a break from people, you become more snarky."

"Snarky?"

"I read."

I laughed.

"And," he continued, "I know that when you start rolling your shoulders, someone's about to face a beating. When you eat, you focus on one thing at a time until it's gone. When you drink, you always lick the cup's edge before setting it down."

I did what?

"When you sleep, you curl on your side and tuck your hands under your cheek. When you're upset, you say things you normally wouldn't. When you fight, you hate hurting the other person...except the Urbat. You worry about the people around you and resent what you do to them. You think you need to be alone for the rest of your life and that scares you. You love stretchy clothes because you can move in them. You need to condition your hair in order to comb through it. You think makeup is a waste of time."

"Stop. How can you possibly know all that?" He was right, of course, but how could he know?

"Because I pay attention, Isabelle. Because I care more than you can imagine."

I stared at him for several heartbeats while everything he'd just said sank in.

"So, you do know me. And you think that makes us ready for what? Being engaged? Living happily ever after?"

"I think it makes us ready to see each other for what we really are."

"And what are we?"

"Meant to be."

His certainty thrilled and scared me.

"What if I don't want what you want?"

"And what do you think I want?"

"Biting...running...mating."

He smiled and shook his head.

"No, Isabelle. I just want you."

My heart stumbled. Carlos was right, I was afraid of hurting him. My one attempt at a date stuck out in my mind. All it took was the thrill of a first touch, allowing myself to feel it, and I'd nearly killed the boy. Ethan had known the risk. He'd kissed me, but I'd never let myself feel anything. I couldn't. It would have killed him.

But Carlos was different. I couldn't pull emotions from him or push them into him. What would happen if I kissed him?

My pulse jumped as I considered it.

"I'm afraid I'll hurt you," I said softly.

"I know you are. But you won't."

My imagination continued to explore the possibilities as my gaze drifted over his face, and my neck grew warm.

He inhaled deeply and closed his eyes for a moment. When he opened them, his pupils seemed a bit dilated.

"I've waited so long for that."

"What?" I said, afraid I already knew the answer.

"Your desire."

He stayed in his spot, his gaze devouring me. If he'd made a move toward me, I would have bolted or kicked him in the face. He was smart to wait me out.

"This is a stupid idea," I said.

"It's the best idea in the world."

"What if I knock you out?"

"I'll be the happiest, unconscious man ever."

"Gah!" I turned my head away but didn't get up. Why was I fighting this internal battle? Was I fighting what I felt for him, just for the sake of fighting? Didn't I want to know something more than that? Didn't I want to have someone I could spend my life with? I rubbed my face in frustration. I didn't want someone; I wanted Carlos.

With a slow exhale, I swallowed hard then turned to look at him again. Yep, he was still there, watching me with the same lack of expression. My stomach twisted and flipped at the sight of him.

Wiping my hands on my leggings, I gathered my courage and moved to kneel beside him. I wasn't imagining the change in his pupils because, as I stared, they grew larger. I inched toward him. My hands shook, and I felt lightheaded. What was I doing? How could I risk this? Him?

Carefully, I set my right hand on his left shoulder. He shuddered at the contact. My heart started to hammer, and I withdrew my hand.

In a quick move, he wrapped his hands around my waist and lifted me up and over so I was straddling his lap. Both my hands rested on his shoulders as I stared down at him with wide eyes.

Despite the shaking, his expression, though intense, remained void of any emotion.

"What are you thinking?" I asked, unable to go further without knowing.

"I'm trying to think of what I can say, what I can promise you to get you to finish what you've started."

His desperation made my lips curve and eased some of my tension. I was still in control.

"And what did I start?"

His fingers twitched at my waist.

"Just kiss me already, Isabelle."

Nervousness at hearing him say it aloud had me wondering if he'd let me escape. As I stared into his deep brown eyes, I realized I didn't want to run. I wanted to stay. I wanted to try. Slowly, I reached up and set my hands along his jaw. His pulse jumped under my fingertips, and the shaking grew more pronounced. Mindful of his bruises, I lightly ran my fingers over his stubble. He held still, letting me explore the arch of his brow, the slight bump on his nose, and the curve of his bottom lip.

My pulse raced as I traced my finger over his mouth once more. What would it feel like to press my lips to his? I desperately wanted to know. I leaned in, watching him as I closed the distance between us.

An inch from his lips, I paused and tried to control what I felt. I didn't want to drain him.

Carefully, I brushed my mouth lightly across his. A zing of excitement and need ripped through me, and I quickly pulled away to check him. His eyes immediately popped open. The pupils were extremely dilated, but very much human.

Reassured, I dipped my head down to try again. Setting my

lips against his, I explored the warmth and texture of his skin. I nibbled at his fuller bottom lip, and a faint growl rumbled in his chest. His hands, still curled around my waist, gripped me more firmly when I opened my mouth and licked his lip.

He didn't stop me or take over. He continued to let me explore one little nip and lick at a time. My skin tingled but not in the negative way I'd grown so used to. Finally, I pulled back and gave him a tentative smile.

When he opened his eyes, the pupils were far too large for his face.

"Does this mean you're ready?" His voice was rough, deep, and hard to understand, and each word he spoke exposed his elongated canines.

I swallowed hard and slowly shook my head. Whatever he was ready for, I definitely was not.

"Too bad," he said a moment before he had me on my back, his weight pressing me into the couch.

Before I could inhale a decent breath to tell him to get off, he buried his face in the curve of my neck. His tongue traced a wet path up to the little dip below my ear. I shivered and gripped his shoulders. His teeth scraped my skin there, and a rather girly sigh escaped me.

"Carlos, wait," I said on another breathy exhale.

His tongue blazed a trail back down to my collarbone, played there for a bit, then traced its way up the other side of my neck. By the time he nibbled that side, I was panting. He left my neck and pulled back enough to look down at me.

"Bite me, Isabelle."

Like a bucket of cold water dumped over my head, his words brought clarity to what we were doing.

"It's time for you to get off me," I said, giving his shoulders a slight push.

He dropped his forehead to my chest.

Why did that cause a burst of heat inside me?

"Seriously. Up now." I pushed his shoulders again, with very little effect. He wasn't ready to stop. I needed to make him.

"I'm going to start pulling and won't stop until I have enough strength to push you off me. Is that what you want?"

He lifted himself off me, stood, then stiffly left the apartment.

I watched the rest of the movie alone.

AFTER TAKING A VERY LONG, hot shower, I sat on the couch and brushed my hair while I contemplated if I should go and find Carlos. I didn't think he'd been mad when he'd left. Annoyed, maybe. Disappointed, most likely. But not mad. What was the point of tracking him down, then? I wasn't ready to pick up where we'd left off.

Yet, a small part of me continued to wonder if I was wrong, and that he really was upset with me.

I tossed the brush aside and drew my legs to my chest. I recalled our kiss and blushed at the memory. I had allowed myself to feel every wonderful emotion and nothing bad had happened. If Ethan were here...I sighed. He would be happy for me, happy that I wouldn't need to spend my life alone. Well, if Carlos ever came back.

I was just about to get up and wander around the apartment when a key slid into the lock. I stood quickly and watched as Carlos opened the door. His gaze immediately found mine.

The worry I'd harbored surged forward as he eased the door closed behind him and stood still, watching me.

"Are you mad?" I asked.

"Why would I be mad?"

I shrugged, unwilling to speak my doubts if there wasn't a reason.

He inhaled deeply.

"You're worried." Slowly, he approached me. "I've smelled your anger, your amusement, your annoyance, and even your fear, though it was brief. I've never smelled worry on you like this. What's causing it?"

I'd worked in an office full of women. Not only had they oozed their emotions, they'd also talked about their moods endlessly. It was as if feeling all of that emotion wasn't enough. They had to talk about it, and I had to listen, too. I wasn't about to turn into a female like that.

"Just thinking about tomorrow."

He tilted his head and studied me.

"Do you lie because you don't trust me with the truth or because..." He inhaled deeply again. "You're uncomfortable."

"You keep sniffing my emotions like that, and I'm going to punch you in the nose."

"Fair enough. Are you ready for bed?"

I nodded hesitantly.

"Are you going to make me sleep on this very short couch?"

I glanced at the couch. It wasn't that short. Well, for me, anyway. Carlos would need to curl up a little. But if I was honest, I didn't want him on the couch, so I shook my head.

He held out his hand, and I took it. Turning off the lights as we went, he led me to the bedroom. There, he let go of my hand and moved to fold down the covers. When he looked over his shoulder at me, I still hovered in the doorway, watching him. I wondered what he was up to. Did he think sharing the bed meant I was ready to pick up where we'd left off?

He motioned for me to get in bed.

Setting aside my concern, I crossed the room. Once I was settled, he covered me like a child, placed a kiss on my forehead, then turned off the light. In the dark, I listened to him walk around the bed. He lay on top of the covers, yet against me, and draped an arm over my waist.

"Goodnight, Isabelle."

"Goodnight, Carlos."

I listened to his breathing for a while, still thinking about the reason he'd left.

"I don't share feelings; I steal them."

Carlos remained quiet behind me.

"When I was thirteen, a boy asked me on a date. I liked him and knew from what he was feeling that he liked me too, so I said yes. I nearly killed him when I held his hand.

"Ethan was there. He pulled the boy away from me. Probably saved his life. But Ethan and I both knew after that...I couldn't be with anyone. So, I never tried. I had Ethan, and he was enough. He was my first kiss. He tricked me, took me by surprise. I was terrified and wouldn't let myself feel anything. I think he knew, and it made him feel even more sorry for me. I've always loved Ethan, but not the way he wanted because I couldn't."

I wiggled under the covers, turning myself so I faced Carlos.

"The things you're asking for, I've never considered. I don't understand relationships. They scare the hell out of me. And the idea of a relationship with you is even scarier. I have no clue what you're thinking because I don't know what you're feeling. We kissed. Then when I asked you to stop, you walked out the door without a word."

He reached up and gently ran a finger along my jaw.

"I left because if I had stayed, I would have kept kissing you. The idea of a relationship is new to both of us. I'll work on sharing what I'm feeling with words. And you can work on just letting yourself feel."

I sighed, letting my tension drift away, then nodded and closed my eyes.

"Isabelle?"

"Yeah?" I said, opening my eyes again.

"I want to kiss you goodnight."

"Okay."

He didn't go for my forehead, as expected, but settled his lips against mine. My pulse leapt, and I reached for his bicep. I almost pushed him away but stopped myself. Relax, I thought. Let go. Slowly, I did.

His tongue traced the seam of my lips, and I opened my mouth. He started to shake as he pressed deeper, playing with my tongue. Then, just as quick as the kiss started, it ended. He pulled back, kissed my forehead, and rested his chin on the crown of my head. I stared at the column of his throat. Dark whiskers already started to poke through the skin. I moved closer and rubbed my lips against the rough texture. Lying as we were, curled around each other, felt right...yet so alien.

Sighing, I closed my eyes.

I wore Carlos like a blanket. Sweat slicked every inch of exposed skin. Mine and his. At some point during the night, the whole sleeping on top of the blankets thing had disappeared. Along with his shirt. I didn't mind the missing shirt, though. I loved his corded chest. The sweat I could live without. The air, I couldn't.

"Too close," I said against his throat.

He growled at me like a dog defending its chew toy.

"Can't breathe," I said.

He gave me an inch. Cool air caressed my face, and I took a large breath. His arms, one over my waist and the other tucked under me, held me prisoner. Somehow, I knew he did not intend to let me go any time soon. That was bad news. I had to pee.

His lips brushed my temple.

"Good morning, Isabelle."

"Good morning. Uh, can I get up and go to the bathroom?"

His arms loosened around me. I lifted my head and stared at the ebony orbs that had replaced his human eyes.

"Everything all right?"

He nodded. When he blinked, some of the white of his eyes returned.

Unsure what it meant, I chose to pretend I hadn't noticed and slipped from the bed. I grabbed my bag on the way to the bathroom. I needed a shower badly. It wasn't until I stood under the hot spray that I realized how relaxed I felt. As if I hadn't absorbed a thing overnight, which was odd since I'd felt wisps of emotion the night before.

As I shampooed, I tentatively opened myself to what might be around me. I immediately felt the neighbor's anxiety and closed myself off again. The emotions were still there. Weird.

I conditioned my hair and grabbed the razor I'd set on the ledge of the tub. By the time I finished with the forest on my legs, the blade was dull. How long had it been since I'd shaved? Since before Ethan died. I lifted my arm.

"I am so gross," I mumbled, lifting the razor.

Why on earth would anyone be attracted to me? Most days I wasn't even attracted to myself.

Yet, since Carlos had laid eyes on me, he'd made his attraction very clear. What did he see in me? I shook my head, ran the blade under the water, and set it aside to rinse my hair. Whatever it was, I hoped I didn't lose it. I didn't like the idea of losing Carlos.

When I stepped out of the bathroom, I smelled breakfast. I carried the bag with me to the kitchen. Carlos manned the stove, moving a pan back and forth over the burner. With a quick jerk and toss, he flipped the omelet in the air.

"Hey, do you think this place has a washer and dryer?"

"They're in the closet right behind the entry door."

I glanced around the room and saw the double door closet in the living room. And sure enough, a washer and dryer waited inside. On the shelf above them, I saw a bottle of detergent and a box of dryer sheets. I started tossing the dirty items from my bag into the washer.

"Do you have anything you need washed?" I asked over my shoulder.

"I'll add my clothes when we're done eating."

I closed the lid and set the bag on the shelf before I joined him in the kitchen. He had two plates out on the counter along with orange juice and silverware.

"Any word from anyone else?"

"Most everyone is awake. Charlene reached Penny. According to Grey, it was a tense conversation. There's some kind of history between the two, but Charlene isn't saying much. Regardless, Penny has agreed to meet with Charlene to hear what she has to say."

"Just Charlene?" I asked, sitting at the breakfast bar.

"No. We will all go."

"What time?"

"Tomorrow morning."

He turned, and I was surprised to note his bruising had completely faded. His skin was once again smooth and unblemished. As I studied him, he eased half the omelet onto my plate and the other half onto his. When he lifted his gaze to mine, I quickly looked at my plate and sniffed appreciatively.

"What's all in here?"

"Ham, mushrooms, onions, and cheese." He sat beside me.

I cut into the egg, watched the steam rise, and decided to wait a minute. Carlos took a bite right away.

"So what are the plans for today, then?"

"No plans."

"Do you still want me to bite you?" I said.

Carlos froze mid-chew.

I was equally shocked. Where in the hell had that come from? Stupid hairy legs and self-doubt. It must have been eating at my subconscious. Hot or not, I forked a large bite of eggs into my mouth and then another bite while I prayed Carlos would move or say something before I choked myself on eggs.

He swallowed—it looked difficult—set his fork aside, then turned to face me.

"Why do you ask?"

I shrugged as I chewed and swallowed my mouthful.

"I just wanted to know if you changed your mind yet."

"I won't. Ever. If you're ready, so am I." He paused and studied me. "Are you ready?"

"I don't know. What exactly does being engaged to a werewolf mean? For humans, the guy gives the girl a ring, and if she gets pissed, she can chuck it at his head and tell him to get lost. What's the point of the bite?"

"Do you want a ring?"

"Gah, no!"

The idea of Carlos getting down on bended knee freaked me out way more than me biting him.

We stared at each other while I waited for him to say something.

"The bite is more permanent than a ring. And when you get angry, there's nothing for you to throw at my head."

"Probably a good thing," I said.

"Probably."

He sighed, and a hint of frustration showed in his face. Before I could see if it was directed at me, he spoke.

"Grey wants to know if we can join the group."

I nodded and quickly devoured my eggs. Carlos likewise cleared his plate. I found myself staring at his throat as he tilted his head back to drain his orange juice. He set the glass on the counter and looked at me.

"You don't need permission," he said.

"For what?"

"To bite me."

"I'll keep that in mind."

I stood and took his empty plate to the sink with my own.

CHAPTER SIXTEEN

WE WORKED TOGETHER TO QUICKLY CLEAN UP BREAKFAST THEN LEFT the apartment. Down the hall, to the left and around the right corner, one of the apartment doors gaped open. I felt the familiar emotions and headed toward the opening.

"I don't like it," I heard Thomas say before I stepped in.

"Sorry, we're late," I said when all eyes turned to us.

"It's all right, Isabelle," Winifred said. "We were just discussing Charlene's conversation with the news lady."

"Penny," Charlene said.

"Yes, Penny. The woman was insistent that they meet but then said she wasn't available until tomorrow."

Bethi caught my blank look.

"It's fishy," she said. "The woman practically screamed yes when Charlene asked if they could meet to talk but then became cagey about a time. She wanted Charlene to give her a number so she could call her back. Charlene insisted on a time before they hung up."

"I expected her reaction," Charlene said. "And it's nothing to worry about."

"It's everything to worry about," Thomas said. "The woman knows what you can do."

Charlene and Thomas shared a look.

"She does," Charlene said, agreeing with him. "And that's why she's willing to meet with us. And why, come tomorrow, there will be cameras ready."

"She's in for a bit of a shock, then," I said. I could only imagine how the woman would react to Winifred changing into a werewolf.

Charlene's lips curved into a slight, sad smile.

"She is." She laid her hand on Thomas' arm. "There's nothing to worry about. I'll have an idea of what she has planned before we even reach her."

"How?" I mean, I knew Charlene could control people, but could she read minds, too?

"I can feel the wills of the people around me. When they are consciously focused on something, it's in their will for me to feel."

"So you're reading everyone all the time?" Thoughts instead of feelings. I didn't envy her.

"No. I have to make an effort to read a person's will. I usually don't, respecting their privacy. However, tomorrow, I will be reading everyone."

"We should go early," Bethi said. "To keep an eye on things."

"I agree," Thomas said. "We'll go an hour early tomorrow morning, but we also need to check on things today. Isabelle, Carlos, and Grey, I'd like the three of you to go to the station now and see what you can feel and learn."

"Isn't that dangerous with Blake's men out there?" Michelle asked.

"It's not too bad," Gabby said. She looked rested for a change. "There don't seem to be many Urbat in the city."

"And those who are here would have to be walking right next

to us to catch our scents," Grey said. "There's too much going on in this city."

Thomas nodded.

"Right now, I'm more worried about Penny and the humans than I am the Urbat."

I didn't relish the idea of going outside or lingering near a busy news center. My skin would be crawling in no time. Bethi seemed to have the same thought.

"It's not going to work. Isabelle won't be able to stay out there for very long."

"Bethi said you're an emotional siphon. Yet, you pushed out your emotions before," Thomas said. "Have you ever tried to stay in a constant state of pushing instead of pulling?"

The possibility of what he said exploded inside my head. All I could do was stare at him in shock. If I stayed in a constant state of pushing, there would be no build up and no dangerous release. No need for fighting. No need to hold myself back. An ache began in my chest as I thought of Ethan and the future we could have had if I'd figured out how to push out the emotions years ago. I could have tried to love him like he'd deserved. Oh, Ethan, I thought. I'm so sorry.

Carlos wrapped his arms around me and turned me. As soon as I faced him, I leaned my forehead against his chest and struggled to swallow my grief.

"I apologize for upsetting you," Thomas said, clearly clueless as to what part of his suggestion had caused my reaction.

I nodded but didn't turn yet.

"I've never tried what you're suggesting. I need to go for a walk and see if it works." I lifted my head and slid out of Carlos' arms without looking back at anyone.

In the hallway, Carlos reached for my hand. The move was too reminiscent of Ethan and made the ache eating through my heart more pronounced.

"Ethan didn't need for you to love him in return. He loved you freely. No conditions. And he would hate to know you carried any regrets now because of him."

His eerie ability to read the direction of my thoughts annoyed me.

"I don't have regrets because of him. I have regrets for him. He deserved so much more."

Carlos tugged my hand until I stopped walking and turned to face him.

"What could be better than your love?" He pulled me close and brushed a thumb over my cheek as he held my face. "A smart man would welcome it in any form. Ethan was smart and knew what he had."

I exhaled slowly, knowing Carlos was right.

"Thank you."

"Anytime, Isabelle."

We resumed walking down the hall and left the building through the parking garage again. Outside, I shivered.

"I need a quiet corner," I said, setting out at a brisk pace.

As soon as I felt sufficiently warm, I stepped up to a jog. Following last night's path, I found a discreet place and stopped. Carlos halted beside me. When I glanced his way, he nodded.

I pushed everything out, and instead of relaxing the force to push out, I maintained it. It felt like I'd done a cannonball into a pool. The emotions that surrounded me couldn't touch me, and I floated in a blissful void. The bliss only lasted for a few seconds.

"This feels weird," I said.

Siphoning was a part of me. Not pulling in anything started to make me panic. Though I knew I continued to breathe, I felt oxygen starved, like a fish out of water, gasping for air. I wouldn't be able to maintain a push indefinitely.

I relaxed the effort behind my force to keep emotions out and once again started to feel the emotions around me. Relief flooded me. It was like regaining feeling in a sleeping limb. I immediately pushed out again, then relaxed the push to let a little in before repeating the exercise once more. Like treading water, I kept myself submerged in emotions but afloat.

"I think I can do this."

We started back toward the apartments. When we neared people, I kept an eye on their reactions. Most of them frowned and looked around. I wondered what they felt from me. But there were no severe reactions. No staggering or nosebleeds.

Everyone was waiting for us in the garage.

"How did it go?" Bethi asked.

"Well, I can't just keep everything out like Thomas said. If I push, I can't feel what everyone around me is feeling, which would defeat the purpose of sending me. But if I push and pull, like breathing in and out, there won't be a buildup to bother me or anything that might hurt someone else. It should work."

"And there are no adverse effects?" Winifred said, looking at Carlos.

"Nothing adverse," he said.

"Then, let's go," Grey said, motioning us to the car.

"We'll see you at dinner," Winifred said. The rest of the group started moving to the stairwell.

"Be careful," Bethi said before she and Luke followed the others.

"We need to stop and get a coat for Isabelle," Carlos said as he opened the back door for me.

I slid over, hoping he'd join me in the back. He did. He also reached out and threaded his fingers through mine. The feeling of his thumb brushing over my skin helped ease the lingering ache from Thomas' comment. Ethan would have been happy I was giving Carlos a chance. And with that realization, my remaining guilt vanished.

Giving Carlos' hand a slight squeeze, I focused on Grey. I'd continued to exercise my emotional purging but hadn't notice any reaction so far since he'd started the car and steered us out of the garage. Then again, I didn't feel much from him, either.

"Do you know where we're going?" I asked him.

Grey's eyes twinkled as he glanced at me in the mirror. "Winifred and Michelle are checking for a store, so we can get you a coat. After that, we'll go to the address Penny provided."

He maneuvered the traffic well, and once it slowed to a crawl, he turned into a parking garage that charged a ridiculous hourly rate.

"We'll walk from here," he said.

People crowded the sidewalks.

Let it in. Push it out. No one twitched or stilled. No one dropped or bled. In and out. I continued to siphon and drain with each inhale and exhale. Carlos stayed right beside me, probably watching me as closely as I was studying the crowd.

We hadn't walked far when Grey paused before a boutique. The mannequins in the windows modeled upscale clothes.

"They're never going to let us through the doors," I said, glancing at Carlos. He at least didn't look like a bum. No offense to Grey, but he and I didn't rise above the bum bar.

"They will," Grey said.

He pushed his way into the store. A woman looked up from the display she'd been dressing.

"Can I help you?"

"Winifred sent us for a jacket."

"Of course. Mr. Cole, correct?"

"Yes, ma'am."

The woman's gaze traveled to me.

"Winifred said you might need more than a coat." She kept her tone level, but I inhaled her feeling of agreement before I blew it back out again.

"Yeah, maybe something new would be a good idea." Where

we were likely going, I needed to fit in; and my just-from-the-gym look wasn't what I was seeing on the streets.

I turned to Grey.

"I don't have a wallet," I reminded him quietly.

He winked at me.

"Winifred took care of it."

"If you'll follow me, I'll show you a few options. Gentlemen, if you'd care for a drink, we have a waiting area to the left."

Grey and Carlos stepped away, and the woman and I drifted toward the sparse racks. For a clothing store, they didn't seem to have much. She led me to a rack with some cool black leather looking pants.

"My butt will never fit in those," I said bluntly.

She glanced at me, eyeing me up and down, not judging but assessing.

"Would you consider a dress or a skirt?"

I would probably need to kick some serious butt later and didn't want the world to see my undies. But I couldn't say that.

"I'm not much of a lady," I said instead. "I like being able to move my legs."

"Let's just take a peek at what we have."

I FOUND Carlos and Grey sipping cider in the waiting area while they watched passersby. Both turned to look at me as I approached. I wore a red-brown leather jacket, a trendy scarf, a comfy long-sleeved shirt, and the most awesome stretchy jeans ever. The woman had tried to get me into a pair of ankle boots with a heel, but I drew the line there and kept my sneakers.

"Wow, Isabelle," Grey said. "You shop fast."

I grinned at him. The sales woman had commented on my

ability to change quickly, as well. I hadn't wanted to mess around in the store too long.

"We're all set. She's billing this to the card Winifred gave her."

"Then we need to get moving," Grey said, standing and looking serious.

Carlos stood and moved toward me. As usual, I remained his focus. He didn't say anything, but I saw appreciation in his sweeping glance. Not wanting to blush, I turned and made my way to the door. Together, we left the shop and walked back to the car.

It seemed to take forever for Grey to turn out of the parking garage.

"Are we going to get anywhere in this traffic?"

"Not far, but it will cover our scent better."

We chugged along in traffic until we got close to the building we needed. Grey took the first parking spot he found.

"The station is a few blocks from here."

We got out and started down the street. Having a jacket made the walk enjoyable. Grey pointed out the building when we got close enough to see it. People continued to crowd the streets, and I found I needed to siphon and drain faster than I needed to breathe.

When Grey stopped walking just outside the building, I kept going.

"Isabelle, wait." He caught me by the arm and leaned in. "Not inside. We just need to read the people leaving the building."

"There's too much out there to read any one thing. I need to go inside." Worry surrounded him. "Watch and learn, Grey. It'll be fine."

I tugged my arm free and kept walking. Inside the building, I barely spared a glance to the grand lobby or reception desk. Veering to the right, I headed toward a bank of elevators. The three of us joined a group of five going up.

Once the door closed, I noticed a change in the other

passengers' behavior. One of the women started breathing quickly, a man reached for his cell phone, another started to sweat. Before it could progress, I inhaled lightly, then kept the emotions. It seemed to stop their growing discomfort, but it didn't remove it.

The panting woman looked at me. "I think I'm having a panic attack."

"It's probably just the elevator. Closed spaces get to everyone," I said.

She nodded slowly and seemed to get a hold of herself as she reached around me and pressed the next floor. When the elevator dinged, four of the five got off.

I turned to the remaining man. "We're supposed to meet with someone, but I'm not sure where to find her. Can you help me?"

Though the initial emotions I'd released were missing, he still held a hint of panic. I pulled that away from him and didn't release it again. He exhaled his relief and nodded.

"Sure. Who are you looking for?"

I glanced at Grey.

"Penny Alton," he said, adding the news station's name.

"That would be the twelfth floor. There's a directory just outside the elevator."

"Thanks. I appreciate it."

The man got out when the elevator stopped at his floor. After the door closed, I pressed the button for twelve. As soon as the doors opened, I stepped out confidently and started walking without glancing at the directory.

The man at the long desk glanced up at us and stood when we didn't pause. I stole his concern as soon as it started to surface, then his curiosity, and finally his indignation. He idly sat back down, looking as if he'd forgotten what he'd been about. I knew he still remembered us; he just didn't care anymore.

As soon as I was far enough away, I pushed what I'd siphoned out again. Two coworkers started arguing.

I walked down a hallway and used people's emotions like a dog sniffing for food. When I scented a flurry of secrecy and excitement, I headed for it. A few times, it was a person working quietly at a desk. I stifled a yawn and passed those by. Whenever anyone grew curious about us, I took that emotion away, held onto it for a bit, and then pushed it out as I moved along.

For the most part, we blended with the people around us. At least, I did. I doubted Grey blended.

I yawned again and wondered if I'd ever find Penny. Maybe she wasn't as excited about meeting Charlene as I'd been led to believe.

Finally, I located what I was looking for. Massive excitement and righteousness behind a closed door.

I knocked and, without waiting for an answer, opened the door and poked my head in. Grey's anxiety coated me.

"Hey," I said. "Is Burke in here?"

The woman holding the ladder turned to look at me in annoyance. "Who?"

"Burke Bently. Never mind, I can see he's not."

I closed the door before either could respond, then turned and started walking down the hall. The people in the room remained focused until I walked out of range.

Neither Grey nor Carlos said anything as we made our way back to the elevator banks.

"You can breathe now, Grey," I said once we were on the street again.

"What did you see in there?" Carlos asked.

"It was a fairly small meeting room. A man was on a ladder, installing something in the ceiling panel. I'm guessing a hidden camera. A woman, most likely Penny, was holding the ladder. The back of one of the chairs was off and on the table. No idea what for. And that's about it."

"Let me discuss this with Winifred and see if we should stay."

"I don't think I can keep this pulling and pushing up anymore, Grey. I'm getting tired. And if I stop pushing—"

"Let's go," he said.

The walk to the car exhausted me. I was yawning almost nonstop. The drive to our building wasn't much better. Carlos and Grey remained quiet.

Back at the apartment building, Carlos and I parted ways with Grey. Grey had agreed that I didn't need to be present when he told the others about the building and what I'd seen.

With relief, I followed Carlos to our apartment.

"Are you hungry?" Carlos asked as he opened the door.

"No. Just tired."

I kicked off my shoes by the door, then removed my jacket and scarf and tossed them on the couch on my way to the bedroom. It didn't surprise me that Carlos followed. I fell onto the mattress and curled on my side. Carlos closed the blinds and joined me, pulling me close.

My STOMACH WAS MAKING weird noises. It brought me out of my sleep enough to know I was alone. Frowning, I sat up. The clock said it was close to six. The wonderful tang of spicy food scented the air, and I heard faint noises from the kitchen. Bounding out of bed, I could only think of food.

I found Carlos in the kitchen.

"That smells so good." I walked up behind him and peeked around his broad shoulders. He was stirring beef, onions, and peppers. Reaching forward with every intention of stealing a piece of browned beef, I was surprised when he caught my hand.

"You'll burn yourself." He lifted my hand to his mouth and kissed the back of it in an old-fashioned way that made my pulse dance. Then, he took a fork from the counter beside him and skewered a piece of meat. He handed it to me.

"Thank you."

"You're welcome, Isabelle."

Spontaneously, I leaned against his back and wrapped my free arm around his waist for a quick hug. He tensed, and I knew I'd surprised him. Before he could make a big deal out of the embrace, I went to my stool on the other side of the breakfast bar.

"Have you heard from anyone?" I popped the bite of meat into my mouth. It was hot but so good, and I savored it. Grey had been right about Carlos' fajitas. They might just make it into the trinity. After all the fast food, burgers had lost some of their appeal.

"Nothing noteworthy," Carlos said, answering my question. "Everyone is staying in and enjoying some quiet time."

Another night alone with Carlos. I wondered if it would be a repeat of last night.

"Sounds good. Want to try watching a movie again?" I let the question hang for a moment. "Or we could skip the pretense and just make out."

He stopped stirring and glanced over his shoulder. Shock was plain on his face, but was quickly replaced by a look that warmed the room.

"Okay. Movie it is," I said.

"Isabelle." His voice was rough and full of warning.

"Carlos," I mimicked.

He breathed deeply and turned back to the stove.

"Would you like to go for a walk?" he said. "After we eat?"

"Sure."

I honestly didn't care what we did. After my nap, I was wide awake and ready to do something.

He turned off the stove and brought the pan to the island where our plates and tortillas already waited. My stomach rumbled in anticipation as I made up two fajitas. Carlos seemed less enthused about eating, spending more time watching me. So I made a fajita for him and set it on his plate. He took the hint.

We ate together in silence. I didn't mind it, but I thought him extra quiet. I wondered if my teasing had hurt his feelings. I'd told him I didn't know what I was doing relationship-wise.

As soon as I stuffed the last bite of fajita into my mouth, he reached for my plate. He still had half a fajita on his.

"You're done?" I was surprised he'd gone through all the effort of cooking if he really wasn't that hungry. Not that I would complain about it; dinner had been delicious.

"Yes. I've had enough." He stood with the plates and brought them to the sink. He set them on the counter and turned toward me.

"Let's go for the walk."

I glanced at the plates behind him. He hadn't scraped the plates, rinsed them, or anything. That wasn't like him.

"Um. Okay."

I went to the couch and grabbed my jacket and scarf. It was a struggle to loop the scarf the way the woman had shown me, but I finally got it, then put on my shoes. Carlos waited by the door the entire time. Though he was an emotional void as usual and didn't fidget in the slightest, something about him rang with impatience.

"Don't you need a jacket or a sweater or something?"

"No." He opened the door and gestured me out.

"Are you impatient?" I asked, eyeing him as I walked out the door.

"Yes, Isabelle. Very."

He closed the door.

"Are you going to tell me why?"

He held out his hand. I took it, and we started down the hall. I had to hustle to keep up with his long strides.

"I'm hoping we can go for a run."

"Aren't we already?"

He slowed down as we jogged down the stairs. Though I kept glancing at him, I couldn't read anything from him.

"Where are we going to run?"

"Outside."

I laughed at him, and the sound of it echoed in the garage. He pulled me toward the exit door, barely nodding to the guard there. As soon as we were outside, he stopped and turned to me.

His fingers glided over my cheeks, and he leaned in close to my ear.

"Run, Isabelle."

I jerked back at his roughened voice.

"Whoa! Wait. Is this like the last time? You can't..." I glanced around. There were still people everywhere. The guard watched us through the security window. "People will see."

"I won't change."

His shaking, fisted hands didn't convince me.

"And what are you going to do when you catch me?"

His gaze heated.

"Make out."

My stomach thought it was a great plan and started doing aerobatic maneuvers. Anticipation coursed through me.

"I want a head start," I said.

"I'll count to ten."

"Fifty."

"Twenty-five, starting now. One. Two..."

I pivoted and sprinted away from him, pushing people aside. My stupid grin helped keep everyone's alarm down. I pressed myself to run fast, then faster, using the emotions I accidently siphoned from those around me. Behind me, the sound of Carlos' counting faded.

What was I doing? This was crazy. Crazy exciting!

I gasped for air but didn't slow. My sneakers hit the pavement with resounding thumps. I turned a corner then dashed across the street, weaving between still moving cars. One almost hit me. I didn't slow.

Was he still counting? Had it been twenty-five seconds? I bolted around another corner, putting more distance between us, and spotted a little café ahead. I briefly considered ducking into it, but that thought came to a screeching halt when I was grabbed from behind and lifted into the air.

I squealed and laughed.

"That wasn't the reaction I expected," a strange voice said a moment before the man spun me around and hit me in the face.

Pain exploded. I widened my stance to keep from falling as my ears rang. My vision was grey and blurry, messing with my equilibrium more. I tried to shake the feeling free and pull, but pulling made my stomach heave. I gagged.

The guy swore and grabbed my arm, spinning me away from him. My pulse throbbed in my upper lip and cheek.

"I've got one," I heard him say. "She was alone but running. Get a car here, quick."

Like hell.

I shook my head again and pulled hard. His grasp slackened, and I almost lost my fajita but the pull worked. I'd gained what I needed. Clarity returned in time for me to see the man fall to his knees. I punched him in the face. Twice. Then grabbed the phone from his hand. The man blinked at me stupidly.

Across the street, someone was yelling. I ignored that and put the phone to my ear.

"Who is this?"

"This is Blake," a man politely said on the other end.

I saw red.

"Who is this?" he asked.

"Hi, Blake. Not nice to meet you. My name is Isabelle, and I'm out for your blood."

He laughed.

"So refreshingly honest, Isabelle. I am truly sorry about your loss," he said, becoming serious. "I hope we can meet, so I can apologize in person."

I clenched my fists and looked at the man still kneeling beside me. He was starting to look a bit too alert. I pulled again, taking some of the anxious emotions from the people starting to crowd around the café. The coppery tang of blood coated my mouth, and I spat.

"The human's death was unnecessary," Blake said. "We only wanted to separate you from the filth with which you've been traveling so we might discuss the future."

"The future," I said. "Yeah, we have a lot to discuss. And I'm on my way to you. But not with your guy here."

Carlos came around the corner at a run but when he saw me, he stopped and started to shake violently. Crap. He was going to go fur. I glanced around at the people staring at us from the café across the street. Not good. This would end with the kind of exposure Bethi didn't want for the werewolves.

"Gotta go," I said quickly, then disconnected.

I dropped the phone to the sidewalk, stomped on it, then pulled hard enough that the guy next to me slumped to the ground. Just as quickly, I pushed everything out.

Hurrying forward, I went to Carlos. His teeth peeked out from his upper lip as he stared at me.

"You caught me," I said, cupping his face.

He growled, not at me, but at my bruised and bloody face. His gaze flicked to the man on the ground behind me.

"No way, Carlos. You promised me a make out session."

His gaze shifted back to me, and I tilted my head back, offering my lips. He didn't move to meet me, and I couldn't reach him. We didn't have time for his hesitation. No doubt some idiot had already called the cops. They were probably snapping pictures. Carlos needed to find his happy place fast.

"Hey, I'm the one who's supposed to be playing hard to get, remember?"

I set my hands on his shoulders then jumped up and wrapped my legs around him.

"I feel like a frontwards backpack," I whispered before touching my lips to his. It hurt. And I was pretty sure he tasted my blood. But I didn't stop.

After a moment, his arms wrapped around me. His lips feathered over mine oh so gently, then skimmed over my hot and throbbing cheek.

"We can't leave him. He'll trace our scent back to the others," Carlos said against my skin.

"We can't kill him," I whispered against Carlos' throat. He shuddered. "Too many witnesses. Take me for a run. We'll get a taxi, then go home." I pulled back enough to look at Carlos. His teeth had receded.

His gaze drifted to those around us, then he turned and headed back the way we'd come. At the street, he didn't cross but kept going straight. When I saw a taxi over his shoulder, I whistled—my cheek felt ready to fall off—and waved. The car pulled over.

"Got your wallet?" I said in Carlos' ear.

He nodded and set me down. I got into the back and slid over for Carlos.

"We'd like to see some sights," Carlos said, pulling out a benny and showing it to the driver. "What do you recommend?"

I didn't catch the driver's answer. My face was killing me.

Carlos had the driver stop for an Italian ice, just so I could hold something to my cheek and lip. While he was paying the vendor, the driver quickly asked me if I was okay. His disinterest belied the question. No doubt he was just asking to cover himself in case I showed up dead on the news. So, I told him I'd run into an ex and Carlos had helped me.

The driver didn't ask any more questions as he showed us the sights.

IT WAS LATE when we got back to the apartment. Grey was inside waiting for us.

He let me escape to the bathroom while he spoke quietly with Carlos. I looked in the mirror and winced at my bruised face. I should have kicked that guy harder. Despite the Italian ice, I would be looking like a battered woman for a while.

"I have a bag of ice for you," Carlos said through the closed door.

I opened the door and took the bag from him.

"Thanks. Are we grounded?"

Carlos stepped aside and let me into the hall where I could see Grey still waited near the door. He wasn't smiling.

"Can you tell me what happened?" he asked.

I glanced at Carlos, wondering just how much he expected me to say. As usual, I couldn't tell.

"Um, well, Carlos and I went for a run. We were separated for just a few seconds, and when someone caught me from behind, I thought it was Carlos. Until that someone spun me around and punched me in the face. Then, I figured it out. With my ears ringing, I couldn't pull right. The guy called Blake to say he had one of us—"

"How do you know it was Blake?" Grey asked.

"Because I pulled again, knocked the jerk who'd hit me to his knees, and stole his phone."

"What did Blake say?"

Some of my sass left me as I remembered his apology.

"That he didn't mean for Ethan to die. He was lying, though. I told him we were coming and that I would kill him."

279

"All right. I'll let you two rest. Stay inside for the rest of the night." Grey left, quietly closing the door behind him.

I turned to Carlos.

"Yep, we're grounded."

Carlos wasn't amused. At least, I didn't think so.

"Come on, big guy. Let's go to bed. I'm beat."

Grinning at my pun, I held the bag of ice to my face and walked back to the bedroom.

CHAPTER SEVENTEEN

SEVERAL TIMES DURING THE NIGHT, A COOL CLOTH PRESSED AGAINST my cheek as I lay in the circle of Carlos' arms. Each time, his care brought a drowsy smile to my lips before I drifted back to sleep.

In the morning, I woke alone and stretched slowly. My face hurt, but it was nothing new and nothing to cry about. I'd been hit hard plenty of times in my life. And each incident was my own fault. This time was no different. I shouldn't have played quite so hard to get.

"Good morning, Isabelle."

I looked over at the bedroom doorway. Carlos stood there, dressed for the day in his pressed pants and pastel polo shirt. His hair was neatly combed, and he looked freshly shaven. The sight of him made me feel light and happy, and not just because he was holding a plate of food.

"Good morning."

Patting the bed beside me, I pushed myself up into a sitting position. He joined me and handed over the plate. Scrambled eggs and hash browns.

"I'm so glad you can cook," I said, loading my fork. "I suck at it, and TV dinners like to go straight to my butt."

He didn't say anything. I paused with my fork halfway to my mouth as I eyed him. I took my time studying his features, trying to guess at his mood since I couldn't feel anything, as usual. Something about his eyes seemed almost sad, but the set of his lips was slightly tight.

Four days ago, I would have thought his expression neutral. Now what I was seeing was the barest of changes. That I was really starting to know Carlos warmed my middle.

I set the fork back down.

"What part are you upset about?"

"The part where I took you outside."

"Really? Because I liked all of it. A lot. Until I got hit in the face. That guy pissed me off."

He closed his eyes and inhaled deeply. I took the opportunity to lean forward and kiss his neck.

"Isabelle." The warning in his voice made me grin.

"Carlos," I said, using the same tone. "Does this mean you'll chase me again?"

"No."

"Not even around the couch?"

His lips twitched, and I grinned.

"Did you almost smile?"

"Almost. Eat your breakfast."

I took a quick bite, chewed, and swallowed.

"You're thinking about it, aren't you. Chasing me around the couch."

"I love you, Isabelle."

My heart stopped then restarted with a different, faster beat.

"I saw you fighting in Ethan's bar and wanted to kill the man who was trying to hurt you. When I saw Ethan touch you in the field, I wanted to kill him, too. Then, I started seeing you for what you are. A fighter. I'm not okay with that," he said, touching my bruised face, "and I'm always going to want to protect you. But fighting is part of who you are, and I'll need to learn to deal with it."

I swallowed hard as he continued to watch me.

"Wow. Uh, that was a lot." As soon as the words were out of my mouth, I wanted to cringe. I was screwing this up. He'd just told me he loved me, and I couldn't say it back because I always hurt the people I loved.

I set my plate aside and pushed back the blankets to get to my knees. He watched me closely.

Swallowing hard, I wrapped my arms around him and hugged him. Just a hug. He hugged me in return, smoothing a hand down my back.

"You feel like home," I whispered, hoping he'd understand.

I turned my head, laying it on his shoulder. We held each other for a long while before I pulled back. As he let me go, he reached up and ran a gentle finger along my cheek.

"How is it feeling today?"

"Better than it should be. Thank you for taking care of me last night."

"Last night and every night."

His words made me warm. How could he make me feel everything like he did? Happy being with him, more loved than I ever had in my life, and sad on his behalf because I wasn't ready to bite him. I held his gaze. Why wasn't I ready? It was too soon. Too soon since meeting him and too soon since Ethan died. Yet, so much had happened. It didn't feel too soon. It felt like months. Still, I couldn't bring myself to bite him.

I looked down at my hands.

"I know what you want," I said quietly. "That level of commitment seems..." I exhaled heavily and met his gaze. "I still feel like I don't know you. I need a hint of what you're feeling sometimes. I feel so blind with you. Everyone else I can read. Not you."

"I see what everyone else's emotions do to you. I don't want what I feel to hurt you."

"So, you're going to hold yourself back forever? When you're mad, I want to know it. When you're happy, I want to laugh with you."

"Once you Claim me, I won't be able to keep it locked up."

"What?"

"When you bite me, you'll feel what I feel."

I frowned.

"So, the floodgates would always be open?" I remembered the few times I had felt what he'd felt. Emotions so intense they'd taken me over. How would I deal with that? I couldn't. Letting a bit out here and there would be fine, but if I had access to everything...

"You'd end up like my parents," I said, thinking aloud.

"I don't think so. Grey and I discussed this at length. According to Bethi, you siphon the emotions you feel around you. What you and I would have...it's different. We will feel each other in our minds."

Slowly, I shook my head.

"It's not a risk I'm willing to chance."

"I understand. But what if I told you we could try it, and if you didn't like it, you could break the Claim?"

"Really? How?"

He shrugged.

"There are several different ways. The point is that we could try."

I thought back on Bethi's conversation. She'd said mating was the only permanent bond.

He watched me as I thought it over. We'd already kissed, and he'd been fine each time. I could bite Carlos and know what he was feeling. If the connection made me twitchy or took over, I could say I wanted out. There didn't seem to be a downside, nothing to lose. A thread of excitement filled me.

"So do I need to light candles for you or something? Or just pounce?"

His pupils dilated and a shudder ran through him.

"Pounce." The word was already rough with his slipping control.

It amazed me that I did that to him. With a grin, I knocked him back onto the bed.

His shaking grew more pronounced as I set my hands on his shoulders and buried my face in his neck. I inhaled deeply, smelling Carlos. The urge to nibble at his skin gripped me.

A small, happy noise escaped me as his hands settled on my waist. He pulled me over him, so I straddled his stomach. It made it easier to run my lips over his skin, trailing kisses. His hands moved from my waist to my back, pressing me closer, until we were chest to chest. My pulse pounded with the need to bite him. I opened my mouth and scraped my teeth along his skin. He groaned.

I grinned at his response then gave him what he wanted, a nip on the neck. It wasn't as satisfying as I'd thought it would be.

He shook as I pulled back.

"Well?" I said, looking at him.

His arms tightened around my waist.

"More." The word came out a broken growl.

He wanted me to bite him more? I looked at the red mark I'd left on his skin. It was already barely visible, even though I'd bitten him pretty hard.

"Whatever floats your boat," I said, bending down to nibble his skin again. I trailed little nips down to his collarbone. Without a doubt, I was enjoying what I was doing and so was he. His shaking grew worse with each pinch of my teeth.

"Isabelle." The drawn out syllables of my name sounded pained. "Break the damn skin."

I pulled back in surprise.

"You want me to what?"

His arms wrapped around me, and he slowly drew me back to his neck.

"Bite me. Bite me like you're mad at me. Bite me like it's the only way you'll get free. Because it is. I'm not letting go until it's done."

I tried pulling back again, and he didn't budge. Instead, I turned my head so I could see him.

"You really want me to hurt you?"

"It won't hurt. I promise."

I continued to stare at him, doubting his words, even as the urge to bite him like he'd asked rode me hard.

"Please."

The begging won me. I turned my head and bit hard enough to draw blood.

His yell shocked me.

"You said it wouldn't hurt!" I jerked back from him, wiping my mouth while looking at him with concern.

He exhaled heavily and closed his eyes.

I felt relieved and relaxed and very turned on. I wasn't that turned on a minute ago. I wanted to kiss him but held myself back, waiting. What was I waiting for? My heart swelled with love for him. He was perfect. Everything I wanted. And so beautiful. Whoa, what? Carlos was handsome. Hot. Rugged. Intense. Nowhere in there did I think him beautiful. It was way too girly a term for him.

"What the hell is going on?" I said, staring at him.

Emotions continued to tease me, but not in the way I was used to. They weren't filling me. They were just in me.

"How do you feel?"

286

"I wouldn't know. You're in my head."

"I mean, is what I'm feeling causing any problems?"

"Yes, you're so horny I can't think straight."

He grinned. A full, show-me-your-teeth grin. It was sexy as hell.

"Is there a volume control for this?" I asked.

He closed his eyes again and some of the feelings gradually mellowed. The love didn't. That emanated with an intensity that made it hard to breathe.

I eased out of his arms, slightly overwhelmed by the new experience. He let me go and sat up, watching as I grabbed my plate. I began to eat the cold eggs while I considered what I was feeling from Carlos. I was used to sorting through a whirlwind of emotions, but this was different. The emotions were strong but not in a way that brought me to my knees. Instead, they wrapped around me like a warm blanket on a cold day.

His love was the easiest to feel and know. Then awe and pride. Because of me. Because I'd found him worthy enough to Claim him. He humbled me with those emotions. But behind them hid a layer of anger and pain so thick that it took me by surprise. Was he feeling that way because I'd messed up the bite? How was I supposed to know I had to bite that hard? I ate another mouthful of eggs as I blushed, thinking of all the unnecessary nipping I'd done. A slow heat crept up my neck.

"Why are you worrying?" Carlos said once again looking at me.

"Why are you mad?"

The anger melted away, but the pain remained.

"The bite didn't hurt, right?"

"The bite was perfect." He leaned toward me and kissed my forehead. "Do you need more ice? Biting didn't hurt your cheek further, did it?"

I shook my head, still trying to puzzle out the anger and pain.

"We need to meet up with the others," he said. "It's almost time."

I nodded and watched as he stood and walked out the door. He was more complex now that I could feel his emotions, not less. If I hadn't screwed up the bite, then why was he in pain? What had hurt him that much?

Forking the last bite of eggs into my mouth, I stood and made my way to the kitchen. Carlos was by the dryer, taking out our clean clothes. I'd forgotten about them.

I left my plate on the kitchen counter and went to the bathroom. Only my hairbrush and toothbrush waited by the sink. He'd already packed up his things. We were obviously not staying longer.

Brushing my teeth hurt. A few of my molars protested, and I eased up on the scrubbing. When I spit, there was pink in the foam, and I got angry all over again at the man who'd hit me. Blake had so much to pay for. I wished I could be a fly on the wall when the crap-storm we were about to create hit home for him.

After running the brush through my hair, I packed up my things and opened the door. Carlos was waiting with my jacket, shoes, and our bags.

"Everyone is waiting for us by the cars."

"We're not staying?"

"We're packed just in case. We don't know if Charlene's contact will be able to get us on the air or not. If she doesn't, we'll need to wait until she can. If she does, it would be better to leave the city."

"More long car rides...sounds fun."

A wave of love washed over me.

"Was that a mental hug?"

"Something like that."

My insides warmed, and I tried to send what he made me feel back to him.

"All right, big guy, let's roll. If we're lucky, I'll get to hit someone today."

"THIS TIME, Charlene will get us in," Grey said as we stood outside the news building.

I nodded, more than willing to let someone else take the lead.

People moved around us, keeping up with their everyday chaotic rush. Since leaving the apartment, I'd maintained my balance of near emptiness by siphoning and draining. In those brief moments when I inhaled the emotions of those around me, I got a read on our group. Anticipation was heavy, but trepidation was a close second.

Carlos stood behind me, his hands wrapped around my arms. I wasn't sure if it was a loving embrace or restraints. Either way, his touch helped calm some of the storm as did the gentle surges of love I felt from him.

Charlene and Thomas started out, followed closely by Winifred. The rest of us fell in loosely behind them. As a group, we entered the building and made for the elevators where we split into two groups.

"We'll meet on the twelfth floor," Winifred said.

Bethi, Luke, Gabby, Clay, and Grey stepped into the elevator with Carlos and me.

"Congratulations," Clay said quietly, looking at Carlos.

Behind me, I felt Carlos nod.

I was puzzled for a moment until Carlos gave me another one of those mental hugs.

Bethi's eyes went wide as she stared at me.

"Shut up..."

I gave her a crooked grin.

"Bet you didn't get a hand shoved in your face," she said.

"Will you ever let me forget that?" Luke asked.

"Nope."

Gabby glanced at me.

"It's strange at first, but you'll get used to him being in your head."

Hearing her say that relieved me. It was weird having Carlos in there. Not really in a bad way, just...weird.

"I hope so," I said.

"We're standing right here," Luke said.

Gabby grinned at him and leaned back against Clay.

"In your head is a good place to be," Clay said. He wrapped his arms around her and kissed the top of her head.

The elevator slowed and binged. When the doors slid open, we stepped out. The other elevator was three floors behind, apparently having stopped to pick up passengers.

We lingered by the elevator bank, waiting. I carefully breathed the emotions in and out. Bethi's ran all over the place.

"Tone it down, girl."

She nodded and immediately her emotions muted. They weren't nonexistent like Carlos', or silent like the Elders', but they were quiet enough that she didn't overwhelm me. She was getting better.

Behind us, I listened to the quiet conversation of the receptionist with another woman and the approaching click of heels. The doors opened to the second elevator. Winifred and Sam stepped out, followed by Charlene and Thomas.

A wave of panic hit me, and the sound of heels stopped. I turned and saw Penny in the hallway, her gaze locked on Charlene.

I stole her panic as she spun on her heel.

"Charlene," I said in warning before the woman took a second step.

"Penny," Charlene said. The woman stopped walking and slowly turned.

In an eerie display, all other movement in the large room stilled as well.

The man behind the desk laid his head down, and the woman joined him. Another man, who'd been reading the paper while he waited in one of the reception chairs, folded the paper on his lap then closed his eyes as if to take a nap. A maintenance worker, who was sweeping the floor with an extra-long dust mop, set the mop on the floor, then took a seat. The unnatural actions had me glancing at Charlene.

Bethi had said Charlene could control people but seeing it was scary crazy. I wasn't the only one affected by the display.

Penny's fear spiked.

"So much for not abusing your power," she said, anger shaking her words.

"I don't abuse my power," Charlene said. "I only use it when necessary. And you've made it necessary."

"Me?"

"Do you forget what I can do? I know you have a camera in the room, a voice recorder, a new lock on the door, and the police on speed dial. You planned to tape me doing something amazing and then turn me in. It didn't work the last time you tried, and it won't work now. That's not why I'm here."

"Then you're wasting my time."

"I promise I'm not. I have something much more newsworthy to show you. If you take me to one of your recording studios, you can broadcast live."

Penny narrowed her eyes as she studied Charlene. I could feel her mistrust.

"I don't have that kind of pull," Penny said.

"I do." A wave of regret and fear rolled from Charlene with

those words. I could understand her regretting her power, but why the fear?

Penny studied Charlene for a moment. Then a surge of the woman's triumph hit me, and I wanted to grin. She had no idea what she was in for.

"This way." She turned and started walking.

When she looked back and saw all of us following, I felt her hesitation and soothed it away. As we left the reception area, I noticed the maintenance worker stand and head toward his mop. Scary.

Carlos threaded his fingers through mine, bringing my focus back to our group as we entered the corridor. After yesterday's wandering, I didn't feel so lost when we made several turns before entering a hall with a few glass-windowed doors. Penny reached for one of the darker ones and opened it.

As she stood aside to let us in, she caught Charlene's eye.

"Someone is going to ask what I'm doing," Penny said.

"I'll worry about that," Charlene said to her then stepped into the room. The rest of us followed. It was a bit crowded.

"Isabelle, Carlos, Winifred, would you go with Penny into the studio to explain? I'll wait out here for whoever may come."

"I'm not taping you?" Penny asked as she shut the outer door.

"No. You're bringing the world bigger news than me, Penny. The news you were meant to reveal."

Penny was surprised and self-satisfied by Charlene's last words. Yet, there was still a layer of annoyance and frustration as she opened the studio door for us and led the way in. She turned on the lights, flooding the second room with a brightness that almost made my eyes water. It was a small area with a fake backdrop of the city hanging on the wall behind a couch. Two chairs were positioned on either side of the couch. The staged area faced the equipment inside the room, just in front of the recording booth window.

When the door shut behind us, I enjoyed a new kind of emotional silence. The well-insulated room kept more than sound out.

"I need one of these," I whispered to Carlos.

Penny's gaze drifted to me, and her eyes widened in recognition.

"Hi, again," I said with a smirk.

She glared at me a moment then turned to Winifred.

"So, what are we revealing?" Penny asked.

"The existence of another species," Winifred said, walking toward the couch. She set down the bag she'd carried and turned to face Penny. Carlos and I stayed by the door.

"What kind of species?" Penny asked, not moving to join Winifred.

Winifred glanced at me, probably wondering if I was really ready for the freak-out this lady was about to have. I nodded.

"The shapeshifting kind," Winifred said.

Penny laughed then grew quiet when she saw we didn't share her humor.

"Before I put you on the air, I need some kind of proof. I will lose everything," her gaze drifted to the booth, "if I don't have proof."

Charlene nodded to Penny then pointedly looked at Winifred. Penny's gaze followed. I could see her frustration with the situation as much as I could feel it.

"You have proof?" Penny asked.

"No. I am proof."

Winifred held out her hand and changed it to a white paw, then back again.

Disbelief and panic surged from Penny. I took both.

"I'm willing to demonstrate what I am on live TV," Winifred said. "And will answer your questions after I explain why I'm coming forward."

As if in a trance, Penny slowly crossed the room to join Winifred by the couch.

"Do it again," she said, staring at Winifred's still outstretched hand.

Awe filled Penny as Winifred's skin slowly disappeared under a layer of fine white hairs. Her thumb shrank back a moment before the rest of her fingers. A paw at the end of a human arm. It was surreal to see. Winifred didn't leave it like that for more than a heartbeat before everything went back into place.

"Incredible." Penny sat heavily in the chair.

The door behind us opened.

"We'll be ready in five," a man said.

Penny turned with wide eyes.

"Seriously?"

When the man nodded, Penny's gaze drifted to Charlene, who watched us from the inside of the booth.

"And you're okay with this?" Penny said, once again looking at the man.

"Of course," the man said. "It's breaking news. The public needs to know."

He withdrew again, closing the door.

"Have a seat," Penny said to Winifred. Then she looked at Carlos and me. "There's plenty of room if—"

"They will remain by the door," Winifred said, moving to sit on the couch at an angle to Penny's chair.

Behind me, the door opened. Two men came in to operate the cameras angled at Penny and Winifred. A woman came in and stood near some sort of panel. Carlos moved closer, positioning himself between me and the door. Penny patiently watched the booth.

I glanced that way, too, and saw a digital countdown in the window.

When it reached one, Penny turned to Winifred and started to speak.

"You're coming forward with some astounding information I know our viewers won't believe. A new species exists among us."

"Not new," Winifred said. "We are as old as humans. Here since the beginning."

"And what are you?"

"The most popular term is werewolf."

Disbelief and irritation wafted from the others in the room. I breathed both in and watched them closely. They continued to record, or whatever it was they were doing.

"You can't expect us to believe something like that without proof."

"Of course not," Winifred said, standing. Penny stood, too.

"You might want to move back," Winifred said.

After Penny withdrew two steps, fur sprouted on Winifred's skin as she began to change forms. It wasn't a burst like I'd seen during battle, but it wasn't the slow shift into a paw either. We were on a schedule after all. If this were a live feed like Charlene meant it to be, we needed to reveal then peel out of there.

Winifred stayed upright long after her legs shortened and recurved. Her boobs shrank as her chest expanded, so when her shirt split open with a loud rip, there was nothing but fur to see. Her pants caught on her tail, but she shook the material free before everything fully formed. Her pearl necklace burst apart, sending the little beads everywhere.

As the panic and fear swelled in the room, I breathed it in. For just four people, there was quite a bit of it. My skin started to tingle.

Penny's mouth had popped open at some point during the display. Seeing a hand was a bit different than seeing the whole thing.

Winifred dropped to all fours and stepped out of her shoes. She was completely transformed, now. I'd never seen a dog or wolf so big. She turned and padded to the bag she'd brought. The cameras followed her every move. She stuck her head into the bag and pulled out her white hotel robe. When she took a step toward Penny, Penny backed up.

"She wants to change back," I said, off camera. "All she's got now is her birthday suit."

Penny glanced at me, then at Winifred, before she extended a shaking hand toward the robe. Once Penny held the covering, Winifred turned away from the camera and sprang back onto her hind legs. The transformation back took the same amount of time.

The stunned Penny didn't cover Winifred's exposed backside right away, and Winifred turned her head to glare her overly large human eyes at the woman. The look motivated Penny. She stepped close and held the robe up to cover the almost smooth skin and receding tail. But she left the covering lowered enough to show Winifred's back.

After the fur disappeared, Winifred threaded her arms through the sleeves and cinched the robe before she turned and sat.

It took Penny a few moments to do the same. Her stunned expression had me grinning while Winifred waited patiently for the first question.

"Are you dangerous? How many of you are there? Was that dog attack earlier this year one of you?" The rapid questions flew from Penny before she took a calming breath then asked, "Why are you coming forward now?"

"I've come forward because we are all in danger. We are not the only species hiding within the human population. There is another species, Urbat, who are very similar to us in appearance but not in nature. They would see the human population devastated."

"Urbat," Penny said slowly as if testing the word. "Why do they want our population devastated?"

"Because your numbers are a threat to their goal. They want to rule. The population, the planet, everything."

"What are we supposed to do?"

A very muted knock on the window startled Penny. Winifred and I both looked over and saw Gabby motioning for us to hurry up.

"Our time here is over. The Urbat are coming for us because we've shared what they didn't want us to. Find Blake Torrin, their leader. Cut off his connections. He's everywhere and has enough money to do much damage."

Winifred stood and grabbed her bag.

"How are we supposed to tell you apart from the Urbat?" Penny said, standing.

"There isn't much difference. Only the nails. Ours are grey, theirs are black. Good luck, Penny."

Winifred stepped toward us, ignoring the cameras that followed her. Carlos opened the door, and I quickly stepped out. The emotions in the booth were thick. I pulled as much as I could.

"How close?" I asked Gabby.

"Two are in the building."

"Isabelle, I need you to lead," Charlene said. "I need to maintain my hold until we are out of the building."

"Perfect," I said with a nod. "Gabby, Clay, and Grey can ride down with Carlos and me. I'll see you on the bottom, whole and healthy," I said to Bethi, pulling away her fear.

She nodded.

Our small group struck out the door, the rest following. The people we passed in the halls and open workspaces watched us, but no one moved to stop us. The emotions were a blend of disbelief and curiosity.

When we reached the elevator bank, the main part of the group hung back near the reception desk while we took the first elevator that opened. As soon as Gabby was in, she ran her hand down the first twelve floors.

"Um..." I gave her a questioning look.

"They're right here," she said as the doors closed and the elevator started to descend.

"What do you mean?"

"They're standing right in front of us. On one of the floors."

I looked at Grey.

"Tell Charlene to hold the other elevators so the Urbat can't jump onto one."

"Done."

I stared at the doors with Gabby as we slowed. Clay nudged her behind him. Grey made to step forward so he was at the front.

"Stay by Gabby," I said. "There are only two, and I need the fight." Too many emotions were floating around the building. As we descended, I absorbed mostly fear and suspicion.

The door slid open. Two people stood waiting.

"Not this elevator," Carlos said, holding up a hand when they would have entered.

Puzzled, the man and woman stepped back; and the door slid closed.

We checked each floor down to the third. Before the doors glided open, I knew we'd finally found the two we were looking for. I felt the impatience and anger rolling off them.

"Get ready," I said.

The doors slid open to reveal two men standing side by side. On the floor behind them lay a bloody security guard. The rest of the area near the elevators was empty.

"Hello, boys," I said with a smile a second before I stepped forward and planted my fist in the right one's face. His head snapped back, but he quickly brought it forward and growled at me.

"Which one are you? The dreamer or the fighter?"

I hit him again. The blow drove him back a step, spiking his anger.

"Which do you think I am?"

I ducked under his next swing and danced around him so he was further from the elevator. Not that he noticed. He dove for me, and I stepped back several more feet.

Carlos didn't touch the other man. Instead, he dodged the blows and neatly maneuvered him away from the elevators as well.

"Let the doors close," he said to Grey.

I could have hugged Carlos.

As soon as they shut, I pushed. The men fell to their knees. Carlos hit his opponent hard enough to knock him out, then turned and knocked out mine before I could protest.

"We need to move. The rest are coming down. Charlene says police are coming."

He pulled me toward the stairwell, and we raced down two flights of stairs. It was good to get my heart pumping and relieve some of the lingering tension.

On the main floor, we burst into the lobby and complete chaos. Clueless visitors to the building stood in frozen panic as police poured in through the front doors. Gabby, Clay, and Grey had almost made it to the exit.

"No one leaves!" one of the uniformed men shouted.

I glanced at Carlos, wondering how the heck we'd get out of there. He reached for my hand, and I gladly held on. He pulled me close to his side as someone shoved past us. The police were using their shields to push people back into the room. People began to panic and shove against the barriers, causing a ripple effect of jostling bodies. Carlos was my rock, my mountain shelter. No one touched me. Yet, despite his physical protection, the emotions of everyone in the room were getting to me. I started pulling and pushing emotions, just to keep from going under.

Across the room, the elevator doors opened, and Charlene stepped out. All motion stopped. Just froze.

She walked forward, weaving her way between the bodies. The rest of her group slowly followed. Carlos started leading me through the crowd as well.

"We are not the ones to fear," Charlene said, her voice carrying the length of the room. "The ones you seek are on the third floor."

She continued to move toward the door, joining Grey, Clay, and Gabby. A few of the people around us slowly started to move toward the exit, too. The police and security remained stationary.

As soon as we cleared the doors, everything inside went back to normal speed. We walked among the crowd of those who also sought to escape the madness. As we walked, I breathed in and out, barely sampling the emotions around me.

On the sidewalks, people were stopped, staring down at their phones or other devices. Disbelief ran rampant.

"They will discredit what they saw," I said, walking beside Winifred. Oddly, no one seemed to notice her walking around in a robe.

"They might have. But they now have two Urbat," Charlene said.

I felt her disquiet at the thought. Was she imagining what the government would do to them? I was. Because, since the day I'd figured out what I could do, I'd wondered what would happen to me if the world knew. I shivered.

CHAPTER EIGHTEEN

"W̲H̲A̲T̲ ̲D̲O̲ ̲Y̲O̲U̲ ̲S̲E̲E̲,̲ G̲A̲B̲B̲Y̲?" W̲I̲N̲I̲F̲R̲E̲D̲ ̲S̲A̲I̲D̲.

We walked together in a cluster—the same arrangement we used for practices—toward our vehicles that we'd parked several blocks away.

"Mass movement in their facility to the north. So many are fleeing it. I see Olivia's spark moving too."

"Keep an eye on her," Bethi said.

Gabby nodded.

"So what now?" I asked.

"We wait and see where they take Olivia and go after her," Bethi said. "She's the last of us."

"And when we find her?"

We entered the parking garage, and my last word echoed around us.

"The Taupe Lady has been a little vague on that part."

The who?

"But I'm still having dreams and learning. By the time we find Olivia, I hope I'll know more."

I didn't like the sound of that. It was a huge maybe. I could see Bethi didn't like it, either.

"For now, I think it's safe to head back to the apartments," Charlene said.

Carlos and I went to the car. This time Grey and Jim joined us. As soon as Jim settled into the front seat, he turned to Grey.

"Think we can stop somewhere to eat? Our fridge is cleaned out."

If their food supply had been like ours, I didn't see how that was possible.

"Where do you put it all?" I said.

"In my stomach." He winked at me, which earned the bottom of his seat a nudge from Carlos.

"Nice bruise, by the way," Jim said, studying my face. "What's the other guy look like?"

"He's still breathing," I said.

Jim grinned then faced forward.

Grey pulled out of the parking garage, stopping to pay before joining the slow stream of traffic.

"Gabby says Olivia is moving," Grey said. "She thinks a car maybe."

"What direction?"

"So far, north."

I nodded and hoped we wouldn't need to follow her north. It was cold enough here.

Grey turned a familiar corner and pulled toward the garage door. The security guard opened the door and waited while our three vehicles drove in.

The security guard's gaze stayed on Winifred as she got out. Because of the robe she was wearing, she showed quite a bit of leg in the process.

"Excuse me, ma'am," the older man said, looking at her.

I grinned at his emotion and waved everyone to keep moving.

"We'll see you upstairs, Winifred," I said.

Sam frowned at me and lingered enough that he walked beside me.

The guard watched us leave, making no move to say anything more to Winifred.

"Why are we just leaving her?" Sam asked as he stepped into the stairwell.

The door shut behind us, and I turned to peek out the narrow security window. The guard was slowly walking toward Winifred.

"Because he's sweet on her. And worried that she's walking around in a robe," I said quietly.

"Sweet?" Sam said.

I glanced at him when I felt his unease.

"As Elders we can't—"

"Hush. Every woman wants to know she's pretty. Winifred just exposed herself on national TV. Let her have this moment."

I watched the man speak, though I couldn't hear what he said. Winifred blushed, smiled, said a few words to the man, and left him with a small wave. She caught me grinning at her through the door.

"Time to go," I said.

When I spun around, ready to sprint up the stairs, I almost took out Carlos. He moved aside and followed me up.

It was a relief when he closed our apartment door behind us.

"Well, that was an exciting morning. What should we do this afternoon to top it?"

"Rest," Carlos said.

I wrinkled my nose and walked toward the fridge.

"Boring. What are you going to make me for lunch?"

"What would you like?" he asked from just behind me.

Since leaving the building that morning, I'd felt very little from him through our connection. Now, however, it surged forward. His complete devotion wrapped me in a mental blanket.

"What are my options?"

His hands settled on my shoulders.

"Burgers, pizza, cereal?"

I grinned and slowly turned. His gaze found and held mine.

"You speak my language," I said.

He gently touched my face.

"How long will it take for this to fade?"

I shrugged.

"I dunno. A week. Maybe a bit more. Why?"

"Because I want to kiss you."

My pulse leapt.

"So kiss me."

He shook his head slowly.

"I won't hurt you."

I put on a fake pout, and he swatted my butt.

"Hey," I said. "What happened to not hurting me?"

"Go sit, and I'll cook for you."

I went to the couch and turned on the TV. A news feed ran on the bottom.

"Check this out," I said as I read it.

Carlos closed the refrigerator and came to stand beside me.

Live air interruption causes widespread speculation. Are werewolves real? Tune in at 10.

"Well, we seem to have gotten the attention Bethi wanted," I said, lifting the remote to check other stations. Similar messages displayed on several of the channels. One mentioned Blake by name and had a phone number for anyone to call with his whereabouts.

Carlos drifted away from me. While I continued to watch the coverage, he made burgers.

"Crap," I said when one of the stations cut over from the regular programming with images of Carlos hitting one of the Urbat in the head. The angle was from behind the Urbat so the camera caught me too. Full face.

Carlos came to stand by me again. We watched the replay together as the men fell to their knees, and Carlos knocked them both out. The screen changed to close ups of both of our faces.

"Well, the good news is that I'm barely recognizable thanks to the bruise and swelling."

"Grey and Winifred are coming to watch."

A second later, the door opened. I kept my eyes glued to the TV. Someone had obviously gone through the security footage. In addition to the close ups of Carlos and me, there were grainy images of Gabby, Luke, and Sam. Clay was fairly ambiguous because of his hair, and Bethi often walked with her head down. Somehow, each image only managed to catch the back of Grey's head, and he consistently blocked any clear image of Charlene.

Well, that's convenient for her, I thought.

"Perhaps we should leave New York," Winifred said.

"We don't know where we'd be going yet," I said. "I think we should hole up, let this blow over a little bit, and give Gabby a chance to figure out where Olivia is headed and Bethi a chance to dream some answers."

"I think Isabelle is right," Grey said. "We are safer here than driving around out there."

Winifred sighed heavily and nodded.

"Reach out to everyone, Grey, and let them know of the aftermath of what we've done. We need to keep our people safe."

He nodded as she stood and walked toward the door.

"I'll speak with Bethi and see if she has any guesses where we might go from here if she doesn't receive any new information from her dreams."

Grey ate burgers with us as we continued to watch the news stream. When he finished, he left to check on the others. I didn't move from the couch.

Reporters took to the streets, asking random people what they thought of the day's revelation. Some were still unaware and showed their shock. Many claimed it was a hoax, as I'd anticipated. That, in turn, led to several very detailed analyses done by "experts" on the live footage of Winifred shifting.

"How detailed can this report be if it was done in just a few hours?" I said under my breath as I listened to the current analyst claiming Winifred's change to be a hoax.

I wanted to applaud the news anchor when she asked, "If this is a hoax, why then is there a large scale search being done for Blake Torrin, the named Urbat leader?"

They continued their debate for several minutes before the station cut to commercials.

"This is kind of fun," I said, standing to get myself a glass of water. "Who would have thought mere minutes of air time could turn into hours of speculation? Do you want something to drink?"

"No, thank you."

I went to the cupboard, grabbed a glass, and filled it at the faucet.

"You haven't said what you think of everything," I said, turning off the water. I took a drink as I turned and almost spit water all over Carlos.

I swallowed quickly and scowled at him.

"You've got to stomp when you move around. You're going to kill me with this sneaking."

"I like surprising you."

"Really. Why is that?"

"The surge of adrenaline," he inhaled deeply, "changes your scent."

"Um, I'm guessing in a good way?"

"Yes."

"Hmm. Well, you're just going to have to find a different way to make your sniffer happy because scaring the daylights out of me for the rest of our lives isn't going to cut it."

He stole my glass and took a drink before handing it back.

"The rest of our lives. I like the sound of that."

"Of course you do," I said, moving away from him. "Because you like how I smell."

"And move," he said.

I exaggerated my walk and heard him make a small, pained noise.

"Come on, big guy. Let's snuggle."

He made it to the couch before I did.

Barely containing my smile, I curled up against his side and laid my head on his shoulder. We watched the news like that for almost an hour. Most of our faces were displayed, but our poster child remained Winifred.

"What's everyone else saying about all of this?"

Carlos was quiet a moment before he answered.

"Bethi is freaking out. Grey's words, not mine. Gabby is quietly watching the Urbat movement, which appears uncoordinated, and Michelle is on the phone with her lawyer, seeing what she can do to help Bethi."

"Why's Michelle trying to help Bethi? They didn't get a good image of her."

"Bethi's mom recognized her and called the station. Bethi can't reach her mom, now."

My heart went out to Bethi.

"Let's have them over for dinner. We can order takeout. Pizza."

Carlos nodded.

A few minutes later, someone knocked on the door.

Carlos had just stood to answer it when it burst inward. A sobbing Bethi flew toward me.

I caught her in my arms and held her tight, pulling away the worst of her emotions until she breathed normally again.

"You can hit me all night long," Luke said. "Thank you." His hair stood out in disarray like he'd been running his hands through it in frustration for the last hour.

"No problem," I said over Bethi's head. I tried to ease away from her hug. "Hey, what do we want on our pizzas?"

"Valium," Bethi said. "Lots of it."

"Michelle has the connections to help find your mum," Luke said. "Trust her."

Bethi nodded despondently.

"Could you manage to hug *me* for a while?" he said, still watching her.

Her lips twitched, and she finally loosened her hold on me. My skin felt tight and my stomach full, as if I'd just eaten.

Carlos and I looked at each other as the other two went to sit at the breakfast bar and find pizza places in the phonebook.

"Want to go for a quick run?" he asked.

"Can we?"

"We don't have a choice, do we?"

I shook my head.

Bethi looked up from the phonebook as I grabbed my jacket.

"I'm sorry, Isabelle."

"Nah, don't be. I'll get rid of this, then come back for seconds in a bit."

She gave me a weak smile.

"And I like extra cheese on my pizza. None of that deep dish crap, though. I want the toppings to overpower the dough." I slipped on my shoes as I spoke.

"Got it," she said.

CARLOS and I ran for a long while. My breath gusted out under the streetlights. We wove our way through the streets, sticking to the nicer neighborhoods. Whenever I found a quiet spot, I pushed out some of the emotion I carried. We kept moving until a bakery's display window had me slowing.

"Something catch your eye?" Carlos said.

I nodded and pointed, unable to speak normally.

He glanced at the decadent chocolate mousse tuxedo cake decorated with artistic dark and white chocolate shavings and drizzle.

When his gaze returned to me, I felt his love and his need to make me happy.

"All right. Let's go in."

"I'll stay out here. My face was on TV more than yours, and with the bruise, I'm hard to miss."

"Stay put."

"Bring me cake, and I will."

He nodded and stepped inside. Through the glass, I watched him approach the counter. I stepped back and turned away as he pointed to the cake in the window. The woman looked down at the register as she said something to him. Carlos frowned and said something back. Too bad I couldn't read lips.

A sliver of frustration poked my mind. It wasn't my own. What could possibly frustrate Carlos?

He turned, without my cake in hand, and walked back out the door.

"Um, you're missing something pretty important, buddy."

"They take orders for their cakes. They don't have any premade."

"That's bull."

More frustration crept in, and I realized just how much he'd wanted to get me that cake.

"It's all right. Cake's overrated. I would have ended up splitting my new stretchy jeans."

Disappointment filed in with the frustration.

"You're just a barrel of emotions tonight," I said, stepping close to him and wrapping my arms around his waist. "What else can we throw in there? I know. How about some anticipation? You can chase me again."

"No."

I'd hoped he'd say yes.

"Why not? Now that I bit you, I'm not a challenge? It's no fun anymore?"

"Oh, it'd be fun." He leaned forward and gently kissed my cheek. "But I don't want to risk any more damage."

My heart melted just a bit.

"But what if I really, really wanted you to chase me back to the apartment?"

He took a slow breath.

"Not happening."

"I think it just might." I stood on my tiptoes and moved my arms from his waist to around his neck.

His hands smoothed down my back, stopping just at the curve before my swerve. I nipped his neck.

"I can feel your excitement," I said against his skin.

He shuddered.

"Race you back," I said a moment before I ducked out of his hold and bolted down the sidewalk.

Before I reached the garage door, Carlos caught me from behind, spun me, and backed me against the building.

Out of breath, I did nothing to deter him. He pressed lightly against me so I felt his heart beating as he rested his forehead against mine.

"Do you know how much I like watching you run?" he said. "You're in my blood, Isabelle. Without you, I would die."

"Sweet words," I said, "for a man who forgot my cake. For a man who won't kiss me because my bruised face scares him."

He pulled back and frowned at me.

"Kiss me, Carlos. Kiss me like you meant every word you said about not leaving me alone. Ever."

He growled lightly and lowered his head. I closed my eyes, ready to feel without fear of hurting him. His lips settled against mine, light and loving. He kissed me until I shivered then reluctantly put some distance between us.

"Let's go see if we have pizza waiting," I said.

We walked into the garage and up the service steps together. The quiet, emotionless hall worried me more than relieved me, though. I impatiently waited for Carlos to open our door. Inside was empty as I'd suspected. We found a note on the breakfast bar along with an untouched pizza.

You took forever.
~Bethi

THAT GIRL NEEDED help in a major way. I just wasn't sure that what I could do for her was helpful. I wasn't kidding when I'd told her I was like crack. Hopefully, with the worst of her emotions gone for now, Luke would be able to comfort her.

Pushing aside my concern, I grabbed a lukewarm slice of pizza and took a big bite.

"So good."

Carlos walked to the cupboard, removed two plates, and handed me one.

"How are we going to live together forever? I'm such a slob compared to you. Don't think I haven't noticed how you move my shoes and line them up next to the door. They are at a perfect ninety degree angle to the wall."

He smiled slightly.

"I like being the center of your storm."

I tilted my head and studied him. He really was the center to my storm. He was everything I needed and more. Giving me an out had been smart. It had given me enough courage to grasp for something I'd never dreamed I'd have. A future with someone I cared about. A future that didn't involve the need for long breaks.

He held my gaze as I settled my mind and let what I felt for him surge, hoping he'd feel it and understand without me having to say the words.

"Good," I said. "I wouldn't want you getting tired of it."

"Does that mean—"

"I'm not going anywhere. I'll keep my Claim."

THE NEXT MORNING I woke alone and shuffled into the kitchen, looking for Carlos. Instead, I found a bowl of cereal waiting on the counter and our bags next to the door.

Our time was up. Not cool. The group's uncertainty over what would happen next worried me. I mean, look what had happened so far.

I ignored the cereal, grabbed my bag, and closed myself into the bathroom. Ten minutes later, I reappeared, clean, fresh, and repacked.

Carlos sat at the island, waiting for me. A smidge of worry drifted from him.

"You should be worried," I said. "I saw what you did. Who folds underwear? Seriously."

He shook his head slightly, clearly amused as I'd intended.

"We'll have company soon."

Someone knocked on the door before he even finished speaking.

"Come in," Carlos called.

Grey opened the door and stood aside as everyone poured in. My gaze found Bethi's. She looked tired and sad but wasn't broadcasting like she had the night before.

"What's going on?" I asked when Sam shut the door.

"Gabby's been tracking Olivia," Bethi said.

"Olivia's not alone," Gabby said. "Someone's with her. Urbat. I can't tell who beyond that. But I've been watching and think they might be heading toward the Compound."

"First, what's the Compound? And, second, why do you think they are going there?"

"The Compound is where we live," Charlene said. "A collection of buildings in Canada that we've made into a home for any werewolf."

"Canada?"

Gabby nodded.

"And I think that's where they are going because they are consistently making their way west. Sometimes they detour, but they always correct and return west. What else is up there for them?"

"But why the Compound?" I said.

"Because he knows we need to be together," Bethi said.

He. Blake. He wanted us together to do that Judgement thing she'd mentioned.

"What exactly are we supposed to do together?"

"Make a Judgement. Change the world."

"And how do we do that?"

"I'm not sure yet. But the dreams keep coming. I'm sure they will give me the answer."

GREY, Carlos, and I rode together in the car. As we slowly made our way out of the city, Grey kept us informed on Urbat movement.

"Gabby's reporting that most of the Urbat have scattered, and their movement appears random. However, they are generally heading toward the southern and west coasts."

"Makes sense. We announced where their home base is. They'll want to move in the opposite directions," I said.

Carlos glanced at me in the mirror. He did it often, not liking that I'd insisted that Grey ride shotgun.

"Eyes on the road," I said. "Any word on Bethi's mom?"

"Nothing," Grey said.

It was a good thing they were a couple of cars ahead of us so I couldn't pull in what she was feeling.

We rode in silence for several minutes before I unbuckled and reached forward to turn on the radio.

"You could have asked," Carlos said, annoyance lacing his words.

"But then I wouldn't have been able to brush up against you." I continued to search for a station with good music or interesting news.

"Isabelle, buckle up."

Grinning, I found a station talking about the possibility of werewolves and then sat back. Carlos watched me in the mirror until I clicked in again.

"You're such a worrier."

"Only with you."

He said the best things.

The two men on the radio claimed our attention for the next hour as they took numerous callers with opinions on the subject. It was entertaining, for the most part, until one man came on over the air breathing heavily.

"I got one," he said to the host. The thrill and vindication in his tone sent chills through me. "I woulda thought it was just a big dog running through the alley before that white one showed herself on the news—"

"Grey," I said, getting worried.

"I'm telling the others to listen," he said.

"But when I saw it, I knew. I shot it and it turned into a f—" an annoying bleep covered the speaker's word, "man as it fell down. Butt naked. I called the cops, said what happened, and they said they'd send someone over. Only it wasn't just the cops who showed up. It was the Feds too." The man was talking so fast and in the background, his steps echoed. He was running. Why?

"They circled him, guns drawn. The guy pulled himself off the ground and growled at them. Dumb sh—. He didn't even try to hide what he was. They shot him up, but not to kill him. When I saw them dragging him into the back of one of their vans, I bolted. I've got pictures of this sh—." The radio's censors bleeped it out again, then went straight to commercial.

Neither Grey nor Carlos spoke.

"Is it one of your kind?" I asked.

"We don't think so. No one has reached out to us. We've sent a call to report any injuries and instances involving humans."

A minute later the radio host came back on air.

"Our anonymous caller has sent over his photos. They're on the station's website. Check them out, but hurry because I don't think they'll be there long."

Talk turned to government conspiracy, and Grey reached over to turn the radio off.

"Winifred and Gabby checked the images. They believe it was an Urbat, one of the few remaining in the city, according to Gabby."

Grey spoke with quiet regret, an emotion I didn't share.

"They killed Ethan," I reminded him. "They tried to take Gabby and me. Don't expect me to pity them."

"Not them. You. The six of you. If your purpose is to maintain balance between humans, werewolves, and Urbat, I think we've just made your job a lot harder."

I sat back against my seat and looked out the window. He was right. We'd started a crap storm, and it was only going to get worse.

Thank you for reading *(Dis)content*, book 5 in the Judgement of the Six series. I'm so excited to share *(Sur)real*, the conclusion with you and can't wait to hear your reactions.

Keep reading for a sneak peek!

AUTHOR'S NOTE

Just one more book then the series is over. Yep! That's it! If you're not ready to say goodbye to the characters you've fallen in love with, be sure to check out the *Judgement of the Six Companion Series*, written from each man's point of view. Thank you to all of the readers to demanded more! The Companion Series was written just for you. :)

If you want to keep up to date with my current projects be sure to sign up for my newsletter at melissahaag.com/subscribe.

And I will be forever grateful if you'd leave a review or tell a friend about this series. Your support keeps me writing.

Happy reading!

Melissa Haag

SCENE EXTRA

FINDING ISABELLE AND LOSING GABBY

CLAY...

"She's stopped moving," Gabby said from beside me.

We all sat squeezed inside the car. Tensions were still high after our run in with Isabelle.

Gabby rested her head against my shoulder, tickling my beard with her hair. Over the last few weeks, since she Claimed me, we hadn't had the time to talk about where we were in our lives or what we wanted from the future. It wasn't something I would have normally thought of talking about, until this morning. Seeing Gabby crumble to the ground and being unable to do anything about it had ripped me open and left me raw. Her nearness helped ease some of the concern I still felt. But, I knew my tension would remain until Gabby and I were back home, and she was safely going to school once more.

"I think we should give her a little while to calm down," Bethi said from the seat behind us.

I didn't need to turn to look at Luke to know what he was thinking. After shaking Bethi awake, he'd repeatedly said we should leave Isabelle alone. Bethi had been just as adamant that we get her.

"There are Urbat not far from Isabelle," Gabby said. "I'm not sure how long we can wait."

"Keep an eye on them. We can't let them get to her," Bethi said.

Gabby inconspicuously laced her fingers through mine. I gently squeezed her hand, giving as much comfort as I was taking while I continued thinking about our relationship.

Every night when we lay in bed together, I told her that I loved her. She no longer tensed up at the words. She'd accepted me, despite what I was sure was her accidental Claiming of me, but I knew she wasn't yet ready to be my Mate.

Mate. The idea of a permanent bond with Gabby still made my heart race, as did the idea of losing her. I turned and pressed my lips to her forehead. This morning had been too close.

We sat quietly for almost an hour before Gabby spoke again.

"We need to go know. They turned back and are heading right for her. Something must have tipped them off."

Grey started the engine and backed out as Gabby gave him directions. Her heart accelerated, and I knew what she saw was upsetting her. When I gave her hand another light squeeze, she turned to meet my gaze. Worry flooded her soft brown eyes while the scent of her fear teased the air.

"It'll be all right," I said quietly as we pulled into the parking lot of a hotel.

I would make sure of it.

As soon as I opened the car door, I could smell the others. According to Bethi, these were the ones after the girls. The same ones who had sent a wolf to challenge me for Gabby. My canines lengthened at the thought of anyone trying to take Gabby from me.

"Two of them," Carlos said, already heading for the hotel doors.

Grey waved for us to follow Carlos. Reluctantly, I let go of

Gabby's hand; and she immediately followed me out of the car. I would have rather Gabby stay in the car with Grey.

"This isn't a good idea," I said, walking close to Gabby as we entered the hotel. Fear still drifted from her, clouding her usually sweet sent.

"I agree," Luke said.

Normally, I would care less if Luke agreed with me. I didn't like him and doubted I ever would. That he now had a Mate of his own didn't erase the fact he'd hit on Gabby.

Bethi rolled her eyes at Luke but kept walking, following Carlos down the hallways.

"She only knocked us on our asses because she's scared, Luke. It wasn't personal."

"Like hell," Luke said under his breath.

I had to agree. Again. I took anything that happened to Gabby very personally.

"I think they are already in the room with her. It's hard to tell with so many floors," Gabby said.

"How much further, Gabby?" Carlos asked.

"End of the hall, I think."

When we neared, I let my claws lengthen. Gabby brushed against me, unknowingly making my possessive anger worse. I wanted to grab her and get out of there.

Carlos pushed the door open, the wood splintering under the strength of his anger.

"Empty," he said, turning toward Gabby.

"Then it's gotta be the room above us."

We hurried up the emergency stairs, and I saw Carlos inhale deeply. I did the same, scenting the woman, too. If she was in there, then so were the Urbat. I nudged Gabby behind me and saw Luke do the same to Bethi.

Carlos didn't pause. He crashed through the door, Grey just behind him.

Luke and I had only made it into the room as Carlos tossed the first mongrel out the window. The girl, Isabelle, hadn't even had a chance to tug her friend toward the door when the second one cleared the broken glass. I understood Carlos' anger and concern as he watched her.

Bethi stepped around us. Gabby moved to join her, gently touching my arm as she passed. A wave of reassurance washed over our connection. She was getting the hang of being Claimed.

"We need to leave," Carlos said, still looking at the girl.

"Come on, son," Grey said, moving to help lift Isabelle's friend. The guy didn't look so good. But then, humans didn't hold up well to chokeholds.

"Isabelle, I'm Bethi," Bethi said, stepping forward quickly. "I dream our past lives. Mine, yours, hers." She nodded toward Gabby, making me want to tuck Gabby behind me, out of harm's way.

"More of them are coming," Gabby said, the fear in her scent spiking.

Bethi nodded to show she heard, but kept addressing Isabelle.

"Gabby can see their locations and the locations of the others like us. We need to leave. We can't let them find us."

My palms grew damp and tensed, waiting for that strange feeling to wash over the group again, bringing us all to our knees. The need to shield Gabby had me stepping closer to her. But the bone weakening sensation didn't come.

"Yes, let's leave," Isabelle said, suddenly agreeable.

Bethi and Luke moved out to the hallway as Grey helped Isabelle's friend. No one seemed suspicious of Isabelle as we quickly left the building. I didn't like it but kept quiet, until the hair on the back of my neck started to stand up.

"How many?" I asked quietly as we trailed the group.

"It's hard to say. They are moving in from all over. Twenty?

Maybe thirty?" Gabby said softly. Her gaze remained slightly unfocused as she continued to watch.

We followed Isabelle as she led the way to her car. Gabby glanced at Grey and motioned for him that we needed to hurry. He nodded and moved away as Isabelle's friend slid into the front seat. Isabelle tried taking the keys to drive, but Carlos took them first.

"I'll drive," he said.

"No thanks," she said, holding out her hand.

"We don't have time for this," Gabby said. "They're grouping to the east. We need to go."

Gabby's fear wrapped around me. Her fear and the feeling creeping along the back of my neck had me eyeing the parking lot, watching for signs of movement.

"Fine," Isabelle said. Carlos opened the back door and waited for her to get in.

Gabby turned, snagging Bethi as she moved to the car. I had to hurry to keep up with the pair.

"We need to move. Now," Gabby said.

Grey was already in the front seat with the engine running when we reached the car. Luke beat me to the back seat, sliding in beside Bethi. I quickly got in the front.

"Tell me what you're seeing, Gabby," Grey said as he backed up.

"They are closing in from all directions. Turn right out of here," Gabby said from behind Grey. "Speed Grey. Don't stop for anything."

I turned slightly in my seat. Her eyes were wide and her face pale. I sent a wave of reassurance and love over our link.

"How close are they?" I asked, watching her.

"Very close. Wait. There's a small opening. Here! Grey, turn here!"

Grey jerked the wheel hard, and I faced forward to watch the trees lining the old side road. I spotted movement to the right a second before four half-shifted men sprinted from their cover. They ran straight for our car, the leader jumping up on the hood and hitting the window with his fist. As the glass splintered, Grey slammed on the brakes.

All hell broke loose. The man on the hood went flying over the top of the car as we came to a stop. Wolves poured from the trees. The glass beside me folded in as an arm reached for me. I growled, my half-shifted mouth and extended canines ready for the fight. Claws raked my skin as the owner of the arm tried to grab my shirt. I thrust the arm down, hearing a quick snap of bone.

Glass splintered around us as more crashed upon the car. Arms reached through glass while others pulled at the windows to make bigger openings. Grey growled and thrust his door open, using it to push men and wolves back. Behind me, a passenger door opened.

Gabby screamed. The sound tore through me. I turned my head in time to watch her disappear into the crowd of Urbat. My control slipped. The change consumed me as I burst from the car. Men grabbed at me. I clawed and savagely tore into anyone trying to stop me from reaching Gabby.

She yelled again, further away. I roared. A wave of love washed over our connection.

I fought harder. Bones snapped and blood poured. Still they came. A wall of bodies determined to keep me from her. Until, suddenly, the wall was gone. And, so was Gabby.

I howled at the same time someone else did. Turning, I saw Grey near a gore covered Carlos. Carlos was shaking, the tremors so violent, I wondered how he was still upright. I realized I wasn't much better off. They'd taken Gabby. I hadn't protected her.

"We'll find her, but we need to move, now," Grey was shouting at Carlos.

Bodied littered the ground. Sirens howled in the distance. With a shudder, I pulled back the change.

"Here," Bethi said, thrusting a package of baby wipes at me. "I've learned it pays to start carrying something for cleanup with you guys around." Her voice warbled as she spoke, and I noted the long bloody blade in her other hand.

I took the package and quickly swiped the blood off my face. Luke tossed some clothes at me. I tugged on the pants then finished dressing as we moved away from the scene.

Carlos moved beside me.

"Where are they?" he asked.

I concentrated on the connection Gabby and I had.

"East of us."

He nodded.

We stayed within the cover of the trees as we jogged east. The sirens were a distant wail when we stepped out onto another street.

"We need to move faster," Carlos said.

I glanced at Bethi, the one slowing the group down.

"Go. Get them. If you don't, everything we've done so far will have been pointless. They can't have them."

The girl was shaking hard now. Seeing it scared me.

"Let's go," I said a second before I took off. I didn't care who witnessed my unnatural speed. Only Gabby mattered.

My heart nearly stopped when we found a van pulled over on the side of a road. Two men lay on the ground, and the redhead was slowly crumpling to join them. Carlos rushed to her. I barely paid attention. My focus was riveted on the interior of the van. In the shadows, Gabby lay still on a bench seat.

"No. Gabby."

Moving into the van, I gently lifted her into my arms. Her heartbeat reassured me, but only a little. She was so pale and still, her shallow breathing barely moving her chest as I carefully stepped out of the van.

"What happened to her?" I said, looking at Isabelle.

The redhead had puke stains on her shirt and looked just as pale. She also looked guilty as hell.

"Is she breathing?"

I nodded.

"I happened to her. We couldn't go with them."

She sounded like Bethi. I glanced at the men on the ground, the ones who had taken Gabby. I wanted to kill them. One of them moved, and I growled but before I could even think of setting Gabby down, Carlos stepped forward and finished him.

"Thank you," I said softly. He nodded once and went back to Isabelle.

It took some persuading, but once he had her in his arms, we ran back to the group. The whole time, Gabby didn't move. Not even a twitch. Fear clawed at me. Would she ever wake up? Just what had Isabelle done to her?

I'd watched Gabby lay sick and motionless too frequently in the short time we'd been together. The helpless fear that consumed me the first time it had happened hadn't eased with each occurrence. It had only gotten worse. How often could she lay in my arms like this before there came a time when she wouldn't wake up?

Sam. Gabby's out again.

What do you mean?

Like at the Compound. She's breathing but not waking up. She doesn't look good.

We're close, son.

A few seconds after we joined the rest of the group, three

326

vehicles pulled up. Winnifred and Sam both rushed over to check on Gabby.

"What happened?" Sam asked.

Before I could answer, Isabelle spoke up.

"I couldn't kick open the door without help. She's not hurt. Just the opposite. She's floating so high, it'll be awhile before she's back. As long as she's still breathing, she should be fine."

Fine? I didn't like Isabelle's attitude, or the fact that she was walking toward us. She'd knocked Gabby down twice now. It was hard to be mad at her, though, when I knew she'd saved Gabby by also knocking out the men who'd taken them.

"She'll be okay. I promise. I accidently did this to my parents a ton of times while growing up." She absently swiped at her bleeding nose, watching me with pain-filled eyes.

I nodded, realizing she felt guilty about what had happened to Gabby.

"We need to go," her friend said.

"Clay, put Gabby in the back with you," Sam said. "Bethi and Luke, there's room for you, too."

While the rest figured out a new seating arrangement since we were down a vehicle, I climbed into the SUV. Cradling Gabby in my arms, I waited for the rest to join us.

We drove for an hour before pulling over.

"What's going on?" Bethi asked.

"Ethan is saying Isabelle needs to stop."

Bethi quickly exited with Luke right behind her. I stayed where I was, watching Gabby's peaceful face. I couldn't feel anything over our link. If she was "floating high," shouldn't I feel something? Gently, I brushed a piece of hair back from her cheek.

"I need you, Gabby. You need to wake up."

She continued as she was. Unaware and unreachable.

Several minutes later, everyone was moving back to the vehicles.

"We need to listen to him," Bethi said. "I know Carlos is thinking he knows best for her, but in this case, he doesn't. Ethan is her friend. When it comes to her ability, he obviously knows how to help her. Carlos needs to chill out and start paying attention or she will die."

I lifted my head to glance at Bethi. She was talking with her hands, and Luke was doing his best to contain most of the wild gestures.

"We understand," Sam said from the front. "Carlos is trying to be patient."

"No, he's not. He's going all caveman on her. He can't do that. This Mate crap isn't what's important here. Hasn't anyone been listening to me?"

"Luv, of course we have. Come here." Luke wrapped his arms around her, and she started to cry.

Turning away from them, I went back to watching Gabby, looking for any sign that she was ready to wake up.

We are in trouble and need a place to stay for the night in North Carolina. If anyone is willing to help us, please reach out to an Elder.

Winnifred's message to all of our kind surprised me. Joshua hadn't been the only Urbat to infiltrate the pack.

"Isn't that a big risk?" I asked, glancing at Sam.

Bethi, who'd been quietly resting her head on Luke's shoulder, popped up.

"What's a risk? What's going on?"

Grey turned to look at Bethi.

"Winnifred sent a message asking for a place to hole up in North Carolina."

"No! Why would she do that?"

"We need a place to stay that's out of the way. Gabby's out, and Isabelle and Ethan don't look good."

"Joshua wasn't the only one who—"

"We know," Grey said kindly. "That's why we're saying yes to each person who is offering. Only we'll know which one we'll take."

Bethi calmed a little. I did, too. It didn't feel any safer. But with Gabby still out, nothing really did.

The place the Elders chose was an old farm in the country. As soon as the car stopped, I was out and carrying Gabby to the door. Sam helped me with the lock and held the door for me. The scents of the family still lingered faintly. Most families had gone into hiding when the Elders had sent out the warning weeks ago.

I followed a hall to a set of steps leading up. There, I found a bed in the middle of an open room.

Kicking off my shoes, I settled on the bed, keeping Gabby in my lap. I hated the waiting, the worrying. It was twice as hard because I knew this wasn't like the last time. It wasn't a simple twelve to fourteen hour wait for her to wake up and ask for water. She'd be out until whatever Isabelle did to her wore off. If it wore off.

As the sun faded in the sky, my worry grew.

At some point, everyone came inside, and I could hear their quiet conversation in the kitchen. Bethi introduced Isabelle to the group and gave her a rundown of each of the other girls' abilities.

Then the conversation quieted when Isabelle went to shower. Downstairs, I heard Carlos asking if any of the girls had something Isabelle could wear. Michelle offered up some of her clothes.

Each second that ticked by, each word that Gabby missed of the conversation downstairs, crawled under my skin. Why was she still unconscious? How long had Isabelle knocked her parents out?

The sound of footsteps on the stairs barely penetrated my worry.

"When I came to, she had my head in her lap," Isabelle said softly as she crossed the room. "She was stroking my hair like my mom used to do before I broke her. It was dark in the van. I could feel we were moving, driving further away from help. I felt Gabby's fear and her barely contained panic. Not far away, I felt the pitiless lust and eager aggression of the men who drove."

I'd known she'd saved Gabby. But hearing what she'd saved her from made swallowing difficult.

I glanced up at Isabelle, ready to thank her.

"I'm so sorry for what I did to her. But what they would have done..."

"I know," I said.

"If there would have been another way, I would have taken it."

I nodded and looked back down at Gabby. There wasn't anything I wouldn't do for her. If keeping her safe meant hours of worry, I would deal with it.

"Give her a few more hours. She's sleeping off the best high of her life. And when she comes to, keep her away from me. I'm crack. Highly addictive."

I nodded. I'd keep her far away. When Gabby woke, I'd convince her we needed to go somewhere else. Not home. At least, not yet. But when the Urbat stopped looking for her, we'd go back. I knew how much finishing school meant to her. Until it was safe, maybe I would be able to convince her living in the woods wasn't so bad.

Isabelle left me and joined the others in the kitchen. Her voice carried when she started asking questions.

"How long are we staying here?"

"It's not safe to move until Gabby's awake," Bethi said. "But, for all we know, the Urbat could be closing in around us now."

Smoothing a hand over Gabby's hair, I hoped she would wake before that happened.

"We should be fine," Winifred said.

"If you need her awake, wake her up," Isabelle said. "A good slap will do the trick. However, she'll still be loopy."

Jerking my head up, I glared at the stairs.

No one slaps, Gabby, I sent to Sam.

"Clay can hear you and doesn't appreciate your advice," Sam said. "Neither do I."

"I'll be outside," Isabelle said after a few moments of silence.

The tension that had gathered at her words didn't leave with her presence because I knew the group was concerned about the location of the Urbat. It was only a matter of time before the idea of how to wake Gabby was mentioned again.

When someone walked past the stairs, my worry escalated. Sam was on my side, I reminded myself. He loved Gabby, too, though they didn't see eye to eye lately. Yet, I could feel the high emotions of everyone downstairs. Their worry was climbing. They needed Gabby awake. So did I, but when she was ready.

I heard Isabelle come back in and pulled back my lips.

"Who the hell is worrying so much?" she said.

I took a deep breath and pushed my worry down.

"Gabby still hasn't woken up. We're trying to decide if we should move on without her guidance or continue to wait."

"I've seen people sleep twelve hours after that kind of hit," she said.

I glanced at the clock beside the bed. It had almost been almost ten hours.

"My dad slept, what? Eighteen?" Ethan said.

Sheeeet.

I dropped a kiss on Gabby's forehead and pulled her closer to my chest. The group wouldn't want to wait eighteen hours. I could already feel the tension in the air after that comment.

"Okay, just hold tight for a minute," Isabelle said.

I listened to her approach the stairs. As much as I wanted to stand up and fight her, I knew it wouldn't end well for me. Or

Gabby. I wasn't about to leave her side, and fighting with Isabelle while close to Gabby would mean that whatever Isabelle did to me would also affect Gabby. Isabelle had said she was addictive. I didn't want Gabby craving what Isabelle could do.

I angrily watched Isabelle clear the stairs.

"What do you think's safer?" she said. "Sitting here and waiting, or finding out if the bad guys are getting closer? I already told you what they mean to do to us."

"You're not touching Gabby," I said.

She smiled. I didn't like it.

"You're right. I won't need to because you'll do it."

What? I glanced down at Gabby, unable to imagine slapping her.

"You'll be gentler," Isabelle reasoned.

She was right. I would be gentle. Because I wouldn't do it.

"Here's the thing. When she wakes up, she'll still be high and loopy. She won't act like herself. But don't let her go back to sleep. The effect will wear off faster once she's awake and moving around."

Not happening.

"You have ten seconds before I start pulling from you. I can't aim, so it'll just hurt her more."

I looked up at her. She knew she had me.

"Ten."

Glancing down at Gabby, I fought against my anger and revulsion.

"Nine."

With a gentle touch, I stroked her cheek. Hopefully, she would forgive me.

"Eight...seven."

Inwardly cringing, I tapped Gabby's cheek.

"Pathetic. And six."

I growled. From downstairs, I heard Grey tell Carlos to settle down. If Isabelle didn't knock me flat, Carlos would try to. Didn't they understand I was trying to protect Gabby?

Son, I don't want to see her hurt any more than you. That's why you need to wake her.

"Five. Better hurry."

I closed my eyes, knowing Sam was right. There were so many threats here. I needed her awake so she could help us get away from all of it.

"Four."

Forgive me, I thought before I slapped her.

Her eyes flew open, but I could tell right away that she wasn't herself.

"Gabby," Isabelle said loudly. "Check your sonar."

Gabby turned her head and tried to focus on Isabelle.

"Check your sonar," Isabelle repeated.

"Is Clay safe?" Gabby asked softly.

I sent a wave of love over our connection as I gently stroked the red mark on her cheek.

"You're sitting on him. He'll be safer if you can tell us if there are any bad guys around."

Gabby blinked again and looked at me. She reached up and ran her fingers through my beard.

"So handsome," she murmured, a tiny thread of desire drifting over our link.

"Focus, Gabby," Isabelle shouted. "Check your sonar."

Gabby sighed, and her hand dropped tiredly to her lap.

"They're netting again. None are close." Her eyelids fluttered.

"Keep her awake, Clay," Isabelle said, heading toward the stairs.

As soon as she reached the bottom, I tapped Gabby's cheek again. Her eyes opened, and she smiled at me.

"I was worried," I said.

She reached up and brushed my hair back from my face.

"You are so handsome."

The small, secret smile that curved her lips sent a ball of need right to my gut.

"I can feel that, Clay," she said, lifting her head and offering her lips.

Normally there'd be nothing I'd want more than to kiss her; it was only my worry for her safety and the sounds of conversation downstairs that stopped me from happily giving her what she wanted.

"Gabby, you're not safe here."

"I'm safe with you. Always with you," she whispered, nestling closer to me.

Her hand brushed over the width of my chest, distracting me enough that I almost went for her lips.

"No. I mean, yes. You're safe with me. But, you're not safe with this group," I said softly, knowing full well anyone paying attention in the kitchen might hear me.

"Clay, I want your lips on mine. Now. I need to feel you."

Hell. Her hand roamed over my chest once more, and I knew I was lost. When her head cleared, we'd talk more.

I claimed her lips, meaning to kiss her sweetly. Her tongue didn't agree with sweet intentions. She kissed dirty, and I lost all thought. The slide of her tongue against mine did that to me every time. With my last shred of will power, I fisted the sheets with my claw tipped fingers. She had no idea what she did to me; how much I adored her.

Her small hands threaded through my hair and held tight as she directed the kiss, pressing her mouth firmly against mine a moment before she pulled away.

"Not good enough, Clay," she whispered against my lips. "Don't you want to touch me?"

Want to touch her? No, I needed to touch her. I burned for it. But I hadn't thought she would welcome it. Not yet, anyway. I'd been wrong, though. That or I'd died and gone to heaven.

When she moved, shifting position so she no longer lay cradled in my lap but straddled it, I gripped her waist. She was my lifeline. I claimed her mouth once more, possessing her lips and tongue. She stayed on her knees for a moment, making a soft sound before slowly settling on my lap.

I groaned. She moved her hands from my hair to my shoulders. Holding me, she tilted her hips against mine. The explosive pleasure that should have robbed me of thought, instead, set off warning alarms. She moved against me again, and I tore my mouth from hers to look at her.

Her lips were wet and puffy, begging for more kisses. Man, I wanted to kiss her again. Lifting my gaze from her mouth, I saw her glazed vacant stare.

Sheeet.

"Gabby, baby. I can't."

"No," she said softly, rocking her hips against mine again. "You can. I can feel it."

Ten seconds ago, I'd been in heaven, now I was certain I was in the seventh ring of hell. Yes, the way she was arching into my lap guaranteed she'd feel just how much I wanted to touch her...and more. But she wasn't herself.

I dropped my head back against the metal bedframe, shaking and barely in control. She pressed her advantage and kissed her way along my neck, tracing her tongue over the place where she had Claimed me.

"I love you, Clay. Don't you love me, too?"

"Gabby..." It wasn't her name but a growl that came out. I let go of her waist and curled my hands into fists. Closing my eyes, I started listing off all the parts in a Ford Escort's exhaust system. There weren't enough to distract me from the feel of her, though. I cleared my throat to try speaking again.

She hummed as her lips skimmed over my adams apple.

"Gabby, baby, I need a drink." My words were desperate, and if she would have been paying attention to our connection, she would have known it was a lie.

"Okay," she said sweetly. She moved off my lap. I wanted to sigh in relief as much as I wanted to cry at the loss.

I didn't mentally kick myself long before I realized she hadn't moved far. In fact, her hands were busy tugging at the edge of my shirt. The touch of her fingers on my stomach had me groaning again, and I couldn't make myself move away.

"Gabby, I'm thirsty. Remember?"

Her lips curved as she tugged my shirt higher and stared at my exposed stomach.

"I really like your muscles," she said.

When she tried tugging the shirt higher, I didn't resist her.

"Especially these," she said, running her fingers over my chest.

I swallowed thickly and let my head drop against the headboard again. The metal made a hollow sound. Empty, like my head. If I were smart, I'd get off the bed and convince Gabby to walk somewhere with me. Where? We weren't safe. I needed to talk to her about—

Her tongue flicked over my right nipple, and I grunted at the needy sensation that gripped me.

When her mouth closed over it, I was off the bed and across the room before she could blink at me. I shook with need. I wanted her in my arms. I wanted her biting my neck as I pushed my way—

Rubbing a hand over my face, I dropped that line of thinking.

"Clay?" Gabby looked at the mattress, then both sides of the bed as if I might have fallen off. When she didn't spot me, she sat back on her heels and looked down at her hands with such sadness that I stepped forward.

"You're not yourself, sweetheart."

Her gaze found me, but the sad frown didn't clear. Her stare returned to her hands, and I knew that I'd hurt her by leaving. She had no idea what she was doing to me. I wanted to make her happy, to give her what she wanted, but she'd hate me later for it. However, seeing her unhappy now was just as bad.

Crossing the room, I stood beside the bed and opened my arms to her. She looked up at me, uncertain and hesitating. Distrust and unhappiness drifted over our link. My chest ached for causing those emotions. Leaning forward, I scooped her up in my arms and settled onto the bed once more.

I knew what I needed to do. Suck it up and make out with my woman without going all the way. There wouldn't be a shower cold enough to help me when we finished.

"I swear I will do my best to give you a reason to be happy...today, tomorrow, and every day for the rest of our lives." I pressed a kiss to her temple, and she sighed, a thread of contentment touching my mind.

She snuggled into my chest, and her hands started roaming once more.

It would be a long night of heaven and hell.

Gabby leaned into me further, and I gripped the counter tightly. Doing that was the only thing stopping me from taking her back upstairs and just finishing what we'd started over an hour ago. If I allowed myself one touch, one tiny caress, tomorrow's anger be damned. I'd have her tonight.

I'd thought begging to come downstairs for a drink would have cooled her off a little after she'd managed to get under my shirt and undo my pants. She'd given into my begging and let me leave the bed without becoming upset again, but she'd touched me in some way the entire time.

My blood was boiling, and I could barely think.

"I want you," I whispered against her lips when she pulled away to breath. "Claiming isn't enough. I want you as my Mate, as my forever, Gabby."

She smiled her beautiful secret smile that made my knees weak, then threaded her fingers in my hair. I knew I was in trouble. I couldn't take any more. I'd give in. She pressed her lips to mine at the same time she arched into me. The ache riding in my pants turned to fire. My hold on the counter tightened, and I arched back into her.

The kitchen door opened. I couldn't decide if I wanted to growl at whoever it was or beg for help.

"Just give in to her already," Isabelle said.

I pulled back to look at her, and Gabby made a small sound of protest and started to kiss my neck. That same damn sensitive spot where she Claimed me. It was like there was a target painted on it now.

Doing my best to remain focused on Isabelle and Carlos, I shook my head. With them present, there was no way I'd give into Gabby. A public Claiming she could handle. A public Mating...she'd kill me.

"Fine," Isabelle said. "Then this is going one of two ways. I can rip that lust from her, which would keep her high; or you can man up and walk away."

I almost growled at her.

"Believe it or not, I'm trying to be helpful. I just can't stick around with all this emotion. And according to grandma, I can't leave either. What Gabby's broadcasting needs to stop. Now."

She was right. It did need to stop.

I kissed Gabby's forehead and tried to move away, but Gabby wasn't having any of that. She pressed against me firmly and nipped my neck, weakening my resolve to walk away.

"Bethi," Isabelle yelled.

A minute later, Bethi joined the crowd of voyeurs. Gabby was going to be so mad at me.

"Help Clay," Isabelle said. "I can't touch Gabby."

Bethi stepped forward and laid a firm grip on Gabby.

"Come on. Clay needs to go, and you need to make Sam some coffee."

As soon as Gabby's hands loosened from my hair, I bolted. Gabby made a small, upset sound; and I wanted to howl as the screen door slammed closed behind me.

With all the crap going on, I should have just given into her. Bethi had said the only true way to protect Gabby was to be Mated, that the Urbat couldn't break that if they ever took her from me again. Why had I hesitated? Because I couldn't have taken advantage of her like that. She wasn't herself. As much as I wanted her forever, I wanted her on her terms. I didn't want her having any regrets when it came to our Mating.

And where did my nobility leave me? Pacing by the damn cars, so stiff I could barely walk.

The kitchen door opened again.

"Now you can help me," Isabelle said, waving for me to follow as she strode toward the barn.

It was only then that I noticed everyone else waiting in the opening of barn doors.

I followed Isabelle and listened to her speak to Winifred.

"Bethi won't be able to handle Gabby on her own, and I can't take anymore emotions. I need you all to go back inside, help Bethi and Gabby, and stay away from me."

The girl either had no idea to whom she spoke or didn't give a damn. I figured it was probably the second; Isabelle had guts.

The interior of the barn was lit. She continued inside as she gave orders.

"Ethan, can you grab our new bags from the car? Carlos, can

you ask around for some blankets? If we have to stay, I can't sleep inside the house tonight."

She turned and looked at me with a grin.

"You look like you need to burn off some energy. How are you at fighting?"

An hour later, I walked back to the main house, more relaxed and a little sore. Isabelle was a fighter through and through.

The house was quiet when I entered. Thomas and Charlene were lying on the couch. Jim and the Elders spread out on the floor. Michelle and Emmitt and Luke and Bethi were missing, probably in a bedroom. I followed Gabby's scent upstairs and found her asleep on the bed. Just seeing her was enough to heat my blood again. The remembered feel of her lips on my neck hit me hard.

I paced for a few minutes before I joined her on top the covers.

"Clay?" she murmured sleepily, reaching for me.

"Yeah, it's me."

"I missed you."

"I missed you, too. Are we safe to stay the night?"

She yawned and nodded.

"Nothing close by. The Urbat are netting out from where they almost had us. We'll need to leave in the morning."

I wrapped her in my arms and pulled her close to my side. She sighed and laid her had on my chest, sleepily nuzzling me.

"Go to sleep, Gabby. I'll be here for you in the morning."

Thankfully, she listened.

I didn't sleep; I just held her. When the sun started to rise, I went downstairs and checked the refrigerator. It was well stocked as I figured it would be.

Setting out three dozen eggs, I started breakfast. Those in the living room started moving, and after a few minutes, Sam joined me.

"Gabby herself yet?"

"She's not up, but she seemed better when I came in last night."

Sam nodded and started making coffee.

"I'm going to talk to Gabby about leaving," I said, cracking the last egg into the bowl.

Sam stopped his coffee preparations to look at me.

"You're not talking about checking the way this morning to get back on the road, are you?"

"No."

"It's not safe out there for her. She's safer with us."

"Is she? She was pulled from a car yesterday. If not for Isabelle..."

Sure Isabelle had saved her, but she'd probably almost killed her too.

"According to Bethi, we need Gabby. We need all of them to finish this."

"Sam, I'd let the world go to hell to keep her safe."

"I know, son, but she would resent you for it. Gabby isn't the type of person to let people suffer just to save herself. And neither are you."

"What are you saying?"

Sam sighed and rubbed his chest.

"I'm saying we all need to be ready to make sacrifices, son."

I stared down at the eggs for a moment.

"I'm still asking her."

"Fair enough."

When Charlene came into the room and took over cooking, I used the bathroom to clean up then went upstairs.

Since Gabby was still sleeping, I joined her on the bed and managed to rest. Her disquiet woke me some time later, as did her attempt to try to sneak from the bed.

"Morning," I said, opening my eyes.

She blushed red.

"Morning."

I watched her stand and smooth her hair. Her gaze was alert, but she was acting oddly. I studied her, trying to get a read from our connection or her body language. When that didn't work, I inhaled subtly. Was she mad? Should I apologize for yesterday?

"I'm going to use the bathroom," she said at the same time I caught a hint of her shy confusion.

I nodded and stayed where I was, giving her time to sort out whatever was going on in her head. After giving her a two-minute head start, I put my shoes on and went downstairs just in time to see Gabby head into the kitchen.

Gabby sat next to Sam. She stared at her hands as I sat next to her. I didn't know what to say or do. If she was confused, so was I.

Charlene set a loaded plate and a glass of orange juice in front of both of us. I thanked her and started eating. Gabby did the same but with no enthusiasm. Ethan came in to use the bathroom then went back outside. Carlos watched the man closely from the doorway. Everyone else went about their morning as usual, eating and packing up. Gabby didn't. She ate slowly and didn't look at anyone. Especially me.

Long after we'd finished and Gabby still toyed with her juice, Isabelle walked in and went straight for the stove.

When Isabelle turned to the table, her determined gaze fell on Gabby.

"I'm sorry about what happened," Isabelle said.

Gabby lifted her head and nodded. A blast of shame and guilt surged over our connection. She felt shame? For what? It wasn't her fault she'd been taken. It was mine. I sent a wave of love over our link and felt a wave of love and guilt return. Guilt? I wished Gabby would just look at me and help me understand what was going on.

With a sigh, Isabelle pushed her chair back and stood.

"Come on. Let's go for a walk."

When Gabby stood, I stood too.

"No boys allowed," Isabelle said.

I kept my gaze on Gabby, hoping for a clue about what was going on in her beautiful head.

When Isabelle moved to leave the kitchen, Gabby followed, and I stayed put. Ethan moved Isabelle's plate to the stove and made a new plate for himself, grinning the whole time.

Watching the clock, I leaned against the kitchen wall and waited. After a few minutes, a random wave of love washed over me. Then a thread of guilt followed. She was killing me.

She walked in a short time later. Her face was still flushed, but she moved straight for me and gave me one of her small smiles.

I let out a breath I hadn't known I was holding.

While Isabelle threatened Ethan for eating her breakfast, I led Gabby from the kitchen and out to the barn. Carlos paced in the yard and nodded to us as we passed.

In the barn, I pulled Gabby to an out of sight corner.

"I'm not good at guessing what you're thinking," I said.

She grinned slightly.

"I disagree. I think you're really good at guessing." She wrapped her arms around my waist and leaned her head against my chest. "You do make me happy, Clay. Every day."

I hadn't been sure she'd remember everything. But, I was glad she did. What I felt for her wanted to consume me, and I knew I needed to tell her.

"Before I met you, I thought I wanted a family, kids. But now...it's you, Gabby. Just you. You're all I want."

"So no kids?" she asked as she lifting her head to look at me.

"I'd love kids. Little pieces of you running around."

She grinned and set her head back on my chest.

"I want to leave, Gabby. We can't go back home, but there are some places I know where we'd be safe. Safer than if we stayed here."

She was quiet for a long time.

"I want kids, too, Clay. Someday. I know what happened yesterday scared you, and I'm sorry for that. But I don't think I can leave. I don't think there will be anywhere safe for me to hide. You heard Bethi; they hunt us down. Her dreams, her memories of dying…they're too real."

She lifted her head and met my gaze.

"I have to stay and see this through to the end. And, I hope we'll get our someday."

Her eyes were sad when she said it, and I felt how shallow her hope was. Yesterday hadn't just scared me. It had scared her, too.

That sounds so ominous, doesn't it? *evil grin* Be sure to check out (Sur)real, the final book. It's epic!
If you liked getting inside Clay's head, there's a whole Companion Series just so you can delve deeper into what these amazing Judgement men are thinking. Go check them out! They aren't just a retelling of the same story. They are the men's stories. Enjoy!

There's still a sneak peek of (Sur)real. Keep reading!

(Sur)real

Judgment of the Six: Book 6

Now Available!

I sat in the backseat and listened to Frank's impatient tapping on the steering wheel. We'd been driving for hours since our last break near dawn, and I needed to use the bathroom.

"Can we stop?" I asked.

He growled angrily.

"Bathroom or food?"

"Both." If I only asked for a bathroom, he would find somewhere to pull over and make me go on the side of the road... with him watching.

In silence, I waited for his answer. It took a few minutes.

"There's a station up ahead," he said. Anger laced his words.

I felt the vehicle slow.

"Don't try anything when we get in there."

"Do I ever? I know where my loyalties are."

When the car stopped, I remained in the back until I heard my door open. He tapped impatiently on the frame as I unbuckled and slid out. The shadows of the Others zipped around us, painting my world grey so I could see my way toward the gas station door.

I pulled the sunglasses from my pocket and placed them on my face.

"Take 'em off," Frank said from behind me.

"We're not supposed to call attention to ourselves. And, my eyes will do that," I said.

He growled and opened the door. As I stepped past, he leaned in.

"He's not here to know," he whispered.

I kept moving, not allowing any worry or fear to surface.

345

In the bathroom, I exhaled shakily and splashed water on my face. Frank was dangerously close to losing control. Since the moment Blake had called him back into the office and told him to drive me west, Frank's resentment had grown. Why would Blake tell him, a pure and strong Urbat, to listen to a weak, blind Judgement? Frank's failure to obtain the provider had cost him much within the Urbat ranks. He'd lost Blake's respect and was desperate to get it back. That's why he'd been ideal to drive me across the country. However, his desperation wasn't keeping him in line as planned.

After quickly using the facilities and washing, I opened the door. My sense of smell wasn't anything compared to either the werewolves or the Urbat, but it was better than most humans. Even without the shadows dancing around Frank's body, I knew he was standing right outside.

"I'm sorry I took so long." My quiet apology was sincere. If Frank lost any more of his composure, I would suffer.

Frank didn't immediately answer or move. I hesitated, listening. Although the shadows gave me basic outlines, there was much I still couldn't see. Things I needed my other senses for…like the faint sound of Blake's voice.

"You called him?" I said in surprise and concern, not bothering to suppress either emotion.

Frank disconnected the call on Blake's recorded message.

"Yeah, and he isn't answering. It's your turn."

"He was clear when we left. He doesn't want to hear from either of us until we get there. If I try contacting him and he asks why, what am I supposed to say?"

Frank stepped close.

"Something is wrong. I can feel it."

My pulse jumped in panic, and I looked around as if suspecting whatever he sensed was within the gas station.

"Not here. With Blake," he said.

One of the shadows started swirling crazily around the person behind the register.

"We have the attendant's attention," I said softly, facing Frank. "We should make our purchases and go back to the car."

"Do you know how close I am to not giving a shit about what Blake says?" Frank asked with menace.

"Yes."

Other Titles

Touch
Moved
Warwolf
Nephilim

APPENDIX

The Judgements:

- Hope — Gabby, recently reluctant mate to Clay [*Book 1: Hope(less)*]
- Prosperity — Michelle, mate to Emmitt, son of Charlene [*Book 2: (Mis)fortune*]
- Wisdom — Bethi, mate to Luke [*Book 3: (Un)wise*]
- Strength — Charlene, Emmitt's mother, wife to the werewolf leader Thomas [*Book 4, (Un)bidden*]
- Peace — Isabelle [*Book 5: (Dis)content*]
- Courage — [*Book 6: (Sur)real, anticipated release early 2016*]

The lights Gabby sees:

- Werewolf — Blue center with a green halo
- Urbat — Blue center with a grey halo
- Human — Yellow center with a green halo
- Charlene — Yellow with a red halo
- Gabby — Yellow with an orange halo
- Michelle — Yellow with a blue halo
- Bethi — Yellow with a purple halo
- Isabelle — Yellow with a white halo
- Olivia — Yellow with a brown halo

CPSIA information can be obtained
at www.ICGtesting.com
Printed in the USA
LVHW111952080720
660120LV00004B/720

9 781943 051847